Copyright © 2013 by Barbara Ann Derksen
Second Edition

All rights reserved. No part of this book shall be reproduced, stored in a retrieval system, or transmitted by any means without written permission from the author

Shadow Stalker

-a Finder's Keepers mystery-

Prologue

Her vision seeped through the louvers on the utility room door. The images seemed broken as in a jigsaw puzzle until she leaned forward and placed her forehead against the wood. Her insides tightened. Everyone was shouting. She willed her body to stop trembling but it seemed to have a will of its own. The gun that the stranger held, just like on TV but different, was pointed at her father. This was real. Daddy had hid her ... *told me to stay where I am until* ... She couldn't remember.

Daddy's voice sounded like it did when he talked on the phone sometimes. "What do you want with us? You have no business being here. We said no contact."

She watched his face get redder than she'd ever seen it, even when he'd been out in the sun too long. Mommy was shaking her fist. *She never did that.* The stranger smiled, totally silent. *Not intimidated*, it seemed to the five year old. A shiver walked its way up her spine. She'd seen guns like that in the cartoons she watched. This one was a little longer though. Only business, the man said. *What business*, she wondered.

The man straightened his arm, the one holding the gun. Her vision blurred for a second, horror filling the empty spaces in her brain. The explosion echoed in the foyer. The bullet seemed to travel in slow motion. *Just like the cartoons*, she thought. Her daddy's body slammed into the banister of the staircase heading up to the bedroom area and the maid's quarters. The railing shook. Her father's body flopped forward. His head smacked the floor. He lay still then.

Blood covered the wall behind where her father had stood. Her mother screamed and then was silent. Before her father's body hit the tiled foyer, she watched the side of her mother's head explode. Specks of blood and other gooey stuff splattered all over the walls, mixing with the blood from her father. Her stomach lurched. She wrapped a hand tightly across her mouth. A silent scream rattled around in her head seeking an escape. *Get up*, it said. *Daddy. Mommy. Get up. Please.* The scream evaporated, as if it had never been. They weren't moving. In the cartoons, they always got back up. *Why don't they get up?*

Tears filled her eyes, blurring her vision again. Daddy just lay there. Mommy lay beside him, covered in the blood that flowed from her body. Her sightless eye stared toward the girl, hidden. The girl felt as if she was going to throw up but she swallowed instead. She swiped at the tears that silently trickled down her pudgy cheeks. Her mother told her she had cute dimples, whatever that was. Her mother liked to touch her cheeks. Now...

She watched as the man, the monster, moved toward the entrance. Then he stopped. He looked up the stairs, then down the hall. He looked toward her hiding place, his eyes cold, calculating, wondering. Her stomach lurched, the fright almost real enough to touch. Could he see her? Her daddy had told her to hide here. He knew they were in danger. *Why? Who was this man? How did daddy know him? Maybe it was mommy the man hated. Why?* Footsteps interrupted her questions. The man was moving down the hall straight toward her.

She crept backwards, crawling on all fours as if she were a spider. Her gymnastics teacher had taught her that. *I need to get out of here. He will kill me, too.* She remembered her discovery when she'd hidden in here last week. Her cousins had come for a visit. They loved to play hide and seek in the large, multistoried mansion that was her home. She'd found a door leading to the garage where her daddy's cars were kept under the chauffeur's apartment. She'd sneak out that way.

Several hanging tools brushed her shoulders as she crept under them toward safety. They swung to and fro. It was as if they whispered, "*She's in here.*" She twisted her head behind. She couldn't see through the slats in the door anymore but the heavy tread of footsteps grew louder, closer. She reached the hidden door. It creaked as she slipped through.

"Wait." His voice echoed through the tiny room, resonating off the walls of the small space, the sound carried over the creak of the door as he pulled it open. The menace in his voice was gone, replaced by enticement.

She scurried into the large garage. Ignoring the man, she skirted the three cars stored there. Her heart pumped so loudly in her ears, the sound blocked out the rustle of the man's clothes as he squeezed through the same opening. She turned slightly and saw his shadow. Her short legs pumped toward the door leading to the stone walled courtyard and the gated entrance to the back yard. The wrought iron gate was open. *Good.*

Her feet flew over the paved driveway toward the gate. She turned once to see if the chauffeur was nearby. Benson played with her sometimes. He was nowhere to be seen. Then she remembered. Benson had asked for the day off to take Maria, the maid, to the beach. *There's no one to help.* She streaked through the wrought iron gate.

The yard was tree filled, almost like a park. She ran like the wind, as if the devil himself was after her. *He is.* She reached the second gate in the high wrought iron fence that surrounded her parent's property. It was slightly ajar. Her parent's always kept this one locked but now... She almost forgot to breathe as she raced through it and into the street. The sidewalk led to town. Her legs pounded the pavement hard. "Wait." The shout came from behind her. The man was following.

The sound of his footsteps bounced off cement walls and rock enclosures, the attempt of homeowners to protect what was theirs. Trees, thick for privacy, lined the street, hiding nearby houses from view. Traffic was non-existent along this street at this time of day. She ran. Her instincts told her that life, her life, depended on it. She rounded a corner but then peeked back. He was still coming, walking briskly in her direction. *I need to hide.*

She crawled under a nearby bush, *its dense foliage the perfect cover*, she thought. The picture of her mother's head scattering debris all over the walls played like a ticker tape through her brain. Her stomach roiled again and she gagged. *Mommy. Daddy. Please help me.* Footsteps rounded the corner. The sound grew louder. *He'll find me. I have to leave.*

She stood. He reached for her with one hand while the other, the one that had held the gun, was in his pocket. She ducked just out of his reach. She raced like the wind, staying off the sidewalk this time. She flew through the trees as if someone carried her, her feet barely touching the ground long enough to make an indent in the leaves. Her body slammed into low branches that scratched and tore at her clothing. She was shorter than the man so movement for her was easier here, she reasoned. The heavier footsteps had slowed, proving her right. She heard a twig snap. He was still coming. Maybe a policeman…

The girl ran. Her legs hurt. Muscles contracted painfully. Trickles of blood from scratches marred her perfect skin, skin that her mother would caress from time to time. *Mommy.* The thought hurt so much. Her daddy liked to swing her over his head. She almost smiled at the thought but then tears flowed again when she remembered. *He's back there. Lying on the floor. Blood oozed from his forehead. He never got back up.*

The race continued. She rounded another corner. Her body slammed into legs encased in dark blue pants. Strong hands steadied her but she wriggled to be free. She looked over her shoulder, twisting this way and that. "Hey there. What's the hurry?" The voice sounded kind, different than the one she ran from. She looked up.

"Melissa?" The man's smile turned quickly to a frown, concern written all over his face. "What's wrong?"

She pointed in the direction she'd come from. Her breaths were mere gasps, words impossible. Tears fell unhindered. She slipped behind the legs. *Would the man shoot this person too?* She pointed again as the man rounded the corner. She saw him stop before the policeman could look in the direction she pointed. The man ducked his head as his foot stepped backward. She watched him, silently and as quickly as he'd come, step behind the nearest tree, out of sight. Her heart felt as if it would leap out of her chest. Then she was sick. All over the shiny black shoes of the policeman she'd collided into.

"I don't see what you're trying to tell me, Melissa. Calm down. Just take a deep breath." He saw her looking at the mess at his feet. "Don't worry about that. I can clean them. But what's got you in such a tizzy?"

She swallowed. Tears streaked down her cheeks as if they'd never stop. "He-he," She hiccoughed. She pointed in the direction she'd come from. "He shot mommy and daddy." She gasped for another breath. Her finger shook as she continued to point toward the corner where the monster had disappeared. "He shot them."

Chapter One

Christine sat up in bed, her back straight. She swiped at the streaks of perspiration on her face only to discover they were tears. Images of her parents disappeared like wisps of fog. She shuddered. The dream always felt so real, just like it happened yesterday. *The face of that monster never fades. One day ...* She swung her legs to the floor and hung her head. The loneliness was always overpowering after the dream left. She rose from the bed and looked at the twisted sheets. She sighed. *Nights like this are never restful.*

She stepped into her tiny bathroom, turned on the pewter coated hot water tap, and splashed her face. Images swam before her eyes. She shuddered. *I hate that dream.* She grabbed the lace edged towel that hung near her right hand and covered her face, escaping into its folds. A cold nose brushed her bare leg. "Chief." She looked down at her large German shepherd. The dog wagged his tail in response and then cocked his head as if to ask if she was okay.

She patted his head. "I'll bet you wanna go for a run, don't you?" She ran her fingers behind his ears. Then she looked at the clock on her night stand. "Man. It's only 7 a.m." Christine groaned and then slipped through the door on her way back to bed. Chief blocked her progress. "Aw, come on. It's too early." He whined and then wagged his tail harder.

"Oh, all right. I guess an early start will do us both good." She stepped toward the hook behind her bedroom door where she kept her running clothes.

She tossed the shorts and t-shirt she wore at night on her bed. Chief barked. "Sh-h-h. You'll wake the neighbors." She grinned at her pet/partner of three years and then pulled the sweatshirt she used for her early morning excursions over her head. She stepped into the matching pants. The gray fabric warmed the cold spots on her leg. *I like wearing shorts to bed but some nights they're slightly inadequate,* she decided. *Maybe it's time for flannels.* She turned toward the door to the hallway. *Oh, right. Running.* She slipped her sweatshirt off again and retrieved her sports bra from the chair beside her closet. *I hate these things.*

Finally ready, if still a little groggy, she looked at her patient animal. "Okay Chief. Let's go." Christine walked briskly down the hall, past the other two rooms that would one day be an office and another bedroom, and through the living room of her modest home. She opened the drawer in the coffee table and located her taser. With one hand, she pocketed her weapon and with the other, turned off her home alarm system. The front door was double bolted so she turned the bolts and then took the industrial strength chain off before stepping into the early morning air. *The sun isn't even up yet.* She groaned. *Oh, well.* "We won't have any traffic to contend with at least." She looked down at her companion and then locked the door behind her.

Christine had chosen this area to live in because dogs didn't require leashes in the nearby park. She wanted Chief to be able to run free. She looked at her pet as he lifted his leg at the closest oak tree. Her heart filled with love. *Even if he does push me out of the house before sunrise.* Her stride increased as soon as Chief was able to keep up. They moved toward the walking path through the park the city had devised for just this purpose.

Christine made a point of never doing things the same way or at the same time each day but she'd go for a run when she had the time. She felt it kept her agile. She chuckled. It also cut down on how stringent she needed to be with her diet. *Can't leave the junk food alone.*

The morning air felt like an early fall was descending. She noticed the beginning of some red hues appearing within the green leafy trees that were in abundance along her street and into the park. She inhaled the crisp air, coughed as the cold air hit her lungs, and then inhaled again enjoying the smell of smoke from nearby chimneys. *I love that smell. But not the thought of winter coming.* She smiled. The cobwebs of the dream were finally dissipating.

A bird, hidden among the leaves of a nearby tree, chirped it's greeting at them, as they made their way along the path. Christine kept a steady pace, running defensively, looking for shadows that moved. She kept her pace slow enough that she could enjoy the beauty around her, what she could see of it at this early hour. *If it weren't for Chief ...* The dog had no trouble keeping up. His muscles rippled beneath his sleek fur and his breath gave off wisps of cloudy emissions. His training kept him alert.

Christine turned her head toward the east. The yellow gold rays of the sun could be seen through the branches of the trees in the distant landscape. As the duo made their way down the path that wound around the circumference of the park, more birds could be heard as the sky lightened. Christine began to relax a little, her vigilance not as worrisome. Then the sun slipped up over the horizon illuminating everything in its path.

Christine led the way past the walking bridge that led to a favorite ice cream stop for area residents. *I love living on the edge of the park. It gives me a place to get away from the search.* She grinned as she picked up the pace a little. *I won't need to work out at the gym today, I think.*

Large open areas of well-kept lawns filled the left side of the path, places where people often enjoyed picnics after a long day at the office. Now the area was empty. Christine enjoyed the serenity that surrounded her. Dew twinkled on the blades of grass as she sped quickly by. Instead of cavorting across the wet grass as dogs loved to do, Chief matched her pace right beside her.

Thirty minutes had passed, she guessed, when Chief whined and then stopped just off the path. She stopped as well but continued to pump her legs up and down to maintain her heart rate. She reached into her pocket, pulled an empty bag out of her pocket and turned it inside out. She slipped her hand inside and when Chief was finished, she bent forward to clean up after him. The nearest trash receptacle gained a deposit.

"Come on, Chief. Time to get home. I have a busy day today and so do you." She reversed direction and began the trek home. Chief fell into step beside her and then stretched out when she expended an added burst of energy. The run cleared her mind as it always did, and gave Chief his early morning exercise as well.

By the time she reached the yard of her little bungalow, Christine was panting almost as much as Chief. She bent forward resting her hands on her knees and then stretched her legs, one at a time, to cool down. Chief rolled around on the grass giving his back an extra work out on the prickly twigs hidden in the thatch. Christine laughed. "I guess that's your way to cool down, huh Chief?" She reached over to scratch him behind his ears when he walked beside her to their back door.

I feel so lucky to have this house, she thought, not for the first time. *Once I get my agency up and running, I'll be able to cover the costs from my salary but for now ...* Christine took long strides toward her back door, continuing to stretch her tired muscles. "Mr. Goodman did a good job finding this house for us, didn't he Chief?" The dog panted in response. *If I can't have parents to advise me, then a lawyer is the next best thing, I guess. And it doesn't hurt to have a trust fund.*

Christine unlocked her door, stepped inside and allowed her vision to sweep the premises for anything that might be out of place. She relocked the door as soon as Chief slipped through behind her. Her habits had been ingrained in her since childhood. She'd been taught to always be aware of her surroundings and to make sure her house was secure ... just in case.

Her thoughts heightened her insecurities, as always. She jumped when the phone rang as soon as she was inside the kitchen. She reached toward it. *Wonder who could be calling so early.* She popped it open. "Hello."

The voice on the other end was from a new friend at the local police detachment. "Oh. Hi, Charlie. What's up?" She listened as the man on the phone gave her some disappointing news. "But, can't you tell me anything else? I mean ... they're my parents." She listened as Charlie reiterated his reasons. "Yeah ... well ... I'm going to find him. I'll just ... Yeah, fine." She slammed the phone closed.

Christine banged her fist on the counter. "Darn regulations. Just because I'm family. They say I'm too close to the situation. Phewy." She scowled toward her dog whose ears were folded back on his head. Then she marched toward her bedroom. She punched the doorframe as an added inflection over her unsatisfactory phone call. "I'll just have to find another way, won't I, boy?"

She straightened the crumpled sheets on her bed, threw the duvet over the sheet and then straightened the pillows and the shams. *I'll never be free if I don't get some answers.* She grabbed a pair of jeans from the closet. Christine inspected the shirt she'd worn once before to make sure it was still suitable and deposited it on her bed post to keep it free of wrinkles. *Now for a quick shower.*

Before he finds me. The thought traveled across her brain as quickly as any she'd had that morning. She looked at her reflection in the mirror. The frown lines were back. She slipped out of her running clothes and tossed them in the hamper under the vanity. She reached past the shower curtain and twisted the knob in her shower stall. Hot water erupted from the rain shower head. She folded the plastic lined floral fabric back and then stepped inside.

That's why I cultivated my friendship with an officer of the Royal Canadian Mounted Police. They're federal. I thought ... but it seems not. She soaped her hair and massaged her scalp. Her hair was a lot shorter than when she'd grown up but it still got greasy if she didn't wash it every day. As she ran fingers through her curls, she assessed her situation again. "I'll just have to get a little friendlier with Charlie. Get him on my side." She grinned.

The hot, gentle spray worked its magic on her senses, helping her relax for the first time all morning. She stood still, letting the overhead shower head pour water over her as if she were standing in a rain forest during the afternoon deluge. Her mind returned to the conversation with Charlie.

He said they never let family members know the details of an on-going investigation. *They've had twenty years.* She leaned her head back allowing the spray to rinse her hair really well. *And they're no closer to knowing the truth about my parents' killer than they were the day it happened. Their regulations are ridiculous. Who else has a better right to know? I guess I'll just have to find out what I need to know a different way. Maybe the lawyer ...*

Christine stepped out of the shower, grabbed a nearby towel, and began drying her slender body. Her muscles rippled. Maintaining a high degree of fitness was always of personal interest to her. She looked toward Chief. His body seemed relaxed as his head lay over his large paws but she knew he was watching her every move. "You ready for a busy day, boy?" The dog lifted his head and then opened his mouth, his tongue hanging out one side. His intelligent eyes spoke volumes as if to say, "I'm ready. Let's go."

She chuckled. "You like the added training, don't you? One day, you'll be the one to solve one of those missing kid cases." She hoped so. Then it would all be worth it ... the six months spent training hard every day in order to open her agency for finding missing children.

She and Chief had been trained to work as a team. The training was for finding any missing person, but she hoped it would help them specialize in children. That's where her heart was. Since her move to this location, she'd found a private instructor. They could hone their skills and keep sharp. It did keep her out of her office part of the time. "And that's the problem, Chief. I can't find out what I need in my parents' case if I'm not there."

Christine walked past her dog, dodging his sharp claws with her bare feet, and removed clean lingerie from her dresser drawer. While she dressed, she thought about her life until now. Born Melissa Ramport, she'd been raised by a distant cousin of her dad's after her parents were murdered. They had changed her name to Christine Finder ... to protect her, they said. *I'm glad I kept my adopted name, though.*

But the Finders had given her a good life. She thrived as a small town girl in Texas. She'd learned to shoot, ride a horse, and herd cattle right along with her guardian's ranch hands. She'd become a legal permanent resident of the United States as soon as she was old enough to understand but she'd retained her Canadian citizenship. The nightmare had ended ... almost ... a long time ago but the details of that night were as clear as if it had happened yesterday. Now that she was living near the city where it all began, the dreams had surfaced again.

"Chief, after we've spent some time at the office, we need to go see Mr. Goodman." She watched the dog's ears perk up as if he understood all she was saying. She buttoned the top button on her shirt, and then reached with her right hand to scratch the dog between his ears. "Maybe he will answer some of my questions since he's been looking after mom and dad's estate all these years. Surely he wants to see their killer caught just like I do." A tingle walked up her spine from her tailbone. She'd been warned, hadn't she?

Christine pulled on her comfortable shoes, grabbed her handbag from the dresser, and then walked briskly through the door of her bedroom, with Chief right on her heels. She wobbled in her haste and struck one of the photographs she'd mounted on the wall with her shoulder. It was the one of her mother and father on their last anniversary. They seemed so happy. She straightened it and then shook her head. *Can't think about that now. Gotta get to work.* "Come on, Chief. Let's get some breakfast and then hit the road."

Chapter Two

Jeremy slipped his arms through the shoulder holster and settled it into place before slipping on his black leather jacket. He zipped the jacket up concealing the weapon from curious spectators. Then he plopped his black helmet over his sandy colored curls, leaving a fringe of hair showing beneath the helmet. *One of these days, I think I'll get a haircut.* He walked through the back door of his two bedroom side by side condo and strode with purpose toward the black and gold BMW motorcycle sitting in his driveway.

Taking a soft cloth from one of the saddle bags, he wiped off the dust that had accumulated overnight. This was his pride and joy. Jeremy stowed the rag, threw a leg over the seat, and, with his feet still firmly planted on either side of the bike, added goggles to his attire. He stuck his key in the ignition, and smiled as the powerful machine roared to life. He lifted his legs to the pegs as the bike rolled slowly to the end of the driveway.

Traffic, he noticed, was light this morning. But then it was only eight o'clock. He looked both ways and then left again before maneuvering into the street. Soon he was zipping past parked cars and, when he turned left, he was into heavy morning traffic. He watched his mirrors for drivers still not fully awake and unaware that he was even there. Motorists often had a hard time seeing someone on a motorcycle, so he drove extra defensively.

Fifteen minutes later and a few more turns, he arrived on the street where his office was located. Goodman Investigations worked primarily for the lawyers in the city who needed some research done. Sometimes, he located a missing husband, or tailed a suspected adulterer for his angry suspicious wife ... through her lawyer, of course.

Jeremy backed the bike into his parking spot as soon as he arrived in front of his business address. He pushed the kickstand in place, leaned the bike and then locked the ignition. *Can't be too careful in this neighborhood.* He looked around before slipping off the bike.

His hand automatically caressed the gleaming black and chrome on his gas tank. He chuckled. *Dad's probably right. I need a girlfriend.* He chuckled again. *Naw.* This time he laughed out loud. Then he took the steps leading to his front door two at a time. He used the same keychain to unlock the door. As soon as he opened it, he heard the phone ringing.

Forgetting to lock up behind him, his long legs covered the distance to his receptionist's desk in two quick strides. He reached for the phone, wondering who could be calling so early. "Hello. Goodman Investigations." Then he smiled. "Oh. Hi, Dad. What's up?"

Jeremy listened as his father reminded him that he'd not been to see his mother in a couple of weeks. "But that's not why I'm calling," the older man reiterated. "Melissa Rompart ... er ... I mean, Christine Finder is coming to my office at 4 pm today. I think you should be here."

"Dad, I have a lot of paperwork to catch up on. James Dickinson wants to get all the charges for his investigation settled so his client can move to Florida. Then ..."

"Jeremy, Christine is coming to get some details about her parents' case. It's time you met her since you've been the one traveling to Texas and back for the last ten years. Keeping track of her has been your job, not mine. So be here." The request had become a command. Jeremy was used to that. He and his dad had a great working relationship but sometimes he could be a little abrupt when it came to Christine or Melissa, whichever name she was using these days. He'd lost track of her since she'd moved back to Canada two years ago.

"Okay, sir. I'll be there. I guess she needs to know what we know. She's old enough now. See ya later." Jeremy hung up the phone. He stepped away from the desk. He frowned as he moved toward the door, jangling his keys from one hand to the other. It was too early to be open for business yet.

He pulled the door handle with one hand and was about to insert the key in the knob when the door was yanked out of his grasp. A large man stood framed in the doorway, his countenance about as gruff as any that Jeremy had seen in the last few weeks. Jeremy was tall but this man towered over him. "Mr. Finder."

The scowl on the face of his visitor softened. He reached his hand out to shake Jeremy's hand, the corners of his mouth lifting a little. "Mr. Goodman. I am here on official business. I want to hire y'all." The southern drawl was unmistakable. "We need to conduct our business before any of yur other employees come to work. This has to be kept between you and me."

"You have me intrigued. Come in, Mr. Finder. I almost didn't recognize you."

The man, his stern countenance gone, spoke in his southern drawl. "Call me Conrad."

Jeremy clutched his hand firmly. "Ok. Conrad. Now, what can I do for you?"

Conrad Finder stepped fully into the office, his welcome assured. "Let's sit where we won't be interrupted. And go ahead and lock yur door. This won't take long." The larger man moved toward the hallway leading to the back of the office area. He turned as Jeremy slipped his key in the lock to secure the front door.

Jeremy stared at the man who'd treated the little five-year-old as his own daughter for so many years. He pointed the way to his office, and stepped around the older man to open the door. He noticed the worried countenance that the man wore but remained silent until Conrad was settled on a comfortable chair.

The seating arrangement in the room was designed to seat a few people at a time around a sofa and chair configuration, There was a work station across the room complete with more than one computer and a couple of extra computer screens. Jeremy was all about hi-tech. "Sorry I have no coffee to offer you. My office assistant is not in, as you can see." Jeremy sat on the sofa facing Conrad. "Now, what can I do for you?"

Conrad cleared his throat. "Two weeks ago, one o' my ranch hands was murdered. The investigation went nowhare but a couple of my hands said Jose spotted some smoke coming from one of the line shacks. No one from the ranch was workin' thare so he went ta see what or who might be trespassing. Anyway, they found his body a few miles from the cabin. He'd been shot in the head, execution style. For the almost 20 years that Christine lived with us, there were no incidences that gave us a reason to suspect that her parents' killer had found her. Now ..."

"You mean, you think this is tied to her. But why? Couldn't it have been a random killing ... maybe a rustler? They do still have cattle rustlers in Texas, don't they?" Jeremy sat forward, placing his elbows on his knees.

"The killer was careless ... or maybe deliberate. He left a picture of Christine behind at the cabin. I think it was one of them computer generated pictures but it looked close enough. I think she's in danger. I want you to protect her. I will pay whatever it takes." The man cleared his throat. This was an issue that affected him deeply, it appeared. "I care for Christine, like a daughter. I do not want her to be hurt any more. Her decision to move back to Canada was against my wishes but I was only a guardian. Once she became of legal age, your father, her lawyer, told her she was free to live wherever she wanted. I cannot protect her in this city."

Jeremy stood, his hands on his hips. The scowl that had been on Conrad Finder's face was now on his. "Is there any way one of your ranch hands may have ... well ... fallen for her and had her picture, left it at the cabin?"

"No. No way. They're all married. I haven't had an unattached caballero in five years. My men are loyal and wish to remain on the ranch to raise their families. I don't need to hire anyone else. Besides the murder, there is stealing but no one is stupid enough to go up against the Texas justice system these days. Our courts are tough since we have so many illegals. And they only want to remain hidden. This man seemed to flaunt his power ... I mean ... he killed Jose in broad daylight only a few miles from the main house." He wiped his face with a handkerchief he'd removed from his pocket. "Do you have some water?"

"Sure." Jeremy walked over to the small bar he kept for his clients. He pulled a bottle of water from the tiny fridge.

Conrad took the bottle, snapped off the cap, and took a long swig. He swiped the extra moisture from his lips before continuing. "I had my ranch hands search every inch of the property. Other than that photo, he left nothing behind. There's not a trace of him and I have no way of knowing what Jose told him before he died. There were a couple cigarette burns along his jaw line."

"Your ranch hands know Christine's history?" Jeremy frowned, creases flowing from side to side across his forehead.

Conrad scowled. "You think I'm a stupid man, don't you? Of course they don't know anything about her except what is right before their eyes. They do know she's not our daughter. But that's all." He took another drink from the water bottle.

"Then there was nothing for Jose to tell his killer. But …"

"That's not the point. It's what he does know that could endanger her. Are you going to protect her or not?"

"If you think this man is after Christine, what makes you think he didn't follow you here, to this city?"

"I didn't want to make a phone call in case he had some way to trace the call. I didn't travel straight here. I went by way of Los Angeles, then Denver, then Calgary. Each time, I changed my appearance." He took off the cowboy boots he was wearing and pulled the lifts out. Then he took his cap off for the first time and with it came a wig, leaving him almost bald.

Jeremy chuckled. "No wonder I was confused. Those things in your boots make a big difference. And don't you usually wear a cowboy hat? That baseball cap seems so out of character."

"I figured the disguise was enough to throw off anyone if they didn't get too close. I practiced for a few days before I left home, to walk and to do the make-up for the changes I wanted to make." He swiped his brow again with the handkerchief and then took a long sip of water.

"Anyway, let's assume you weren't followed. If this man had trailed Christine to your ranch after all these years ... well ... do you have anything at the ranch to identify her as Melissa Rompart? How could he know what she looks like after all these years?"

Conrad rubbed the stubble along his jaw line. "It was that computer thing." His eyes looked more troubled than when he'd first arrived. "We never kept anything once she was sent to us. We got rid of anything that could identify her as Melissa. Even her teddy bear. She became Christine through and through ... once the nightmares stopped. That took a couple of years and a lot of love from my wife and me. I don't know how he found out or what all he knows … and that's what worries me. He could have already picked up her trail." He stood and then returned the lifts to his boots. "I will leave here as I came, but from the hotel, I will be in a different disguise."

"You've gone to a lot of trouble, Mr. Finder … er … Conrad. I will do what I can. I'm meeting with Christine this afternoon at my father's office. We'll devise a plan to keep her safe ... at least until that monster is caught. I wonder if she can even identify him after all these years." Jeremy opened the door to his office. The jangle of the office phone and the subsequent voice answering it, told him they were no longer alone. "Jenna's here."

"Mr. Goodwin … er … Jeremy. Christine remembers what he looks like, alright. Her nightmares made sure of that. She used to sketch him all the time until about five years ago. Now she's determined to find him herself since the authorities haven't succeeded." Conrad walked through the door behind Jeremy. "I tried to talk her out of that but that girl is one stubborn woman. I guess that's my fault. I treated her just like one of the hands."

The younger Goodwin led the way to his outer office. "Hi, Jenna." Conrad followed close behind but neither made an attempt to introduce him to the office receptionist. "Oh, wait. We haven't talked money and I should have you sign a contract."

"The contract I'll sign but just bill me for yur expenses. I don't care 'bout the cost. Just keep m' girl safe." Conrad switched his path to follow Jeremy to the receptionist's desk.

"Jenna. Hand me a blank contract, will ya?" Jeremy reached for the sheet of paper she handed him before he'd finished his sentence.

She grinned. "I kinda figured."

Jeremy smirked and then handed the contract to Conrad for his signature. He nodded in Jenna's direction. "She's worth her weight. Just sign and I'll fill in the details later."

Conrad scratched his name along the appropriate line,

handed the sheet back to Jeremy and then headed toward the outer door. He turned back and reached his hand out for another handshake. He looked intently into Jeremy's eyes. "I'll be in touch." He slipped through the opened door.

Jeremy stood for a moment staring after the man who had taken on so much responsibility all those years ago. He remembered the first time he'd traveled all the way to Texas as his father's representative. He was only 20 but had been trained at the police academy by then. He'd wanted to become a police officer, but seemed to have a head for investigative work. His father needed an investigator so here he was. *Christine was 16 then, a young tomboy who loved to ride horses and herd cattle with the men.* Conrad was the one he always met with but the brief visits left a lot to be desired.

Jeremy would hand over the support check that came from Christine's parents' estate. He'd leave as quickly and as quietly as he'd arrived. Christine and he had never met. Now ... today ... he'd meet her for the first time. He wished he didn't have to give her this new information. But she had a right to know. She also had a right to know what her father did for a living, but that was an on-going discussion he'd had with his father for many years.

He turned toward the large reception area. Jenna held a cup of coffee out to him. "Thanks. I need this."

Jenna grinned. "This is early, even for you. Who was that, anyway? A new client, I take it."

Jeremy took a long sip. He felt the hot liquid flow all the way down to his stomach. "More like an extension to the work we do for an old client." He took another long sip. *Only she's not so old*, he thought.

Chapter Three

Christine pulled into the vacant spot, the only one at Larson Canines, a local dog training facility. They trained service dogs but she and Chief had been using them to stay in shape. She unlocked the back door and took out the harness that Chief wore when they went through their paces. "Come on, boy. Let's go play."

She walked around to the large open door of the big barn-like structure. Inside, several dogs, a variety of breeds, were attending to the commands of their trainers. A couple of animals were learning how to open doors at the structures designed to look like front doors or inside doors. "Hey, Christine." The sound of her name brought her face to face with Denny Larson, the owner of the facility.

"Hey Denny. How's it goin'?" Christine grinned, her friendly smile an open invitation for a long conversation. "You look a little tired. Out partyin' last night?" She punched him on the arm. In the short time she'd been in this part of the country, she'd become friends with the large Norwegian.

"Aw. Ya know I'm not the partyin' sort. Here to put Chief through his paces?" He reached down to scratch the dog behind his ear. "You ready to work, Chief?" Denny led the way toward the far end of the building where he had an obstacle course set up. "I'll go get the kid scent pack. You can get started." He walked away, leaving Christine the freedom to choose which end she'd start from.

"Come on, Chief. Let's do er." For the next two hours, Christine and Chief worked hard stretching their skills. Chief thrived on the exercises and Christine worked alongside him as if they were one mind. She used subtle hand signals part of the time and at others, she spoke a single word to get the dog to do what she wanted him to do. Chief was very cognizant of his mistress's needs and wishes.

Before long, and a little too soon for Christine and Chief, the training was over. Chief was panting by then and if Christine could have, she would have been panting too. "Good work out, boy." She patted his head and then took one of his favorite treats out of her pocket. This was the one reserved for the end of the training, for a job well done. Chief chomped on the bacon flavored biscuit. She turned toward Denny, as he walked in her direction.

"All done?" The oversized teddy bear grinned at her.

Christine smiled back. "It was good. Thanks, Denny. See you next week."

"Hey. When you gonna let me take ya dancin'? Pretty girl like you should have some fun. All work and no play ... well, you know." Denny chuckled, his flirtatious mannerisms meant to tease and nothing more.

Or so Christine thought. "Well, you know, Denny. With those large size thirteen feet of yours, I may be taking my feet's life in my hands if I accepted that invitation. Besides, all your other girlfriends may object." Their verbal sparring worked to keep a distance between them, a distance Christine fostered. Just before she turned to leave, she lifted her hand in a casual wave and then strode toward the door and her car. She missed the look of disappointment on the man she left behind.

Christine ushered Chief into the back seat, closed the door and stowed his harness in the trunk of her car. She slipped into the front seat and turned on the ignition. "That man is a big flirt, isn't he Chief?" She smiled to herself as she turned onto the gravel road that led back to the city. "Now let's go see what the office has for us."

A short trek on the gravel road led to pavement and then the highway that took them into the downtown area of the city. Once they'd encountered heavier traffic, Christine slowed to the appropriate speed limit, and traveled the familiar route to the building that housed the office of Finders Keepers, her agency for locating missing children. She hoped the sign company would be there today.

Soon the large gray edifice appeared on her right. She maneuvered into the appropriate parking space and turned off her engine. Chief stood on the backseat, waiting to be released from his moving cage. Christine unlocked the back door as soon as she closed hers and grabbed Chief's collar to add a leash. The owner frowned on dogs let loose in his building, even service dogs. "Come on, Chief. Let's go see if we can get the office into some semblance of order. Can't have clients coming into the mess it is now."

They strode side by side through the front door, waved a greeting to the security guard on their right, and walked through the door in the glass wall in front of them. Chief walked as if at attention, his footsteps matching Christine's. "Good dog," she praised her partner. Another door separated Finder's Keepers from the rest of the tenants in the building. She pulled on the handle and walked down the hallway to her office.

Christine unlocked the door and then looked around. The lone desk looked as if a mountain of paperwork had been dumped on it. Christine glanced toward the filing cabinet to make sure she could access it easily to complete the task she'd left the day before. Just as she was about to sit down, the phone rang. She jumped and then laughed a little nervously. "I guess the phone's been hooked up." She picked up the handset. "Hello. Finders Keepers."

Christine listened, her smile quickly turning to a frown. "When did you notice him missing?" she asked the person on the other end of the call. Chief stood nearby but then sat on his haunches. His eyes never left Christine. "I just got in but you're welcome to come over. Bring something with the boy's scent on it." Christine looked toward her partner. "Yes, I use a dog." She listened some more. "Okay, see you in fifteen."

She replaced the handset and then turned toward Chief. "I guess we have some work to do. Already." She looked around. "I need to get this mess cleaned up before she gets here. Can't instill confidence if I look disorganized, now can I?" Christine began to sort through the papers she'd left from the day before. She soon had them ready for filing.

Chief walked over toward his water bowl, lapped up some of the refreshing liquid, and then stood facing the door. His low growl told Christine someone was entering the hallway. She straightened her desk a little more and then stood in preparation to answer the knock when it came.

The fur on the back of Chief's neck stood up and then a soft knocking sound could be heard through the office. "You're better than a doorbell, boy." Christine walked to the door and pulled it open. "Hello, Mrs. ...?"

"Brent. I'm Teresa Brent. Not missus, yet but my boyfriend said ... never mind." She swiped her hand across a nose that continued to run. Her eyes looked as if she hadn't slept in a week. "Nathan is four years old. Two days ago I went to get him up for breakfast, wondered why he hadn't come out of his bedroom yet. I couldn't find him. The screen on the window was ripped open. The sergeant who came to investigate asked me if he sneaks out on his own. He don't."

Christine motioned for the woman to take the only other chair in the room. "Please excuse the mess. I just moved in a week ago. It's been hectic. Can I get you some water? Don't have the coffee on yet."

"Naw. I just need you to find my boy. I'll pay whatever you want. You come highly recommended." She swiped her arm across her nose again and then reached into her handbag for a tissue.

"Who recommended me?" Christine was curious since she'd not had a chance to establish a reputation here yet.

"A Sergeant Charles Major. He said you done this a lot." She blinked. "Lots of kids go missing. Is that right?"

"Well, not lots but yes, we've done this before. Tell me about Nathan." Christine took out a note pad.

"He's four years old. Oh, I said that already. Anyway, he's a good boy. Never runs away like that officer suggested. The screen was cut, they said, from the outside. Nathan likes dogs. He'd like your dog. The officer found some doggie poop under Nathan's window but that's all he found. They did that Amber Alert thing right off but it's been two days. My boy is scared and he has asthma. If he can't breathe, he needs his inhaler. You gotta find him."

"What makes you think the police aren't looking? I mean …"

"They aren't and if they are, they have a lot of cases. Do you have other cases?" She sniffed and then her eyes filled like a dam ready to burst.

Christine shook her head. *Sure. Charlie will recommend me for this job but won't let me know about my parents' case.* "No, I don't have another case. I just got into town a couple of weeks ago. I'll see what I can find out from the police and drop by after I've seen them, okay? Then we can discuss my fees and get this investigation under way. He's been gone two days, you said."

Teresa Brent looked at her watch. "Two days and four hours, the nearest I can figure. O' course, I don't know what time he was snatched. You gotta find him." The tears started leaking down her weary face. She handed Christine a slip of paper with her address on it. Then she stood. She glanced toward Chief who had also stood. "He gonna bite me?"

"No, Mrs. ... er ... Teresa. Chief wouldn't hurt a soul unless ... well ... you don't need to know that. He's a good track dog and a trained service dog so you have nothing to worry about. He's with me wherever I go and has never bitten anyone who didn't deserve it." She looked toward her pet. "Isn't that right, boy?" His tail wagged a couple of shakes but then he watched Teresa Brent as she made her way to the door.

The distraught woman turned, her hand on the door handle. "I'll see you soon. Right?"

"As soon as I get the information I need from the police." Christine smiled, hoping to encourage the woman a little.

"You need this?" Teresa handed a small bag toward Christine.

"Not right now. Sorry, I guess your call startled me. When we come to your house, Chief and I will try to recreate Nathan's movements that morning and then we'll need the scent. Hang onto it till then." She walked toward the door as Teresa nodded her head and walked through. "See you soon. I promise."

Christine watched the slumped shoulders of her first client disappear through the door that connected to the front of the building. *I wonder why the guard never called to make sure she was expected.* She decided to find out.

Christine motioned for Chief to stay put and walked through the same door Teresa Brent had just exited. She walked to the guard's station. "Hey Mitch. How come you never called to make sure that woman was expected? Isn't that what I pay security fees for?"

The guard lifted his eyes from the newspaper he'd been scanning. "Well, she looked harmless enough. I thought ..."

"In the future, you call before you send anyone to my door, understand?" Christine huffed and then turned on her heel to go back to her office. The guard grunted but never said another word. *He does that again and I'm gonna have him fired.* She pushed the door to her office closed and then picked up her phone.

Chapter Four

The streets were congested, making the short trip to Teresa Brent's home take longer than she wanted. Her patience worn thin, she finally turned her vehicle down the street where the child lived. Chief stood at attention as soon as Christine applied the brakes. She quickly exited the vehicle and pushed open the little gate in the white picket fence that surrounded the tiny front yard. Christine released Chief, and walked to the front door.

She rang the doorbell. It opened a crack and then swung all the way to reveal the same petite woman with red puffy eyes who'd paid her a visit earlier that day. "Oh, thank goodness." Teresa Brent stepped back to allow Christine, followed by Chief, to enter. "Can your dog wait outside? Tommy don't like no dogs in the house."

"No, Teresa. He can't. Chief is a vital part of the investigation." She stood still as she watched various emotions crisscross the features of the woman in front of her.

"Okay. I guess it's alright. My boy comes first, right?" Her steps quickened as she indicated the way to her son's bedroom.

Christine commanded Chief to stay close beside her and then followed Teresa to the back of the house. The house was immaculate, although well lived in. The furnishings seemed in good condition. As she walked down the hallway, she noticed two other doors, closed for the time being. "Mrs... er ...did you search the other rooms in the house that morning?"

The distraught woman stopped, her hand on the doorknob for the third room. "I looked everywhere before I called the police. He wasn't anywhere in the house." She turned the knob almost reverently and then stepped aside to let Christine into the tiny room.

Christine strode toward the screened window, located at the head of the little boy's bed. She examined the tear as she fingered the edge. "This has been cut. And the way the mesh is bent, it looks as if the perpetrator came at him from the outside. Teresa, where's that item of clothing we can use. One of your son's." She watched as Chief followed a scent down the hall back toward the front door.

Teresa handed her the brown paper sack she'd had with her earlier. Christine whistled. Chief was large enough that they could hear his feet hit the hardwood floor and his nails click on the wood as he barreled down the hallway. His appearance in the bedroom doorway was almost instantaneous.

Christine pulled out a pair of socks. Teresa nodded in the direction of the socks. "Nathan took these off the night before he disappeared when he got ready for bed."

Christine held them for Chief to sniff. "Find," she commanded. The dog raised his head in the air, turned around a couple of times, and then headed back down the hallway. He scratched at the first bedroom door. Christine looked to Teresa for permission and then opened the door.

"Good boy." The room was definitely a little girl's domain with stuffed animals laying everywhere. She watched as Chief sniffed, looked around, and then left the way he'd come. He stopped at the next room.

"That's our bedroom. My husband … er … boyfriend and I. The other one was Darcy's. She's our seven year old. Our neighbor has her." The woman's eyes released a lone tear that made its way down her already wet cheek. She heaved a sigh and then rubbed a hand over her face to stem the flow.

"Teresa, we'll find him. Don't worry." Christine placed her hand on the cold arm belonging to the distraught woman, hoping her belief in Chief's abilities could give some hope. She grimaced. She really couldn't promise anything.

She pursed her lips. *Think, Christine. What am I seeing … or not.* She watched as Chief followed the scent trail all over the house but nothing revealed the whereabouts of the little boy. She looked toward Teresa. "I think we need to take Chief to Nathan's bed, see if your son's scent leads him to the window and outside."

Teresa nodded and led the way. Christine followed with a slight hand signal for Chief to go with her. Chief immediately walked over toward the bed. His ears perked up. He jumped and landed in the middle of the bed. His nose sniffed the air. He lowered his head, his nose twitching as he used it to push aside the blankets. Then he moved toward the window. He placed his paws on the sill and pushed his head toward the hole that had been cut in the screen. Christine held on to the leash. "Okay boy. Let's go outside."

Chapter Five

Breathing heavily, the man rubbed the inside of his thighs. He swung his right leg over the hind quarters of the horse that had been his method of getting around this rugged country, far longer than he'd wanted. His foot hit the ground with a thud and then his left leg followed. He bent at the waist to stretch his back rolling his body from side to side. He looked over the back of the horse. *Nothing.* His eyes scanned the horizon. *What kind of people live like this?* He placed his hand on the small indent of his back. A soft groan escaped his lips as he stepped around the horse's head.

This should have been so easy. He lifted his eyes to the far distant horizon again. *They probably gave up by now. They figure I'm long gone.* He could see the ranch in the distant foreground. He slipped his binoculars off the saddle horn, raised them to his eyes and scanned the landscape near and around the ranch buildings. A few ranch hands ambled slowly toward a corral that fenced in some horses. *Don't look like they're plan-*

ning to ride anytime soon.

He searched closer toward the main house, or at least he assumed it was the main house. So uncivilized, he groused. No activity there. *I'll wait till nightfall. Sneak down for a closer look.* He picked up the reins that trailed down from the bit in the horse's mouth. "Come on. Let's find some shade."

A stand of tall trees ran along the ridge that bordered the back of the ranch. Casio walked his horse toward a low hanging branch just under the largest tree inside the grouping. He tied the reins loosely so the horse could graze a little. He grabbed a canteen from his saddle bag and took a long swig. The horse whinnied as if to say, "Me too."

Casio removed a bowl from the other saddle bag where he kept some extra clothing. He poured a little of the precious liquid into the vessel and placed it down by the horse's feet where the animal could slurp it up as he wanted. The horse complied as soon as his rider took his hands off the bowl.

Casio loosened the cinch on the horse's saddle, threw the saddle to the ground with the blanket and made a bed for himself. He eased his body to the ground and stretched out. *I'm not cut out for this. It's too bad that dude didn't know more about the girl but at least I have a name. He was sure surprised I had a picture of her, though.* He laid his head back and closed his eyes. Weariness seeped from his pores as his muscles relaxed against the hard ground. *If only ...*

The years had not been kind to him. At one time, the ladies competed for his attention. He had access to all the luxuries his heart desired. He was well respected. *Rompart. That was the beginning. Yeah. Of the end*, he thought. Why he ever went into business with that scum ... well, that was water under the bridge. He chuckled, remembering the kill. *It was clean. No witnesses.* So he thought. *Then the brat. Now look where I am.*

Weariness took over. His memories faded as sleep replaced the thoughts in his head. *Nothing to do but ...* Soft snores emanated from the man as the horse lifted his head. His soft brown coat glistened in the summer heat as he tossed his head from side to side. Then he lowered it. His large brown eyes focused in on the perfect patch of sweet grass.

The afternoon shadows faded as the killer continued to sleep undisturbed. He turned onto his side, his arms wrapped around his weary body. A soft breeze moved the tree branches overhead, taking away the Texas heat. A few birds sang simple lullabies in the bristly evergreens nearby as the sun dipped behind the escarpment on the other side of the ranch. The scene was peaceful, for now.

Casio stirred. The sun had disappeared and shadows darkened the landscape. *Soon.* He raised his head, grabbed hold of the canteen and took a long pull on the tepid water. He swallowed thirstily and then reached behind his head. He had some jerky left in one of his saddle bags. He grabbed a piece and then sat straighter. *Shoe leather probably tastes the same*, he thought miserably. His stomach grumbled its protest at another jerky deposit.

Dark mysterious shapes began to creep from the trunks of nearby trees. Overhead, stars twinkled as if tiny holes had been torn in the canopy of the sky. Casio marveled. *The one redeeming factor for this damnable country.*

His meager meal complete, the once respected crime boss, dug around for the binoculars again. He spotted the horse looking his way. "What're you lookin' at?" He growled as he raised the glasses to his eyes again. *All's quiet.* He watched as the last light, emanating from a window of the ranch house, flickered and then went out. *Time to go.*

Casio stood, stretched his battered muscles, and then swung the blanket into place on the horse's back. The horse turned his head and, with a glint in his eyes, used his teeth to pull the blanket off. Casio smacked his haunches. "Stop that." He replaced the blanket and picked up the saddle where he'd dropped it. He threw that piece of equipment on the horse's back just as he'd done for the past few weeks.

Gathering up the saddle bags, binoculars and canteen, he placed them along with his rifle on the horse. His left foot fit perfectly in the stirrup as he swung his considerable body aboard the tall animal. He groaned. *I hate riding a horse. Archaic.* He lifted his nose in the air as if sniffing to see which direction worked best. He signaled the horse to move and was soon on the path that led down to the ranch far below.

He hummed an old Italian drinking song, one that his ancestors had celebrated with at weddings. He'd missed his daughter's wedding, thanks to Rompart. His wife wanted nothing to do with him now. He was obsessed, she said. The girl was young, she would forget, she said. He wanted the loose ends tied, tightly, permanently, and he would not stop until he found her. Now, at least, he knew where she fled to after that day. The ranch hand was forthcoming ... after a little persuasion.

Now to find out where she went from here, if she went anywhere. Maybe she's in that house, right now. *I can taste freedom.* He swayed in the saddle as the horse took another cautious step along the narrow path. His hatred for the girl burned. *If not for her ... I would be czar by now. I'm going to like this kill.*

Chapter Six

Jeremy sank down on the cushioned seat of the sofa. He'd asked Jenna to hold all his calls, as was his custom, and opened the Bible that always held a prominent place on the side table in his office. He opened the book to the place he'd finished reading yesterday and bowed his head. "Lord, teach me from your word today. Holy Spirit, help me understand what I'm reading. Amen."

He focused his attention on the ancient passage about Abraham's trek through the desert, following a God that he barely knew but trusted implicitly. *I pray Lord, give me that kind of faith.* He read some more. He read about Abraham's belief that what God promised, He'd deliver. *Lord, You made him wait so long. But Abraham was faithful. He believed You'd keep Your Word.*

Jeremy thought about the promise he'd made to his father, years ago. He'd been sixteen. His father had asked him to promise not to marry a woman who was an unbeliever. Now, he was thirty years old, and so far no woman had turned his head from that promise. Jeremy continued to talk to His heavenly Father. *Lord, I'm lonely. I want a family. I want what Abraham wanted ... children. But You haven't brought a woman to me so I guess I need to search harder for one. Maybe the Internet ... no, not yet. I'll wait until Your timing, Father. Amen.*

Jeremy completed his time with God by praying for Christine Finder. He'd have to tell her that the man who had murdered her parents had discovered the Finder ranch ... and killed again. He didn't know much about her, but surely she'd want to know what had transpired. He hoped she wasn't one of those prissy females who'd faint at the news. He shook his head. *No, Mr. Finder described her as a tomboy. Sounds like she can handle the news.*

Jeremy said, "Amen." and stood. He stretched his back muscles and strode toward his office door. He peeked out. Jenna was sitting at her desk going through some papers, "Jenna, any calls I need to return?"

"No, boss. Quiet morning so far." The smallish woman ran a hand through her unruly curls. Her freckles danced along the lines in her face.

"You look tired this morning, Jenna. Feeling okay?"

"Yeah. The effects of my last chemo are finally gone. It always takes me so long to bounce back, though. I appreciate you asking." She slumped her back for a few seconds and then straightened her spine. "I'm just going over these bills. Boss, you've let some of these slide since I've been gone. Want me to pay them all ... now?"

Jeremy grinned. "I'm lost without you. Go ahead. Make out the checks and I'll sign them." He chuckled. "Glad you're feeling better. When's the next treatment?"

"Doc says not for another six months. He wants me to rest awhile before we do another one. That'll be my last, he said. Then we'll see if it worked. God already knows. By the way, thanks for that little devotional you gave me. Two-Up. What a name for a devotional. Focuses on the freedoms we enjoy as believers. The ones listed in the book lifted my spirits." Jenna grinned, her age spots dancing across her cheeks.

"I'm glad. I thought it was meant just for you ... in light of ... well, you know." He walked back into his office and closed the door. He bowed his head again. "Father, take care of Jenna. Heal her of this cancer. For me and for her family, who still depend on her so much. Amen."

He walked toward the telephone and picked up the receiver. His finger punched in the right numbers. "Don. Good morning. Free for lunch today?"

He listened for a short minute. "Great. I have that report for you. I'll bring the final bill, too." He chuckled. "Well, you're getting a divorce anyway. This'll just give the lawyer something to fight with." He listened to the distraught man's response. "Okay, see you at the Forks. Let's meet at the Pancake House. I'm hungry for a Giant Apple pancake. Not good for my physique but ..."

Jeremy patted his stomach, his mouth watering. "See ya later." He hung up and then dialed again. "Hi Dad."

For the next two hours, he looked after some other phone calls, answered a few new ones and even gained a new client. The woman was scheduled to come in later that afternoon to sign the contract. He sighed, leaned back in his chair and put his feet up on his desk. He checked his watch. *Need to leave in half an hour.* He sighed again. *Wish I could go for a long cross country ride on the bike. Oh well.*

He opened the bottom drawer on his desk, extracted the file he'd need to take with him, and then stood. He placed the file on his desk top and walked down the hall to the restroom. His days were always full. *I guess that's a good thing,* he mused. *Thank You, Lord.*

Chapter Seven

Christine finished walking Chief over the entire front yard of the Brent's home. Her own tracking skills had kicked in. Yet Chief had lost the scent of the small boy. Her hands encased in rubber gloves, Christine picked up a small deposit made by an animal much smaller than Chief. She deposited it into a plastic bag she always carried in case Chief felt the need.

Just as she inserted the bag into her pocket, Teresa Brent walked outside. Christine looked at the photo in the older woman's hands. "Is this a picture of your boy? We need to send it over the airwaves and email the picture to the Amber Alert people so they can transmit the information to all their people across the country."

"I think the police did that already. No results, though." Teresa handed the picture to Christine.

"Well, repetition can't hurt and maybe it'll get some attention this time. Do you own a small pet?" Christine pocketed the photo. "I found a fecal deposit near your son's bedroom window. Chief couldn't find the boy's scent. The perpetrator must have carried him out of the yard."

"Great. Now what? We don't have a dog. Tommy. Remember." The tears began to flow freely at this piece of news. Teresa placed her hands on her hips, exasperation written all over her face.

"I saw a footprint in the dirt by the window as well. Could someone from your family have stood outside? If not, it may be the culprit." Christine knelt down beside Chief. "It's okay, boy." She patted his neck.

As she was about to stand, she spotted something glinting in the grass along the fence. "What's this?" She stood and walked closer. She bent at the waist, spread the blades of grass, and reached into her pocket for an evidence bag. Maybe ...

She turned the disk over in her hand. *It's a coin. But not one I'm familiar with.* Christine looked toward the house and scanned the neighborhood. The houses, for the most part, were bungalows, built in the 70's or 80's, she surmised. Most had brick facades with stucco on the other three walls. *Probably a housing development.* Lawns were well kept with an accumulation of flower beds and shrubs. *Pretty normal, quiet middle class neighborhood,* I think. She sniffed the air. *Someone has a fireplace.*

The front door slammed, the sound traveling like a ball bouncing down the street. A tall, rather gaunt looking man stomped down the front steps. "Teresa told me the questions you been askin'. We don't got no pets and no neighbor or family member would stand in the flower bed. They good folks here." He glanced at the plastic bag in Christine's hand. "You find something?" He rubbed the back of his neck. "I hate this. Children should be safe, especially in their own homes. That a coin or somethin'?"

"I think so, but not one I recognize. Could be something. Might be nothing. But I'll check it out." She held out her hand as she introduced herself. "I'm Christine Finder. You must be Tommy."

He wiped his hands on the leg of his jeans before extending it toward Christine. "Name's Tom Devine. Only Teresa calls me Tommy. I told her to let the police handle this but she don't listen a hill o' beans." He sniffed, and frowned as if to get his message across.

"So you think the cops are doing a good job? They haven't found your son, yet. Teresa thinks ..." Christine wiped the hand he'd shook on her own jeans in an attempt to remove the wetness.

"That's the problem. Teresa don't think." He inhaled again. "Her little kid coulda run off but she don't wanna believe he could do something bad."

Christine positioned Chief between her and Tom Devine. The dog sat. "Nathan have a habit of running off, did he?"

"Well, no, but kids are always doin' somethin'. Anyway, I don't think he was abducted." He turned back toward the house. "This is a waste of money." He threw the last remark toward her over his shoulder as he walked up the steps.

Christine watched his back disappear inside. *That man sure has his priorities straight.* She huffed. *Must not be his kid.* She took another glance at the coin in her hand and slipped it into her pocket.

Teresa Brent pushed open the door to the house again and walked hurriedly down the front steps. "I heard what he said. Don't mind him. Not his kid. Anyway, you still gonna look for my Nathan, right?"

"I will do whatever I can to bring your son home. Chief, scent." She opened the bag of dog feces from her pocket and let Chief get a good whiff. "I think Chief can follow the scent of whatever animal made this deposit. Could be the perpetrator used an animal to lure the boy outside after he cut the screen. And I found this." She held her hand out with an evidence packet for the woman to see. "Are you familiar with this?"

"What's that?" She grabbed the bag and turned it over. "Where'd you find this? I never saw this before."

"Over by the fence. It appears to be one of those coins the collectors would be interested in acquiring. Maybe our perpetrator is a numismatist."

"A what?"

"You know, a coin collector." She stuffed the bag back in her pocket. "I'll catalog it as evidence as soon as I get back to the office. I'll call Charlie Major and have him check it for fingerprints before I make the rounds of the collector's shops to see if anyone can identify this coin. Now ..." She looked at Chief, lying in the cool grass, licking his front paw. "Chief. You lose the scent?" She opened the bag again to give him another chance.

Chief's sensitive nose twitched. He walked slowly around the area where Christine had found the deposit and lifted his head to sniff the air as if to say, "It's gone." He bounded toward the fence. Christine followed. Chief whined a little until Christine opened the gate and stepped to the curb in front of the house. He sniffed the grass as he paced back and forth. Then he lay down, right where he was.

"He's lost the scent again." She glanced toward Teresa. "Maybe ..." She patted Chief on the head. "Good boy." She knelt closer to the ground. She felt the cement markings on the curb and reached toward the pavement. "A car was parked here. See that spot of oil. It's fresh."

"How'd you know that, Miss Finder ... er ... Christine? The police never said anything about some car out here." Teresa grunted her skepticism.

Christine shifted her weight from one leg to the other. "I'm a trained tracker. From the time I was a little girl. Learned from the best trackers in Texas. This is fresh oil and if we can get someone from forensics here, I'll bet they'd be able to get enough evidence to tell us which make of car and even how old it is. See the black markings over there. He left in a hurry. You sure you didn't hear anything unusual that morning or in the night?"

"No. This neighborhood doesn't go to sleep till the wee hours. There's always lots of traffic and people about."

"Did the police canvas the area ... in case someone saw anything?"

Christine watched Teresa shake her head. "If they did I know nothing about it."

"I'll ask Charlie. Teresa, was Tommy home all night or had he gone out sometime in the evening?" Christine's eyes scanned the houses on either side of the Brent's as she pulled her cell phone out of her pocket.

"Why you askin' 'bout Tommy? He's a good man. Never hits me or nothin'." The woman's cautious gaze caused Christine to file that piece of information for a later conversation. *She's protecting the man. Why?* She punched in the numbers to the Winnipeg Police Department. She listened for a few seconds and then, "Hello. May I speak to Charlie Major." After his initial response, she responded, "Okay, I'll hang on." Christine looked around the neighborhood again. *I wonder if anyone saw anything.* "Yes. Hi Charlie. Yeah, twice in one day. You know anything about the Brent case ... the missing boy?"

Teresa hung on every word spoken from Christine's side of the conversation. "Yeah, well, I think he's been taken and so does Chief. I found some interesting markings and an oil spill right near the curb at the house. Do you think you could speak to the person in charge, have them send someone from forensics out? This could be important."

Christine listened as Charlie told her the sergeant wasn't all that convinced the boy was abducted. Then in the next breath, he said Tom Devine was a person of interest. "You think ..." She looked quickly toward Teresa and then toward the ground as she angled her body out of earshot. "The sergeant ... Yeah, but ... Okay. I won't be here but Teresa can tell them where the oil spill and the tire markings are. Make sure they understand I'm experienced in tracking so if they ..." Charlie cut her off.

"I know. I know. But I could help. By the way, can you tell me if they've done a canvass of the neighborhood?" Charlie's voice boomed through the connection. "Okay, okay. Don't get all hostile. Nothing, eh? I'll be by to see ya later. Need you to get some fingerprints off this coin I found." Christine snapped the phone shut. She turned a disgruntled face toward Teresa. "I'll never understand why the police won't use civilians to help in cases like this. Anyway, they're sending someone out. And Charlie says they talked to the neighbors but no one saw anything." She spotted the movement of a curtain in the window of the house next door. "I'm going to leave so I can follow-up on this coin. I'll keep you posted. Will you be able to handle the team when they get here?"

"Yeah. I guess. They still not believing he was taken, right?" She sniffed, forcing a tear to escape her lower eyelid.

Christine wanted to encourage her but nothing she'd heard gave her anything to say that would bolster the woman's demeanor. She shook her head. *The police have not done a thorough job, to say the least*, she thought. *Maybe, when I bring in the evidence I picked up, they'll work with me to find this little boy.*

"I need to call the Amber Alert people. Let's get them on board, if they aren't already." Christine punched in the numbers. As soon as she heard a voice on the other end, she began transmitting pertinent information about Nathan Brent, but the voice stopped her. She listened for a second and then, "Oh, that's great. You have the details already." She smiled toward Teresa. "Yes, I agree. The more people, the better." Christine fingered the picture in her pocket. "I have a photo. I'll scan it and send it to you as soon as I get to the office." She snapped the phone shut.

"Apparently the police have sent information to Amber

Alert. They wouldn't do that if they didn't believe you. At least a little." She turned to her dog. "Come on, Chief. We've got work to do." She lifted her hand toward the woman standing on the porch. "See ya later, Teresa. I'll stay in touch."

Chapter Eight

Jeremy's eyes paced the room, his impatience over his client's tardiness written all over his body language. "Come on, Don. I'm hungry." His stomach growled as if to make his point. He perused the menu again as his mouth watered. "Right now, I could eat two of these things."

The sound of shuffling feet caused his eyes to lift without raising his head. He spotted Don Rembreau, coming toward him. "It's about time," he muttered, before allowing a welcoming smile to light up his face. After all, clients like this one put food in his cupboards. "Hey, Don. Last minute customer?"

Don Rembreau stripped his arms, one after another, out of the sleeves of his jacket. He plunked it over the back of his chair. His pudgy index finger pushed his coke bottle glasses up the bridge of his nose as he sat his squat body opposite Jeremy. "Yeah."

His nasal tones when he said the word 'yeah' was another thing that irritated Jeremy. So many things about this man just seemed off. Jeremy was never able to figure out why. "I asked the waitress to hold off so we could order at the same time. Check your menu. She's heading our way."

"I guess I'm paying for this, too. Right. Expenses and all that." Don opened his menu and used his index finger to scan the page. "This whole thing has cost so much and it's not changed a thing. She's still going to divorce me."

"Well, you won't care after I show you the file on her. That woman is not discriminating." Under his breath he muttered, "Probably has a disease by now."

"What'd you say?" Don's eyes glinted, his anger just below the surface. "She's my wife. I love her."

"Let's order. We'll talk later." He looked at the petite woman standing patiently beside their table. "I'll have the giant apple pancake ... with a side of sausage."

The young girl wrote his selection on her pad of paper. "Links or patties? she asked.

"Links. Some coffee, too. Is it good today?"

"Don't know. Don't drink coffee but no one's complaining. And you sir?" She looked at the late arrival.

Don almost smiled in her direction. "I'll have the Western Omelet. Dry toast, no butter."

"Whole wheat, rye, or white?" The waitress spoke as she wrote.

Jeremy glanced at the man's Adam's apple as it bobbed up and down a couple of times. He looked as if he were making a life and death decision.

"Rye," Don finally said. He then proceeded to wipe each utensil beside his plate with a clean napkin. Both men saw the waitress disappear around the corner. "Okay, let's see the paperwork."

Jeremy reached down beside his chair, brought his briefcase to his lap and opened it. He removed the only file inside and placed it before his client. The man had paid a hefty sum for this bad news. "Here. It's all in there. Your lawyer will have no trouble getting her to pay alimony."

Jeremy watched as Don slowly opened the file folder. The man's eyes filled with unshed tears almost immediately. "Oh, Carol. How could you?" His eyes focused on every picture, distress seeping down his face unashamedly. He was halfway through when the waitress returned with their order. She discretely placed their plates of hot food in front of them, poured fresh coffee, and left the way she'd come. Jeremy knew she had to wonder what was going on. Don sniffed. He closed the folder, placed it on the floor beside his chair, and used his fork to cut a chunk off his omelet. "Oh, right." He'd noticed Jeremy waiting for him to put his fork down.

Jeremy bowed his head, but Don peered with vacant eyes toward the wall across the room. Jeremy began, "Lord, thank you for this food. Bless it to our bodies. Thanks for the hands that prepared it and may the conversation around this table be in honor of You. Amen."

"Why?" Don's whiny nasal tone erupted again. "Why do you say that? That our talk honor Him. It has nothing to do with Him, if there even is a Him." He stuck a forkful of food into his mouth and began to chew with a ferocity that startled Jeremy. "You religious types bore me."

Jeremy blinked. *Don's in rare form today.* "I work for the Lord, no one else. You may be paying the bills but He's my boss and I want to honor Him with everything I do. I take it you're not a believer."

"Pfffttt. Doesn't make a difference. The world is a rotten place and my wife is still a slut." He filled his mouth again. "I can't believe she'd do something like this."

"Keep reading. She's done it more than once." Jeremy decided to switch gears. His Lord did not need defending. "With that evidence, you'll be set for life. How'd you ever end up with a woman who was that wealthy, anyway?"

"What? You mean a guy like me?" He swallowed another large forkful and reached for the jelly to lather his toast with jam as he talked. "She loved me as much as I loved her ... in the beginning. About two years ago, things changed. She wouldn't let me touch her."

"I'm sorry, Don. You still love her. I didn't mean ... well, you know. I've included my expense report and a final bill. The file is yours to do with as you see fit. If your case goes to court, I'll testify. That's part of my fee."

The two men ate in silence for the next ten minutes. As Jeremy savored his food, he could see that Don was just going through the motions. "Don, you seem antagonistic toward all things Christian. Why is that? If you don't mind my asking?"

"I come from a long line of people who are independent. Don't use crutches. I run my own business and have for years. It's doing real well so I don't need any religious mumbo jumbo. Don't take offense." He slathered another piece of toast with some fruit preserve. He motioned the waitress for more coffee. "You seem like an intelligent sort. Why do you need that stuff anyway?

"To me, it's not stuff. It's a relationship. But, you have to acknowledge that He's a real person before you can understand the meaning." Jeremy gathered his briefcase and prepared to leave. "When you want to know more about Jesus Christ, let me know. I gotta go. I have an appointment with my dad and a meeting tonight that I try never to miss. Let me know if you need my services again ... you know, court or anything. Take care, Don, and ... well ... God cares."

"Yeah. Right. Pfftt. Don't hold your breath about any more questions, eh." Don stood as well, grabbed the file folder in one hand and the check in the other. "Thanks, I guess." He waved the check toward Jeremy as a farewell and left as slowly as he'd arrived, his shoulders slumped in an attitude of complete rejection.

    Jeremy walked outside to his motorcycle. Before leaving, he talked to His best friend. "Lord, I know you're sad and hurt when someone rejects You. Use the words I spoke to Don as seeds. Water them and bring in the harvest."

Chapter Nine

The traffic roared along Portage Avenue. Horns honked, and tires screeched, as traffic lights blinked from red to green and back again. The lunch hour pedestrian traffic marched across streets toward office buildings prepared to complete the rest of the day on the job.

Christine tapped her foot near the gas pedal impatiently. The Amber Alert people needed the photo as soon as possible so their network would be on the lookout for the little boy. As she neared her office building, her cell phone buzzed. She quickly pulled into the nearest available parking space. "Hello."

Chief's ears perked up. He stood on the seat of the car, waiting. Christine glanced at him as she listened to the caller. "But, I thought ..." She listened some more. "Right, Charlie. I'll wait for you." She snapped the phone shut, unbuckled her seatbelt, and released Chief from the car restraints.

She looked toward Chief and shrugged her shoulders. "The sergeant is bringing the boyfriend in for questioning. I guess I'm not the only one who didn't like the guy." She shook her head and grabbed Chief by the collar till she attached his leash. She slammed the car door shut just missing Chief's tail. "Sorry, boy." The pair walked toward the back door. She used her key to gain entrance.

"I guess I'd better tell security I'm here." Christine led Chief toward the front foyer. She rounded the corner and peeked into the small office housing all the monitors from the cameras located around the building. "Hi. I'm back and just thought I'd let you know that I'm expecting a police officer in a little while. You can let him come on back." She waved her hand at the man whose mouth full of food restricted his words. He waved back as Christine turned on her heel and went back toward her own private domain.

She unlocked her door and stepped inside. "Probably should put on some fresh coffee. Charlie likes his brew." She completed the required tasks for a fresh brewed pot and sat at her scanner. Inserting the photo, she scanned it, making sure that the image was clear. She clicked on the email button to send it to the Amber Alert people. Chief watched her intently. "I guess you'd like something to eat and drink, right boy? Man, its lunch time already."

Christine filled the appropriate bowls with food and water for her partner and reached into the tiny fridge for an apple and some cheese for herself. She took her small meal to her desk. *I need to find some coin collectors. I'll bet Charlie will take the coin to the lab for me. We'll see what they tell us about the perp. Hopefully this lead will tell us what we need to know to find that little boy. Nathan has to be terrified.*

As she was about to make the first call from the list she'd found in the yellow pages, there was a soft knock on the door. "Come in." Christine quickly swallowed the bite of apple in her mouth as a tall man with blond hair stuck his head around the door frame. "Hi Charlie. Come in. Want some coffee." She stood as he walked farther into the room.

"Hi Christine. How's it going?" He folded his long legs as he sat on the only other chair in the room. "When you going to get some furniture in here?" He chuckled.

Christine walked over to the coffee maker. She poured a cup for each of them. "You never answered but I'm assuming you want some coffee. You always do." She handed him the cup. "As far as furnishings, I've got what I need. I usually entertain only one client at a time." She sat at her desk again and placed her steaming cup of coffee on top. "Now. What did you need to tell me?"

"Christine, if you tell anyone where you got this information, it'll be the last time I help you. I figured you had a right to know a little about who your parents were and who they worked for." He took a sip from the steaming cup in his hands. "What do you remember about their lifestyle?"

Christine propped her head in her hands as she prepared to listen to the first piece of information she'd been able to get from the police. "I know my dad left the house early every morning and came home pretty late. My mom didn't work outside the house but they said when I went to school, she was going to work for dad."

Charlie set the cup on her desk. "Your dad was laundering money for the Colombian cartel out of Bogota."

"What, no way. My dad was a good man. He loved me and my mom. He'd never put us in danger. I don't believe ..."

"Christine, this is hard to hear. But, he was a banker so he'd take in their money, and deposit the funds into a bogus company account where they were able to withdraw it anytime they wanted. These facts are all in the evidence file. The police haven't figured out why they killed him, though. He had to be an important asset to them." Charlie saw the look of devastation that crossed Christine's face.

Tears welled in her eyes. "So all the years ... I thought ... Uncle Conrad never ..."

"He might not have known. But your lawyer … he was your dad's lawyer, too, wasn't he? He might have been part of it. We haven't found anything on him but he is a person of interest." Charlie took another longer sip from the coffee cup and then replaced it on the desk top. "What do you know about him?"

A tear slid down Christine's cheek. She remembered the last hug she'd received from her dad and the scared look on her mother's face when they'd made her promise not to leave the closet under the stairs. *They loved me. They weren't the people Charlie describes.* "I only know that someone brought a check to Uncle Conrad every month. The money was from my parent's estate. That's what paid for my house. I'm going to prove you guys wrong. There's no way the parents I remember could be criminals. No way. I have a meeting with my lawyer this afternoon. He'll tell me and then … If my dad was laundering money, why didn't the Feds confiscate his property? His … their house is still sitting there and is part of the estate I inherited." She lifted her chin is defiance.

"Christine, I'm only telling you what I found in the file. I haven't discussed this with anyone. Remember. I'm not supposed to be talking to you about this. But that certainly is a good question. Maybe one that you can get answers to when you see your lawyer." He tipped his cup for a final sip of coffee. He stood as he replaced the cup on Christine's desk. "I gotta go. You said something about a coin."

"Yeah." She reached for the baggie that contained the silver disk. "How fast can you get the lab to lift any prints. I want to make the rounds of the coin shops this afternoon. That boy has been missing for two days already. I need to hustle on this one. I don't have a good feeling. What makes the police think that Tom had anything to do with this?"

Charlie shrugged. "Nothing much. They always look at family first. You know that if you've worked on these cases before. By the way, how many missing children have you found?"

Christine sighed. *Why do I always have to prove myself?* "Look Charlie, I've been working in missing persons for two years, but before that I could track anything that Uncle Conrad hid and any person who was hiding from me anywhere on the ranch. Calico Joe taught me to track like a native. I know my stuff."

"Yeah, but how many have you found." He smirked.

The man needs to be taken down a peg or two. "You remember the case when a little girl went missing two years ago? She was found in the middle of a corn field." She watched Charlie's head nod up and down. "Well, I was the one who found her. There was the case about 15 months ago when an elderly gentleman walked away from a nursing home. I found him in some nearby woods. He was sitting amongst the roots of a large tree. If it wasn't for Chief, that man would have died of exposure. I know what I'm doing. In those cases, the police thanked me for helping them."

"I'm impressed. The sergeant figures we've got this taken care of. We don't hire outside help. We've a large force in Winnipeg with trained people. Maybe those other cases were in smaller precincts, eh?" Charlie moved toward the door. "I'll get this done asap. I'll call when you can pick it up again." He raised his hand as Christine was about to protest. "That's the best I can do."

"Charlie, talk to them. I can help find this kid. They can talk to the other police departments I've worked with. I don't care. We just have to get serious about finding this boy." She looked at the floor as Charlie waved before turning down the hall. "By the way, thanks. I know you went against regulations to get me that information about my parents."

"No prob. See ya later." He tossed his hand in the air again before he slid through the door to the lobby.

"Tell them to hurry." Christine hollered after him and then turned to go back in her office. She almost tripped over Chief. "Oh, sorry boy. Didn't see you."

Christine plunked down at her desk. The frown lines on her face deepened as she contemplated the information Charlie had given her. It seemed so inconsistent with the image she'd carried in her heart of her parents. *Why would my dad risk his family? Why had my parents been killed if they were cooperating with the drug lords? There are too many unanswered questions.*

Christine took a bite of her half-finished apple and sliced off another hunk of cheese. *I need to compartmentalize. The murder of my parents has gone unsolved all these years so a few more days won't hurt. The little boy, on the other hand ... his life could be hanging by a thread. First things first.* She picked up the telephone directory and began her search for coin shops.

Chapter Ten

Casio slipped down toward the main house. The shadows had deepened so he had plenty of places to hide. The night air silently swam around him, interrupted occasionally with a screech owl flying overhead or some crickets rubbing their legs together between blades of grass. He edged closer to the side of a long rectangular building. *Must be the bunk house.* He peeked around the corner, and moved to a window. Darkness greeted him as he peered inside. Nothing moved, not even the dust highlighted by the moonbeams flowing through the opening. The building seemed empty.

He slithered toward a house, a little smaller than the main one. *Must be nice. These ranch hands have homes ... not just a bed to sleep in.* He spotted an open window. The air was still now. Earlier breezes had vanished so the curtain didn't move. But he heard voices.

He crept closer, his feet a silent indent in the hard earth under them. Soft voices floated through the screen covered window. Casio hunkered down beneath the window, keeping his profile as small as possible. He slowed his breathing, his ears strained to hear every word.

"Maybe the boss be home tomorrow, I think." The voice belonged to a man, his tenor spoken with a slight Spanish accent. "What happen wit Diego, eh?"

A woman's voice spoke in little more than a whisper. Casio had to rise up closer to the window to hear her answer. "He get in fight at school, that's all. Teacher say next time, he go home for de day. You need speak to heem."

Casio grunted. *Nothing here. Except the boss is away. Business trip? I wonder.* He squatted a little longer. Nothing else was forthcoming except more talk about the kid. He moved, as silent as death, to the next building, another small house. All the windows stood open but the only sound erupting from the interior were soft snores. *If she's here, she's at the big house, I'll bet.* He crept toward the large two-story with its porch illuminated by one lone light beside the main door.

This building, covered in cedar siding, looked like a log cabin. The windows on the first floor were all closed but, when he craned his neck backward, he saw several open to the night air. *Someone in the house knows something.* He stepped close to the outer edge of the first step leading upward to the covered sitting area on the porch. Silence. He took another step. Solid. No creaks.

Slowly, believing that he had all night, Casio crept upward. He crouched as soon as he landed on the deck. He stopped, listened, and rotated his body to make sure no one could surprise him. Nothing moved nearby. *I am one with the night*, he hissed, and reached up for the doorknob. He twisted it slowly. Silently it opened. Casio stood, moved stealthily past the door frame and closed the door after him. He waited while his eyes adjusted to the darkness inside.

A soft light filtered toward that part of the house from somewhere toward the back. Casio assumed it probably was the kitchen. *I might stop for a snack after I've killed the girl.* He looked around until he spotted the staircase, a circular one large enough for anyone to make a grand entrance when descending. Humphh. *They think they're rich.* He moved toward the first step.

As he was about to place his foot on the carpeted wood riser, he felt something poke him in the back. He stopped as if frozen.

"Don't move. Don't turn. Don't breathe. Or I'll put a hole through you so big a bird could fly through." The voice was mellow but had the husky timber of someone who meant what he said.

Casio remained as a statue, his foot still in mid-air. "Can I at least put my foot down?" He dropped his voice a little lower hoping to intimidate his prey. *I am still the hunter.*

"I told you not to move. I mean it. Now, place your hands behind your back ... slowly." He spoke the word as he wanted the man to move ... slowly.

The gun dug further into Casio's backbone. He lowered his hands to his side and as he did so, a small knife dropped into his palm. He whirled as fast as the flash of the gun as it went off. His arms struck out as the bullet whizzed by his shirt, missing contact by a hair's breadth. The knife hit its target, sinking deep into his assailant's chest. The gun clattered to the ground, echoing through the once silent house.

Casio's peripheral vision spotted lights coming on outside. His hand, still firmly attached to the knife, reefed it upward. He felt the man's chest cavity open as his last sigh filled the darkness around them. He took a moment to relish his kill. Blood covered the blade as he stuck it in his pocket. He removed it again. *Might need it.* His hands were sticky. He headed straight toward the part of the house where the only light came from.

Casio reached the back door as footsteps sounded overhead. The steady beat of running feet prefaced the crash of the front door as shouts filled the once peaceful night. Casio was already outside when lights illuminated the death scene he'd left behind. A lady's screams wafted over the sound of crickets as he found his horse, mounted, and raced for the cover of nearby trees. Shots buzzed near him but were too far away to make a difference. *I'll be back. You wait.* He lay over the back of the horse. *Can't shoot at what they can't see.*

Chapter Eleven

Christine patted the large overstuffed doggie bed in the corner of her office. "Chief, drink what you need now. We're going to check these coin dealers, see if they have any idea who collected coins like the one we found. Charlie says the lab found nothing on the coin so that's a dead end." She slipped her taser in her pocket. "Never know, right?" Chief whined. He stood to follow her. "This won't take too long. Only three shops."

She waved her partner out the door. Christine smiled, feeling as if she'd forgotten something. *I guess I did. Better tell Mitch I'm going out.* She walked down the hall leading to the lobby.

When she rounded the corner, she spotted Charlie again. "Hey, what are you doin' here? I was gonna come down to the station to pick up the coin."

Charlie smirked as he turned from the security booth. "I had to go out anyway so thought I'd save you a trip. By the way, the sergeant's let Tommy go. But that lug only added to his idea the boy just ran off. I don't know how women can allow men like that around their kids."

Christine waved to Mitch. "I'm going out for awhile. Don't send anyone back there till I get back." She glanced at Charlie and motioned for him to join her in the seating area of the lobby. She sat and patted the seat beside her. "Some women are not always good judges of character when they're lonely. Anyway, I don't think Tommy did anything. He's too much of a slug. You know ... lazy."

Charlie chuckled. "So laziness is an alibi now. Anyway, I agree. He's not smart enough. The sergeant has asked him to stick close to home in case he has more questions. As far as the coin goes, he says there's no evidence proving it has anything to do with the boy's disappearance. I have to agree with him. It's just a coin. Could have been left there by anyone."

Christine closed her eyes. "Teresa's yard, if you noticed, is trimmed and spotless. If that coin had been there the day before, she would have seen it. She didn't. What about the forensics guys who were supposed to stop by the house and check out those tire markings and that oil spot?"

"First of all, I wasn't at the kid's house. This is not my case, remember. And those guys aren't back yet so I have no idea what they found." He stood. "I need to get going. I'll call your cell if I hear anything more. The Sarge finds out I'm filling you in, he'll have my head." He took a step toward the door. "I know you want to solve this case. I hope you do ... before it's too late for the kid."

Christine watched him leave through the front door. She sighed as she stood to follow him. *I guess I just have to find the boy, and then the police will believe I'm an asset in cases like this. I wish Nathan was a little older and more able to defend himself.* She walked out into the bright sunshine.

She fingered the coin in her pocket. *No use worrying about fingerprints.* She pulled it out as she strode toward her car. *Can't be too many coins like this. At least I hope not.* She popped the disk back inside her pocket and zipped the pocket shut. Opening her car door, she sat down wearily and looked at her watch. *Man, 1:30 already. Gotta move if I'm gonna make that meeting with Mr. Goodman.* She started the car and backed out of her parking space.

Christine moved slowly into traffic. The first address was on a street not too far away. She drove cautiously, checking her mirror regularly. Chief relaxed on the passenger seat, looking out the window beside him. She was good at noticing which cars kept pace with her and which ones had joined the line of vehicles headed in her direction. *Uncle Conrad was probably a little paranoid but one can't be too careful, I guess. At least he thought so.*

She put her mind on remote as she remembered her childhood. They'd loved her. She'd felt the same once she'd gotten used to them. *Uncle Conrad and Aunt Connie gave me everything I needed growing up including a need to be careful around strangers. They attended all my games, came to parent interviews and tucked me in at night.* She couldn't remember her parents doing any of those things. *Of course I was only five years old.*

She turned onto the street where the first shop was located and checked her mirror. No one followed and as she passed the ramshackle buildings, she could understand why. *I guess coin collectors aren't rich.* Christine spotted the shop, one of the nicer ones, and found a parking spot with no trouble.

"Chief, stay." *He can guard the car.* She glanced around as she exited her vehicle. Two sleazy looking guys with long greasy hair and pants around their knees returned her stare. One waved toward her obscenely. The other hooted as he took another slug from the beer bottle in his hand. *I hope this doesn't take long.* She swallowed and moved toward the door to the coin shop, her hand holding the taser weapon in her other coat pocket.

Dust clouds swirled around her as she stepped into the dark recesses of the shop. Dust covered glass display cases lined one wall with books of all shapes and sizes along the other wall.

Her eyes dropped to the first display case. Her hand wiped the dirt off the glass and she peered inside. As she was about to move to the next one, a voice spoke right behind her. "Can I help you?"

Her insides jumped but she turned a calm countenance toward the voice. The voice belonged to a little man, shorter than she was, wearing wire rimmed spectacles that looked as if they belonged in the 19th century. He wore a sweater vest over a long sleeved gray shirt. "Yes. I hope you can." She pulled the coin out of her pocket after pulling the zipper down.

Christine handed it to the little man. "I assume you're a collector. I hope you can tell me about this coin."

He took out a small round magnifying glass that he fitted to his right eye. He remained silent as he studied the coin. Then, almost to himself, Christine heard him mumble, "Three Cent. New York Coat of Arms. Light porosity." He looked at her. "This is a Feuchtwanger, made in 1837. It's worth about a thousand or so but I'm not interested. Only private collectors would want to buy that coin." He handed it back to her.

"Oh, I'm not looking to sell it. I want to know if you've met anyone who might own one like this. Do you keep track of individual collectors?" Christine's breathing had accelerated. *I'm right. It was an important clue. No one would just drop something this valuable.*

"Naw. Don't know anyone who had a coin like that. I'm just a small collector. One of the other shops …" He scurried back behind the first glass case and reached down by his feet to retrieve a dust rag. "Dust gets in here easy. Can't keep up with it." He began to move the dirt around.

Christine sneezed. "Well, thank you mister … er …" She held out her hand. Instead of shaking it, the man placed a business card in her palm. She read the tiny print. "Mr. Fine." She handed him one of hers. "If anything comes to mind, could you give me a call? You know, if you remember anything, anything at all." She smiled and headed toward the door. *One down …*

She walked back out into the sunshine and took a deep cleansing breath.

She glanced at the store front where the two creeps had stood when she went into the shop. They'd disappeared. She unlocked her car, sat down as quickly as she could and relocked the door. Taking a pad of paper out of her glove compartment, she wrote the information about the coin. *I'll have to look up the spelling of that name but this'll remind me. 1837. Wow. This is rare.*

Putting the car in gear, she looked at the list sitting on the dash in front of her and plugged the address of the second shop into her GPS. She pulled out onto the street and as she drove past the store, the two thugs waved. She saw them throw their heads back and laugh, as if they'd pulled the best joke on someone. Christine shook her head in disgust. *Get a job. Man, some people have too much time on their hands.*

Christine turned her radio on. The first thing she heard was the Amber Alert announcement about little Nathan Brent. They were asking anyone who had any information to come forward. They said a small reward had been offered. Christine grimaced. *That should bring the crazies out of the woodwork.*

Chapter Twelve

Jeremy shuffled the sheets of paper around on his desk. *This is the part of running a business that I dislike.* He wrote on the bottom of the first page and added a sticky note for Jenna to pay the bill. Just as he was about to tackle the next invoice, the phone rang.

Jenna spoke in a hush. "Boss, there's a woman here to see you. Says she has an appointment but I can't find one."

"Did she say what she wanted?" Jeremy began to gather the scattered reports and invoices. When Jenna answered in the negative, he told her to send the woman in. "We could use the business now that Don's case is taken care of."

"By the way. Did he pay you?" Jenna handled the receipts and the banking.

Jeremy stood after putting the phone on speaker. He slipped on the jacket hanging over the back of his chair. "He said he'd mail it. I did give him the invoice, though. He's usually punctual."

"Yeah, he is. Your visitor is coming your way, now. She looks upset or maybe just impatient." Jeremy heard the sound as Jenna replaced the receiver.

He walked slowly toward the door. Just as he was about to place his hand on the handle, a light rap sounded. He opened it and stared into the green eyes of a woman about his age, maybe younger. "Hi. Come on in." He led the way to the conversation area with the soft chairs. "Can I offer you something to drink?"

Her voice flowed like maple syrup heated in the microwave. "What do you suggest? I like anything Rye." She sat on the edge of her seat and crossed her shapely legs at the ankles.

Jeremy swallowed. Then he smiled. "I was thinking more of a soda or water. I can also get you some coffee, if you'd prefer."

She returned his smile. "Good. Water, please. I like it that you don't drink on the job. I'm here to hire you to find my father."

Jeremy reached into the small apartment sized refrigerator and pulled out a bottle of water. He grabbed a tumbler from the shelving above the short counter. As he poured he asked, "How long has he been missing?"

She settled back into the chair and lifted one leg delicately over the other. "He walked away from the assisted living home on Meadowood Drive yesterday. He hasn't settled in there as I'd hoped he would."

Jeremy handed her the glass of water. "So he never contacted you?"

"No," She looked down and picked some lint from her skirt. "He blames me for putting him there but I had to do it. He was forgetting to turn off things like the stove and the light bill was astronomical. He was always leaving them on. I'm his executor so I handle all the bills." She looked worried.

Jeremy decided to test her sincerity. "How old is your dad? How long has he been living there?"

"My father is 72 years old. He's been in the home for three years. I visit when I can but he's never satisfied. Says he's lonely." She smiled but this time the smile did not reach her eyes.

Jeremy moved toward his desk. He opened the drawer where he kept blank contracts. "Do you have any idea where he might have gone?"

"No, not really. Although he had a friend who used to visit him fairly regularly. I called her …"

"A woman. Could he be hiding at her place?" Jeremy approached the seating area again, this time with a clipboard and the contract attached for the woman to fill in. He handed it to her.

"I called her but she said she hasn't seen him. I really don't know who she is or how she knows my father but … By the way …" She held out her hand. "My name is Amanda. Amanda Prescott."

Jeremy gripped her hand. He shook it and then took his seat opposite her again. "Is that Miss or Mrs.?"

"Amanda will be fine." She began filling in the forms. "So you'll take the case?" She lifted her elegant eyebrows and smiled, her features showing interest beyond that of a business relationship.

Jeremy cleared his throat. His countenance remained friendly but his insides were clenching. *This woman just chucked her father in a home and left him. I'd bet on it.* "Those are the usual forms for an investigation of this sort. It outlines my fees and how often I'll send you an update and an invoice. This is a large city so it could take a while." He'd start with the friend. "I'll need you to keep me informed about any changes along the way. You know, if he shows up on his own or something."

"Certainly." She handed the clipboard back to Jeremy. "I assume you are Mr. Goodman." She stood. "How soon will you be able to get started?"

"Whoa, hold on there. I need a lot more information than that. Like what's the friend's name?" He leaned back against the chair cushion. "I'll also want a recent photo. Is he healthy? What are his medical conditions, if any?"

She returned to her seat. "Oh, of course. But I already called Mrs. … er … his friend. I told you. She knows nothing." Amanda Prescott continued to fill Jeremy in on the aspects of her father's health. She reached into her handbag and pulled a picture out. "This was taken three years ago but he's not changed much."

Jeremy looked at the photo in his hand. The man was tall, slender, and a little stooped over but, otherwise, looked as if he was in command of his life. "When did the Alzheimer's start?"

"Oh, he doesn't have that. He just forgets sometimes." She brushed at her skirt again.

She's lying. "When did you take over his finances? I assume you have power of attorney."

He watched the woman fidget a little, straighten her jacket, and then stand once more. "I don't think that's any of your business." Her voice was no longer syrupy but had a harsh edge to it. "Just find my father." She stalked toward the door. "The sooner, the better."

Jeremy held the edge of the door to his office as the woman stalked through. He decided not to follow her, even though she was now officially his client. She'd paid the retainer, filled in all the blanks as far as information about her father. He believed her motives for wanting her dad found were suspect. *Why was he in this home in the first place if there was nothing medically wrong with him and how had she coerced him into giving her control of his finances?*

Jeremy closed the door as soon as he heard the outer door swing shut. He went back to his desk and began making notes about this new client and placed all pertinent information in a new file folder. He pressed the intercom button for Jenna. "Jenna, would you begin an expense account for Amanda Prescott, our new client. And get me Meadowood Assisted Living on the phone, please." He removed his hand from the button after hearing his personal assistant reply in the affirmative.

Jeremy had no time to think about anything else before the phone on his desk buzzed. He pressed the answer button.

Jenna's soft cadence seeped through the box on his desk. "It's the home, Jeremy."

Her voice just doesn't fit her appearance. He chuckled, remembering the reaction of a few of his male clients when they'd heard her for the first time. "Thanks, Jenna." He picked up the phone. "Hello. May I speak to the administrator." The woman on the other end put him on hold while she buzzed her boss. "Hi, my name is Jeremy Goodman. I'm a private investigator hired by Amanda Prescott to find her father."

He listened to the man on the other end of the line. "I can come over right now, if that works." The man seemed reluctant to divulge any information without checking Jeremy's credentials first. *As it should be.* He wrote the address on a piece of paper. "See you in a few minutes. My office is not too far from you." He hung up.

Then he pressed the intercom again. "Jenna, do I have any appointments before my meeting with Dad?" He stood as she responded to his question. "Good. I'm going over to Meadowood. Then I'll go straight to Dad's office from there. You can lock up when you leave." He removed his sport coat and slipped on his leather jacket. He grabbed the folder from his desk with the name Mr. Jeremiah Burton on it.

Chapter Thirteen

Christine pulled into the parking lot, noticed her spot behind the office building was already filled, so decided to take an empty one beside the building. The traffic along Portage Avenue was beginning to look like rush hour. She looked at the clock on her audio system. *It's only 2:30.* "Come on, Chief. Let's get you some water." She locked the car after extracting her dog. Chief followed closely beside her as she walked the short distance to the front door of the building.

She waved toward Mitch, as she made her way past his security booth. Her hand grasped the door knob for the entrance to the hall where her office was and she pulled it open. Then she walked all the way toward the back door to make sure it was locked. *Others used this hallway. The one drawback to being here*, she thought. *They're supposed to leave it locked.* But one time, she'd discovered it had been left propped open. So she made a habit to check it now and then.

She walked down the hall toward her office, *The door is*

ajar. Someone had broken in. Some papers were strewn across the floor and Chief's dishes were turned upside down. *Vandals?* She marched back the way she'd come. "Mitch." She almost shouted the guard's name.

He peeked his head around the corner of his cubicle. "Yes, Miss Finder. What's up?"

"Did you go into my office for anything?" The hands she placed on her hips and the look on her face were meant to let him know she was not pleased if he had.

"No. Why?" He stepped into the lobby, his massive frame almost blocking the doorway.

Christine stared daggers toward him. "Someone has. Either that back door was left open again or someone slipped past you. Did you go away from your post any time since lunch … since I left a little while ago?"

Mitch put on his best defensive posture. "I did not. And I can't help it if someone leaves that door unlocked, now can I? Anything taken?"

"You're supposed to check that door every now and then, aren't you? I mean … that's what Mr. Putnam said when I complained about that door being left open last time. He said he'd …"

"Well he never. And besides, how can I be in two places at once?" He began to walk toward the door separating that hall from the lobby. "Want me to call the police?"

"No. What good would calling the police do? I want the locks changed on that back door and on my office door. Now. This afternoon. You got that. I have to go out in about an hour and a half and that locksmith better have been and gone by then. I pay a high price for the added security here and …"

"Miss Finder. Calm down. I'll get right on it as soon as I get the owner's approval." He retraced his steps toward his office. "I'll ask about checking that door more often, too."

"By the way. Someone is parked in my spot. Do I need to get the plate number for you or do you have time to trace who that is and ask them to move?" She turned her back on him before he had time to answer. She knew that was part of his job description but ... *I wonder just what he does here all day.*

Christine walked back toward her rented space. The office was only one room but she'd felt it was a necessary expense in order for people to take her seriously. *Now I'm not so sure. Maybe I'd be better working from home and meeting people in a public place so no one knows where I live or work.* She picked up the paper from her floor.

Near the corner of her desk, she noticed one of her business cards and bent to pick that up too. One corner was bent. *This might be one I handed out. Man I'm an amateur. I'm inviting people to find me. My address is on all these cards.* She looked at it a little more closely. *All I really need is a phone number.* She picked the stack up that she'd placed in a receptacle on her desk. *That's it.* She tossed them into her waste basket by the side of her desk. Chief whined beside her. "Oh. Sorry, boy. I promised you some water, didn't I?"

She turned his bowls right side up, scooped the food scattered about back into the bowl, and then went to the small sink to fill his water bowl. She opened the small fridge and grabbed a bottle of water for herself. Chief lifted his head to look at her as she swallowed almost half the bottle. She smiled at him. "Getting that angry makes me thirsty. Maybe getting scared does it too." She watched his ears perk up and then he bowed his head to his food again.

Christine walked back toward her desk and began rummaging around to see if anything was missing. It didn't appear so. *Not much for anyone to take. Nothing of value. But ...* the file for Nathan Brent was open. The papers she'd picked up came from that file. She checked each one out. *There's the contract with Teresa Brent. The report from Charlie about the dog feces and ... wait. Where's the report about the coin?*

She looked under her desk and then stood, walked to the

restroom to see if she'd left it in there. *Nothing. It's missing. But why ...* Someone had taken that sheet of paper and nothing else. *What did that report say?*

    Christine picked up the phone. She punched in the numbers and then listened as it rang. "Charlie. Do you have a duplicate of that forensic report on the coin?" Charlie reiterated that he had the original. "Good. Make me a copy, will ya?" She listened as Charlie spewed his objections to being her personal assistant. "My office was broken into. Someone stole that report. I need to see what's on it. Someone thought it worth stealing."

    Christine confirmed that she would pick it up this time. "I have to see my lawyer, remember. In about an hour. I'll pick it up on the way. Thanks, Charlie." She hung up and then leaned back. *I wonder what was so important that someone took the risk to break in here to steal it.*

    It took only a minute or two for Christine to have her desk in order again. She leaned back in her chair. A sigh escaped, as she closed her eyes in frustration. *Maybe this office is redundant. I could rearrange my living area to include a desk. Ohh, I need to order new cards.* She picked up the phone and punched in the numbers for the printer she'd used last time.

Chapter Fourteen

Meadowood Manor was nestled back from the street, surrounded by trees, and built with several wings that flanked courtyards of all sizes and descriptions. Residents sat in wheelchairs enjoying the last vestiges of a warm fall day. Jeremy locked his ignition as soon as he'd rested the bike on its kick stand.

He ran a hand lovingly over the fairing, and stepped up on the sidewalk. He noticed several residents watching from their windows as he passed on the way to the entrance. He waved and a couple waved back. *Must be lonely*, he thought as he pulled the heavy glass door open. He signed his name, jotted his license number in the appropriate spot and then the name Jeremiah Burton where he was supposed to indicate who he'd come to visit.

He pressed the automatic door opener and waited patiently as the heavy door slid sideways to let him enter. The lobby had several comfortable chairs situated strategically so seniors could gaze at the birds in one of the courtyards. Jeremy spied a few bird feeders hanging from trees. One of the home's inhabitants was adding some birdseed to a wooden feeder.

Jeremy approached the nurse's station. "Excuse me."

A young, blond nurse dressed in casual attire, not hospital garb, glanced up from the chart she'd been writing in. "Yes, what can I do for you?" She smiled, her eyes traveling over the length of him, at least the parts she saw from her seated position, Jeremiah surmised.

He cleared his throat, a little self-conscious at the close scrutiny. "Yes, well. I'm here to visit with your administrator. What's his name, by the way?"

"Oh," she giggled. "His name is Mr.Levey. Randall Levey." She picked up the nearest telephone. "I'll call him for you."

Jeremy listened as the girl spoke his name into the instrument and emitted another short giggle at something the person on the other end of the line said. *She's actually blushing*, he noted.

"He'll be right out." The nurse motioned for him to take one of the chairs in the lobby while he waited but Jeremy preferred to stand.

He walked over to the bank of windows and watched as a stooped shouldered older gentleman replaced a scoop into a bucket of bird seed and took a seat on a nearby plastic patio chair. His head hung, as his chin rested on his chest and within seconds his eyes were closed.

"They like to sit in the sun when the day is warm … like it is today." Jeremy started as the man at his elbow nodded his head in the direction of Jeremy's gaze. Then he held out his hand. "I'm Randall Levey, the administrator of this facility."

Jeremy clasped his hand, feeling the sweat the man's palm contained. He wiped his hand on his pant leg and glanced toward the old man in the patio chair again. "I'm Jeremy Goodman. I called about Jeremiah Burton. Did he spend much time on the patio?"

"Oh, my no. Jeremiah preferred to stay in his room ... most of the time. He never got used to being here so, I guess, we shouldn't be too surprised he escaped." He emitted a slight cough. "Well, what I mean is ... he left. Would you like to come to my office and we can talk in private." Mr. Levey's short, robust stature led the way. He waved toward the blond nurse as he passed the station. Jeremy heard another giggle.

Their two sets of feet clattered down the silent hallway. A woman hollered unintelligibly, and a man shouted that he wanted his lunch. Mr. Levey just kept going as he took it all in stride. Jeremy looked around. *If I hear about these people being abused ...*

"Mr. Levey ..."

"Please, call me Randall." The man closed the door to his office as soon as Jeremy had walked through. He moved, rather gingerly considering his size, to the back of his desk and sat down in his chair. "Have a seat." He motioned to the only other chair in the room.

"Randall, how long was Mr. Burton a resident here?" Jeremy decided on the way over he'd do what he could to double check Amanda Prescott's story.

"Let's see." He opened a file folder on his desk. "Jeremiah joined us on September 30, three years ago. His daughter was with him but he didn't seem happy about being here. Most people don't at first. He knew nothing about what we could do for him. Even after he experienced the way the staff treated him, and all the wonderful food we provided, he hardly spoke to any of us. We tried. In fact, this report says Mr. Burton was forgetful so we assumed he was in the early stages of dementia although the daughter didn't say anything about that. Later, after a doctor gave him a good physical, we told her ..." He looked toward Jeremy. "You know, she was the only one who visited him ... oh, except for Franny."

"The doctor. Did he confirm dementia?"

"No. Jeremiah was in good mental condition and we told her that. Did Amanda mention Franny?"

Jeremy glanced at the notes he'd jotted down from his interview with Amanda. "Yes, Amanda told me about her. But she didn't know where she lived or what her connection was with Jeremiah. Are you familiar with her?"

"Oh my yes. Franny loves to visit the residents. Especially the men. She perks up their day, let me tell you." He chuckled. "Franny lives nearby and since she became a widow ... well ... she has a lot of time on her hands, she says. So she visits and brings home-baked treats. She checks with us, of course, to make sure they can eat the stuff she brings but they do enjoy her visits. Jeremiah was no exception."

"Where does she live?" Jeremiah had a phone number but no address apparently. At least Amanda said she didn't know what it was.

Randall Levey swung his chair toward the credenza behind him and searched through some files. He grabbed the one he wanted. "She used to live at 89 Wellington Crescent but when her husband died, she might have moved. I don't have another address for her but she says she lives close."

"I'll call her." Jeremiah made a few notations in his folder of the Burton case. He looked at the man across from him again. "What happened the day Mr. Burton disappeared? Anything unusual?"

Mr. Levey scratched his head. "No-o-o. I don't think so. His daughter visited ... oh, right. He threw her out of his room. We heard him cussing her out all the way over here. He was mad as a wet hen about something." He grinned. "I almost forgot that. He could be real ornery at times ... mostly after one of her visits. I guess they didn't get along."

"Did he ever tell anyone here why?"

"No-o-o but I'll bet Franny knows. The guys would tell her everything for a cookie or two." He chuckled again.

"What are you doing to find him?" Jeremy gazed at the older man with expectation.

Randall Levey cleared his throat. "We called the police right away. They came here, searched his room, trying to find a clue to his whereabouts. They combed the neighborhood. I haven't received a call from them today but I assume they've been in touch with Mrs. Prescott."

Jeremy pondered the information Mr. Levey had just given him. *Need to remember to add a Mrs. to the woman's name.* "I need to find Franny. By the way, do the cops know about her? And what's her last name?"

Levey coughed. "I guess I forgot to mention her to the police. She's such a fixture around here. Anyway, her name is ..." He peered into the folder again. "Morris. Yes that's right. Morris. You have her phone number, you say. Maybe we ought to give it to the police."

"I'll leave that up to Amanda Prescott, since she's so intent on finding him without the aid of law enforcement, it seems. He's only been gone a day, is that right?"

"Yes. No one has seen him since he threw his daughter out. His aid came by to remind him that it was supper time and he wasn't in his room. We searched the entire facility and by bedtime, no one had located him ... anywhere. I called Mrs. Prescott. She was livid, let me tell you. Threatened to sue and everything. We phoned the police right away." His forehead displayed a slight shine as if the telling of his side of the story was stressful.

Jeremy pursed his lips. "How long was it from the time you, or someone, last saw him to the time you called the police?"

His face slick by now, Randall paused. "You have to understand ... we're busy here. We have a lot of people to look after.

Getting them fed, put to bed … it was probably about 8 hours since anyone had seen him. We notified the authorities at eight pm as soon as it quieted down after supper."

"A long time for an old man to be walking the streets alone, don't you think? Did he take a coat with him?" Jeremy noticed his questions were distressing the administrator a little but he didn't care. *Some people should never be in charge of the elderly.*

Randall cleared his throat. His face appeared a smidge redder than it had a few minutes earlier, further proof, as far as Jeremy was concerned, of a guilty conscience. "I believe the police discovered his coat missing ... so, yes, he had a coat. Now if you'll excuse me, I have work to do. You can find your own way out, I'm sure." He began to fuss with another file on his desk, his head bowed in dismissal.

Jeremy stood. "Can I use your phone?"

"Use the one at the nurse's station." The man almost growled his response. He lifted his chin high as Jeremy reached for the door knob. "I don't appreciate you accusing me of negligence, Mr. Goodman. We take care of our people."

"Did I accuse you? I only asked questions. If your conscience is clear, why are you so upset? Find the answer to that, Mr. Levey." Jeremy left the room, leaving the door ajar and walked hastily to the front lobby. *I really need to locate the woman who might have befriended Jeremiah.*

He leaned his head in through the opening in the glass partition surrounding the nurses' desk. The pert little blond was nowhere to be seen but a young man of Asian descent glanced up. "May I be of help?"

Jeremy smiled, in spite of the turmoil churning though his system. "Your administrator said I could use the phone." He looked expectantly at the younger man.

Reaching for the phone closest to the window, the male nurse handed the instrument to Jeremy and then turned back to the task he'd been engrossed in before Jeremy's interruption. Jeremy opened the file folder in his left hand, located the number that Amanda Prescott had given him, and punched the numbers in. He placed the device to his ear and listened.

As he waited he glanced around the lobby, filled to capacity now with several people in wheel chairs and some relaxing on the more comfortable chairs with walkers in front of them. A few were deep in conversation with the person beside them but most were just sitting, staring into space or out the window. A common thread of loneliness pervaded the place. *Hope I never have to live in one of these places.* Jeremy shuddered. *Or put Dad in one.*

The phone erupted with a pleasant "Hello". Jeremy responded and asked if this was Franny, the friend of Jeremiah Burton from Meadowood.

"Oh, my, yes. Such a wonderful man." The woman sounded younger than Jeremy had pictured but, he mused, voices over a telephone can be deceiving.

"I'd like to meet with you about Jeremiah. Would ten minutes be alright"

He heard the huff though the phone connection. "Who are you and what do you have to do with Jeremiah?"

"Oh, sorry. I guess I should have introduced myself. I'm Jeremy Goodman, a private investigator looking for Jeremiah. I was hired by his daught …"

"A piece of work, that one," the woman interrupted. "Why are you looking for Jeremiah? Why is she looking for him? She only came when she needed something from him. You calling from Meadowood? See for yourself. He's in room 203."

She doesn't know. "No. You don't understand. He went missing yesterday. I'm trying to find him before he comes to harm. Amanda said he called you all the time and you visited him … here … a time or two. According to Mr. Levey, anyway."

"Amanda, eh? So that's how it is. Well, I can't tell you anything. I don't know where he is." She harrumpff loudly into the receiver, her disdain for all things Amanda clear as a bell.

Jeremy sighed. *Protective, too.* "I just thought … maybe … you could tell me more about the relationship. What is your address, anyway?"

"I happen to live around the corner from Meadowood. 2013 Fisher. I can fill your ear about the Prescott dame. Come on over, if you're not afraid of the truth."

"I'll be there in a few minutes. Thank you Mrs. …"

"Morris. My last name's Morris. But, you already knew that, didn't you?" She hung up and Jeremy listened to the silence from the other end of the line. *This woman is shrewd. Comes straight to the point, it seems.* He chuckled. *I wonder what Jeremiah Burton thought of her?*

He strolled toward the exit, punched in the security code, and his gaze followed the door as it slid shut behind him. It moved slowly so anyone walking fast enough would be able to get through easily. *Jeremiah had his coat on which would have been an obvious giveaway about his intentions to leave. I guess no one noticed.* Jeremy walked toward his bike, grabbed the handle bars as he swung his leg over the saddle, and righted the bike before kicking the kickstand back and out of the way. He pulled his key out of his pocket, slipped it into the ignition and turned it on.

A few seconds later, he was roaring around the corner looking for 2013 Fisher St. He spotted a small bungalow, set back from the street, and tastefully landscaped in easy to care for shrubs. The numbers 2013 were displayed above the door of the attached garage and again beside the front door. A small Ford Focus was sitting in the driveway, gleaming in the late afternoon sunshine.

Jeremy parked at the curb, shut his engine off, and noticed the curtains in the window billow a little as he strode toward the front door. The door opened before he had a chance to ring the doorbell.

"Why you driving one of those widow makers? Got a death wish?" Her words of welcome were anything but. She motioned him inside; a scowl seemed permanently plastered in place. Then she smiled, and ten years disappeared from her face. "Hi. I'm Franny Morris."

Jeremy blinked. "I'm Jeremy Goodman, Mrs. Morris. Thanks for agreeing to meet with me."

"Just call me Franny. Everyone does. Come sit. Take a load off. I hate those things." She waved toward the front entrance and the street. "Noisy enough to wake the dead. And dangerous too."

"Have you ever been on one?" Jeremy snickered. *She's a feisty old broad.*

Franny punched his arm and proceeded to pour some coffee from the carafe in front of her. "Cream? Sugar? I'm too old to try riding one of them things. Now what's all this about Jeremiah gone missing?"

Chapter Fifteen

Christine watched as the locksmith cleared away the tools he'd used to change her lock. "Here're the keys for yur new lock. This dead bolt should make it a lot harder to break into yur office but not impossible, ya know. Might wanta invest in a safe, too. I could help ya wit that." He handed her the clipboard with the invoice attached. "Sign here and I'll send the bill off to Replex. They're good for it."

"Did you replace the one for the back door? You'll have to get keys for everyone in the building, I guess." Christine handed the bill back to the wiry man standing in front of her. He seemed to know what he was doing.

The man grinned. "No, I supply one key. The rental company gets a duplicate for everyone else." He turned to exit Christine's office. Lifting his hand good-bye, he opened the door, checked his workmanship again, and proceeded to close it firmly. Chief moved to Christine's side.

"Think we're secure now, boy. He did say the lock was not foolproof. Maybe a safe or a home office would be less expensive. A lot safer, too. Although, we're supposed to have security here. I need to check out Mitch. Wonder if he can be bribed." The dog's ears perked up and his head tilted to one side. She snickered. Chief looked as if he was trying to understand her. She ran a hand over his head between his ears, scratching his favorite spot. He leaned into her hand as he always did.

"Let's go see Charlie and get that forensic copy. It's almost time for our meeting with Mr. Goodman, too." Christine gathered her purse, Chief's leash, and the file folder with all the information about Nathan Brent. "This little boy needs us, Chief. We have to get busy. I suspect, since the report about the coin was taken, one of those dealers knows more than he lets on." She led the way to the door, locked it behind her and tried the knob again. "The lock definitely seems firmer than before."

Christine kept up a steady chatter with Chief all the way to her car. The dog tugged at her coat sleeve to let her know he was listening. Once they reached their destination, she turned toward her assigned parking space. A tall, athletic looking man slipped his body into his car parked where she should have been. She decided to tell him he'd parked incorrectly.

She opened her back door, scooted Chief inside and shut it again. Briskly, before he could get away, she walked toward the interloper. The engine was running but the man was talking on his cell phone. She knocked on his driver's side window.

The man glanced at her, scowled, and ended his conversation rather abruptly, it seemed. He pressed a button to roll the window down. "May I help you?" His words did not match the look on his face.

Christine cleared her throat. "You're parked in my spot. We are assigned parking slots by the landlord. I don't think I've seen you here before."

"I'm here to meet with someone. I couldn't find another empty spot when I arrived so I took yours. Sorry." He grinned. His face had relaxed now that he understood what she wanted. "I'll remember next time." He started to push the button to close his window and then stopped. "Don't I know you?"

"I doubt it. I'm Christine Finder of Finder Keepers, a detective agency specializing in missing children. You are?" Christine smiled coquettishly. Some men responded better to a flirt.

He reached his hand through the window. "Desmond Caputo." He clasped her hand in a firm grip that he held a little too long, as far as she was concerned.

"We've never met. Your name is memorable. Italian, right?"

"You're new to this area. I can tell but you do look familiar. Maybe I met your mother ... or father. Oh well. I must be going. I hope we run into each other again. Detective agency, eh? I may need one sometime."

"See ya. My parents are dead." She waved and turned her back to him as she moved toward her car. *I hate greasy men.*

She slid into the front seat and kept her eye on him as Desmond Caputo eased his car into traffic and disappeared. *I wonder who he was meeting with.* She looked toward Chief to make sure her pet was lying down and then turned on the engine. She backed out, headed to the main exit and eased into traffic. She headed in the opposite direction from the Caputo car.

Uncle Conrad would say I probably told him too much. I forget sometimes that someone wants to kill me. She watched for her chance to change lanes as she neared the RCMP Detachment. *I probably should be looking behind me, too, to see if I'm being followed. I've gotten sloppy since I got to this city.* Christine pulled into visitor parking in front of the large gray building that housed the federal police agency.

She snatched her cell phone from her purse and punched in the numbers for Charlie Major. "As soon as he answered, she responded. "Hi Charlie. I'm out front. Can you meet me in the lobby? I'm running late for the meeting with my lawyer in ..." She glanced at the timepiece on her wrist. "Yikes. Ten minutes."

Charlie agreed to meet her halfway. So she clicked the phone shut. She turned off her ignition, and angled her body toward Chief, who was already standing on the back seat, waiting to go with her. "You stay here, boy. I'll be back in a jiff." Chief answered with a whine of protest but settled on his hind quarters to wait all the same.

She exited the vehicle, skipped up the five steps leading to the front door of the detachment, and slipped inside. Charlie waved the sheet of paper in her direction as soon as he saw her. She walked swiftly toward him, grabbed for the paper but Charlie whipped it out of her reach. "You owe me Finder. If the staff sergeant finds out I'm giving you a copy of evidence in an ongoing investigation, he'll take my badge."

She managed to grab the sheet. "Thanks, Charlie, but the staff sergeant missed this evidence. If it wasn't for me ... You can be grateful I'm sharing." She turned toward the exit and ran toward her car. Chief stood as soon as he saw her, his tail doing the happy dance as she slipped into the front seat. "Hi, Chief. Told you I wouldn't be long. Now we gotta hustle." She punched the address to Barkley Goodman's office into her GPS and headed back into traffic.

Chapter Sixteen

Jeremy took a long sip of the coffee still cooling in his cup. He gazed at his watch. *Time I left.* He glanced toward his hostess again. The woman had shed a lot of light on the character of Jeremiah Burton. "I gotta go. Thanks for the coffee and the cookies." He stood and handed Franny one of his cards. "When ... if ... Jeremiah contacts you, will you get in touch with me? My father's a lawyer. He may be able to help Jeremiah get his life back."

"I certainly will." She wrapped her arms around one of his as she walked him toward the front door. "I believe the broad is up to no good. I'm afraid for Jerry, though. He has no place to go and the weather gets pretty cold at night."

"I'll do everything I can to find him. In the meantime, if you're a praying woman, some prayers on his behalf will certainly help." Jeremy stepped through the door into the afternoon sunlight. He took the few steps to the sidewalk and walked toward his BMW.

He tossed his hand over his head at the woman he knew still stood in the doorway. *She certainly seemed pleasant enough. No wonder the residents at Meadowood like it when she visits them.* He straddled the bike, turned the machine on and let it idle for a few minutes as he pulled on his gloves. He grinned toward the figure watching his every move and pulled onto the street. He waved again as he cranked the throttle and roared out of the neighborhood.

The traffic had increased ... a lot ... since Jeremy left his office. *I may be late. Oh, well. Work is work.*

His father's office was clear across town, near the St. James Bowling Alley and the new Mazda dealership. He'd take Grant Street to the new bridge that crossed the Assiniboine River. *This route would shear off a little time anyway. Most people will be going the other way at this time of day. Wonder what Melissa Rompart is like these days? I guess I'm about to find out.*

Jeremy zigzagged through traffic, careful to stay within the speed limit. The temperature was getting a little chilly already so he didn't relish being out on his bike after dark. *I hope this meeting is a short one but it sounded like Dad had a lot of information to give to Melissa ... er ... Christine. I'd better get used to calling her by her adopted name. Wouldn't want someone hearing her real name from my lips. Must be awful to know someone's out to kill you?*

Jeremy rode back down Portage Avenue toward the neighborhood where, for the last twenty years, Barkley Goodman's office was located. Some of the buildings were in need of repair, he noticed, but others had been newly renovated and decorated to fit into a more modern era. He pulled up at last in the small parking space in front of the brown and red brick facade that housed Barkley and Son. *I wish he'd take that 'And Son' off the sign. I won't be moving into this space anytime soon and he knows it.*

He sat on his bike for a second, waiting for the evening shadows to creep a little further along the parking pad. No car, yet. *At least I'm not the last one to get here.* He swung his leg off the bike after engaging the kick stand. He locked the ignition, stowed his helmet in the trunk alongside his gloves and secured that lock, too. As he was about to walk toward the front door, a Jeep Cherokee pulled into the lot and parked right beside his bike.

He turned slightly to get a better look at the occupant of the vehicle but decided to head inside so she wouldn't think he was nosy. After all, if she was Melis ... er ... Christine, he'd meet her soon enough. Out of the corner of his eye, though, he spied a large dog jump to the pavement. *It's Christine, all right, and her dog, Chief.*

He walked through the door, greeted his father's secretary, and walked down the hall toward the older man's office. He knocked and let himself in. When he stuck his head around the door frame, Barkley Goodman stood to welcome him. "Right on time, son. Christine just pulled up."

"I know. She just got out of her car. At least, I assume it was her. Been a long time since I've actually seen her. All my business was conducted with Conrad. Speaking of which, he came for a visit." Jeremy took one of the three leather chairs flanking a coffee table. There was a fireplace along one side of the sitting area.

Barkley stopped mid stride. "Conrad? Here? How come?" He glanced at the door as his young client strode through the door. "Hi, Christine. Glad you could make it. Just in time to hear Jeremy tell us about a visit from your uncle."

"Not like I have much choice. Not if I want to find out who killed my parents." She walked closer to the older man who'd made sure she was looked after since her parents' death. "How are you, Mr. Goodman? Say hello, Chief. I told you about him, right?"

"Barkley, please. And, yes, I remembered you own a service dog. Search and rescue trained, I understand." Barkley shifted his gaze to Jeremy. "This is my son Jeremy. Do you remember him? He's been my liaison between you and this office for the last ten years. Now, son, what is this about Conrad visiting you?" Barkley took one of the empty chairs after grabbing a file folder from his desk. He motioned for Christine to do the same.

****

Christine sat on the only other chair, closest to the fireplace. Chief made himself comfortable at her feet. She rubbed her hands together. "Oh-h feels good." Her glance at Jeremy was filled with curiosity. "I don't remember you. Why would my uncle visit you and not come by to stay with me or even give me a phone call?"

Jeremy cleared his throat. "What no small talk." He chuckled. "He didn't want anyone who might be following him to discover your whereabouts. He asked me to protect you ... act as your bodyguard. Apparently someone on the ranch was murdered. A picture of you was found at the scene. He believes the man who murdered your parents caught up with your Texas address."

Christine's sharp intake of air appeared totally involuntary. *He's found me*. Her insides crumbled but she sat straighter in the chair, stiffening her back-bone. "I need to find that man before he tracks me here. Did Uncle Conrad have any description, anything to identify who this man is?" She glanced at Barkley Goodman hoping for some answers.

"I found out some disturbing news today myself. The police think my parents laundered money for the mob. Could this man be a mob hit man?" She saw the look exchanged between the two men in front of her.

Barkley moved toward the credenza that held the makings for a cup of coffee. "Let's get some coffee and we can fill you in on all the details we kept from you over the years." Jeremy reached over to pat Chief on the head. The dog growled, low in his chest. The menacing thunder sound caused his lips to curl slightly at the corners. Jeremy snatched his hand back.

"He doesn't like strangers and as a service dog, he is working so don't touch." Christine's eyes traveled over the tall man, dressed in leathers. *Must be his motorcycle in the parking lot. Another crash test dummy.* Her stomach rebelled a little and she remembered she'd not had any lunch.

She stared at Jeremy as he settled in his chair. The man crossed one long leg over the other, his smile confident. *He thinks he's charming. Well not to me.* She decided to begin the conversation. "I don't remember ever hearing about you before. As liaison between this office and me, how come we never met?" His smile quickly disappeared.

"My instructions were to leave the check with Conrad ... so ... he was the person I went to see. I understood what ... er ... who the money was for but I saw no reason to pull you into it at that time. I am aware you are an adult now and ..."

Jeremy's pause gave Christine an opportunity to share her displeasure at being treated as a child. "I've been considered an adult for the last ... oh ... eight years. You should think about that instead of ignoring my existence."

Jeremy sputtered. "Why ... you ... I never ..." He stood. His full six foot, three inches usually an intimidating sight. Christine stood as well. Chief stood in front of her.

Barkley strode hurriedly toward them, a cup of coffee in each hand. "Come on, you two. Jeremy followed my orders, Christine. We thought since Conrad had always controlled your affairs, he continued to be your adviser, even when you moved back to Canada. Now, we'll deal with you directly." He handed each of them a cup.

Christine sat down gingerly, holding her hand steady. *Where did that come from?* She glanced toward Jeremy who had also taken his seat. *Never reacted to anyone with instant anger before.* "Sorry, Jeremy. I know you did what you felt was right. No lunch. Must be hungry ... or something."

"Yeah ... or something." Jeremy grimaced. She could tell his smile was forced. "Anyway, as investigator ..."

Christine was about to take a sip of her coffee but stopped midway to her mouth. "You're an investigator, too?"

"Yeah. I work for dad mostly but I also have a few other clients. Other lawyers who need some snooping done. Then there's walk-in traffic as well but mostly word of mouth. I understand you specialize in missing people, mostly children." Jeremy relaxed a little. His eyes held hers as he took a drink from the flavored beverage his father knew was his favorite.

"I do. Chief and I. But I'm just getting started. Nothing big like you ... yet." She looked toward Barkley. "I need to know everything you know about my parents. I remember the day as if it had just happened. Or at least, I think I do. It's a reoccurring nightmare. Some of the details may be distorted." She shivered, her memory of last night vivid once again.

"Your father's profession was as a banker, a very successful one, but he owned, and now his estate owns, the large bank building on Portage Avenue near Polo Park, to the right of the shopping center. And there are several other businesses along the street that he owned as well and are very successful. He was CEO at the bank but controlled all the other assets, too. There are others in place, now, to control all the real estate but the estate ... you actually ... own everything outright. I oversee the operation and I made sure to appoint trusted men to assure your assets were protected. It's been a full time job for me over the last ... well, since your parents were killed." His brows crinkled over his nose when he spoke the last words.

Christine listened intently. "I'd been told they were well off but ..." She had a hard time processing just how rich. "Exactly how much am I worth?"

"I never sold the house so you own it as well as the bank. You're worth close to one hundred million dollars. I sold the boat a year after your parent's death but I kept the house because … well, I thought you might want to live in it someday."

Christine shuddered. "All I can remember about the place is the murder. I don't think …"

Jeremy interjected. "Maybe you need to visit it before you decide what to do with the property. After all these years, it may not hold just those memories."

Christine scowled toward him. "If your parents had been murdered right before your eyes, would you want to live in the house again?" She glanced back at Barkley. "Besides, the killer certainly remembers where it is and probably waits for the day I show up."

Barkley appeared to consider this for the first time. "If there's been anyone keeping their eye on the place, no one noticed. People have rented the house over the last twenty years. The estate has paid for the upkeep, but on paper, as far as the public records go, they are the owners, not the tenants. So, no … I don't think he expects you to return there."

Jeremy interjected, "Dad thought of everything he could to keep you safe in Texas. And the Finders did as well. But now that the killer discovered your connection to them, you may want to change your name again. Finder is not a common name and since this is your home city … he'll put two and two together …"

"… and come up with Rompart. I understand." Christine reached toward Chief and patted his head. "I thought of moving my office home. More secure. I had a break-in earlier today. I'm looking for a missing four-year-old and someone stole some evidence I had gathered, or at least, the forensic report of the evidence."

Jeremy scrunched up his face. "I suppose you could move into my office. We could operate separately but under my name …"

"What?" Christine almost choked. "You can't be serious."

Chapter Seventeen

Casio walked confidently across the tiled floor of the airport. His boots made a steady clatter as he approached the ticket counter. "I need a one-way ticket to Canada ... Toronto, Canada." He placed his one suitcase on the scale to be weighed and sent to the baggage area.

The ticket agent looked at his computer screen. "There's a plane leaving in one hour."

"I know. That's why I'm here." His gruff, no-nonsense mannerism made the agent cringe. "How much?"

"First-class or business?"

"First-class. Near a window." His tone softened. *Wouldn't want to be remembered.* He smiled.

Casio kept his eye on the agent as the younger man punched in the particulars. His uniform was pristine as he printed off the ticket and boarding pass, secured them in a folder, and then looked toward Casio. "That'll be Houston to Toronto, Canada, United Flight 8541, first class, departs 7:35 this morning and will arrive at 11:37 this morning in Toronto. Trip duration is three hours and two minutes. Will that be okay?" When Casio nodded, the flight agent secured a luggage tag to Casio's bag. "That'll be two thousand, four hundred, and three dollars, please."

    Casio handed over the money without any further comment, took the packet, and then, after reading which gate was boarding that flight, made his way down the concourse toward gate 16. He handed the agent at the security gate his boarding pass, emptied his pockets into the basket provided, and walked through the portal beside the x-ray machine. His belongings back in his pockets, he made his way toward the waiting area until he was called to board.

    Casio sat on one of the hard plastic chairs. He crossed his legs and sighed. *Can't wait to get back to Canada. That kid must have gone somewhere. I ain't waiting for her any longer. They might find me if I wait around. She may never come back anyway.* He switched his legs, crossing one over the other again. *Maybe she's at home ... her parents' home.* He sighed again and then growled. *I hate loose ends.*

Chapter Eighteen

Without thinking, Christine muttered an expletive. "I don't run errands."

She saw Jeremy cringe. "You have some mouth. I guess working and living on a ranch in Texas never taught you how to be a lady." He scowled at her. "I don't run errands, either. Right now, for instance, my client wants her father found. He went missing from a nursing home. We could help each other … with your tracking skills … oh, forget it. Dumb idea."

"No, I don't think it is." Barkley Goodman sat up straighter. "Christine needs a new location for her office and you need to protect her as Conrad Finder asked you to do. It's a win-win situation."

Christine protested in her most masculine tone of voice. "I work alone ... with Chief. I don't need a babysitter."

Jeremy chuckled a little and then squelched the chuckle. "You said that, not me." He smiled toward her but then removed the expression off his face, too. "I mean partners. You buy into my practice and we're equal partners. There's an extra office with all the furniture."

"The rental company requires a month's notice."

Barkley decided to add his two cents. "But you were thinking of leaving sooner, weren't you?"

"Yes. Well. I don't feel safe in my office anymore." She leaned back in her chair placing the coffee cup on the side table. "Chief warns me when we're in residence but when I'm not there, things happen. I figured I could meet prospective clients at a restaurant or something."

"Sounds like a plan and one you probably should implement even if you decide to join Goodman Investigations." Jeremy drained the last of his coffee and placed his empty cup on the coffee table in front of him.

Christine swallowed. She glanced at a grease stain on her jeans and then lifted her eyes toward the younger man. "We don't get along."

Jeremy bent his head as if in agreement. "With the Lord's help …"

Christine groaned. "Wonderful. You're a religious fanatic, too. I don't do religion."

"It's not relig … oh never mind. I can't be a partner with someone who's not a believer, anyway." Jeremy threw his hands in the air.

"Come on. You guys." Barkley squinted at Jeremy. "Not a partner, then. She can simply rent space from you." He turned to face Christine who was getting ready to leave, it seemed. "You don't want to find out whether what the police said is true or not?" He motioned for her to be seated again. "Jeremy is not a religious fanatic. Neither am I. We believe. That's all. The Lord is important to us but our faith doesn't need to affect a working relationship between you two."

Christine returned to her seat. *The man is impossible. He is so sure of himself.* She thought the last with every ounce of sarcasm she could muster. "What? I'm not good enough to be partner, now, cause I don't go to church?"

Jeremy decided to let the comment drop. "The rent will include utilities for the percentage of space you're renting since it's all on one account. This is for convenience sake, only. Nothing else."

"Fine. I'll think about it. Now what about my parents laundering drug money?" Christine pulled Chief by the collar toward her legs and settled him at her feet. "I can't remember what they were like but I don't remember ever being scared before that day."

Barkley began. "The real estate company your father owned was having financial difficulties. He had acquired too many properties and with the crash of the banks in the US and their economy in dire straits, people were not investing as much as they once did. A wealthy man came to the office looking for investment opportunities so the company … your father … sold him a whole bunch of properties both commercial and residential. However, your dad didn't check him out initially. He was just so glad to get out from under the expense of keeping those properties in saleable condition; he jumped at the chance to unload them. When he did decide to get to know the man better, it was too late. He was in bed with the mob. They kept coming back to him. They threatened to expose him if he didn't continue to launder their money." Barkley shook his head. "Your dad was so naive in the beginning."

"So if he was working with them, why did they kill him … and my mother … 'if'" She made quote marks with her hands. "… they are the ones who did this?" Christine's face clouded. Years of unanswered questions filled her mind. As much as she hated knowing the truth, not knowing why someone killed her parents had been worse.

Barkley cleared his throat while Jeremy sat rigid. Christine felt his eyes on her. The urge to stick out her tongue at him was almost over-powering. Barkley continued, "Your dad decided that he wouldn't do it any longer. He wanted out. That's why they killed him. He threatened to go to the authorities to clear his name. The RCMP had already approached him and told him they were looking into his activities."

Christine laid her hand on Chief's collar. "The RCMP know so much about mom and dad because they were investigating them. I tossed around the idea of joining them in order to find out what they had in their files about my parent's murder, but made friends with one of the corporals instead. He's become a good friend."

Jeremy asked, "Is that all they told you?"

"Yes. He wasn't supposed to tell me that much but figured I ought to know. He figured I wouldn't be able to do anything with the information anyway." She gazed at the toe of her shoes and then raised her eyes to Barkley. "What else? How did you deal with all this after their death?"

"One good thing was your dad never used me to act as a lawyer for any of the real estate business. I was his personal lawyer. I only knew what he was doing after he told me the trap he'd fallen into. Make no mistake. It was a trap. He had no idea who these people or this man was or he'd never have done business with them. Your father was a highly ethical man." Barkley stepped over near his desk and opened a file cabinet. He retrieved a sheet of paper and reached toward another drawer to get a second sheet.

Jeremy decided to interject. "Your parents, as far as I can see, tried to do what's right. The RCMP should have protected them but ... maybe he hadn't told them how far he was willing to go to clear it all up and clear his name in the process. Didn't you tell me, Dad, that John Rompart told you this group of hoodlums comes from the Toronto area. I don't know what the police have on them or how far they've come in their investigation."

Barkley handed Christine the sheets of paper. "The top one is a contract between you and I, allowing me to continue acting as your lawyer. Now that you're here, we can meet on a regular basis so I can bring you up to date on all the assets. We can inspect each individual property and I'll introduce you to the property managers, or ... I'll continue to handle things as in the past, keeping you out of the picture. Frankly, in light of what Jeremy was told by your uncle, I think that's the way we should proceed. For your safety. The fewer people who know who you are, the better. Don't you agree?"

Christine stared at the older man for a moment. "I hate being managed. But ... I agree. If he finds me before I can find him, I'm a dead person. You've done a great job so far, or at least, I think you have, so we'll continue along that vein until I find out differently."

"Are you suggesting my dad ..."

"Jeremy, never mind. Christine has a lot to be suspicious about. Other than the Finders, she's not known anyone she can trust." His eyes followed as Christine signed the contract. "Now the other sheet of paper is an affidavit to change your name legally."

"Is a legal name change necessary? Can't I just call myself something else? Especially since I'm not going into partnership with Jeremy." She leaned back into the chair, lifted the now cold coffee and sipped enough to wet her lips. All this was beginning to feel like information overload.

"I suppose, but you'll need to change your license and everything." Barkley glanced at the affidavit as Christine sighed and signed in the correct spot. "Have you thought of what name you want to use?"

"I thought I'd find the most popular name in the phone book. That way, it'll be hard to find should the name ever crop up on their radar. I don't want Uncle Conrad and Aunt Connie knowing what it is either. I'll keep in touch with them some other way ... maybe through you Jeremy, since you have a contract with him."

Jeremy stood. "I have to go. But yes, that'll work. You will let me know when you want to move in ... if you want to move in. I can help."

She bristled. "Don't bother. I can do it. I'll let you know in a day or two. Right now a four-year old needs to be found." Chief's ears perked up and he stood to his feet with his tail wagging as soon as she stood. "We've a kid to find, don't we boy?" She smiled at her partner.

Jeremy squinted his eyes at the interaction between the woman and her dog. "How come you can be so nice to the dog but you treat me as a pariah?"

She smiled for the first time since she'd arrived. "Want me to scratch your ears?"

"If it'll improve the situation between us." He turned the side of his head toward her.

Christine chose to ignore him. "I'm glad you told me about my parents, Mr. Goodman ... er ... Barkley. Habits are hard to break. Anyway, at least now I understand my Dad wasn't a criminal. The police ..."

"Yeah. I know. To them everyone is guilty until proven innocent. We'll get all this straightened out. In the meantime, be defensive. Don't do anything dangerous. Let the authorities handle things." Barkley gave her a pat on the shoulder.

"The authorities? Yeah, right. The cops had twenty years. No, I think this is something I need to do." Christine continued to walk toward the door. "I may have to feed the information I come up with to them ... like I had to do with this little boy's abduction I'm handling. They missed so many clues because they didn't want to think there might be a pedophile in the city preying on kids. But I gave them the information so things can be all legal like and we'll get a conviction ... if we find the guy. I'll do the same with my parents' killer."

Jeremy walked slowly behind her toward the door. "I can help, too. I have resources you don't have. By the way, how good is Chief at tracking missing people? He could help me find the old man. Dad, I may need you to do some legal work for him when I do find out where he went."

"No problem, son." He walked slowly toward his office door with the two younger people. "By the way, Christine. Can you still remember what this man looks like after all these years?"

Christine frowned. She rubbed her temple as if she had a headache. "Every night, or at least most nights. I have a reoccurring nightmare. The dream stopped for a while but its back now. I visit the entire scene as if it happened yesterday. That man's face haunts me."

"How about going over some of the photos the police have on file?" He placed his hand on his hip, his pose thoughtful.

"I haven't done anything like that, and the police haven't suggested it, but that's a good idea. If this guy is organized crime, they may know all about him." Christine reached toward Chief again as if trying to reassure herself. "There's been little time to really do some digging but I guess I'd better get serious about tracking this creep down. Maybe even go back to Texas …"

"Hold on a minute. I said don't do anything dangerous." Barkley and Jeremy spoke almost at the same time.

"I can go but not you." Jeremy interposed.

"Right. And if he's still there, he'll follow you right to your office … where you want me to work." She looked toward the younger man with disgust. She turned her head toward Barkley. "It was a thought. He's probably long gone now anyways. What about a sketch artist?"

"I can arrange things." Barkley walked back toward his desk. He opened a drawer.

Christine moved toward the door again. "Gotta get going. Let me know when you get things set up with the police and a sketch artist. Thanks for everything, Barkley. Jeremy, it's been different." She tilted her head up a little as she breezed past him. Chief let out a low growl and followed her footsteps as he'd been trained.

Barkley glanced at the door and stepped around his desk. "Fine. I'll be in touch. Take care you two and try to get along. Life's too short. The Lord ..." He stopped when he saw Christine's face. "Okay, okay. But one day you will listen when I tell you about what God did for me." He waved as he shut the door behind them.

Christine turned to face Jeremy. "Is this God thing going to be a problem between us? Otherwise, I can move my office home instead."

"No. No problem. Tell me when you want to move." Jeremy threw his leg over the seat of his bike. He pulled the zipper of his jacket all the way up to his neck before placing his helmet on his head.

Christine glanced toward him before opening the door to her vehicle. "Those things are death traps, you know."

"Yeah, heard it all before. See ya." She watched as he kicked the bike into gear and roared out of the parking lot. She shook her head. Chief whined beside her. She opened the back door and the dog jumped inside. He immediately lay down. "Time for home, eh boy? We'll go get some dinner and then prepare for a long night of surveillance. We'll find out what happens after dark at the first coin shop."

Chapter Nineteen

  Jeremy rounded the corner heading to his office. He pulled into the parking slot in front of the converted residence, switched off his bike, and put the kickstand down. *I forgot to give Christine the address. She doesn't have my telephone number either. That woman has me all fuddle brained. I wonder what her problem is, anyway.* He walked up the few steps to his office's front door. He knew Jenna would have already gone home, so he took out his key and unlocked the door.

  His brows furrowed as he thought about the young woman he'd just met. *She sure seems to have a bee up her bonnet.* He stomped down the hall toward his office after making sure the main door was locked again. Before heading into his personal domain, he opened the door to the empty space he'd mentioned to Christine. *This should work nicely for her. Should be large enough.* The furnishings were sparse but he knew she had some of her own to add to the stuff already in the room. *Probably has a bed for Chief, too.*

  He closed the door and went across the hall to his own office space. Like his dad, he enjoyed the comfortable seating arrangement where clients could feel at ease. He stepped around the sofa and sat in the chair at his desk. He turned on his computer. Entering his password, he searched for the file he'd already started for Jeremiah Burton.

When the Word document popped up on the screen, he entered the date, Franny's name, and then began to add the information he gleaned from his visit with her. As he typed, he thought of the man he was searching for. Franny had told him a lot about the older gentleman. Jeremy typed widower and the date four years earlier. Apparently, at least according to Franny, Jeremiah went into a slump after losing his wife of fifty two years.

"He doesn't remember much about that time," Franny told him. "He just couldn't cope with her death so he'd left the funeral preparations for his daughter. She'd had a lot of papers for him to sign in the months that followed, and one of them, he'd found out later, was the power of attorney, making her executor of his estate. She controls all his money now."

Jeremy typed a note to himself to check out Jeremiah's bank, see if he could get a copy of that document from them. *They must have a copy on file*. He shook his head. How could a daughter do that to her dad? But then Franny said that he'd been at a low point for a few months. Maybe she thought he needed to be placed in there for his own protection.

Then he remembered another thing that Franny had said. "Jeremiah told me that he was admitted to Meadowood a year after his wife died. By then he was doing fine on his own, although he still missed her. He had forgotten things a few times and his daughter started treating him as if he were a child." Franny had looked rather disgusted when she'd told Jeremy that. She'd offered her opinion. "I think this is a case of elder abuse, myself."

Jeremy used his computer to investigate the law concerning elder abuse. He looked up what constituted abuse, and what could be done to protect the victims. He glanced around the room. *Boy, I'd never get away with this stuff with dad. I wonder why Amanda felt she had the right to treat her father that way.*

He finished the report, shut his computer down, and then walked back down the hall to the front door. Franny had mentioned something about a pub near Jeremiah's home address. She thought he was friends with the owner or someone there. *I can get some dinner there while I check it out.* He pulled the picture of Jeremiah; the one Amanda had given him, from his pocket. *Shouldn't be too hard to recognize.*

He stepped out into the early evening air. He shivered. *Getting cooler, need to get the truck from home.* Jeremy zipped his jacket all the way to the neck as he walked toward his motorcycle. He ran his hand over the gold and black paint job, a custom finish. *Adds pizzazz,* he thought. He headed down the street toward home. Keeping his speed a little lower than he had that morning, he soon spotted his truck in the driveway. *Heat will be good,* he decided.

He sat on his BMW for a minute, letting the last rays of sunshine warm his chilled body. Almost time to put the machine away for the winter. *I need a place where I can have space for all my toys.* He straddle-walked his bike around the truck and parked it on the tiny bit of lawn in front of his condo. *This was alright as a temporary place to live but I need more room.*

Locking his bike, he placed his helmet on the front seat of his truck, stepped up into the cab, and stuck his key in the ignition. The vehicle roared to life almost immediately so he backed down the driveway again. He sat at the edge of the street until he punched the address of the pub into his GPS. *Where would we be without gadgets like this?* He snickered. *Dad has no use for them. He can be so old-fashioned about some things.*

Better conceal my gun. Jeremy took his jacket off, unhooked his holster, and placed his weapon in the glove compartment. *Probably won't need this where I'm going.* He put the leather garment back on, fastened his seat belt and then turned his heater on. *Ah-h warmth.* He put the truck in gear and headed toward the pub. The GPS said it was thirty minutes away.

Chapter Twenty

Christine pulled into the driveway. She sighed as she stared at her home. *I love this place but I'm never here. When this case is over ... but a new client could walk through my door any day. Oh, well. The place is a refuge at the end of the day anyway.* She unlocked the back door of the car before stepping out of the vehicle. Chief barked once and bounded out as soon as she opened the door. "Chief, stay close."

She glanced at him as he rolled around in the dead leaves under the trees lining her property. His feet kicked up in the air as he scratched his back, wiggling his body back and forth. "You love this place, too, don't you boy?" She walked toward her front door.

Inserting the key into her deadbolt, she turned the lock and pulled the door handle with her other hand. "Come on, Chief. Let's get something to eat." The dog flew toward her at the mention of food. She chuckled. "Hungry, are we?"

She slipped inside and, immediately, locked the door behind her. "I'm gonna wear sweats tonight." She spoke to the dog that was waiting by the kitchen door. "Let me change first."

Chief followed, as she moved down the hall to her bedroom. *Seems as if I've been gone a week instead of a day,* she thought. She bent her neck from side to side to stretch her spinal column. Quickly exchanging one outfit for another, she walked back the way she'd come and entered her tiny kitchen. She pulled open the door to a large cabinet, slipped the lid off the fifty pound container of dog food and used the scoop inside to fill Chief's bowl. His eyes were filled with gratitude as he wagged his tail to say thanks. Christine patted his head before he bent it to the bowl.

"Now for me. Let's see." She opened her freezer. "Yuck. TV dinners. I need to take some time to add some nutritious meals to this freezer." She took one out, popped it into the microwave, and walked to her back door. It wasn't quite dark yet, so she saw clearly into her back yard. *The trees have lost more leaves today,* she noticed. *Gonna have to find time to rake or they're gonna kill the grass. Home ownership has a lot of responsibility.*

She thought for a minute about Connie and Conrad Finder. *I wish he'd stopped by or at least tried to get in contact with me. I miss them. A trip would be nice when this is over.* She remembered all the work running the ranch in Texas. *This house is not as much work but maintenance takes some time.* The microwave buzzer sounded.

A few steps to the fridge, she grabbed a bottle of pomegranate juice. She opened a cupboard door to nab a plate to place under the hot meal from the microwave. Once she had everything in front of her, she sat at the table to enjoy her meal. Breakfast was a long time ago.

She thought about the conversation she'd had with the two Goodman men. *Jeremy is so different from his father. His ego is almost bigger than he is. He thinks he knows it all. Barkley seems so thoughtful. I'm glad he's my lawyer, for now anyway. Boy, Jeremy sure didn't like me saying I might not have reason to trust his dad in the future.* She chuckled. *Serves him right for acting so smug.* She frowned. *Don't like him. Don't understand why. Maybe it's that religion thing.*

She chewed a mouthful of the steak dinner as she pondered the idea of sharing an office with him. *Might work, would be convenient.* Grudgingly she admitted that his resources could come in handy. *At least, if he actually has some. Chief could find the old guy he's looking for, too.* She placed another forkful of food into her mouth. *Maybe I'll try renting the space for a few months to see how it goes. Better than compromising my home address.* She looked toward Chief. "All finished, boy?"

The dog lifted his head after slurping water from his bowl. He wagged his tail once she acknowledged him. He walked toward the back door, sat, and turned his head toward her as if to say, "Okay. Now it's my turn to refresh myself."

Christine chuckled. "All right. But don't leave the yard." She opened the door and gazed toward the back as he bounced over the grass at full speed. She re-closed the door, and walked into her living room and the desk she'd placed in one of the corners. *I'll do some checking on those coin dealers. See which one appears the most suspicious. My instincts tell me the first one is not all he's cracked up to be. He creeps me out. And those guys across the street sure seemed interested in what I was doing.*

Christine plugged the information into the search engine for the first shop. Nothing bounced back except for an address and phone number. No web page. She walked to the front door, grabbed her briefcase and placed it on the desk. She removed a folder marked with the shop's name. She typed the owner's name into the search engine this time. *Nothing. Now how come, if he wants to be known as a serious collector. I can't find any information on the internet. No one can find him.*

To prove her point, she inserted the name of the second shop and the third. Both had a website, and lots of pages of information. *If I wanted to sell my rare coin, I'd find these guys easy enough. I think I'll follow my instincts. Something's not kosher with Mr. Fine.*

Christine closed her laptop, shut the lid on her briefcase, and then headed toward the back door. Time to go. She called, "Chief. Come, boy. Time to go." Chief trudged reluctantly, head lowered, to the back entrance. "Looks like you were having fun. Did you find a squirrel?" Chief sauntered past her into the warm kitchen, panting.

His eyes never left her, as she put on her warmest jacket. "We'll pick up some coffee at the convenience store. Wait, I'll bet you'd like some treats, too. I'll bring a bottle of water for you and your dog dish. Don't know how long we'll be up tonight."

The dog's answering tail wag was all she needed to confirm he would be happy with the water and treats. She placed everything in a plastic bag and headed out the front door. Securing it behind her, she led the way back to the car. *I'll be glad when this is all over and I don't have to be so paranoid over my locked doors.*

About a half hour later, Christine pulled up in front of Mr. Fine's shop. The evening sky had darkened considerably since she'd left her house but sporadically spaced street lights lessened the gloom a little. She parked a few doors away hoping to remain un-noticed. She turned off the engine and settled into her seat. Taking a sip from the freshly brewed coffee she'd picked up, she allowed her eyes to become accustomed to the dark and glanced around. No lights shone from any of the nearby windows, even the residential buildings. Quiet, with almost an ominous cast, flooded down the street. Christine reached over and locked all her doors. She shivered. *I hate this.* She reached toward Chief for reassurance.

A car sped past. The exhaust backfired and Christine jumped in her seat. *Wow. I'm spooked tonight. Must be lack of quality sleep.* She leaned her head back against the seat, willing her body to relax. She peered toward the shop. *I could get out and take a stroll toward the back. See what I can find.* "Whatta ya think, Chief? Up for a stroll?"

Christine unlocked her driver's side door. She stepped out and made room for Chief to exit the car from the same door. She locked the car again and crept to the front of the coin shop. A narrow alley separated the shop from the building next door. She angled her body sideways and inched toward the back lane. Chief crept quietly behind her. Before they reached the back of the structure however, he let out a low growl, so quietly Christine was sure she was the only one who heard it. At least she hoped.

She pressed her body so tightly against the facade she almost felt the walls move. A dark figure walked past her, not looking from right or left but staring straight in front of him or her. Christine couldn't make out what gender the person was. *The person seemed young, about the same age as those hoodlums who'd hung around earlier when I was here. Maybe this is a male.*

She stared as he approached the back door to the coin shop. He took a key from his pocket, and unlocked the padlock securing the door. *Sure mustn't want anyone to get in from here.* The person used his sleeve to wipe his nose and entered the shop without looking to see if anyone else was about. Christine was close enough to hear the lock click into place from the inside. It sounded like another padlock. She inched her way back to the front of the edifice urging Chief to move ahead of her.

She slid back into the front seat of her car. She rubbed her hands together for warmth, and kept her eyes peeled for any sign someone was inside the shop. *Nothing. No lights.* She opened the thermos of coffee, poured some into her cup, and took a sip. "Want a treat?" She turned toward Chief.

As she turned, she saw someone's head disappear behind the car. Chief noticed the intruder, too. He began to bark as soon as Christine pounded the door locks into place. Not one, but three interlopers stood behind the car, and slowly, menacingly walked around to her side.

They had baseball bats in their right hands, using the wooden instrument to pound their left hands. Their intent was clear. Christine fumbled with the ignition switch. She glanced at the thugs. They were young, heads shaved, with a myriad of tattoos along their necks and down their right arms. Even though the night air was cool, they wore no jackets. Studs the size of pennies hung from each of their ears completing their intimidating appearance.

The first punk raised his bat before Christine was able to get the car started. He swung the wooden baton with such force at the windshield that the glass caved inward and shattered. *I have to get out of here.* Chief was about to go through the windshield at them. She'd never seen him so menacing. *Probably the only reason they haven't reached inside yet.*

Her car roared to life as a second bat connected with the hood of her car. She realized if she didn't get away soon, her car would be disabled. She flipped the lever into drive and raced out onto the street, nearly hitting the third thug. They threw their bats at her as she squealed her tires in escape mode. She glanced at her rear view mirror. They were laughing. They thought this was funny. The wind whistled through the windshield.

Chief was standing on the front seat, his growl intimating and ferocious. She reached toward him. The fur along the back of his neck was standing straight up. "Calm down, boy. Everything's alright now." She patted him and made a left hand turn to skip a few streets to disguise her route home. *Just in case.*

She drove a little slower to accommodate the absence of a front window. Her legs and the front seat were covered in tiny shards of broken glass. She needed to find a heavily populated parking lot to clean up a little and call the police. *Jeremy.*

She looked toward Chief. "Now why did I think of him? I don't need a body guard." Her instincts were telling her, though, she needed to find a way to protect herself ... *something better than a taser.* "I'll call Charlie. He'll tell me whether this is something I can pursue. Those guys are the same ones who were standing across the street from the coin shop earlier today. At least I think they are." But would Charlie help the way she wanted him too?

Christine drove a little further and made another left hand turn. She continued down the street until she was on the main drag. She turned right. Before long she pulled into a McDonald's parking lot. The restaurant was very busy since it was not late yet. She pulled into the nearest empty space and took a deep breath. She picked up her cell phone and punched in the numbers.

Chapter Twenty-One

Jeremy slid his backside into one of the booths that sat on the periphery of the small dance floor. Country music played softly in the background. The bar was sparsely populated for this time of night but he figured later it would be packed. The noise level would be off the charts. He leaned forward on his elbows as his eyes scanned the people sitting nearby or at the counter.

He slipped his hand inside his shirt pocket. The picture of Jeremiah Burton was not a recent one, his daughter had said, but Franny thought it was close enough. He checked it again and looked toward the counter. An older gentleman stood near the end sipping something from a can but Jeremy saw no resemblance to the photo. He leaned back and checked the other patrons. No sign of Jeremiah Burton.

A waitress approached with an order pad in hand. *I guess she knows that I'm here to eat.* He smiled toward her.

"Good evening sir. Do you want a menu?" She shifted her weight from one hip to the other.

Sir, he thought. *I'm not that much older ...* "Yes, please." He watched the woman walk back toward the bartender and grab a menu from its location near the cash register. Her jeans were skin tight but she wore a loose fitting blouse over top. *A tunic, I think they call those.* He saw her approach again.

      The woman handed him the menu. "What would you like to drink?"

      Jeremy decided she was a lot younger than his first glance. "Just bring me a Coke … in a can, please, and a Reuben with fries."

      "Will do." She turned her back on him and walked toward the bar.

      This time he checked out the menu. Making a selection from the sandwich list, he placed the menu on the table. As he did, the young woman returned with his can of Coke. She set it down and opened her order pad. Jeremy told her his selection, and asked, "Have you met a man by the name of Jeremiah Burton?"

      "No, but I've only been here for the last six months. Jock …" She pointed toward the bartender. "He's been here a long time. He knows everyone." She flipped her order pad closed and walked to the kitchen area. Jeremy decided to step up to the bar. He looked around. His drink would be okay left where it was.

      He slid out of the booth, sauntered toward the bartender who was completing an order, and sat on a vacant stool in front of the older man. Jock seemed as if his health had been better. *He should have retired a few years ago.*

      "Yeah. What can I get ya?" His voice had the gravelly sound of a lifetime smoker.

      "Nothing. My drink is over there. Do you know a man by the name of Jeremiah Burton?"

      The man coughed. He looked at Jeremy through bloodshot eyes. Placing his elbow over his mouth, he coughed again. "Maybe. Who're you?"

Jeremy stood straight and tall, giving the man a serious perusal. "I've been hired ..."

"That daughter of his again. Jeremiah was okay until she took over his life. Now ..."

"So you do know him?" Jeremy sat back down. "I need to find him, before something happens to him."

The man glared at him. "Ain't nothin' goin' ta happen ta Jerry. He can take care of hisself. Besides, she put him in that place. Don't care nothin' for her dad." He used a damp rag to wipe at some water spots on the counter. Then he busied himself wiping around the sink behind the counter.

Jeremy considered how much he should tell him. "You a friend of his? You care about him?" He watched Jock's body language. The man knew something.

"Why should I tell you?" He placed both hands flat on the counter and scowled. "If I'm his friend, I don't tell you nothin'."

Jeremy handed Jock his business card. "I'm with Goodman Investigations. When I talked to his friend, Franny ..."

"You've met Franny? When she called, she didn't say nuthin'." He hung his head as if considering this situation hurt his brain. "Jerry's a good man. Don't deserve what that daughter of his did to him."

"I figured she was not what she seemed. So I went to the retirement home and then to see Franny. My father is a lawyer. He can help ..." Jeremy spotted the waitress approach his booth with his food. "I need to find him. Hear his side." He noticed Jock didn't seem too surprised that Jeremiah was missing from the home.

"I see him, I'll tell him. He can decide whether to meet with you or not." He moved farther down the bar to assist another customer.

Jeremy returned to his table. He slid into the booth and looked at the Reuben sandwich he'd ordered. *Looks good.* His stomach growled. He bowed his head. "Father, you know where Mr. Burton is and how he is. Please protect him, but bring him here so I can talk to him. Bless this food and the hands that prepared it. Amen." He picked up the sandwich and took a big bite.

While he ate, he gazed around the bar again. More patrons had arrived while he talked to the bartender. There were still some tables available but only about half the number since he'd arrived. The noise level had also increased. He chewed a couple of fries, and took a long drink from the can of Coke. As he was about to pick up his sandwich again, a tall man, a little bent over, walked into the bar. Jeremy glanced in the man's direction as he headed straight for the bartender.

He pulled the picture out of his pocket. *Could be him.* The man wore a knitted cap pulled low over his ears. His jacket collar swept the back of his neck and hid the lower part of his jawline. Jeremy took a bite and scanned the room.

Jock recognized him. Jeremy glanced at the bartender and moved quickly when he noticed the older man looking in his direction. *Don't want the man to get spooked.* He stepped around a couple swaying to the music from the jukebox. *Didn't know there were places that still used those.* He reached his hand toward the newcomer's shoulder but the man sidestepped him and headed to the door. He was older than Jeremy but moved as fast as a man twenty years younger. "Hey, wait. Jeremiah. I need to talk to you."

Jeremy tried to catch up but a couple of other men blocked his path. He peeked around them. He tried to shove past but when he stepped left, so did they. He glanced toward Jock. The man grinned. Jeremy looked back toward the door. No one was there. Jeremiah had left. He shoved the first man aside and made a beeline to the door. His grip on the handle was strong as he pulled the door open but when he looked outside, the older man was nowhere in sight. He'd vanished.

Jeremy went back inside. Jock was busy wiping his counter. The other two men were watching his every move from the far end of the bar. "You could have stopped him. I can help. I haven't contacted Amanda Prescott since she was in my office this afternoon. She doesn't know what I know."

"I ain't helpin' ya put my friend behind locked doors again. If Jeremiah wants to talk, he'll contact you. I gave him yur card. Now finish yur supper and get out. Yur not wanted here." Jock scowled toward the two men at the end of the bar and they nodded their heads.

Jeremy plunked himself back down in the booth, and slowly took a long drink from the can of Coke. He motioned for the waitress to come back to his table. When she arrived, he asked for a box. The sandwich could be reheated at home. While he waited, his mind went over what he'd found out.

Jeremiah was a regular here, or at least, had been at one time. He had friends who were loyal to him. But most of all, he discovered that the man was certainly in control of his faculties. *He'd made himself scarce pretty quickly when he was told why I was here.* He also didn't look frail as Amanda had led him to believe. *I think I'll believe his friends. I also think I'll stake out this place after I leave. Maybe Mr. Jeremiah will return.* Just then, his cell phone buzzed.

Chapter Twenty-Two

The house looked peaceful. He couldn't tell whether someone was living there or not. *I'll need ta take a closer look.* He sat quietly in his car, watching. Not too much traffic on this street. He took a sip from the flask he kept for cold nights and long hours.

Through the wrought iron railing that circumvented the yard, he could see well-manicured lawns but no flower gardens. *Looks like there used to be lots of flowers.* He suspected the sprinklers would automatically begin as soon as it got dark. *They probably didn't want the grounds to be all wet when kids went out to play in the morning.* The stone façade made the building seem cold to the man sitting in his car. *But then it should be cold if no one's living there.*

He watched a bird fly from one tree to another, its song of invitation echoing through the neighborhood. He lifted a set of binoculars from the seat beside him and focused on the front driveway. It was clean, free of weeds. *Someone is taking care of this place. I wonder.* He sat back, took another sip, and then closed his eyes, laying his head on the head rest behind him.

A loud tapping on the window beside his head made him jump. His heart rate accelerated to dangerous levels as adrenaline coursed through his veins. *What the ...?* He looked at the uniform of the man who'd interrupted his rest. Police? He sighed.

Then he pressed the button to open the window enough to hear what the man said. "You waiting for someone?"

Rent-a-cop. "I just got tired. Needed a short pick me up." He looked toward the security guard. "The street was quiet so I thought ..."

"Well, move along. We don't allow loiterers or vagrants in this neighborhood." The guard had his hand poised on his gun still in the holster.

He could tell the safety was off, though. "Okay, officer. I'll move. Maybe get a motel. Got any nearby?"

The guard glared at him. "Do I look like the yellow pages? Move along and ask someone else for directions."

This guy don't know who he's messin' with. "Sure officer." He turned the key in the ignition. The car roared to life. "See ya 'round." He waved, his demeanor as friendly as he could make it. His anger was held tightly in check. He'd been warned. The boss wanted no trace.

He steered his car down the street and drove around the same corner he'd traveled an hour ago. *I need to find the broad. The boss thinks she's livin' in that house now. I'll go back after dark. I wonder if there's a security system on the house.* He headed toward the main street where he hoped to find some accommodations. Tonight he'd get some questions answered.

Chapter Twenty-Three

Christine listened as the instrument in her hand rang the number she'd punched in. *I hate this.* She sighed and listened as Jeremy's voice was transmitted back to her. "Uh. Hello. I ... you ... you said we could be a team, utilize each other's expertise. Well, I need yours ... right now."

She listened as Jeremy began to chuckle, but seemed to think of a better response. In all seriousness, he asked what the problem was. She hesitated, heaving a deep sigh into the phone. "I've been hit ... or at least my car's been hit by a baseball bat. I need you to come get me. I called a tow truck to come pick up my car so I need a ride home."

Jeremy cleared his throat. Christine surmised he wanted to chide her about needing his help so soon after their brief meeting. Her declaration 'she was capable of looking after herself' rang in her head like a gong. She added, to fill the silence, "Chief is with me."

"Where are you? I can leave right away." His unmistakable, irritating self-confidence transmitted across the lines. Christine's hackles rose. "Never mind. I can get a cab."

She heard his sigh of exasperation, wiping away the distance between them. "No trouble, Christine. Where are you? Quit being so stubborn." He began to sound like a boss. "Cabs won't allow a dog to ride with them."

"Oh-h. Alright. I'm at Portage and ..." She glanced at the building to see if there were street numbers. She spotted the address up high. "1251 Portage Avenue, near Wall Street. I'm at McDonalds, in the parking lot."

"What the heck are you doing in that area of the city? Never mind. We'll discuss the details when I get to you. I'm only about fifteen minutes away." The line went dead. Christine stared at the phone, indignant all over again. *The man is infuriating.* She folded it shut. Her eyes blinked in Chief's direction. The hair on the back of his neck was still raised, his ears alert to anything that might harm his mistress.

She patted his neck and wrapped her arm around him. "Good dog, Chief. We're okay now. Goodman is coming." *O-h-h I guess I'm going to have to sound more gracious.* "Chief, when he gets here, don't bite him ... too hard." She chuckled, thinking about the look on the man's face if Chief did take him down a peg or two.

Chief turned his head to gaze at his mistress as if to say, "Really?" She grinned. "No boy. I'm kidding. We'll need to be nice."

She sat back again. Her seat still sparkled with the light from the restaurant bouncing off the shards of glass. Most of the splinters had been swiped to the floor with the edge of the folder she'd brought with her. Chief was sitting gingerly in the passenger seat. She'd told him to 'stay' so he wouldn't get any cuts. When Jeremy arrived, or the tow truck driver, she'd move outside but until then ...

Christine pondered what she'd seen behind that coin shop. The back door was certainly locked up tight as a drum. *I wonder who the person was who had a key. He was taller than the shop owner and walked more sprightly. Might be one of those thugs. I wonder what the connection is between those hoodlums and Fine. I'll have to find out.* "Won't we boy?" Her voice filled the night air inside the car.

She glanced around to see if anyone was near enough to have heard her conversation with Jeremy. His laughing brown eyes trotted across her memory. *Something about that guy. I don't know if I can stand being in the same office.* Her brow furrowed. *And yet, who do I call when I need help? Yuck.*

The God thing, too. I'll bet he's praying for me right now. Well, he can have his delusions. If there is a god, why'd He let my parents get killed? I needed them. Impossible. There's no such thing as a god. Yet the picture of Jeremy praying for her seemed comforting somehow. *Yeah, I don't think so.* She tried to wipe the thought from her mind. *Why would he? He doesn't like me anymore than I like him.*

Her internal argument was interrupted by a horn. The ear bending sound came from just behind her car. Christine did a shoulder check. The large tow truck was parked right on her back bumper. As she twisted her neck to see more clearly, the driver approached her driver's side door. She opened the door and stepped out. "Fast service."

The driver pulled his collar up higher. "Slow night. What can I do for you?"

Christine pointed toward the front window. "My windshield was smashed. I can't drive like that. Would you tow my car to Speedy Glass Repair? It's just down Portage. I already called them and they said to leave it in the lot and drop the keys in a slot in the service door."

The driver shifted his weight and walked back toward his truck. He talked over his shoulder." I know where it is. But you can't ride with me. Regulations."

"I know. I called a frien ... someone. He should be here any minute." She let her eyes travel around the parking lot. "There he is now." *Oh, good. A truck. I hadn't thought about how we'd all fit on his motorcycle.* Her look of appreciation followed Jeremy as he pulled into an empty space two cars down from her.

She turned back toward the driver who held a clipboard in his hand. "I need you to sign here and here," He pointed to the two spots. "Your roadside assistance will cover the cost. Did vandals do this?"

"Yeah. A few streets over. I got away as fast as I could."

"You shoulda called the cops. They'd a ..." He took the clipboard from her and began to walk to the rear of his truck. "Does the car still run?"

Jeremy stepped beside her. "What happened?"

"Later," Christine hissed. She smiled toward the tow truck driver. "Yes, it does. Want me to move my car?"

"Yeah. I need to get this chain under your back bumper so I can hoist it onto the truck. Let's move your vehicle to that space." He pointed toward the end of the parking lot where several spots were empty. "More room to maneuver."

Christine began to get back into her vehicle. Jeremy placed his hand on her arm. "Want me to take Chief to my truck?"

Christine shifted her eyes to him and then back to Chief. "If he'll go with you." She reached for Chief's leash. "Come on, boy. No wait. Sit." She moved around her car to the passenger side. She looked at Jeremy again. "There's too much glass for him to move around. I don't want his feet to get all cut up."

She opened the door, grabbed Chief's leash again, and wrapped her arms around his torso to lift.

Jeremy sprinted to her side. "Here, let me do that."

Christine scowled. "This wouldn't be the first time I lifted him. I can manage. He's liable to bite you."

Jeremy reached to pat Chief's head. "He knows I like dogs. He won't hurt me. Besides his senses tell him I'm no threat to you." Jeremy's hand landed softly on top of the dog's head.

Christine felt his tail begin to wag as she set him down on the pavement. "Traitor," she whispered. She handed the leash to Jeremy. "I guess he's changed his mind about you. Now you're a friend. Can we follow the tow truck to Speedy Glass?"

"Sure. Which one?" He turned to go to his truck with Chief before she answered. Over his shoulder, he added, "There's one near here."

"I know. I gave the driver that address." *Man, he's insufferable.* "All looked after." She scowled in Jeremy's direction but with his back turned to her, he missed her tongue when she stuck it out at him. *I guess that's kind of childish but darn him ...*

Christine watched as the truck driver moved his vehicle to let her move hers to the spot he'd chosen. She managed to park it so that the back end was accessible and then watched from the sidelines as he crept under the back bumper to add his chain. In a matter of minutes, he had her car on the flat bed of his truck ready for transport. "We'll follow."

She waved him off the parking lot and then slipped into the passenger side of Jeremy's truck. "I never even thought about whether or not you'd have your bike with you. That would have made for an interesting scenario." She buckled her seat belt.

Jeremy pulled Chief closer to his side to give her more room. "This truck is my back-up when the weather turns colder. Otherwise ..."

He buckled his seat belt; made sure Chief was secure, and shifted into drive. As he pulled into traffic, he glanced in Christine's direction. "Are you going to tell me what happened?"

Chapter Twenty-Four

An hour later, Jeremy pulled up in front of Christine's bungalow. He noticed there were no lights in the yard to dispel the shadows or who might be lurking in them. "Christine, don't you have yard lights?"

"Chief is all the yard light I need. If he senses something amiss, he'll let me know. I pay attention." She opened the door and slid to the ground. "Thank you for coming to get me. I need to talk to you sometime, I guess ..." She hung her head, reluctance seeping from her pores. "I need to get something to defend myself. If they'd tried to get inside my car, Chief would have handled them, and I own a taser, but I realized ... all they had to do was shoot from a distance and I'd be toast."

Jeremy turned off the ignition. "Why don't I come in now? We could talk about some ideas ..."

"... No. No, that's okay." She darted a look in his direction, the idea of him entering her sanctuary uncomfortable. "It's late. Why don't I come by your house ... er ... office, early tomorrow morning? What time do you get in?"

"Ah-h. How are you going to get there?" He wrinkled his eyebrows, telling her he'd already thought of that. "This friend of mine runs a car rental agency. I could call him and arrange for him to deliver a car for your use, until yours is repaired. Those dents may take a few days of body work."

"Dents. I'm not paying those glass people to get dents out of my car. They're replacing the glass. Where do I get dents removed?" She leaned her weight on one hip and glanced at Chief out of the corner of her eye. His usual trip around the yard, stopping at a few low-lying shrubs, gave her the sense of security she'd missed since those thugs hammered on her car.

Her glance moved back to Jeremy. "I'll Google a place for auto body repairs when I get inside and call them first thing tomorrow morning. Now about the rental."

"Can I come in?" He leaned over the steering wheel to peer in her direction. "I promise I won't molest you."

Christine gave her usual harrumph. "As if you could. I do possess some defensive moves." She swept her hair to one side with a shake of her head. "I-I guess. Come on in. Chief will keep an eye on you."

Jeremy smirked. "You're so gracious." He stepped down from the truck, his long legs hitting the ground as if the height of the truck was made for him.

Christine glanced at his physique as he sauntered around the front of his vehicle, self-confidence written all over him. "Chief, heel." She motioned with her hand for the dog to stick close and led the way to her front door. She opened the deadbolt first and then the other three locks that made a trail down the edge of her door.

Jeremy frowned. "This house is locked up tighter than a drum. I suppose ..."

Christine reached inside and switched off the alarm before Jeremy had a chance to enter. She said nothing as she led the way inside, head held high.

"I figured you'd have an alarm system in place." Jeremy gave a cursory glance at the device that was located near the door. "Good brand. Are you hooked up to them or is this just a noise maker?"

"I had a security company, a reputable one, install the alarms. Your father recommended them, in fact." She flipped on the light switch. "Would you like some coffee or something?"

"Water would be fine." Jeremy flipped open his phone and scrolled through his contacts until he came across the one he wanted. He pressed the dial button and sat down on the sofa, crossed his legs and leaned back. Christine let her eyes wander across his relaxed form again. Her comfort level was the lowest it had been since she'd moved into her house. *Is my unease over a visitor at this time of night or that he's Jeremy Goodman?*

She strolled to the kitchen, took a jug of cold water out of the fridge and retrieved two glasses from her cupboard. Pouring a glass for each of them, she returned to the living room as Jeremy replaced his phone into his pocket.

"The car will be here bright and early. I told them to drop it off by eight. Is that alright?" He took the glass she offered him.

"Yes. Fine. Thanks. I could have found someone myself. But thanks. Since you're already here, what suggestions can you make about self-defense?" She took the seat across from her sofa and Chief sat at her feet, his eyes watching the man in their midst.

Jeremy leaned forward and smiled toward the dog. "Come Chief." He patted his leg but the dog didn't budge. "Come on. I thought we were friends."

Christine smirked toward him. "Chief is my dog and does what I ask him to do. When I think he's done enough, I let him relax. Then he might come to you but I don't intend to let him relax until you're gone. I don't know you and I'm not sure I can trust you."

"Trusting me is of tantamount importance if we're going to work together, don't you think? Besides, I made sure you were being cared for in Texas. If you can't trust me after all this time ..."

"You dealt with Uncle Conrad, not me. Now about those weapons." Christine crossed her legs and patted Chief's head in approval for his continued obedience.

Jeremy grimaced, noting her clear intention to keep a distance between them. "I'm friends with a guy who owns a company that makes covert bullet-proof vests. They're light-colored, made of very thin, moisture wicking fabrics, not noticeable when worn under clothing. I was wearing one earlier when I met you at my dad's office. They work well under motorcycle jackets. Give some added protection."

Christine leaned forward, resting her elbows on her knees. "They'll stop a bullet?"

"Yes, they will. Like a police vest but lighter. For starters, anyway. Having a taser on you at all times, is also good practice. Some friends of mine, also investigators, have used them for years. Andrea and Brian just got married two years ago and they run an agency in the states. They manage to avoid using guns while tracking down some hardened criminals, with just a taser for self-defense."

"There're illegal, here, I thought. I keep mine hidden but carry it most of the time."

"Yeah, so is pepper spray and handguns. But there are ways around the laws." He opened his jacket and then remembered he'd left his gun in the glove box of his truck. "I have a carry permit. You need to get one, too. Is your agency registered with the police?"

"Yes, but they don't treat us as an asset, yet. After we track down this little boy, they'll have to acknowledge Chief and I can be of some help in cases like this. There's usually no need for a weapon. In this case, some bad boys are involved, I think. I hate to think about what's happened to the kid if those hoodlums are part of this." Christine furrowed her brow, her eyes becoming a little glossy.

"Stay tough, Finder. By the way, I used your Smith alias for the car rental. I hope that's okay."

Christine nodded. "The sooner I get used to another name, the better. How soon can we order a vest?

"Come by tomorrow morning and we'll get started. I saw the old man tonight so I want to stake out the bar tomorrow night, but for the rest of the day I'm all yours. Conrad is paying me to guard you, remember. Think about my offer to amalgamate our agencies or, at least, think about moving your office to my location. I don't think we'd be in each other's way and you'd be able to come and go as you please while I can still watch your back."

"I'll think about it." She stood, effectively ending the conversation. She saw Jeremy do the same. "Thanks for the help. I'll see you tomorrow." She led the way to the door.

"Is your back door and windows as secure as your front door?" Jeremy spoke as he walked behind her, sending a shiver up her spine.

Christine stepped aside to let him pass her. "Yes, the security company did a great job."

"Well, make sure you utilize all their features. I mean, set the alarm as soon as I leave. The killer may not have the information about where you are now but if he's tracked you as far as the Finders …"

"It's taken him twenty years …"

"He may not have been looking all this time. Maybe something happened making it imperative you be eliminated once and for all. You can't assume he'll take another twenty years to track you here. After all, this is where your parents lived ... and died." Jeremy opened the front door a crack and turned back toward her. "Lock up. Make it a habit." He walked through the door.

Christine gazed at his back as he strode across her yard and did as he suggested. She closed all the drapes on her windows, as well. "Come on, Chief. Let's go to bed. There's a lot to do tomorrow."

Chapter Twenty-Five

Jeremy turned on the radio in the truck as soon as he was out of Christine's driveway. Soft music flowed through the cab but his thoughts were elsewhere. He pondered Christine's situation.

She'd remained virtually safe for twenty years but now this man tracked her to Texas. *Why? What was going on that made her presence a liability all of a sudden? Maybe we need to investigate the guys the Romparts were dealing with instead of leaving it all up to the police.*

He thought about the woman he'd rescued. *She's not very trusting. But, I guess I'd be a little suspicious of anyone and everything if someone was trying to end my life. We assume the man is the same one who killed her parents but this may be another one entirely. We don't know if the killer is still alive after all this time.*

I can't imagine dealing with all this without the Lord. Father, You know her heart. Please touch her. Make Yourself known to her. Amen. Jeremy concentrated on the street in front of him. He turned another corner and spotted his driveway.

She really doesn't live far from me. That's good. Maybe I need to install some surveillance equipment so I can keep track of the comings and goings at her place. Maybe even a tracking device on her car. She's sure not going to keep me informed every time she goes somewhere.

He parked the truck, turned off the lights, and looked toward his front door. *I really would like to have a place with more space.* He stepped out of the cab of the truck. His boots hit the pavement and he closed and locked his door. His stride was slow. *I'm tired. It's been a long day.*

Jeremy began to think about the old man. *He's hiding from his daughter. I just know it. I have to convince him that I have his best interests at heart and help him regain his independence, if that's what's good for him. I only have Franny's word that he's doesn't have dementia.*

Jeremy unlocked his front door. He stepped into his foyer and turned on the hall light. His fish tank glowed across his living room beckoning him to feed the tiny creatures swimming from side to side. *Man, I like fish, but that dog of Christine's sure made me wish I had one of them. He's so intelligent and he takes his role as protector seriously. Amazing.*

He hung his coat in the closet, stepped to the underwater landscape enclosed in glass, fed the fish, and then walked to the staircase leading to his bedroom. *Tomorrow I need to make a plan to find Jeremiah Burton, but I also need to convince Christine that moving into my offices would be in her best interests. Lord, change her mind, please.*

Jeremy placed one foot in front of the other as he climbed upward. He yawned, almost tripping when his eyes closed. He wiped his hand across his brow. *That bed is going to feel so good*. He entered and closed the door behind him.

Chapter Twenty-Six

Christine tossed and turned. Chief lifted his head as if he saw the scenes replaying in his mistress' head. She moaned and kicked out as if trying to ward off an attacker. Chief jumped to the floor and stood, his eyes ever watchful. Christine's body relaxed and soft snores let Chief know she was okay. He lay on the carpet beside her bed and closed his eyes.

****

Blood dripped in her eyes. She tried to wipe it off her hands, but she only smeared it, leaving a larger splotch than before. Tears filled her eyes. They washed the blood down her cheeks. Her head .... where was her mother's head? She heard some footsteps as if the person wore heavy boots.

Thump. Thump. Down the hall. She had to hide again. He'd get her, too. She raced for the doorway under the stair-

case. She slipped. Blood covered the floor. The sticky goo became lumps like Jell-O. It jiggled under her feet. Her foot hit something. She screamed. The object was her mother's head ... only ... part of it was missing. She screamed again.

****

Christine sat up. She forced her eyes open, straining to replace the vision in her dream with something else. She glanced at Chief on the floor. She rolled out of bed, crawled next to him, and wrapped her arms around his furry neck. Chief snuggled into her body. Christine shuddered.

Two nights in a row. That dream ... those images. Tears fell unchecked down her cheek soaking the fur of her loyal companion. Chief never seemed concerned when she cried into his fur. Her heart warmed slightly. He always made the dream go away.

Christine turned her head and gazed at the clock on her bedside table. *2 am. A lot of night ahead of me.* She shuddered when she thought about going back to sleep. *I think I'd better read a little ... get my mind off the dream.*

She stood to her feet, patted Chief on the head, and strolled toward a small bookcase on the left side of her bedroom door. The latest Barbara Derksen novel lay on the top shelf. When Charlie had loaned the book to her, he'd said it would give her something to think about. *As long as it's fiction. I couldn't handle a true story right now.*

She picked the yellow and black book up, turned to the first page in the story and sauntered back to her bed. She lay down and began to read. Chief hopped up to join her. He turned his body around in circles until he hit the right spot and plunked down into a coil, moving her legs in the process. "Thanks a lot, pal." She chuckled. *At least he makes me laugh.*

Before long, Christine's eyes began to close. She lay the book down on the nightstand and rolled over to one side. Her thoughts filled with the scene she'd read about and the mystery unraveling in the pages. Chief lifted his head to look at her, as she began to breathe softly once again.

Chapter Twenty-Seven

The sun filtered through the louvers on the blinds covering Christine's bedroom window. She glanced at her clock and then jumped to a sitting position. Chief groaned. His body blocked her legs. She shoved at him. "Come on Chief. The rental agency will be here any minute with a car for us to drive. Get up."

Chief stretched. His legs stiffened and were long enough to flow over the edge of the bed. He rolled his body to the floor. Christine watched as he yawned. "Yeah, I know. Long night ... again. Let's get ready for a run. As soon as the car gets here, we'll go for a short one."

She ambled toward her bedroom door, retrieved her jogging attire from the hook behind it, and started pulling on clothes. She'd no sooner gotten her pants on, when the sound of musical notes flowed through the house. At the time she'd purchased the doorbell, she'd wanted happy sounds and these certainly were uplifting.

She pulled her sweatshirt over her head as she marched down the hall toward her living room. "Coming," she hollered.

She grabbed the doorknob, began to release each of the locks, and then remembered to check to see if the person on the other side was who she thought he was. She peeked through the small peephole the security company had installed.

A short, rather young looking man stood on the other side. He had his back turned toward the street so she had no way to perceive a uniform with a logo. "Who's there?"

The man turned toward the voice coming through the door. "Brookdale Car Rentals for Miss Smith." He pointed toward the logo now visible on his jacket.

Christine opened the door. She stood squarely in the door frame, making sure he didn't expect to come inside. He held a clipboard out for her signature. As Christine used the pen he provided, she noticed a second car with the company logo on its side sitting at the end of her driveway, just behind the first car. "You have a ride back?"

"Oh-h. Yes." He seemed distracted. "Could you show me a driver's license?"

Christine nodded, closed the door behind her as she went back inside to retrieve her purse. When she opened the door again, she pulled her license out of her wallet, showed it to him, and returned it to its leather enclosure.

"Ah-h. Let me look at that again?" He held his hand out for the document this time. Christine handed it to him and waited. "I notice your license says you're Christine Finder. I thought the car was for a Christine Smith."

Christine almost choked. *Nice going Jeremy.* "Uh-h. No Finder. I guess I didn't hear you say Smith. Finder's my name."

"Well, we were told to deliver a car to Christine Smith. Sorry to bother ..." He turned to retrace his steps to the car.

"No. I'm the one the car is for. Your dispatch must have gotten the name wrong. I really need the car today." She used her best pleading voice. *Darn Jeremy.*

"Well, we'll have to do the paperwork again. The address is fine. Must be some mistake. Here, let's scratch the wrong name off and put the right one over it. Your license is right so ..." He smiled toward Christine, a look of hope spreading across his features.

He watched as Christine inserted her real name. "See. I signed Christine Finder. The name Smith didn't register with my brain. Too early, I guess." She smiled again.

The attendant looked where she signed her name. "Yep. You did." He took the clipboard from her and turned, but then turned back. "Say, you wouldn't wanta go for a drink later tonight, would ya?"

Christine lost her smile in a hurry. She glared at the man. "No, thanks. Can I have the keys?"

"Oh-h sure." He reached into his pocket and pulled out a key with a tag attached. "The insurance papers and registration are in the glove box." He stepped backward off the low step at the door. "No harm done. Can't blame a guy for trying, huh?"

Christine continued to show her displeasure, but said no more. She backed up into the house and closed the door firmly. She placed her eye over the peephole to make sure the men left before she and Chief headed out for their run.

Chief barked. He stood beside her right leg. His tail wagged at the same time so Christine knew what he was trying to say. "I know, boy. You need to go out." She checked the house to make sure all was secure, grabbed her cell phone and keys, and opened the front door again.

"Come on, boy. Let's go get some kinks out." She secured each of the locks, slipped the keys into the pocket of her jacket, and jogged slowly down the driveway. She picked up speed as she neared the park.

The morning was brilliantly lit by the sun. Dew sparkled on the leaves that still clung to the trees but Christine knew soon they'd be all gone. She shivered. *It's colder this morning than yesterday. Even this late in the morning. This is gonna be a short run.*

She watched Chief check out a stump at the edge of the tree line. He sniffed and raised his leg. His eyes never left her, though, so she knew he'd catch up. As soon as she thought it, he sped up and was once again racing along beside her. "You're a great running companion, Chief."

The dog yipped as if agreeing with her. He spotted a squirrel and decided to exercise his canine instincts for a few minutes. Christine hollered after him, "Don't be long. We have to get back so we can head over to Goodman Investigations." The dog bounded across the still damp grass.

Christine ran another half mile with Chief always within eyesight before she decided to turn around. She whistled and headed for home. As she ran, she passed another jogger. He stared in her direction until he passed, but kept on going. She glanced over her shoulder. He never stopped. *Something familiar about that man.* She couldn't place him, though.

Chief pounced on a small frog soaking up the sun in the grass near the path. The frog jumped once. Chief pounced again, missing the frog with his large feet by inches. He barked, turned in Christine's direction, and headed home, too. Christine smiled, all thoughts of the stranger gone. She focused on the last half mile, breaking into a sprint.

Huffing, her breath expended, Christine bent over to stretch her warm back muscles. She stretched each leg as well before inserting the key into each of the locks on her door. Just as she was about to push it open, a large body launched itself at her. Her assailant forced her inside. One hand wrapped itself around her mouth cutting off all protest, as the other slammed the door shut before Chief could get inside. The dog began barking viciously from the other side of the door.

    Christine struggled to regain her footing. She kicked out at her attacker but her foot only flailed through empty air. She knew it was a man because of the strength he'd hit her with. She reefed her head out of his grasp, but his hands closed over her throat so quickly, she couldn't let out a sound. Chief was making enough noise outside, though. Hopefully a neighbor ... she hadn't met anyone yet.

    The hands closed more tightly. The man was standing behind her. His hot breathe wafted over the skin along the right side of her neck. "You stay away from the coin shop. You don't, I'll kill the dog, and then you." He licked the side of her cheek. Christine shuddered. She felt like a rag doll. Her feet barely touched the floor. The man held her by the neck. He was strong, and much taller than she.

    Still retaining his hold on her neck, he propelled her toward her sofa. She lost her balance. Christine crashed to the floor. Her body landed against the coffee table. Her head whacked the corner of the table but she remained conscious. She heard the back door slam as the intruder exited her safe haven. She'd thought it was safe.

    Chief sounded as if he would come through the door at any moment. Christine stood unsteadily, grabbed hold of the back of the sofa and walked rapidly toward the front door. She began to open it but Chief finished the process when his body hurled itself inside. He stopped abruptly, looked around and whined as if feeling bad that he'd not been any help to his mistress.

    Christine patted his head before he thrust his body down the hall to the kitchen and the back door. "Chief, no. Stay." She walked quickly into the bright sunlit room and looked outside the open door before slamming it shut and locking it. *No sign of anyone. He must have jumped the fence. He could have gone around to the front again.* She raced toward the front door and flipped the locks into place. When she did, she peeped through the hole. *No one in sight.*

She leaned against the door. Her breathing had slowed, but the side of her head hurt. She rubbed, hoping to relieve the soreness. Her hand came away with a smattering of blood on it. She decided to head toward her bedroom and a first aid kit she kept in the bathroom linen closet.

Chief walked beside her as if glued to her pant leg. He whined some more. Christine ran her hand through his fur, taking note of the still ruffled mass along his neckline. "It's okay, boy. You couldn't help it."

She glanced in the mirror over her bathroom sink. A nasty cut ran along her hairline. The blood had begun to run down her cheek. *May need some stitches.* She ran a cloth under the hot water tap, wiped as much of the sticky redness away as she could, and then checked the cut again. *I hope I have a big enough bandage.*

While she cleaned up the cut with some antiseptic cream and then bandaged it, she began to think about what the intruder had said. He had warned her away from the coin shop. *I guess those guys did follow me last night. Otherwise.... I wonder how come Jeremy didn't notice anyone following.*

If those guys are that concerned about the coin shop, maybe I should be too. I think I'll take another look at that place tonight, see if I can get inside. Maybe I need to give Chief another whiff of Nathan's socks, to see if he can pick up his scent at that back door. If those guys decided they've scared me off, they have another think coming. But it won't hurt to let them consider they've won.

"Come on, Chief. We need to get to Jeremy's office and see what he has lined up for some defensive devices. I could use a weapon or two, it seems."

Chapter Twenty-Eight

Jeremy unlocked the door to his office as Jenna walked up the steps behind him. He gave her his usual early morning greeting, and stepped aside to let her precede him inside. "Christine Finder ... er... Smith will be stopping by to check out that empty room. "

"Finder, Smith? Which is it?" Jenna hung her coat on the rack behind her desk.

Jeremy laid his jacket over his arm. "We talked yesterday, at Dad's office, about changing her name ... make her less conspicuous. Not many Finders around. If the killer tracked her to the Finder ranch as Conrad thinks, he knows the name. So we decided, or rather she made the decision, to use Smith."

He opened the door into the empty space. He glanced at Jenna over his shoulder. "Would you do a little dusting in here, before she arrives this morning? I'll be able to keep a better eye on her if she works out of this office. Let's make the space as inviting as we can."

"Will she become a partner? Am I going to be working for her, as well?" Jenna scowled. "I already have more work than I need with you." She grabbed a dust cloth and walked toward the now open door of the room Jeremy often used for storage. She checked inside. "What are you going to do with all this stuff?"

Jeremy quickly walked into his office, placed his jacket on a chair and retraced his steps. "What did you say?"

"Well, you have all these boxes in here. They'll need to be moved." Jenna began wiping the desk with her cloth. "What's in them anyway?"

"I ordered a bunch of Bibles and tracks from Christian Motorcyclists Association. I keep them in the trunk of my bike and when I run into someone, I can give them something with the gospel message on it. The rest contains office supplies. I ran across a business closing its doors and was getting rid of their leftovers. I thought we might need it so ...."

"It'll take us years to use up all this stuff. Maybe the building owner has some attic space for storage." She smirked in his direction.

"That's me and I do have storage space. I never converted the basement into more offices as I'd planned when I bought this place. So ..." Jenna gave Jeremy a look of exaggerated fatigue. Jeremy chuckled, "I'll do the moving. I guess now's as good a time as any."

"Right. Then I'll be able to make this room presentable. Let me know when you're done. There's paperwork to do in the meantime." She walked past him into the reception area.

Jeremy grinned. "Aw. Come on. I could use some help." He snatched the first box and grunted. "I forgot how heavy a carton of paper can be." He marched out the door with box in hand and grinned toward Jenna again. "I was only kidding. I know you have things to do."

"Yeah. Stuff." She punched his arm before he walked down the hall to the back of the building. He opened the door to the basement. His body disappeared through it just as the front door opened.

Jenna switched her eyes to the newcomer. "May I help you?"

"My name is Christine ...."

"Oh, Miss Smith. Jeremy told me to expect you. I'm Jenna, his receptionist, girl Friday, secretary, all around jack of all trades. Welcome." Jenna eyed the young woman in front of her. "Jeremy will be right back. We'd hoped to have that room all cleared before you got here. Have a seat." She motioned toward the group of chairs in the reception area.

Christine held her hand out to shake the older woman's. "Call me Christine, please. I'm not used to the name Smith yet. If you refer to me by that name, I may ignore you." She placed a hand by her temple as she looked at her shadow. "This is Chief. I hope you like animals."

"I love dogs. Is he friendly?" Jenna glanced at the dog but her attention was on the bandage on the side of Christine's face. "You have an accident?"

"I was mugged this morning." She checked her reflection in the mirror. "It appears worse than it is." She slipped off her coat and sat, bringing Chief to her side. "Chief, this is ... " She perused the other woman.

"Jenna. Hi Chief. Can I pet him?" She took a step toward the large German Shepherd. "I love his coloring. Chief, you're beautiful."

"You can now, but most of the time he's in service mode. Chief is a trained track dog. He's also my partner so, mostly, he has my back. This morning, however, the intruder locked him outside. He couldn't get to me." Chief hung his head as if he knew he'd failed.

"Oh, poor boy." Jenna patted him and leaned forward to wrap her arms around his neck. She released him and walked over to her desk where she retrieved a cookie from her top drawer. "May I give this to him?"

"Sure. He'll be your friend for life. He loves those kind of cookies." Christine gave Chief the nod to accept what Jenna offered. His tail wagged as he bit into the tasty morsel.

It was gone in a matter of seconds. He licked Jenna's hand. "You're welcome," she said and laughed at the look on the dog's face. "I think he wants more."

"No, Chief." Christine opened the bag she'd brought with her and placed a dish at her feet with some dog food inside. "We left the house so fast I didn't have time to feed him after our run this morning. The creep pushed me through my door as soon as we got back. All I wanted to do was get away after that."

"What's this about some hoodlum pushing you?" Jeremy stood at the edge of the reception area with a deep scowl on his face. "What man?"

Christine told him about her run in with the home intruder. "By the way, telling the rental agency the car was for a Miss Smith was a bit premature. My license says my name is Finder."

Jeremy plunked himself down on a chair beside her. "You trying to change the subject. I thought you said no one knew where you lived."

Christine scowled right back at him. "And that's another thing. For a trained investigator, how did you miss someone tailing us last night?'

Jenna watched the exchange between Christine and Jeremy. Her eyes sparkled. "You two were together last night?" She grinned.

Jeremy shook his head at his receptionist. The slight nod of his head was missed by Christine. "Damsel in distress situation. I just helped out." He glanced at Christine. "We, and I say neither of us, had any reason to think the two thugs with baseball bats were going to follow you. Remember. You said ..."

Christine bristled even more. Chief was also reading her body language and had placed his body between the two of them. His throat emitted a low growl.

Jenna laughed. "If you two don't quit sparring, the nice dog will become less so, I think. Anyone want coffee? Won't take me long to make some."

Christine frowned, ignoring Jenna's attempt to change the subject. "I didn't think they followed me. Apparently they found out where I live. The guy was adamant." She mimicked her attacker. "Stay away from the coin shop."

Christine proceeded to describe her feelings. "Something is not right and I plan to find out what it is. They might have Nathan Brent. I intend to be there again tonight. I'll just have to be a little less conspicuous." She observed Jenna still waiting for a response. "No coffee for me. Thanks Jenna. Now, Mr. Goodman, what do you possess in the way of weapons for me?"

Jeremy leaned back in his chair. "There's some things in the office I was clearing out for you. Why not come, take a look at the space and we'll search for that stuff as well. I wasn't expecting you this early."

"I know. I needed to get out of my house." Christine patted Chief who had relaxed a little when their voices took on a calmer tone. "Chief's had a rough morning. He's never been surprised before, not like that. The thug came out of nowhere. Neither of us had a clue he was behind us."

"Do you have motion sensor lights?" They walked side by side toward the office space.

"Yes, but it was fully day-light. They didn't activate for us or him. I expect Chief will be more observant in the future. I can't help but think the man was scent protected." Christine shook her head at the thought. "If that's the case, they found out more about me than just my address."

Jeremy stepped aside to let Christine in the door first. "I think I have just the thing for you. Even if the guy is hiding behind you, as this one was, you'll be able to stop him in his tracks. A little device I obtained for another case I was working."

Jeremy lifted a box off a chair to make room for Christine. He searched through one of the cardboard containers until he found what he was looking for. In his hand was an ominous spiky contraption between his fingers. "I made these from a picture I saw in a magazine for mercenaries. It's called a Ninja Spike. You fit it like this."

Christine watched as he demonstrated how the spikes pointed outward from the middle of his fist. "Looks lethal."

"The device is easy to use. Not intended to be life threatening. It can do some major damage to an attacker, though." He made a fist around the spikes. "You grip this when you're walking to and from your vehicle or when you go jogging. If there's a perp looking to attack and they see you gripping this weapon, chances are they'll pick a less defended person to prey on. If they don't happen to notice it and you're attacked, a quick punch in the eye with this will definitely make them let go so you can flee." Jeremy punched the air over his left shoulder with his fist to demonstrate to Christine how the weapon worked.

Christine scrutinized his actions. Jeremy offered the spike to her, so she wrapped her fist around it. Jeremy decided to come up on her from the rear. Christine punched back at him, almost hitting her target. "That could've made a difference this morning. If I'd had something like this, the guy wouldn't have been able to overpower me. He was pretty big, I think. I never did get a good look at him. What else have you got?"

Jeremy bent toward the box again. He pulled out a hairbrush. "This is by far one of my favorite weapons. It's a functional brush. Innocent looking, right? No one would ever think the "brush" part pulls off." He demonstrated and revealed a three and a half inch dagger. "Keep in mind that this is a weapon meant for stabbing, not a knife used for slashing, so you have to have enough strength to thrust this into an attacker."

He handed the brush to Christine who immediately whipped out the dagger. She lunged toward him. "I think I'll leave this in the car glove compartment. Then, if I need it ... I hope I won't." She stuck the knife back in its hiding place. "Are these things legal to carry in Canada?" She picked up a can from the chair.

"Bear Spray or you can use the stuff for wasps. They are just animal repellants so the government doesn't care about those. They make effective self-defense weapons." Jeremy pointed to the container in her hand. "It's non-lethal and you don't need to be in direct contact with your assailant."

Christine grinned. "Now this would have been a good thing for this morning." She glanced at the label. "This is like the stuff the ranch hands used when they went into the bush after some stray cattle. They carried the spray to protect themselves against mountain lions or bears."

Jeremy turned to exit the room. "I'll be right back." He swiveled to face Christine again. "You hit someone in the eyes with this stuff and you will magically disappear from their view. And the cops won't have a hard time finding the attacker. They just have to find the blind guy walking around like Frankenstein." He continued out the door and hollered at Jenna. "'I'll take some of your coffee now. Smells good."

Christine beheld the can in her hand, and picked up the other two weapon choices. "I hate the idea I need to arm myself but ...."

Jenna walked into the room carrying a steaming cup of freshly brewed coffee. "A woman on her own in this city must be careful. It's not as safe as living here used to be and in this business ...." She sat on the chair beside Christine. "How did you ever decide to become a PI?" She observed Christine's five foot three inch frame.

The younger woman glanced down, the memories fresh from her dream the night before. *How much should I tell this woman?* Then she decided to trust her, as Jeremy obviously did. "I grew up with the memory of my parents' brutal murder. The man was never found. I intend ..."

"Yeah. She plans to find the killer .... herself." Jeremy strolled into the room again. He handed Christine a small semi-automatic pistol. "We practice with this at the gun club after we get you a carry permit. In this province, you can only own one with a membership to a club and you can carry it from home to the range but that's all. There are ways around ..." He picked up his coffee and took a long sip.

"I thought you religious types were about obeying the law." She held the pistol in one hand and then the other, feeling the weight and familiarity. "In Texas, guns are everywhere. We use them for hunting but also for self-defense. I'm amazed the creep managed to get the drop on one of Uncle Conrad's men. They're always prepared."

Jenna glanced from one to the other. "You guys can finish this conversation without me. I have work to do. We'll catch up later, Christine. I hope you'll decide to utilize this spare office. Another female around here would be a good thing."

Christine glanced in Jeremy's direction. "We talked about that idea but never decided anything."

"Why not? Once I move these boxes, I think you and Chief will be happy here. Come. I'll show you the rest of the layout." He led the way to the first door down the hallway. "We have a restroom." He pointed to the door across the hall. "There's my office. And that door leads to the basement where I plan to store all those boxes until we need the stuff in them.

You can use whatever supplies you want. I'll just include it in the rent."

Christine looked around as soon as she returned to the room designated as her space. *The size is impressive*, she decided. *It already has a desk and a chair. I'll have to move my filing cabinet and bookshelf. I want my mini fridge, too.* She looked back toward the door into the office reception area. "Would Jenna field my calls, too?"

Jeremy nodded. "If that's your preference. I know you're not too busy ... yet. We should share our case load sometimes ... maybe ... if you want. A track dog would come in handy, especially with this missing senior I'm trying to locate. And for you, a man with some connections would be advantageous once in a while." He grinned. "This could benefit both of us."

Christine frowned. "I pictured me doing this alone but ... after this morning ... it's obvious I can't work from home. I called the security company on the way over here and they're installing some alarms around the yard I can activate or deactivate by remote control. So no one will surprise me again." She shook her head. "But my office needs to be elsewhere, I think."

Jeremy sat down beside her. "I know we got off on the wrong foot, but we could be good for each other. And I won't butt in unless I'm asked. Promise." He bowed his head and mouthed, "Thank You, Father."

Christine frowned again. "I don't want any of that religious stuff rammed down my throat, either. If you keep your religious views to yourself, I'll take you up on your offer to share space."

"Christine, this is not religion. It's a relationship. I have no expectations as far as your beliefs go, but Jesus is part of me. So I may pray once in a while when you're around or ask the Lord to help us a time or two, but I won't force you to join me in Bible study or anything." He held his hand out for her to shake. "Is that okay?"

Christine reached to return his peace offering. She couldn't help but add, "You study the Bible? Here?"

"Sure. First thing every morning so if you walk into my office, you'll find The Word opened on my desk. The Lord is my boss."

"Oh, brother. I've not met anyone who called him that before. A lot of other uses for His name but never boss. You just keep it to yourself, that's all." She stroked Chief's ears. "You okay with this place, boy?"

Chief glanced up at his mistress and then at Jeremy. He walked toward the man and laid his head on Jeremy's lap.

Jeremy chuckled. "I guess there's your answer. I'll finish clearing out this space." He stood after patting the dog again. "Thanks for the vote of confidence, Chief."

"I'll drive over to my 'soon-to-be former' office and make arrangements to move my furniture here today. I'll need to cancel the lease agreement too. May cost me a bit, but I intend to point out that my office was broken into. I'll also travel to the courthouse and begin the proceedings to get my name legally changed. To Smith." She sighed. "More paperwork to go through."

"Why not let Dad take care of that. He can probably have it expedited."

"Oh, good idea. I guess I should have done that when he suggested it yesterday." Christine headed to the front door. "Come on, Chief. Let's go for a ride."

Chapter Twenty-Nine

Christine drove slowly past the coin shop she'd spent time observing the night before. All was quiet. She drove down the back lane, hoping to catch sight of someone either leaving or arriving at the rear entrance. There was no one in sight. She headed over to the building that housed her current office.

As soon as she arrived, she pulled into the familiar parking spot, making note of the fact the man who'd occupied her spot the day before was nowhere to be seen. *I guess he's taken my words to heart but after today, it won't matter.* "Come on, Chief. Let's move."

She walked beside her dog toward the back door. *It had better be locked.* She pulled the handle and discovered the door was unlocked again. *I'll need a witness.* She looked around the parking lot. A woman had pulled into the visitor's slot. Christine walked over toward her.

She watched the lady lock her car door and head in her direction. They met halfway. "Excuse me, but could you come with me and witness something?"

"Uh. Yeah, I guess. What's this all about?" The woman was about the same age as Christine. She was dressed nicely and walked as if she had an appointment with someone.

"I'm a tenant here, and the back door is supposed to be locked. It's not, but I need a witness to tell the building owner they haven't fulfilled our contract." Christine walked slowly beside the other woman.

The woman stopped. "How do I know you didn't unlock that door?"

Christine paused for a moment. "I guess you don't. Sorry to bother you." She began to walk away.

"No wait. I'll be your witness. I wanted to see what you'd say. I think I can trust you." She joined Christine who was about to walk to the entrance.

Christine pulled the door open. "See. No Keys. I'm supposed to need them to get in this way." She led the way inside.

"Can I come in this way now?" The woman had stopped outside the door.

"Yes. Come in. Don't mind Chief. He won't hurt you." Christine walked rapidly through the door leading to the lobby. "Mitch. The back door was unlocked again. This lady can verify the fact." She turned toward the woman who nodded her head in agreement.

"Do you want my name or anything," she asked Mitch.

The large uniformed guard shook his head. "No. Won't be necessary. I'll lock the door."

Christine scowled at him and glanced at her new friend. "I want your name. Mitch, locking the door is not going to be enough this time. I want to talk to the building owner." She took a notepad out of her purse and handed it, along with a pen, to the woman at her side. "I hope you don't mind getting involved."

"No. Not at all. Say, do you happen to know where Gord Ferman's office is. I've been told he's a good investigator." Christine shook her head and both women turned toward Mitch.

"He's on the fifth floor." He perused the list of tenants he kept on the wall near the door on the inside of his cubicle. "Room 503."

"Thanks." The woman handed the pad of paper back to Christine.

Christine read the name. "Miss Jenson. What kind of investigator do you need?

"I'm going through a divorce and I need someone to tail my husband. He's messing around with another woman. I know it but he keeps denying the fact and has accused me of being unfaithful. I need to prove I'm right. Give my lawyer some ammunition." She allowed her anger to be visible for a moment but reined it in quickly.

Christine caught the moment. "If he doesn't work out, I'm also an investigator. My office, for now anyway, is down that hall." She pointed toward the connecting door they'd just walked through.

"Oh, so that's why you're upset about that door being unlocked."

Brenda Jenson began to move toward the elevator. "If this guy isn't all they said he was, I'll stop by."

"Thanks for your help, Brenda. If the owner needs proof of negligence ..." She scowled toward Mitch again. "... I'll get in touch. I hope everything works out upstairs." She waved and then strode with purpose toward her office.

Christine entered the space she'd thought was so nice a few short hours ago. Now compared to what Jeremy was offering, it seemed a little shabby. *And small.* "Well, Chief. I guess we can pack." She looked around, placed her hands on her hips and tried to decide where to start.

Her door burst open. "Have you found my son?" Teresa Brent stood in the door frame, her face mottled with a combination of fear and anger. "I expected to hear from you before now. Where is he?"

"Mrs. Brent. Come in. Have a seat." Christine pointed the distraught woman toward the only other chair in her office besides hers. She moved behind her desk, placing it between them. "I would have called but I really don't have much to tell. I have some suspicions, but nothing concrete, yet."

The woman dropped her head into her hands and wept, big soul wrenching sobs. "I d-didn't s-sleep at a-all last n-night." She grabbed a tissue from her handbag. As she blew her nose, Christine walked over to her tiny fridge and extracted a bottle of cold water. She handed the beverage to her client. Teresa continued, "I lay in bed imagining all sorts of bad things happening to Nathan and I ..."

"I understand how hard it is to not imagine the worse. I do have a lead and I'm pursuing it. I'll get Nathan back as soon as I can. The police are still looking, too. Have you contacted them? I gave them the clues I picked up yesterday. One of us will find him."

Tears continued to slide down the mother's cheek. "I love my boy. He and Darcy are all I've got now."

"What about Tommy?" Christine tried not to show her disgust. *The man was not a good father figure, that's for sure.*

"I kicked him out. All he thinks about is partying. I don't want him near my kids anymore. Besides, he has another girlfriend, I found out. She phoned him at my house. I told him no more. He laughed, said I was unfit to be a mother, that I was not a real woman, either." Her head dropped for a second. She straightened her spine and stared Christine in the eyes. "I am a good mother, and right now, I don't care about being a woman. At least, not his kind."

The corners of Christine's mouth curled up a little at the

picture Teresa Brent described. *I can imagine how the conversation went.* She grinned in the woman's direction. "Good for you. Be patient with me. I am working on your son's case and I will find him." *One way or the other*, she thought, but she'd never express those thoughts out loud. She stood. "I'll call you first thing every morning. I'll let you know what I've uncovered so you'll know that your money is being well-spent and ..."

"Oh-h, it's not about the money. I want my Nathan back. I'll get more money if you need it, too. Just find my boy." Mrs. Brent stood and walked toward the door. "It's okay if I came by?"

"Oh, of course. Only I'm relocating my business." She scrambled around to see if she had anything with Jeremy's office address. She didn't. She scribbled the address and Jeremy's phone number on a piece of paper and handed the note to Teresa. "I'll be there after today. You can reach me there but you also have my cell phone. The number won't change."

"Thanks Miss Finder. I'll try to wait patiently. When I close my eyes ..."

"Yeah, I understand. I'll keep in touch, I promise." She walked the woman to the door. "Be strong. Nathan will need a resilient mommy when he gets home."

Christine watched the woman walk back down the hall. She continued to keep her eye on the distraught figure until she'd walked through the door to the lobby. She shook her head. *I can't imagine.* She closed her office door.

"Okay, Chief. Let's get to it. I need some boxes. I wonder if Mitch can find some for me. I'll bet they keep a few for vacating tenants ... maybe in the basement." She ended her one-sided conversation and picked up the phone. "Mitch. Hi. Yes, the owner's number, but I was wondering if you knew if there were any empty boxes in the building." She glanced around her tiny office. "I could use about three."

She watched as Chief went over to his bowls and began

lapping some water. He nibbled at the food left over from the day before. "Yes. Great. I'll come ... Oh, nice. Thank You." She wrote hurriedly on the pad of paper in front of her. "Thanks." She ended the conversation and punched in the number Mitch had given her.

"Mr. Jablonsky, please. Christine Finder calling."

Chapter Thirty

Jeremy steered his bike against the back wall of the garage beside his house. He covered his baby, after a final stroke, with a large tarp and sighed. "Just for a few months." He spoke to the machine as if it were alive. His heart felt like he was abandoning a special friend. He made sure nothing could fall on the BMW while it slumbered for the winter. He walked back outside. "Maybe I should move to a warmer climate. Would be able to ride all year then."

He gazed at the stars. "Lord, you know how much I enjoy riding the bike. Help me find as much enjoyment out of my truck." He chuckled. *Like that's earth shattering.* "Sorry Lord. Just feeling sorry for myself."

He walked into his house. The picture of Christine arranging furniture in the office brought a smile to his face. She is one independent woman. He'd walked in on her while she moved her bookshelf. His offer to help had received a stern reprimand with her telling him she was capable of handling things herself. He'd left her to do it, but his manly instincts cringed. *I was taught to help. Thanks Dad.*

He closed his door, the glass panel still letting in enough light to illuminate the foyer. He slipped off his boots, placed his jacket over a hanger in the closet, and strode toward the kitchen. *Need to eat if I'm going to pull another late night.*

He switched on the overhead light. *Soon it'll be completely dark when I get home.* "Let's see." He opened his refrigerator and peered inside. *Leftover Chinese. Sounds good.* He grabbed the boxes and opened the microwave door. Pressing the timer for two minutes, he hit the start button and walked to his bedroom.

A shower would be wonderful. Won't take long. He decided to relieve some of the tension of his day under the hot spray. Jeremy slipped out of his jeans and short sleeved shirt. He gave his body the once over in the mirror that flanked his vanity. *Not bad.* He shrugged out of the rest of his clothes and stepped into the shower.

Ah-h-h. He sighed as the hot spray from the large shower head poured down over him. The mindless task of lathering his body with soap allowed his mind to wander. Christine had made short work of her move to his office, She'd also managed to get out of her lease without penalty, too.

He lathered his hair. His thoughts roamed around the alarm system Christine's security company had installed that morning. *Now, not only will lights come on if someone comes onto her yard but an alarm will sound, loud enough to warn of an intruder. When she's home, she has monitors to scan her entire yard. She'd be able to see who was at the door before they rang the doorbell.*

Her neighbors might not be so happy with those alarms going off but I guess there's no reason for anyone to show up unannounced either. He shut the water off and grabbed one of the thick, fluffy towels hanging beside the enclosure. He dried his hair and wrapped the warm material around his body before stepping onto the mat outside the stall.

He knew the microwave buzzer had already sounded, even

if he hadn't heard anything, so he hurried to get dressed again. He combed his damp hair and walked gingerly to the kitchen. His bare feet made slapping noises on the tiled floor. *Christine will need to learn to use the gun I gave her. If the mugger comes back or if the man who killed her parents finds her, she'll need the protection.*

He sighed again as he took his dinner from the microwave. *The woman has a heap of trouble for someone so young. Maybe she should have stayed in Texas.* He plopped the boxes of food one by one down on a plate, emptying the contents before taking his meal to the living room and the TV. *Of course, now the killer found that location.* He sat in his Lazyboy and pressed the remote for the news channel.

I'm tired tonight. He filled his mouth with a forkful of fried rice. *Yum. Just what I needed.* The news show flashed several scenes of gang activity that had kept the police busy the night before. *I wonder if the gang that terrorized Christine were caught doing some damage somewhere else. Man, I'm sure giving the woman a lot of thought. Lord, protect her, please.* He munched a mouthful of deep fried pork.

There was nothing on the news about gang activity near Christine's location the night before. A mention of the homeless and their plight had the journalist in a tizzy about the approaching winter. No one person was mentioned in that regard, either. *I hope Jeremiah Burton found a place to stay.* He thought about the older gentleman with nowhere to call home anymore. *That daughter of his is a piece of work. How can a daughter treat her father so poorly? Especially when he's her only living relative. I have some disagreements with Dad once in a while but I'd never treat him that way.* He chuckled. *He'd never let me get away with it.*

Jeremy pushed the button on the side of his chair to raise the leg rest. He laid his plate on the side table beside the remote and leaned back. *Maybe a power nap.* He closed his eyes. In a matter of seconds, soft breathing was all that was heard in the room besides the TV.

Jeremy jumped, his legs sliding off the edge of the footrest, Jangle. *Wh-a-at? Phone.* He reached for his cell phone vibrating across the table beside his chair. "Lo."

He blinked sleep from his eyes. The voice on the other end was mad. "Just a minute. Who is this?"

He checked his watch. *Seven thirty. I must have been tired.* "Excuse me, who did you say this was?" He listened attentively this time. "Amanda ... er ... I mean Miss ... Mrs. Prescott." He scowled. "How did you get ... oh, never mind." She'd called his cell phone. She'd no way of knowing he was at home. "What's wrong?"

Amanda Prescott continued to berate him for not finding her father yet. "He's old, sick, and homeless. He needs to be found ... now."

"I'm doing all I can. I plan to go out again tonight. I may have a lead, but I won't know for sure until I follow it up. Now ..." He gripped the phone tighter in his hand willing his mind to concentrate. The woman kept interrupting.

"Where does this lead go? Maybe I need to be with you tonight to help find him." Her screechy voice grated on his nerves.

This was not a pleasant woman, and sincerity was certainly not her strong suit. He saw right through her. "I work alone. Of course, if you want to search by yourself, that's your prerogative, but as long as you're paying me, I'll do the job alone. Now was there anything else?"

He heard sputtering on the other end of the connection. "Well ... I ... I was .... concerned. Nothing more. Call me tomorrow to let me know how you made out." The line went dead almost immediately. Jeremy replaced the phone on the side table and pushed the button on the side of his chair to release the footrest. *I guess I'd better get going.*

Retracing his steps to the front door, Jeremy slipped on his jacket, and pulled a woolen cap over his still damp hair. *Maybe the bar owner won't recognize me.* He grabbed a pair of eyeglasses with clear glass lenses from the desk drawer near his front door and added those to his disguise. Checking to make sure he had enough money in his wallet, he opened his front door and stepped outside.

The evening had become quite chilly. Jeremy pulled the collar on his jacket up a little and walked briskly to his pick-up. *I'll need to be quick tonight if I want to catch this guy. I don't want to give him a heart attack although Franny said he was in good health. One never knows with a man his age.* He inserted his key into the ignition and turned his truck on, letting it warm for a second or two before putting it in reverse.

The street in front of his house was empty. *Folks have either gone where they've planned already or they're staying home,* he surmised. He stepped on the gas as soon as his truck was pointed in the right direction.

Lights flickered all around him as he drove. *One thing about living in the city, too many lights. Might as well be no stars.* He remembered his last camping trip. *Man those stars were so plentiful, hardly a spot in the sky didn't have a few.*

He turned onto the street where the bar from the night before was located. Just as he pulled into a parking spot, he noticed a tall, thin man enter the bar. *That's him.* Jeremy decided to wait right where he was. He stepped out of the truck prepared to wait but changed his mind. *When he comes out of the bar, I need to be ready to follow. I'd better get to the other side of the street.*

He walked across, dodging traffic and hid in the shadows near a back alley. He peeked around the corner and watched the entrance. *He won't get away from me tonight, that's for sure.* He checked his pocket to make sure he had some ID to show Jeremiah when he stopped him.

Jeremy pulled the collar of his jacket closer around his ears. The cement walls were damp and the dampness was seeping through his jacket, giving his skin a layer of goose bumps.

He rubbed his hands together. *I wish I'd thought to bring gloves.*

The wait lasted several minutes. More patrons entered and he saw a few leave. *Certainly more people coming than going,* he thought. *I can't imagine having nothing better to do on any given evening than hanging out in a bar. Lord, thank you for always providing lots to keep me occupied. I never have time to be lonely.*

He crossed his chilled arms over his chest to get some added warmth. *Lord, please give Jeremiah a reason to leave soon.* Just as he spoke, his quarry walked through the door and onto the sidewalk. The older man stopped for a second, swung his head right and then left, and proceeded to saunter in the direction he'd come from initially. Jeremy noticed he carried two Styrofoam containers that may or may not be food.

Jeremy slipped from his hiding place and walked casually down the block after his target. He even weaved a little. *He won't worry about another drunk on the street*, he thought. He did a zigzag step, righted himself, and walked ahead. Jeremiah was a half block away.

Jeremy kept the older man in his sights for the next three blocks until Jeremiah turned a corner and disappeared. Jeremy stumbled a little faster, his pace accelerated enough to catch up to the tall, gaunt form, he hoped. As he reached the corner, he observed Jeremiah as he opened a wrought iron gate and turned to gaze up and down the street. *He's either suspicious or he's taking precautions.* Jeremiah walked down the cement path to a small one-story house. The abode appeared deserted.

Jeremy hid behind some bushes as Jeremiah walked up the steps to the front door. *The guy has a key.* The cartons he'd carried were placed on the step while he unlocked the door. Jeremiah retrieved his packages and walked inside, slamming the door behind him. Jeremy stepped out from his hiding place. *Well, I guess I have the answer to where he's staying. He's not homeless.*

Jeremy decided to check out the house, see if there was another way in. *If I knock on the door, he'll run. So ... I'll have to break in. Surprise him. Then I can explain.* He walked through the gate and around the side of the house. The windows were too high to be able to scrutinize the inside. Jeremy figured no one else was inside since the lights had been turned off until Mr. Burton had arrived. *It's also too early for anyone to be in bed, I think.*

He walked around to the back. A door leading to the yard stood ajar. It was leaning off one of its hinges. The screen was also torn. *Maybe this is an abandoned house where Jeremiah chose to exercise his rights as a squatter.*

Jeremy found a forgotten two by four lying along the broken sidewalk. The cement path led to a garage that appeared as if mice were the only inhabitants.. He took the plank of wood and barred the door ... just in case. *The piece of timber won't hold forever but might be able to slow an old man down if he tries to leave through the back.* Then he retraced his steps to the front of the house.

The street was as quiet as a cemetery. A few lights were lit a couple of houses away, but the one in front of this house was out. *I wonder if Jeremiah made sure of that.* He walked up to the front door. Carefully, he opened the aluminum screen door an inch at a time. A tiny creak seemed amplified in the silence. He opened it just enough to allow his body through as he stepped onto the small porch.

Jeremy heard voices from inside. He listened attentively. *Don't need any surprises.* It appeared as if the old man was talking to someone but ... *maybe the TV.* He stepped closer to the door. His hand grabbed the knob, his grip firm and sure. With one twist, he pushed the door open and was inside in a split second. Voices stopped as Jeremy barreled into the first room on his right ... the living room. Two people sat on the rickety, well-worn sofa munching on a sandwich.

Jeremiah stood, tall and protective. He swallowed. "Who are you? You can't come barging in here. Boy, call the police."

"Now, Mr. Burton. You don't want to do that. Besides, you're scaring the boy." Jeremy walked further into the room. He placed his hand into his pocket and pulled out a card to identify him. He handed it to Jeremiah. "Your daughter hired me to find you."

Jeremiah Burton plunked down on the sofa beside the small boy he'd been talking to. He hung his head as he perused the card in his hand. "I'm not going back. I don't care what Amanda wants. Not anymore."

"Mr. Burton. Jeremiah. Is it okay if I call you Jeremiah? Mind if I sit?" Jeremy inched his body toward the only other piece of furniture in the room. The large chair sagged profusely in the middle. *If I sit in that, I'll not get out in a hurry.* He decided to sit on the arm. "I've seen Franny. I know what your daughter did to you. I'm here to offer you the services of my Dad. He's a lawyer ... a good one. He'll get the power of attorney reversed if you want and help you get established in your own home again."

"She's been siphoning all my money out of my bank account. Nothing left to even pay a lawyer." He patted the leg of the young boy who sat beside him as if to reassure the child. "Franny tell you where to find me, did she?"

"Well, not exactly. But she did tell me about the bar." Jeremy tried to smile but he noticed the old guy was not in the mood for humor.

Jeremiah glared. "Darn the woman. I trusted her."

"She cares about you and was worried about you being on the street, what with winter coming on. Besides, I told her I could help. We'll need you to get a medical assessment ..."

"The doc's in Amanda's pocket. They're in it together." Jeremiah shook his fist.

"You'll see a doctor that we'll recommend and who has nothing to gain by being dishonest. Mr. Levey told me that the doctor who examined you at the home said you were in good mental condition. If we can prove the one Amanda hired lied, we can have his medical license pulled. We plan to fight for you, Jeremiah. I had your daughter pegged the moment she set foot in my office. She's anxious to have you back, so she says." Jeremy crossed one ankle over the other. "Now, what do you say you come stay at my house tonight and we start the proceedings to get you your assets back tomorrow?" He glanced at the shabby surroundings. "This place abandoned or something?"

"Yeah, well it was the only place we could go." Jeremiah scrutinized the little boy beside him. "Chuckie, here, was cold."

"Chuckie, eh? Where'd he come from?" Jeremy scrutinized the child for the first time. "How did you two get hitched up?"

Jeremiah wrapped his long lanky arm around the boy. The child had stopped eating. He stared toward the newcomer, his large round eyes filled with fright. His pants were torn and dried tears left white tracks along his filthy cheeks. His hair looked as if it had never seen a comb. Jeremiah coughed, stalling for time Jeremy figured. Then the older man spoke, his voice filled with compassion. "He'll have to come with me. I found him. Wandering the streets he was, alone. He either can't or won't talk. Don't know his name so I call him Chuckie. Don't have money so can't do better for him than handouts but ..."

"He'll come with us. Okay with you, little guy?" Jeremy wanted the boy to know he was a friend, to wipe away the look of terror from his face. *Why would anyone let a kid like this wander the streets.* "Do you have any idea where your mother is?"

A lone tear slid down the boy's cheek. He shook his head. Then his large soulful eyes shifted to Jeremiah's face.

The man squeezed the boy harder. "It'll be okay. You'll see." Jeremiah stared hard at Jeremy. "We'll go with you, but I want your assurance you won't take me back to that place. Not like it was a bad place. Amanda saw to that, at least. It's just I couldn't come and go as I wanted. I had no money, no independence. Amanda saw to that too." He took another mouthful of food encouraging the boy to do the same. "We'll come as soon as we finish eating. We haven't had any food all day. Ain't that right Chuckie?" The boy nodded and took a bite of the hamburger in his grubby hands.

Chapter Thirty-One

Christine checked her watch. Ten o'clock, just about the time the kid snuck into the coin shop last night. *Hopefully, I'm parked far enough away that no one will suspect I'm back.* She gave her appearance the once over. All black ... jeans, jacket, turtleneck and even her make-up. Her black gloves made sure her white skin would give nothing away. Chief took a more inventive solution.

She glanced at her dog. His drooping ears and lowered head let her know how embarrassed he was. Christine had covered his body in one of her black t-shirts. She'd tied a black bandana around his head. "Might not be enough to disguise you're a dog, but at least they won't recognize what kind or whose." She chuckled. "Come on. It's not that bad. We have to get inside to see if our little boy is there."

Chief whined. Christine patted his head. "You'll feel better when we rescue the kid." She carefully opened the door to her rented car, soundlessly locked it, and stood beside Chief surveying the street where she'd parked. She looked down at her dog. Her hand hid the giggle threatening to erupt. His tail was tucked firmly between his legs. He truly did not like dressing up.

"Come, boy." She ducked between the nearby houses to make her way to the lane. She was a block and a half and one street over from her destination. She figured this back alley would end up right behind the shop. She hoped to scope out the shop from the plot of grass behind and across the lane.

As she approached the first back yard, motion sensing lights bathed the area in harsh light. A dog barked a few yards away. Chief growled. "Sh-h-h." Christine crept quietly back into the shadows the light cast near the garage. From her vantage point, her eyes traveled over every corner and crevice near the house and the yard. No movement, not even from the windows. "These people must not be very curious."

She edged along the wall of the garage until she stood on the broken concrete in the back lane. More garages extended to her right and left. A few quick glances gave her the information she needed to get her bearings. "Chief, come." she whispered. "This way."

They dashed as quietly as their training had taught them toward the back entrance to the coin shop. Christine followed her instincts to the gate for the yard across from the shop. "Let's be quiet." She hoped Chief didn't growl if the murky figure appeared again.

Christine placed her hand in her pocket. She wrapped her fingers around the spike, making sure that the talons of the weapon pointed out between her digits. The night air had cooled since she'd left home, but she was dressed appropriately. She even had hand warmers, just in case. Stars twinkled overhead, at least the few she was able to make out from this cityscape. "Chief." She whispered. "We'll have to take a drive out in the country after this case is solved. See some real stars." The dog nudged her hand.

Christine glanced behind. The yard appeared deserted. A few old tires leaned haphazardly nearby. Weeds spilled out of them as if the tires had been abandoned a long time ago. A broken bed frame decorated another corner of the yard, rusted and fragile looking. She reached down to pat Chief.

She always enjoyed the texture of his fur. Footsteps broke her line of thinking as they echoed off the nearby walls of the concrete lane. The steps shuffled, stopped, and shuffled forward again. Christine flattened her body against the fence. "Quiet, Chief," she cautioned. The dog's ears were perked up, listening. Christine watched through the scruffy shrubs separating the fence from the yard. They kept her well hidden, she hoped.

The slender body of a young male entered her field of vision. He had a cap pulled low over his forehead. Every now and then, she heard a sniffle as if the man had a cold or something. "I think he's a man." She spoke barely above a whisper to Chief.

They watched as the person moved closer to the back of the coin shop. He walked on past. *False alarm.* A current of disappointment rolled through her stomach. Chief growled, a low sound that only Christine was able to hear. "Too good to be true, I guess. Oh, well, we just got here." She relaxed against the fence again.

Her phone vibrated. Christine pulled it out to see who was calling now? She didn't recognize the name so she decided to drop the phone back in her pocket without answering the call. A slight breeze whipped through the alleyway, penetrating Christine's jacket. She shivered and hoped this would not be a long night. Something scurried across the cluttered grass nearby. Chief growled. He stood, turned his head this way and that, but sat back down on his haunches. His training kept him by Christine's side ... for now.

Footsteps echoed once again from somewhere nearby. Christine noticed Chief's fur stood on end when she placed a hand of caution on his warm body. The dog raised his head to sniff the air. Christine peeked through the branches, maintaining her hidden status. Will I know this person? The figure headed in their direction. She saw a dark shadow, a slender form, but that's all. The footsteps slowed, but continued down the lane at a steady pace. They grew louder the closer they got to her hiding place.

Christine held her breath. She patted the dog's collar bone to calm him. She peeked through the shrubs again and kept her eyes glued to the dark shape. *He appears to be the same height as the boy last night*, she reflected. The youth turned toward the back door of the coin shop. He took his hand out of his pocket and inserted a key into the lock. Christine hoped he'd forget to lock the door behind him this time.

The figure, clothed all in black, yanked the door open. Hinges creaked, the sound echoing back to Christine as if warning her that she'd be noticed if she went in that way. The man disappeared inside. He pulled the door closed, shutting out the damp night air. Christine waited a few seconds, impatience seeping from every pore. After a few minutes, she made her way to the gate in the fence, stopping after every footstep to make sure no one would surprise them.

Chief followed when she held the gate for him to pass. She bent down toward him and pulled one of Nathan Brent's socks from her left hand pocket. She placed it in front of Chief. The dog took a long whiff and then whined. He got the message. Christine replaced the sock, and tip-toed across the lane, carefully placing one foot in front of the other. Chief walked beside her, matching each of her steps.

Christine glanced in all directions. The quietness seemed death-like. She reached the door, grasped the handle and pulled just a little. Nothing moved. *Rats. The kid locked the door again. Now what?* She pulled again.

This time the entry opened enough for her to see a crack between the frame and the door itself. *I need ... right ... my flashlight.* She reached into her pocket again and pulled out the small cylindrical utensil. She shone if on the crack to determine what was holding the door. *I sure hope no one can see this light from inside.*

Chief padded his feet up and down impatiently. "Sh-h-h," Christine cautioned. The light reflected on a small hook latching the entrance. She marked the place with her eyes, turned the light off, and dropped the penlight in her pocket. Her heart pounded so hard, she had to take an extra breath. The desire to get inside was intense, but her knees felt like rubber. She felt the metal in her pocket. *This'll work.*

Christine took the spike out and held it endwise. She slipped the metal point into the crack near the latch and lifted. The fastener easily slipped off whatever was holding it. The door opened a little further.

Christine dropped the weapon in her pocket. Using both hands, she pulled the door open enough to allow her slight frame to enter. Chief squeezed through as well. She pulled the door shut, but decided not to replace the latch in case she needed to make a run for it. Chief lifted his head and sniffed the air.

She led the way, carefully placing one foot in front of the other. Nothing indicated another person inhabited the room with them. The smell of mold and dust filled her nostrils. She decided to take her flashlight out again to survey her surroundings.

The small light bounced off several cartons indicating a storage room of sorts. Boxes reached the ceiling on all sides with a narrow passageway between them. Christine wove her way along the path, keeping the light pointed toward the floor. She rounded a corner and with her hand on Chief's neckline, she felt his fur bulge up again. He smelled something.

She shone the light toward him. In a voice that only Chief heard, she asked, "You smell something, Chief?" Then she gave him the command. "Scent."

Chief took the lead and walked slowly, his feet making no sound on the dirt floor. He stopped at a doorway and sniffed, putting his nose on the crack between the frame and the door itself. Christine placed the side of her head toward the door and listened. She overheard the faint strains of some classical music.

She decided to try the door to find out if a lock barred their entrance. The door responded soundlessly. Christine opened the portal just a crack. She waited. She was about to pull it a little wider when the phone in her pocket vibrated again. *Good thing I have the device on vibrate. No one ever calls me at night.* She ignored a second call.

Chief pushed his head into the door opening, forcing a wider gap. He wriggled his body through and Christine quickly followed after him. The dark room they entered was not as gloomy as the one previous. She recognized some items of furniture, including a small table and a bed. Chief propelled his body toward the bed and he sniffed all over the sheet and pillow. He nudged a baseball hat.

Christine picked up the item of clothing. She turned the cap over in her hands. It might belong to a young boy. She watched Chief. The dog pranced in place, clearly agitated. Then she remembered she had the photo of Nathan in her pocket. She decided to check. Sure enough, the hat appeared to be the same as the one the little boy wore in the picture. These people had taken Nathan.

She crept in the direction of the musical notes, giving Chief the command to stay behind her. She wrapped the fingers of her right hand around the spike she carried and pulled it out. Christine grasped the can of bear spray with her left hand, leaving it in her pocket for now. Then she moved, one step at a time, toward the door leading to the music and some light.

Agitated voices grew more distinguishable the closer she got to the door. The heated argument, filled with anger from one person and remorse from the other, echoed through the room. The younger sounding voice spoke his regret. "I have no idea where he is. I walked the length of this lane and two more blocks in either direction. He's gone." The sound of a loud smack advertised someone had been hit.

"Aw-w-w. Why'd you haveta do that?"

"You stupid ...." The air was saturated with cuss words, some totally new to Christine. The louder, older voice fumed, almost irrational. "You get me another kid." The sound of peaceful music contradicted the ominous silence that followed.

Then the younger voice whined, "Aw-w-w Jerry. I'll get a kid for ya, but ain't I good enough no more. I usta ... "

"Shad up. You listening ... a little boy. Now get out and find me one." Breaking furniture followed the sound of another slap. The recipient remained silent. Christine could picture the younger man falling ... if he was a man. She bent her head to the dog's ear. "Come on, Chief. Nathan's not here. Let's go."

She scurried in front of Chief to the door leading through the storage area. Keeping her weapons in hand, she made her way to the exit in record time. Footsteps sounded as if they followed right behind. She scurried through the door. Its creak sounded loud to her ears, but she just kept going.

"Hey." The voice sounded too close. She ran toward the gate and her hiding place. She hoped he wouldn't notice where she went, but she decided not to stop. She went around the side of the house and kept going. Angry voices filled the night air. "Get her."

Christine raced as fast as her morning runs had conditioned her for. She rounded the last corner. Her car was bathed in shadows when she spotted it. She pumped her legs toward the locked vehicle. Chief was right behind, She fumbled with her keys. Her fingers finally grasped the right one. Shaking, and puffing from exertion, she managed to get her door unlocked.

Angry voices filled the night air a short distance away. Chief stood beside her, bristling. A low growl leaked from his throat. Christine yanked the door open. Chief jumped inside. The air seemed blue with curses as she plunked down on the seat. She quickly flipped the locks for all the doors. She twisted the key in the ignition and the car roared to life. A loud crash at the back of the car sounded as if a rock had been thrown. She dropped it in gear and raced away. Another rock landed on the hood of the rental. The distance widened. Her breathing began to slow. Then her phone rang again.

Chapter Thirty-Two

Jeremy replaced his cell phone. *No answer. Where is she?* He should be looking for a place to hide Jeremiah Burton, and his friend, until his father was able to reverse the power of attorney. He had to find a solution but worrying about Christine was clouding his thought processes.

"Jeremiah, maybe Franny would let you stay with her?" He disliked the idea which was apparently as uncomfortable for Jeremiah as the notion was for him. "Never mind. Bad idea. Amanda found out about her."

"How do I discern whether you're trustworthy or not?" Jeremiah began to clear away the leftovers from their meager meal. The old man glanced at the child who was almost asleep. "This kid needs a warm bed." He patted the child's head to reassure both of them.

Jeremy crouched down beside the door. He sympathized with the old gentleman. *I'd not trust anyone either if I was him.* "Let's just say Franny trusts me or she'd never have told me about the bar. I'm on your side. You want your life back? Take a chance on me. I can get it done for you."

Jeremiah shrugged and glanced at the boy again. "I have someone else to think about now. I don't know who this kid is, but I couldn't let him wander the streets all alone. Maybe his momma beat him or there's a mean step-daddy in the picture. He's run away from home and I need to keep him safe until I find out more. He won't or can't say anything so all I can do is imagine. My imaginings are not good." He pulled a plastic bag out of his pocket and stuffed the refuse inside. "I'll go with you but you lie to me ... just once ... I'm outta here. I'll not be put back in the home."

"I'll do some checking, see if a report's been filed about a missing kid. In the meantime, we need a place to keep you both warm and safe. Your daughter, apparently, has found my home address and the location of my office since she hired me. But ... another PI is sharing office space with me. She moved in this afternoon. Amanda never met her. I'm thinking ... " He pulled his cell phone out of his pocket again. "I've tried calling her already tonight. Maybe she'll answer now."

He listened as the device rang somewhere. Three times. He was about to flip the instrument shut when he heard the ring stop. Someone shout, "What? Why are you calling me?"

"You need to get call display. It's me. Jeremy. Where are you?" Jeremy switched his phone from one ear to the other while he listened to Christine's answer. "Christine. Did I not come to the rescue last night because some thugs used a baseball bat on your car? What part of stay safe don't you understand?" His temper had escalated unpredictably fast. He took a long, deep breath and glanced toward Jeremiah who was listening to every word.

He held the phone away from his ear and scowled at the device. *I can't listen to this anymore.* "Christine, you need to use your head. Are you safe ... now?" He used precaution against permanent hearing damage by increasing the distance between the phone and his head. "Christine. Christine. All right. I'll meet you at your house. I need a favor." He listened to the sputter on the other end of the line.

"Be there in a few." He closed the handset, cutting her off, and grimaced toward Jeremiah and the boy. His eyebrows lifted at the consternation written all over Jeremiah's face. "What? She'll love the idea. I can guarantee it. Come on. Let's pack this up and secure this place again." Jeremy led the way to the street exit. Jeremiah grabbed his plastic bag of garbage with one hand and the small hand of the little boy with his other. They marched out of the dilapidated structure and out into the cold night air. Every line of his body, Jeremy perceived, demonstrated reluctance.

As they closed the front door, Jeremy observed his new clients. "Amanda thinks she's hired me, but I don't intend to take any money from her. I don't plan to let her find out where you are or what we are doing until it becomes absolutely necessary. At some point, she'll come to realize that we're challenging her power of attorney."

The conversation remained one-sided all the way to Jeremy's truck. He unlocked the driver side door and walked around to help the older man step up into the cab. Jeremiah considered the younger man at his side. The sense of disquiet was evident for all to see. "I feel as if I'm walking to my death. Not a good feeling to be able to trust no one."

"Mr. Burton," Jeremy began. "What do you have faith in? I mean, do you trust God?"

"Well, yes. But ... "

"I'm a Christian. Why don't we ask God to take your fears away? I think God brought us together. Amanda might have hired someone altogether different ... a person not so much interested in helping you as in getting paid for a job." He bowed his head, not waiting for the older gentleman to agree. "Lord, You know more about Jeremiah at this time than I do and you understand the mess his daughter made of his life, better than even he does. Please help him feel comfortable with me. Renew his trust in people through me, Lord. Amen." He glanced at Jeremiah to see if he felt any better.

The older man did seem somewhat relieved as he used the handle grip to launch himself into the cab of the truck. The small boy had already gotten in. Jeremy closed the door on his passengers and walked around to the other side.

When he was seated, he started the truck. The boy stirred, but soon nestled into Jeremiah. His eyes were at half-mast almost before the vehicle moved out of its parking space.

The short trip across town was conducted in silence. Jeremy sneaked a glance toward Jeremiah once in a while. He caught Jeremiah looking at him as well, but apprehension continued to mar the old man's features. *Lord, help him trust me.* The streets seemed overly congested. *Must be something going on I'm not aware of. I wonder if Christine managed to find the boy she's looking for. I sure wish she'd keep a low profile but she wouldn't be doing her job, I guess.*

He took the familiar route to Christine's home and pulled into her short driveway. No sign of her car. His eyes veered toward Jeremiah. "Christine had an alarm system installed, so if we go traipsing across her yard before she turns the thing off, we'll wake the neighbors. She shouldn't be too long." He settled back in his seat. "The kid is certainly tired. I wonder how old he is."

"I asked him, but it's one more unanswered question. I can't figure out if he's so traumatized he can't speak or whether he won't talk because he doesn't trust me, yet." The older man ran his hand over the small child's hair. The boy didn't move. "I would like to find out what he's running from. His parents might be the ones abusing him, if that's the issue. Too many questions, not enough answers."

The men continued to stare out the windshield of the truck. Jeremiah rubbed his hands down his upper legs before speaking again. "I guess, in a way, his story is a lot like mine. The people searching might be the culprits so I feel I need to shield him, just as you plan to protect me from Amanda." He sighed. The sound displayed his frustration over the turn his life had taken.

Jeremy remained silent, letting the old man talk if he wanted to. His eyes scanned Christine's yard in the meantime.

Jeremiah cleared his throat. "Once upon a time ... I used to think ..." He paused. "When my wife was still alive, we'd talk about Amanda looking after us in our old age. We thought she would take good care of us, but something changed. After Miriam died, it was like Amanda became a different person."

"How long ago was that?"

"Five years now. I miss her." Jeremiah sat looking out the side window for a few minutes. He rubbed his limbs again.

Jeremy decided to approach a new subject. "Are your legs aching, Jeremiah? Do you have arthritis or something?"

"Oh, goodness me, young man. Everyone our age, just about, has some form of stiffness. But no, my legs don't hurt. Just a habit, I guess. Miriam noticed the practice when I worried. She used to make a joke saying I rubbed my legs like the crickets do." He smiled a little. "We had some good times, me and her. Over 50 years we'da been married if she'd lived."

"I'm sure you miss her. What kind of changes did you observe in Amanda after Miriam died?" Jeremy angled his body to better hear the quiet words coming out of Jeremiah's mouth.

The older man glanced at the child as if wanting to make sure he didn't overhear his answer. "She hardly came around like she used to. It was as if, with her mother gone, she couldn't stand to be at the house anymore. When she did show up, she was always complaining about the mess. I didn't keep the place like Miriam did, but it was clean enough for me. She couldn't find any bugs if she tried."

Jeremy noticed the slow anger begin to develop with the conversation. "Women don't always think we men can do things like house-keeping and such. When my Mom was still alive, she'd go over to dad's office and clean, even though he had a cleaning service. She had her standards, I guess. Now we miss her interference."

"It was more than meddling with Amanda. She found fault on purpose, looking for things to start an argument."

"Her husband ... did he visit with her?" Jeremy began to understand some of the things Jeremiah had to put up with.

"Stephen never came by and eventually, when I asked, she told me he'd walked out on her." He thought for a moment. "That was probably about a year after Miriam went home."

Jeremy's ears perked up at the man's use of the term 'went home'. "Did you and Miriam belong to a church?"

"Well, sure. We're died in the wool Baptists, don't you know. Went to Grant Memorial Baptist Church for twenty five years. No, actually, more like thirty. Loved the place. Was our home away from home." He smiled again.

His memory of a happier time supplanted his distress over current events, Jeremy surmised. "So you actually understand what being a Christian means, don't you?"

"I sure do, young man. Miriam and I accepted the Lord when we were still in high school. She was my sweetheart even then. God came first ... in both our lives." Jeremiah stared out the window as Christine pulled into the drive behind them. "Your young lady?"

"Well, she's not exactly my young lady. We share office space." Jeremy stepped out of the truck. "Wait here, Jeremiah, until I fill her in."

He closed the door, and walked back toward Christine's car as she was getting out. *Oh, boy. She's mad.* "Hi Christine. Did you find what you were hoping? I wish you'd let me ... "

"Now, hold on a minute. Just because I called you last night, does not give you the right to run my life. We share office space. Nothing more. Chief and I still have work to do.

And where do you get off shouting at me over the phone?" She poked her spiked right hand toward his chest. "When I need your help, I might ask for it, but I am perfectly capable of ... "

"Whoa. Calm down. I wasn't trying to run your life. But I was hired to protect you. You need to keep me informed of your whereabouts at all times. You can't ignore the fact some maniac is trying to find you, the same nut job ... probably ... who killed your parents." These last words he spit at her in an attempt to keep his voice low enough the occupants of his truck wouldn't overhear. "Besides you didn't find the kid, did you?"

"Oh yeah. Well I did discover he was being held in that place." She yanked the small baseball cap from the pocket of her jacket. "This is his. I found the cap on a make-shift bed in a storage room at the back of the coin dealer's shop. And ... "

"How do you know it's his?"

Christine pulled the photo out of Nathan Brent. "Same cap." She showed Jeremy the picture.

Jeremy grabbed the photo from her hand. "Let me see that." His eyes widened. "Come with me." He pulled her with him toward the driver's side of the truck. He opened the door as the child on his front seat sat up.

The boy rubbed his eyes as Christine looked inside. "What? You found a kid?" When the child lowered his hands, she looked toward him and back at the photo. "Oh, my gosh. Nathan. Nathan Brent. Are you Nathan Brent?"

"He doesn't talk." Christine discerned Jeremiah's presence for the first time. "You're familiar with the kid, miss?"

Christine glanced behind to see the look on Jeremy's face. *Boy, he's going to take credit for finding Nathan now.* She sighed. "Come on inside. Is this the favor you had to ask me?"

"Well, sort of. Come on Jeremiah. I'm sure Christine has something hot to drink. Is your alarm armed, Christine? We didn't want to step out of the truck until we were sure the bells and whistles wouldn't go off."

"It is but not for long." She flipped open a remote she took from her purse and pressed a button. "It's safe now."

Jeremy was impressed. "Wow. Handy. I was wondering how you were going to get inside without scaring the neighbors to death." He moved past the truck and met Jeremiah and the boy by the large grill in the front. He whispered to Jeremiah, "She's really not a bad person. You'll see."

"Does she have information about the kid? What's her relationship with him?" Jeremiah led the way toward the entrance. He stepped inside and Jeremy followed.

Jeremy looked around. *Christine may appear to be self-sufficient and macho, but this bungalow sure reflects a different side to her.* The decor was ultra-feminine with many accents making her tiny space cozy, yet not cramped. "Christine, let me introduce you to these two. This is Jeremiah Burton, a man whom I was hired to find, who'd escaped from Meadowood Care Home. This little chap ..." He pointed to the child who was hiding behind Jeremiah's pant leg. "He's the kid." He looked toward Christine. "But I think you know more than we do about him, right?"

Christine leaned forward to shake Jeremiah's hand. "Nice to meet you. You sure don't need to be in a care home."

"Exactly." Jeremiah glanced toward Christine and then around the room. "My wife liked a lot of the same frou-frou. Pretty place." He sighed. "The boy hasn't told us his name."

"Like Jeremy," she glared at the younger man, "I am a private investigator. Teresa Brent hired me to find her son missing from his home since yesterday morning. When and where did you find him? As you can see," she held the picture for Jeremiah's perusal, "This is Nathan Brent."

"He doesn't talk. I discovered him wandering the streets this morning. He was shivering so much it took several cups of hot chocolate to warm him. I came across a vacant house and was planning for the two of us to stay there tonight but, your friend here ..." He nodded toward Jeremy and grimaced. "He followed me home after I went out for some food."

Christine pulled the baseball cap from her jacket pocket. She handed the hat to the little boy, who grabbed it and clutched the treasured garment to his chest. "I guess that confirms it." She knelt down to eye level with the child. Chief walked close by and Nathan reached out to brush his hand across the dog's back. Chief's tail wagged in compliance and joy. His scent had told him who the boy was. "You wanna go see your mommy, Nathan?"

Nathan backed up next to Jeremiah's leg. Jeremiah turned his eyes to Christine. "There's more to his story, I think." The child remained silent, his large brown eyes filled with fear. Jeremiah placed a hand protectively to cradle the boy's head. "He's not going anywhere until we have all the answers. I am a good example of how things can get twisted."

"Christine, are you planning to let the police know we've ... er ... you've found him? I think we should wait a while. Till we understand more." Jeremy plunked himself down on the sofa. Chief rested his head on Jeremy's leg. Jeremy's hand patted the dog's head as if it was the most natural thing in the world. "Good boy, Chief." He looked toward Christine.

"Make yourself at home, Mr. Burton. Obviously, there's more here than meets the eye. Nathan's mother assured me he was safe in their house. Now, I guess, I need to investigate the family before we send Nathan back to them. Okay, Nathan? We'll make sure your home situation is harmless before you go back."

The boy nodded slowly and squished his body as close to Jeremiah as he could. Christine studied the rapport between the two. "Seems like he trusts you already. I wonder why?"

Jeremiah appeared indignant. "I'm trustworthy, that's why. What do ya think, I'd hurt him?" He sputtered and his face displayed a pink hue. "Kids always liked me. If I'da had grandkids ... " He seemed downhearted at the thought. "Doesn't matter. Don't. The kid ain't going anywhere until he's safe."

Jeremy decided now was as good a time as any. "Christine, since you have all this security and Jeremiah's daughter knows where I live, would it be okay for Jeremiah and the kid ... er ... Nathan, to stay here with you? I mean ... "

"Oh, come on." She looked from one to the other. "I don't have much food in the house. My spare room is a shambles ... but it could be straightened easily enough ..." Her eyes traveled from one to the other. "There's no place for Nathan to sleep. Besides, I'm usually gone all day and ... "

Jeremy chuckled. "Sounds like a bunch of excuses to me. I'll help with the groceries ... "

"I can afford the food, for Pete's sake. I ... oh, alright. Sorry, Jeremiah. I'm not very gracious, am I? I always need a little time to adjust to change. I wish you'd given me some advance warning, that's all." She turned toward the man who seemed to get her hackles up by being in the same room. His mouth hung open. "Yeah, I know. You couldn't reach me."

It was Jeremy's turn to sputter in indignation. "I ... Were you answering your phone?" Then he relented. "Yes I could have ... should have. Jeremiah, did you stash clothes somewhere?"

"I wish. I left the home on a whim, no planning ... just fed up. A change of clothes and a shower would be great." He glanced at his dust coated pants and his scruffy shoes. Nathan wrapped his arms around Chief's neck. "At least the boy's found a friend." They all chuckled as Chief gave Nathan a juicy slurp across his face. The boy giggled. "That's the first sound out of him." Jeremiah smiled.

"I think we're about the same size. I'll head home and bring you some clothes if you don't mind used underwear. Christine, is this alright?"

"Sure. The living arrangements will work. There's two

bathrooms, Jeremiah, so you and Nathan can use the one just down the hall and mine is an ensuite off my bedroom so will be private. Nathan, you can wear one of my t-shirts tonight. Jeremy, will you bring a few items of children's clothing with you when you come over tomorrow morning. I assume we'll need to co-ordinate our investigative procedures to protect these two."

Jeremy smiled. "Good thinking. I'll head home now and return momentarily. Tomorrow we'll talk strategy." He headed to the door. "By the time Nathan has his bath, I'll be back with clothes for Jeremiah." He walked outside, almost slamming it on the way out.

"Okay, Nathan. Let's get you ready for bed. I'll bet you could fall asleep standing up." Christine noticed the apprehension on the boy's face. She motioned for Chief. "Chief, you come too." Nathan smiled for the first time since he'd arrived. "Jeremiah, if you're going to be my house guest, help yourself to anything you find in the kitchen."

"Thank you, Miss ... er ... what is your last name?" Jeremiah stood to his feet and waited for her response.

"Christine is fine. Make yourself at home." She headed toward the bathroom after Chief and Nathan before Jeremiah asked any more questions. *He's not the only one with secrets. I want to keep it that way.*

Chapter Thirty-Three

After Jeremy deposited some clothes on her sofa, he exited her tiny abode a second time. Christine yawned and said a hasty good-night to Jeremiah before walking down the hall to her bedroom. She studied herself in the mirror. *Need a haircut. Man. Another zit.* She plunked down on the bed and turned toward Chief's empty bed. *I hope Nathan will feel safe with Chief beside him.* The little boy had shyly allowed her to supervise his bath, but when the time had come for him to go to sleep, his crying had torn at her heart. *He seems to miss his mom and yet he's afraid to go home, if his body language is any indication.*

The cops cleared the boyfriend so who else could have the boy in such a fit of fright. She lay back and stared at the ceiling. *I hate popcorn ceilings. Gonna have to fix that. Gonna have to figure out what's going on at the coin shop. What do a gang of thugs have to do with an old coin collector?*

She decided, even though her usual bedtime was a ways off, to get ready for bed and read for a while. *Now that I've found the boy, getting up early is not so urgent. I can rest for one night at least. But another stake out is going to be neces-*

sary to figure this puzzle out.

Christine stood and slowly walked toward her bathroom. Just as she passed her bedroom window, she heard something hit the pane of glass. She dropped to the floor as if she'd been hit by a bullet. Her accelerated heart rate felt almost like she imagined a heart attack must feel. Her breathing labored in her chest.

Where's my weapons? Who can it be? Why didn't the alarm go off? Thoughts tumbled over themselves as she considered her options. The sound at the window was louder this time. She crawled beside the bed and over to the window. She flipped off the bedside lamp plunging the room in darkness. *Maybe I can see more clearly who's outside.* She rose to a crouch, and slid up the frame to peer outside. She hoped whoever it was would not be able to see her.

There. Standing just under her window. Thank goodness this home has a raised elevation. The man was tall, built like a football player, and appeared somewhat familiar. He turned, He glared at her. *Goodman. For crying out loud. What's he doing here?* She opened the window she was standing beside. "Goodman, what are you doing? Do you know what time it is? Go Home."

"Christine, you forgot to set your alarm, didn't you?"

Christine thought about the ease with which she'd opened her window. *Should have sent off the alarm.* She hung her head. "Thanks, Goodman. I'll take care of it. Now go home."

She closed the window, locked the latch, and walked to her bedroom door. She made a quick trip to the front door where she pressed the necessary numbers to engage her home alarm. On the way back to her room, she glanced at Nathan, curled in a fetal position on the sofa with Chief laying on the floor beside him. Chief raised his head to glance in her direction, but didn't budge from his post near the boy. *He's on the job.* She grinned and continued toward the back of the house.

Christine closed the blinds on her windows. *He could still be watching the house.* She wondered why that idea didn't seem as distasteful as the thought once did. *He's a bit pushy.* But her brain reminded her that he was also protecting her. For some reason, that filled her with a sense of ease. *Silly.*

She completed her preparations for bed, and lay down to read for a while. The story was a mystery, but her mind kept seeing the deep brown eyes of a man sitting on a motorcycle. She reread the same paragraph at least three times before she decided that a TV drama might help her focus on relaxing ... more than the memory of a muscled bicep encased in leather could.

She closed her eyes as the drone of the crime drama filled the room. *Life has sure taken a twist since meeting the Goodman's,* she decided. She'd engaged Barkley Goodman to expedite her name change that morning, after she'd been released from her tenants agreement. She'd hired a local moving company, using her new last name, to move her meager possessions to Jeremy's office. Now she lived closer to her office. *I really did enjoy making that space mine.*

I'll need to get new business cards printed. No address though. Just a phone number. I wonder if the drug dealers know about Barkley's involvement with my family? Her eyes popped open. *Wo-o-o. Where did that come from? I haven't thought much about that all day.* Images, better forgotten, flickered behind her eyes, in that part of her brain where the indelible remained stamped for posterity, she figured. *Will I ever be able to forget about the past?*

She closed her eyes again. She listened to the TV show, forcing her mind to conjure up those images instead of the past. Her TV was on a timer so she didn't have to worry about turning it off before falling asleep. She drifted for a few moments and then nothing.

****

The woman sitting next to her seemed friendly. She smiled

often and tried hard to put her at ease but her heart ached. She wasn't sure what to call it, but she knew she missed her mommy and daddy. She didn't want to leave them. *Why were they taking her away from her parents?* Melissa's eyes filled with tears and she stared long and hard at the woman, trying to understand. A sob escaped and the woman turned sympathetic eyes toward her.

"Come sit on my lap," she said. Melissa shook her head and moved to the other side of her seat, She turned her body away from the stranger and peered out the tiny window. White fluffy clouds seemed to be holding the plane up in the sky. Her heart ached so she had a hard time enjoying the flight. She remembered the last one taken with mommy and daddy. That time they'd gone to Disney World. They'd had so much fun.

Her shoulders shook. She couldn't help her feeling of fright and mistrust. She knew she hadn't smiled since she'd run away from her house. The adults that had come into her life since, had tried to get her to smile. They were kind to her, but she was so afraid the bad man would get her, too. *Where did they take mommy and daddy? Would they be able to make them alright?* She hoped so.

Melissa leaned back in the comfortable seat. The woman asked if she wanted the seat to lie back a little and she nodded. The pretty lady in the blue dress brought her a pillow, a small one, just the right size. She closed her eyes. *Maybe if I sleep, I'll wake up and mommy and daddy will be here.*

Then as if time had fallen away while she slept, she'd sat up to the sun blazing through the tiny window. When she'd glanced around this time, men all dressed in gray were walking, or driving carts loaded with suitcases and the plane had landed. The woman smiled at her. "Time to leave," she'd said and Melissa's heart leapt in her chest. *Mommy and Daddy will meet us.* She just knew it.

She hurried down the aisle in front of the woman who accompanied her. As soon as she was out the plane door, she ran, but the woman commanded her to stop, to wait for her**.** But she didn't want to be with this woman. She wanted to get to Mommy and Daddy.

But she'd been taught to listen to adults so she obeyed. Her footsteps echoed down the passageway, two steps for each one that the woman took. They moved out into a larger room and they talked to some men in uniform who searched their suitcases. She had three, but the woman only had a small one.

Her eyes traveled in all directions. The walls were glass and people were standing along the other side watching. Her gaze slid from one face to another. She didn't recognize anyone. *Where is Mommy and Daddy?* She tugged at the woman's purse. But the woman stood still, waiting while the uniformed men read some papers she'd handed them.

They glanced at her and quickly turned their eyes away. But not before she saw sadness fill their eyes. She wondered why they were sad. *Do you know about Mommy and Daddy?* she wanted to ask. *Do you know where they are?* She was just about to speak when the men handed the papers back to the woman. Her companion gripped her hand and led her to the end of the counter where their suitcases had been placed on a cart. Another man, also in uniform but with a cap on, pushed the cart through the doorway into the room on the other side of the glass wall. She followed. She had no choice. They kept on walking.

Wait, her mind said but no words came out of her mouth. Her head swiveled from side to side as they made their way through the crowd. Then she spotted them. But something was wrong. They were covered in bright red, sticky blood. Mommy didn't have a nose and Daddy's head had no back. Melissa screamed.

****

Christine sprang to a sitting position in her bed. Her eyes glanced from one familiar item to another in the room. Early morning light seeped through the slats on her blinds and around the edges of the curtains she'd pulled closed last night. Where was Chief? *Oh, right.* She slowly wiped her hand across her eyes and flopped back down, resting her head in the indent of her pillow.

The images were still clear in her mind. She sucked in a breath as if a sob was still trying to escape. Those days were so filled with pain. She'd been so young and a long time passed before she stopped looking for her parents to show up. *Wow. How can the pain be so intense after all this time?*

A lone tear leaked out of the side of her eye and made its way down the side of her cheek to her pillow. She felt the drip leave her skin. She was so alone. *I wonder why my parents never had any more kids.* She closed her eyes and thought about what life might have been if she'd had siblings. *I might even be an aunt by now.* But for all she knew, she was the only member of her family left.

Maybe I need to do a search, see if I have aunts and uncles somewhere. I don't remember my parent's talking about extended family. But ... maybe. She closed her eyes again. *I need more sleep.* A knock sounded on her door. She pulled the covers over her and responded. "Come in."

The door slowly opened. Her eyes drifted down until she saw the small boy standing, framed by the door opening. His eyes held hope, and something more ... trust.

"Come in, Nathan." She patted the bed beside her and glanced at the clock on her night table. *Six o'clock. Early.* She watched the boy creep slowly toward her. He sat on the bed, but near the end, unsure, she suspected, of his welcome. "It's okay. I was already awake. Getting hungry?" She'd no idea when he'd eaten last.

The child nodded, again slowly. *This must be like my nightmare. He doesn't know anyone and yet he feels safer here than in his own home.* "Why don't we lie down for a little while, see if we can go back to sleep? You can sleep with me. Would you like that?" Christine was happy she'd dressed in sweats last night. The boy snuggled under the blankets she'd opened for him. She felt, rather than heard, his sigh.

Christine closed her eyes again. It was comforting to have another warm body next to her. She realized the contact had taken away the sense of loneliness that had enveloped her when she woke up. She had to get this child back to his family. Loving him would be easy. She knew she'd begin to rely on his presence in her life too much.

Christine's thoughts strayed back to the time she'd first met Connie and Conrad Finder. She'd been so frightened and they were so kind. In the beginning they'd allowed her to lead the way in the relationship. They were sensitive to her longing for her parents. They didn't tell her the truth until she was much older.

This child is only four years old. How much does he remember about his abduction? I wonder if he can tell us what actually happened to him. She opened her eyes and peered at him through half-closed eyes. His eyes were wide open, staring back at her. *Oh, well. So much for sleep.*

"Let's get dressed and have some breakfast." She wondered where Chief was. "I need to let Chief out, too."

Chapter Thirty-Four

Jeremy opened his eyes, bleary from the few hours of sleep he'd managed the night before. His brain had refused to shut off and allow him the rest he needed. He lay still for a few more minutes, trying to erase the cobwebs that lingered. *At least the day looks like a sunny one.* His brain felt wrapped in cotton balls.

The light streaming through his bedroom window registered. *Hey! What time is it?* He looked at his bedside table and the clock radio. *Nine o'clock!* He rolled his legs over the side of the bed and sat still for another moment. He shook his head. *I guess I slept more than I thought. Gotta call Dad.*

Need coffee. He walked barefoot into his compact kitchen. He reached for the on-button on his Keurig coffee machine, waited for the water to heat, and inserted his favorite flavor of coffee. He stretched for a moment and walked over to the window in his living room, while he waited for the coffee to brew. His truck was parked where he'd left it last night. *I need to get over to Christine's.*

He reflected on the job ahead of him. Jeremiah is counting

on me to help him become independent of his daughter. *I wonder if he will have any relationship with her after this is over. I believe God can mend families but I'm not sure she's a believer, even if her father is. Otherwise, how could she have done the stuff she did?*

He walked back into the kitchen, grabbed his cup from the coffee maker, and returned to his favorite chair in the living room. His bible sat on the table beside him. First things first, he thought, as he took the first sip of the steaming liquid. The aroma had done wonders already for his fuzzy brain matter. He opened the well-worn leather bound book, and proceeded to read where he'd left off the day before.

He listened quietly, working to still his mind in the presence of his Lord. "I want to hear you, Lord." He'd always found when he spoke out loud to God, he'd concentrate on the Lord's words better. Calmness flowed through him, erasing all the turmoil of the night before. "Lord, I believe you understand where Jeremiah is spiritually. You also have a picture of his daughter's heart. I believe You desire families to be close, to love one another, and support one another. Please show me how I can help Jeremiah and not alienate his daughter from him. Lord, if a way can be found to help Christine in her search for truth, show me how. Also, Lord, prepare her heart. Show her the need for You in her life. Use me to point her in Your direction. Amen."

Jeremy sat quietly for a few more minutes, contemplating the scripture passage he'd read. He took another long sip of coffee. *I wonder if Dad's in his office yet.* He picked up the phone beside him. He punched in the familiar numbers.

The phone rang twice before Barkley Goodman answered. "Good morning Dad. Shirley not in yet?"

He listened to his father's response, telling him he'd given her the day off to attend a funeral. "What can I do for you son?"

"You remember I told you I might need you to reverse a power of attorney for someone. I found the missing man last night. If I bring him by your office this morning, can we get the procedure started?"

Jeremy listened to papers rustle on the other end of the line. His father's disgruntled voice came next. "I'd planned to get some files organized today, but I guess I can spare a few minutes. The process is pretty straight forward. What time do you think you'll be here?"

"I haven't decided. I just got up." He listened as his father chuckled through the phone line. "Never mind. Late night. I took him to Christine's."

Barkley didn't hesitate to share his opinion. "Do you think this is wise? You might be targeting Christine for some notoriety. If the daughter fights this power of attorney reversal, it would hit the newspapers. We don't want to put her in the limelight."

"No, we don't. I agree. Keeping him at her house once we've begun this action is not a good idea. But he has a kid with him. And ..."

"What's he doing with a kid?" Jeremy heard his father's concern in his raised voice.

He sighed. "I understand. It complicates things, but apparently he found the kid wandering the streets ... all alone. This is the kid that Christine's been hired to find."

A long pause flowed like dead weight through the phone. "How do we know your Jeremiah didn't abduct the kid?"

"Because Christine found the boy's baseball cap in the storage room at the coin shop. Nathan identified it as his." Jeremy stood. "Look, Dad. I'll fill you in when I arrive at your office. Right now, I need to contact Christine before she heads out, if she is going to, for the day. There's lots of questions to be answered. Oh, by the way, would you pull some strings with your buddy in the police department and do a background check on Jeremiah Burton ... just to be thorough."

"Sure. Call me ... never mind. Just come when you can.

I'll be here all day." Silence filled the air when his father disconnected the call.

He walked to his kitchen, gently set his empty coffee cup on the counter, and made his way back to his bedroom. Then he remembered to call Christine. He went to the chair where he'd placed his pants the night before, and took out the slip of paper where Christine had written her number. As he picked up the extension by his bed, he punched in the phone number.

His pulse quickened involuntarily when the familiar female voice answered. "Hi Christine. What are your plans for the day?" He placed his hand over his heart and frowned while he listened to her response. "I thought I'd pick up Jeremiah and take him over to my dad's office to begin revocation of power of attorney. Will this work for you?"

Christine reminded him Nathan was attached to Jeremiah. "Yeah, I know. But if you come along, you could ... well ... watch him while my dad and I talk to Jeremiah."

Christine's indignation sputtered to life, but then she calmed down. "Yeah, yeah. It's not babysitting. Shirley not in today?"

"Gone to a funeral. You'd be able to make some phone calls while you're waiting."

He listened as Christine thought about his suggestion out loud, making a few excuses. Jeremy let her talk and then interrupted. "Christine, the sooner my dad and I get this started, the sooner Jeremiah can have his independence back. I recognize you have to find out why Nathan is reluctant to go home, but I can help. Dad and I ..."

Jeremy sighed as Christine reiterated this was her case and she'd handle things. *Lord, protect me from independent women.* "Okay. Okay. But for now, meet me at Dad's office and we'll go from there. Okay?"

Christine acquiesced and reminded Jeremy Chief needed to be put through his paces at the training school. "He's feeling like a failure since he didn't find Nathan at the coin shop. He needs his confidence restored and the best way to accomplish that is to let Denny give him a work-out."

Jeremy reminded Christine she'd have the rest of the day to do what she needed to do. "This is just this morning."

Then she reminded him that the morning was half over. "Yeah, I know. Slept in. How soon can you be at Dad's?" Her answer told him that she'd been ready for quite a while. "Fine. I'll see you there." He was the one who hung up this time. *Better get a move on.*

Chapter Thirty-Five

Jeremy arrived at his father's office about fifteen minutes later than he'd intended. A hasty shower had helped a lot to prepare him for another long day. He noticed Christine had already arrived. With a quick glance in all directions to perceive if anyone was nearby, he locked up his truck and trotted purposefully to the building that housed *Goodman and Son*.

The elevator to the sixth floor brought him to the lobby where Shirley usually greeted him, but today he faced a scowl. Christine, as usual, did not appear happy. "What's up?"

"I was here on time. You weren't." She placed her hands on her hips, a sense of urgency surrounding her. "I called Charlie, my contact at the police station. He said they found some new evidence on Tommy Devine, Teresa Brent's boyfriend. He won't give it to me over the phone. I don't want him to figure out I've found Nathan ... just yet."

"Who found the kid?" He decided two could play her game. "If I remember correctly ..."

"It doesn't matter who actually established his whereabouts. That's not the point. The fact is, Nathan is with me and I need to go visit with Charlie. Can he stay here with you while I head to the police station?" Christine's voice appeared calmer. She added, her tone filled with reluctance all the same, "Please."

Jeremy's posture relaxed. "For someone seeking a favor …"

"Well, if you don't want to, I'll …"

"Jeepers, you're testy. Relax. He can stay with Jeremiah. Most of what we'll talk about, he won't understand anyway. We need to find some common ground here … work together." Jeremy raised his eyes to the ceiling and then glared pointedly at Christine. "Neither of us worked with a partner before …"

"We're not partners. You said we'd simply share office space. Nothing more." Christine returned to the seat she'd vacated when Jeremy arrived.

"But you must admit, this case kind of joined us. We're bound to experience some tension, no matter how we work together. Let's try to make tense moments the exception instead of the rule." Jeremy glanced toward Jeremiah who was studying their interaction with more than the usual interest.

The older man chortled. "You two sound like an old married couple." He chuckled again and he saw the boy check to see what was so funny. Jeremiah patted Nathan's head. "You'll understand more when you're older."

Before Christine or Jeremy had a chance to respond, Barkley Goodman walked out of his private office and down the hall toward the reception area. "Did I overhear bickering?" His eyes roamed from Christine to Jeremy. "Sparks, eh? Like yesterday. Hm-m-m." He placed his hand along his jaw line and crinkled his brow.

His inflection was not missed by his son. Jeremy coughed. A frown told his father what the older man could do with this idea. Jeremy decided to change the subject. "Let's get this over with. Jeremiah, you and Nathan come with me. Christine we'll wait for you here." He stalked toward his father's office, leading the way.

He turned in time to observe the upward tilt to Christine's head and her muttered, "Bossy man." She spoke loud enough on purpose for him to hear. She walked to the elevator and pushed the button to go down. "I'll return as soon as I can. Come on, Chief."

The dog glanced toward the little person who followed Jeremiah down the hall. "He'll be okay." Christine patted her leg. "You need a reminder, I think, of exactly who your master is." The elevator door opened and she stepped inside. She turned her back to the wall and caught Jeremy observing her every move.

He shook his head and the word cantankerous floated back to her before the door eased shut. His wave toward her was not missed by the young woman but when he turned on his heel, his body language indicated she meant nothing to him.

****

"A power of attorney can be revoked by a written instrument of revocation signed by or on behalf of the person who granted the document," began Barkley Goodman as soon as Nathan was occupied with a pencil and some paper. "Can you tell me if the power of attorney you added your signature to was an ordinary one or a durable enduring power of attorney?" He fixed his gaze on Jeremiah.

The older man thought hard for a moment. "I believe the contract was a durable or enduring one but I can't be sure. Amanda took the paper with her after I signed the thing. I trusted her so much."

Barkley observed the older man, his heart filled with sympathy. "Trust is usually why people take advantage of us seniors. Especially family members. We believe in them so they walk away with all our possessions, just like your daughter did.

An enduring power of attorney can only be revoked by the person who made it. That's you. You must be deemed mentally competent, Jeremiah, before that can be accomplished." His eyes shifted from Jeremiah to Jeremy and back again. "We'll need a psychiatric evaluation, but I can already tell you're not incompetent so ..."

Jeremy noticed his father glance at Nathan. His dad's gaze landed on Jeremiah again. "Where did you get the boy?" Barkley leaned back in his desk chair and folded his hands across his stomach. His eyes were fixed on Jeremiah, reading his body language, Jeremy guessed.

"Dad ..."

"Let Jeremiah answer." He waited while the older man collected his thoughts.

"Strange. I understand. An old guy like me caring for a little boy, but ... I couldn't leave him all alone out in the elements. No coat on and so small. The weather is getting colder at night. I just thought I'd take him with me and the next day, walk him to the police station. Only I was afraid they were searching for me too. Anyway, he trusts me. If I had hurt ..."

"Dad, Jeremiah was feeding Nathan when I discovered their whereabouts. Nothing more. Christine found ..." He looked toward Nathan who was watching them intently, listening to every word. Jeremy whispered, after placing a hand in a strategic spot to cloak his words, "His cap. At the coin shop."

Nathan ran to the older man. "He my friend." He wrapped his arms tightly around Jeremiah's pant leg.

"Nathan. You talked." Jeremiah hugged him back.

Jeremy scooted down on one knee beside Nathan. "Can you tell us what happened?"

The child shook his head. "Mr. Miah save me, that's all. I scaped and Mr. Miah found me." The boy clamped his mouth shut again and walked back to the table where he'd been sitting.

Jeremy sensed that was all he'd get out of the boy ... for now. "At least he can talk. So, Dad. Jeremiah is the good guy here."

Barkley nodded. Jeremy wasn't sure he was convinced. He understood the lawyer in his dad was a skeptic until he had all the facts. Barkley continued anyway. He pushed a form toward Jeremiah. "You'll need to fill this out. This is a revocation of a Power of Attorney and the instrument is not effective against your daughter until notice has been received by her. Consequently, it's a good idea to retain a written document as evidence of your revocation to make sure no doubt exists as to your intention to revoke the power. I'll draw that up for you to sign and we can present the paper to her."

Jeremiah perused the form and began filling in the blanks. Barkley continued, "You're not required to explain why you're doing this. As long as your mental capability is intact, you can revoke your Power of Attorney for any reason. I'd like to be told your story in your own words."

Jeremiah glanced toward Jeremy as if saying ... we've already gone over this. Jeremy smiled his reassurance. The older man stumbled over the first few words as he explained about his wife's death and the depression he'd suffered afterwards. "I needed Amanda to get the groceries. She hired a housekeeper to make the meals and clean the house. I couldn't cope for a while. I started reading my Bible again and when I was ready to function as a single man, she'd already had me sign that dang piece of paper. At first, I thought she was interested in only looking after my interests but the next time I went to pay a few bills, I discovered hardly any money in my bank account. Oh, about a hundred dollars, that's all."

Jeremy noticed the appearance of sympathy in his father's eyes. "How much was in that account before?"

"After I was finished paying for my wife's funeral expenses, the account held over ten thousand dollars. A savings account had a whole lot more, about sixty five thousand or so.

"We can go back to the statements once this revocation occurs and we'll be able to find out exactly how much she took and when. What about stocks, bonds, anything like that, or retirement funds?"

"My pension was direct deposit. But those funds are not in the account. I looked. When the people at the bank discovered Amanda had my power of attorney, they never answered any more questions. Every now and again, I'd sneak out of the home and go to Franny's house. I'd make phone calls or she'd take me to the bank ... in the beginning, once I started getting suspicious." He filled in another part of the form in front of him.

"We'll put together a list before you leave today of every asset you had. Once the copy of your Revocation has been presented to the financial institutions and all other third parties where your Power of Attorney may have been used, we'll go after the missing assets. It could mean a court case. Are you up for a battle?"

"Yur darn tootin." Jeremiah smiled for the first time since arriving at Goodman and Son. "I like the phrase. Those words represent gusto and I plan to pursue this with all the passion the good Lord gave me." He returned to the paperwork. "How long will this action take?"

Barkley shook his head. "It depends. I've researched cases where the relatives hand back the funds as soon as the discovery's been made they're missing. They try to avoid a court case and the extra expense. But, if she doesn't co-operate, the procedure could take a while."

"What do I do for money in the meantime? I mean, I need to live somewhere." Jeremiah's shoulders drooped and his chin rested on his chest in despair all over again. "I hate this. No need for a lawyer. Never wanted one. Now ..."

"The first thing we do is file the revocation with any agency where your Power of Attorney was recorded ... like the Municipal Clerk's Office and the deed registry or land titles, if your house was sold. The bank and the company you dealt with for investments comes next. We'll also send a copy to OAS and CPP for government pensions. Is there a pension from anywhere else?"

Jeremiah finished filling out the form and handed the completed list to Barkley. "Mr. Goodman, it won't be necessary to send anything to the pensions. The funds have continued to come into the account. It's the bank that needs to be contacted so she can't take any more out."

"And once that's done, those funds will support you until we get the rest cleared up." Barkley glanced over the document and directed his gaze at Jeremy. "I've made an appointment for Mr. Burton with Dr. Phineas Rogers. He's well recognized with the court system and worked a lot of cases of elder financial abuse." He shifted his eyes in Jeremiah's direction. "He's a good psychiatrist. Now let's go over the duties of a power of attorney holder. Let's find out if your daughter complied with every rule."

Barkley read the list to Jeremiah. When he was through, he explained, "If the agent, your daughter, fails to act in accordance with these fiduciary duties of fidelity and good faith, she'll be liable for breaching, that is, breaking the duty. That's what she'll be charged with."

"But we won't take her to court if Amanda willingly gives back all the money." Jeremiah obviously didn't want to go that route if he didn't have to.

Jeremy walked toward the older man, placed his hand on his shoulder, and squeezed. "The woman who hired me to find you, does not seem sympathetic to you at all. You need to be prepared to follow through. Are you?"

"Yes. As I said before. But I still hope she'll give in. What will happen to her?"

Barkley leaned back in his chair again. "If you are successful in a lawsuit for breach of fiduciary duty or conversion of property, and I see no reason to believe you won't be, the court will order Amanda to return the stolen property. The judicial system may also require that your daughter pay your lawyer. And, if it's found that her conduct was particularly egregious or involved elements of fraud, the judge may award punitive damages to you as well. For example, in a case involving a nephew who was proven guilty of all these charges against his uncle, the jury awarded the victim the full amount of money his relative stole, along with punitive damages, interest, and attorneys' fees. Happily, the uncle was eventually able to collect every penny of the judgment."

"But no jail time?" Jeremiah leaned forward in his seat with hope registering in his eyes. "What's conversion?"

Jeremy gazed with interest toward his dad. His father had done his homework. He waited for the answer to Jeremiah's question.

Barkley shoved a paper aside and picked up a computer print-out. He read, "An agent who uses an elder's assets for his or her own benefit may also be liable for conversion of the elder's property. In order to establish conversion of property, the elder or his lawyer, must show that the defendant managed or used the elder's property in a way that was inconsistent with the elder's rights of ownership. When the agent has used a power of attorney to convert the property, it must also be shown that, first of all, the elder demanded the return of the property, and secondly, the defendant refused to deliver the property to the elder." He placed the paper back on his desk. "And no jail time."

"Good." Jeremiah relaxed once again. "I questioned Amanda about my house. When she said she'd sold it to pay my nursing home bills, I was furious. I went to confront Mr. Levey, the administrator, and he said the fees for my commitment came out of pension income, not assets. Amanda lied, so I demanded she get it back. She laughed in my face. She ordered me back to bed and said I was to leave everything to her. That was two weeks ago. That incident precipitated my decision to get away from there for good. Let's get 'er done." He raised his hand in a salute of victory. "I want my house and everything returned to me."

Chapter Thirty-Six

Christine frowned. The traffic was heavier than usual for this time of day. Horns honked and brakes squealed as commuters worked their way from one destination to another. Christine glanced over at Chief. He gazed with interest out the front window, but she recognized he had a longing to hang his head free to catch the air as they swished by other vehicles.

"Looking forward to another work-out with Denny, Chief?" The dog's ears perk up and he glanced toward her. "I understand. You like Denny." She reached across to pat him on the head, leaving her left hand to the steering wheel.

"Charlie was no help this morning. There was no new evidence about Tommy. I think he suspects we've found Nathan." She viewed both side mirrors and her rear mirror to gauge a break in traffic. Their turn was coming up. Her mind floated to her conversation with the police officer during her meeting with him a half hour ago.

Their friendship had flared up rather quickly after she'd moved to Winnipeg. She was partly to blame since she'd hoped to develop an inside source concerning her parents' case. He'd thought there was more to the relationship than she was willing to give. Thank goodness he chose to remain friends.

Earlier, after she arrived at police headquarters, he'd asked her for a date again. She'd left him smiling anyhow. He had also confirmed what she suspected. Tommy Devine was not a suspect in the disappearance of Nathan Brent. The cops were likewise not checking out any of the coin shops. "There's not enough evidence to obtain a search warrant," Charlie had informed her. "Unlike you, we need to work within the law in order to get a conviction."

"Yeah, well." She turned right onto the freeway exit as she headed for the dog training facility. She figured a charge of break and enter would be initiated, if the police found out she'd sneaked into the shop last night. "We do what we can to find a kid, don't we Chief?" The dog whined his answer.

Once out on the highway, Chief lay down on the seat, and Christine turned the radio to a country music station. *I miss ranch life sometimes. It was so much easier. Now though ... I wonder who died because of me.* Christine's heart felt a twinge of loneliness. *Can't endanger any more lives.* She felt an urgency to remove Jeremiah and Nathan from her home ... *just in case.*

Christine had made sure she'd taken all the precautions necessary to protect herself and anyone within range but ... *the man seems determined to track me down. It's not a friendly conversation he's looking for. Will I recognize him after all these years? I have to find him. Maybe I need to start at my parents' house.* She spied the familiar outline of the barn where Denny kept the dogs he was working with. His training facility was top notch and his animals were sought after by police departments and service agencies looking for companions for their clients.

She pulled off the highway and drove down the gravel lane toward a fenced area. Denny usually put Chief through his paces in the pasture. She honked the horn as soon as she spotted the tall, athletic man emerge from the building. He waved and she pulled up in front, but to one side. "Okay, Chief. No need for a leash today."

As soon as Christine opened the door, the dog jumped across her lap and escaped straight toward his old friend. Denny bent to rub his head with affection. Christine emerged from her vehicle slowly, giving them time to get reacquainted. "Hi Denny."

Denny straightened and glanced at her with his usual grin. "Hello, Christine. What brings you out here today? I wasn't expecting you till next week."

"Chief needs a work-out. His confidence has taken a beating lately." She walked beside her friend as he moved toward the gate to access the exercise yard.

Denny latched the structure again and continued toward the equipment, a permanent fixture in the field. "Why?"

"We've been looking for a young boy. We retrieved his cap from where he'd been stashed, but someone else actually found him. I think Chief thinks he failed. Anyway, an extra work-out can't hurt." She petted the strong shoulders of the dog who went everywhere with her these days. "Go, Chief."

The dog waited for hand confirmation from Christine and raced toward the first piece of equipment. He bounded across the grass as if he'd come home. "We missed our jog this morning."

"Well maybe you're the one who needs to be put through her paces." Denny wriggled his eyebrows up and down.

"You're incorrigible. Keep your mind on the work." She slapped his shoulder with her hand.

"My thoughts are always of work. Where's yours? I'm serious about you working with Chief. It'll do you good to go over the commands. He needs to remember who's boss, too."

Dennys face had become thoughtful. "Besides, I know when I'm not appreciated by the female of the species."

"Oh, but I do appreciate you, Denny ... as a friend." She made her way to the first piece of equipment and began to work with Chief while Denny assessed her performance as well as Chief's. The dog was eager to jump through the hoops she set before him, but every now and again, he'd hesitate for a second or two. "Chief, don't think, do." She called out to him in as firm a voice as she could. She caught Denny's disapproval in her periphery vision. "What?"

"You've been too easy on him. Remember, he's to be your protector as well. He needs to obey the commands immediately. Now let's go over the basics and instill his earlier training again." Denny utilized the tone of voice he always used when teaching dogs. "Chief, come."

Christine stood back and witnessed his performance for a few minutes. Denny was good with the animals. He had a gift. The dogs loved him too, but they also learned to obey their new masters really well. She noted Chief's hard work to do everything Denny asked as quickly as he required it. *I love him. He's so smart. But I guess I need to think of him more as a service dog than I do. If anything happened to him ...*

Another half hour was all they needed to infuse the old training in Chief and in his mistress. Christine was out of breath by the time they finished, as was Chief. His tongue lolled to one side of his mouth and when Denny offered him a cold drink, he lapped the liquid as if he was dying of thirst. Christine reached inside her car for a bottle of water.

"Thanks, Denny. I think we're back in shape." She glanced at the dog loping toward her. "Chief seems much happier."

"Remember it's not happy you want him. It's obedient. Might mean a lot to you one day. Are you any closer to finding the man who knocked off your parents?" He leaned against the fence with his arms crossed.

"No, but he's found the Finder's ranch. Killed at least one person. I have no knowledge, and neither did Conrad when he was here, if the guy is still there or not. He could be anywhere on that expansive property. By the way, I've changed my last name, thanks to him, and my work address." She handed him the new business card she'd picked up before heading to the training facility.

Denny read the information and stuffed it in his pocket. "The guy has no reason to connect us, but I'll keep this in a safe place anyway."

Christine moved toward her car again. "Thanks Denny. Come Chief." She opened the front door of the car and Chief jumped in, walked to the passenger side and sat. She slid into her seat beside him and inserted the seat belt into the latch. "Denny, I appreciate your time. We both needed it."

Denny seemed concerned. "You take care of yourself, hear?" He waved as she backed up and turned toward the highway again. Her return wave as she drove off was not missed as he swung his body in the direction of the barn. *He's a good man.*

Christine glanced at the clock on her dash. *We've been gone a lot longer than I expected. One stop leads to another ... always.* She turned down the pavement, headed to the city, and allowed her mind to wander again. *What Denny said about the killer ... I wonder if I should make a stop at my parents' house now, before I go back to the office?* She decided to pick up her cell phone from the console and call Jeremy. *I'd better pull over.*

She slowed to a speed that would allow her to maneuver over to the shoulder of the road, and picked up her cell again. She punched in the number of Goodman Investigations. "HI ... Jenna. Is Jeremy there?"

She listened to the other woman tell her he'd just arrived. She listened to Jeremy's deep timbre flow through the line. "Christine, where are you?"

"I'm returning from Chief's work-out with Denny but ... I was thinking. I want to go over to my parents' house, check things out. Maybe the murderer's been around there. What's your opinion?" She waited for the explosion to happen.

After a moment of dead silence, Jeremy took a deep breath. The sound appeared to Christine as if he were sitting right beside her. "I don't think that's a good idea, especially not in broad daylight. If he's watching the place ... waiting for you to show up ... you'd be walking into a trap."

Christine had to admit this would be the logical step for someone looking for her who suspected she'd returned to the scene of the crime. "I know but ..."

Jeremy interrupted. His suggestion was worth considering. She spent a second or two thinking it over. "Do you have time?"

Before the conversation ended Christine agreed to allow Jeremy to accompany her later, closer to evening. "I'll get back to the office as soon as I can. How's Nathan doing?"

She listened when Jeremy recommended she meet them at a restaurant nearby. "I completely forgot about lunch. I'm used to skipping meals, but I guess that's not good for a little boy. How's Jeremiah doing?" Jeremy filled her in on the course of action they'd decided with his dad. "He's planning on taking his daughter to court? Wow. That'd be hard."

Her eyes gazed at Chief. "Jeremy, I won't be able to leave Chief in the car while we eat. I'll meet you back at the office. He can stay in my room. I have food and water for him and he's been worked hard so he's tired enough to sleep. I'm about fifteen minutes out."

Christine steered back onto the pavement as soon as the conversation ended. She turned her radio on again and hummed along to the tune playing. *Does Jeremy like country music.* She wondered why the thought had even crept into her mind. *Who cares what Jeremy Goodman enjoys or doesn't like. Not me.*

Certainly not me.

She continued to drive down the highway. Jeremy's face persisted in popping up every now and then. She thought of his faith. *I've never know a man who claimed to be Christian before. I wonder how that happened.* Connie and Conrad went to church and they took me for a while but not when I was a teen. They said it was my choice and I saw no point to it. Those stories they taught in Sunday school were just that ... fairy tales. No one could explain to me why the Bible says God made everything, when we were taught in school evolution was where we came from. The two don't go together.

She entered the traffic off the freeway in the direction of her new office. It had gotten even more congested than when she'd left. *Must be lunch time.*

Chapter Thirty-Seven

"Jenna, where are those tracks we used to leave on the tables in the reception area. Remember the ones I picked up at the Creation Institute." He stood in the doorway off the foyer. "When you find them, could you distribute them around the office? Maybe Christine will pick one up and read it."

"Are you planning on proselytizing? I thought the idea was frowned on in the work place." Jenna dug through her side drawer as she spoke. "Christine may not enjoy having your faith in her face all the time. It's hardly inconspicuous leaving tracks all over."

Jeremy took a few steps into the room. "I hear ya but ... she needs the Lord."

Jeremiah entered as Jeremy voiced his opinion about Christine's lack of religion. Nathan was right behind him as usual, like a shadow. "I've found the best way to point someone to God is by your behavior. With all the bickering you two do, your action's probably not a good witness."

Jeremy frowned, "She's bristly. Everything I say, she takes exception to."

"Did she fight you about going to her parents' house?" Jeremiah acknowledged the surprise as it appeared on Jeremy's face. "Yeah, well ... I couldn't help but hear your side of the conversation. You were slightly loud. Even Nathan noticed." He glanced at the youngster who was quietly playing with some paper Jenna had given him.

Shame washed over Jeremy. Someone had taken note of his rise in temper. "Where that woman is concerned, I get my back up. You're right. She accepted my help with the trip to her mom and dad's house. That's going to be traumatic for her. She hasn't been there since they were killed. I don't even know ..." His eyes shifted to Nathan and back to Jeremiah "My dad probably had everything cleaned up back then but ..."

He noticed Jenna move quietly past him to deposit some pamphlets around the room. "If you can keep your attitude civil, she'll take what these tracks say to heart."

He clutched his heart. "Et tu Jenna. Have I been so bad?"

Jenna glowered at him and then fixed him with a sarcastic grin. "Ya think? She's been independent for a while now. Christine had a killer stalking her since she was five years old. She trusted her mom and dad and finds out that they were laundering money for the mob. How do you think she's supposed to act?"

Jeremy opened his mouth to reply, but Christine walked through the door at that moment. The room went completely silent. She glanced from one person to another, a question mark attached to the frown on her forehead. "What?"

"We were wondering if you'd had an accident or something. Do we have a phone number for you?" Jeremy coughed and Jeremiah went to sit beside Nathan. Chief trotted over to the little boy who slid off his chair and wrapped his arms around the dog.

Christine considered the exchange in light of what Denny had told her about treating Chief as a service dog and not a pet. "Uh-h. Oh, forget it." She shifted her gaze to Jeremy and reached into the pocket of her jacket. "These are my new business cards." She handed him a few and gave Jenna some as well.

"Boy. Quick service." Jeremy examined the information on the card with the name Christine Smith embossed in black script. "Concise. No address."

"They had everything on file from the previous order so it was simple ... a few changes and voila. I picked them up on the way out to the country." She sat down beside Chief and Nathan. "Nathan, how ya doin'?"

The little boy stared at her with large round eyes. He said nothing, however. Jeremy walked over and patted his head. "He spoke this morning. Didn't you, Nathan?"

Christine's face lit up. "You did? Great." The boy nodded and his gaze dropped back to the floor. He moved closer to Jeremiah. Christine decided to wait to ask all the questions she had tumbling around in her brain. "Are we ready to eat? I'll get Chief settled." She took the dog by his collar and led him to her office.

When she returned everyone, including Jenna, had their coats on. "Let's go." Jeremy was the one who opened the door and held it while the others walked through.

Chapter Thirty-Eight

Jenna began filing some paperwork as soon as she arrived at the office the next morning. Engrossed as she was, she didn't hear Amanda Prescott storm through the door until the woman was in front of her desk.

Invisible fire seemed to seep from irate nostrils. "Is he in?" Her distain floated toward Jenna.

Jenna regarded the younger woman, working hard to hide her distaste. Jeremiah was a wonderful man who didn't deserve what his daughter did to him. "I'll check."

Amanda shook her irritated body to make her point, "For goodness sake. Either he is or he isn't. Tell him I'm here. You do remember my name, don't you?"

Jenna picked up the intercom and shifted away from the troublesome woman. "Jeremy," she whispered, "Amanda Prescott has arrived." She glanced at the woman and replied to her boss, "Okay."

Jenna noticed the pink creep up the neck of the irate woman. "What?"

"He said he'd be right out." Jenna decided to ignore Amanda as she perused the situation, out of the corner of her eye. The furious female took a seat. She hoped the temper tantrum to come would not amount to any physical stuff. Jenna glanced around the room to discern if there was anything breakable nearby. She picked up the copy she'd made of the revocation document. Jeremy wanted the form as soon as he stepped out of his office, he'd said.

He was making her wait. *Not good.* Jenna gazed at the clock anxiously. It wasn't like her boss to keep people cooling their heels for the sake of waiting. *I wonder what his plan is. Footsteps. There he comes. I hope he prayed.*

She spied Jeremy step into the reception area. His face appeared all business-like and serious. He walked over to her desk and picked up the form. "Ms. Prescott. I was about to call you.

Amanda Prescott stood as soon as Jeremy entered. "Yeah, well. You didn't. Have you found my father?"

Jeremy handed her the paper. "As a matter of fact ..."

"What's this?" The color pink suffused her neck and turned to red. She waved the sheet in front of Jeremy's face. "You're working for me."

Jeremy stepped closer to her, making sure she understood he wasn't playing games. "I haven't taken payment from you yet and I don't intend to. Your father, Jeremiah, has issued this statement revoking your power of attorney. As we speak, a courier is delivering a similar document to all of the financial institutions where Jeremiah has ... or had any resources. His lawyer will be in touch."

The woman's face turned a mottled gray. "He-he can't

do that. The power is a legal document."

"Oh, but he can. And we have psychiatric proof he's competent enough to make the decision." Jeremy walked over to Jenna's desk again where she gave him another legal instrument, this one larger than the last. He handed the sheaf of papers to the Prescott woman. "This is notification you have been served. You are being charged with elder abuse, financial fraud, and a few other things ... they're all listed right there."

She almost spit the words toward Jeremy. "My father is suing me? How can he do that? I mean ... I understand how but ... "

"Why do you find this so hard to believe? Did you think you'd never be caught? I guess you actually don't comprehend what a fighter Mr. Burton is. I'd suggest you obtain a darn good lawyer." He strode toward the door to the outside. "Have a pleasant day, Ms. Prescott." He waited while she walked silently out the exit.

Before she reached the outside, she turned, as furious as any person Jeremy had ever seen. With venom dripping from her lips, she cursed the ground he walked on and then some. "You haven't heard the last of me. I plan to sue you for everything you own. You breached our contract."

"Because you misrepresented yourself, any agreement we had is null and void. The court will find in my favor. Talk to your lawyer if you don't believe me. Now good day." He slammed the door and the windows shook as Amanda Prescott did the same.

"That went well." Jenna stared, her eyes large and serious. "I hope that creature gets everything she deserves." She turned to the pile of paperwork on her desk. Then she glanced up at Jeremy. "You know, if the woman hadn't hired you, we'd never have been able to help Jeremiah. I guess God has His ways."

Jeremy walked slowly toward the hallway leading to

his office. "It's not fun dealing with disagreeable people, but we were prepared, thanks to dad. Now we can find Jeremiah a place to live until he has possession of his house again, if he gets it back. Did Christine say how long she was going to have Jeremiah and Nathan at the park?"

"No. At lunch she just told me she thought it would be a good place to try to get Nathan to talk to her. She said she needed to understand what happened so she could plan the next step ... whatever that meant." Jenna stared at her paperwork for a few seconds before glancing back up at Jeremy. "Are you actually planning to take her to that house tonight?"

Jeremy stopped for a moment. He leaned his head against the frame of the hallway entrance. "I was hoping to talk her out of it, but the sooner we get it over, the better I guess. I hope no one's watching the place."

"Maybe you should have a police escort, lots of flashing blue lights and stuff." Jenna wrinkled her brow in concern.

"I thought of the possibility but ... Christine wants this guy to show himself. She hopes he'll tip his hand so she can nab him. She's one gutsy woman."

"Kinda admire her, do ya?" Jenna grinned.

Jeremy huffed and turned on his heel. "She's courageous is all. Don't make up stuff, Jenna." He stalked back to his private domain.

Jenna laughed, loud enough she was sure Jeremy overheard even after he closed his office door. *Better get some work done or he'll fire me.* She bent to her task, but a stray snicker escaped every now and then.

Chapter Thirty-nine

Christine sat on the rubber matting that was the seat of the swing. Nathan sat on her lap and she pushed her body back and forth. Every once in a while, a giggle escaped from the little boy's mouth. "This is fun, isn't it, Nathan?"

She observed his nod, but nothing more. Chief lay on the grass at the edge of the playground equipment in the park. Christine and Jeremiah had taken the boy through the maze, down the slide once or twice, and even helped him maneuver the monkey bars. She hoped he'd come to trust her enough to answer a few questions. She decided to get Chief involved.

"Nathan let's go sit with Chief and talk to him. He'd like to become better acquainted." She stood with Nathan in her arms and walked to the place where Chief lay. "Chief wants to know what happened to you." Nathan was more than ready to cuddle into the dog's soft coat so Christine joined him on the grass.

"He does?" The boy gazed deeply into Chief's face, his nose almost touching the cold black one of her canine friend. Chief licked him.

"See, he does. Why not tell him how you got out of your window." Christine scooted on her seat a few paces away from the two companions. Still within ear shot, she would be able to listen to everything. She waited for a response.

Nathan peeked at her from his position beside Chief. He laid his forehead on the dog and whispered, "Tommy got me out."

Christine's heart skipped a beat. *He was involved. I suspected as much.* Then her ears received some news she'd never expected. "He sold me."

Her insides went cold. *How does a kid survive such evil?* She scooted closer and put her arms around the little boy. "Who did he sell you to?"

Nathan's gaze focused on her. She saw the indecision flash across his face. Would he trust her? Or not? The boy glanced in Jeremiah's direction. He sat on a bench a couple of feet away. Christine saw him nod, encouraging the child to continue. Nathan hung his head. "Tommy said I not worth much, but he get money anyway from the man so I come live with him. Tommy said I had to love him. I couldn't. He's a stranger. Mommy said not to."

Christine sensed, from past experience, the story could probably get a lot worse. "Who was the man who paid Tommy money for you?"

Nathan bowed his head a few brief moments. When he raised it again, the pain of the last three days leaked from his eyes along with slow flowing tears. "The man where I forgot my cap. I only see him a couple of times, but he's not a nice man. I won't love him. He said I would get to like it, but I won't so I left. When the other bad man came, he left the door unlatched one time. I 'scaped. Mr. Miah found me. I was scared at first, but he's a nice man."

"Oh, Nathan. I am so sorry this happened to you." She scrutinized the boy as he leaned into the warmth of Chief's furry body. "Chief likes you. He doesn't let everybody grab hold of him that way." She glanced at Jeremiah. The older man had tears in his eyes. Jeremiah shook his head.

"Nathan, do you want to go home to your Mommy?" Christine hadn't thought about how they would protect him at home, at least until Tommy was taken into custody. She wondered what the relationship was between Tommy and Mr. Fine, the coin shop dealer.

"Tommy said Mommy doesn't want me anymore. That's why he sold me. He told me she was tired of me and wanted only my sister." Tears streamed down his face this time. Christine hoped his pain would seep away with the tears.

Christine sucked in her breath. *How could he?* "Tommy lied. Your mommy hired me to find you. She cries every time she thinks about you. She misses you so much."

Nathan, hope replacing the glistening pain, stared at her as if he wanted to believe, but wasn't sure. "Really?" He sniffled and wiped his arm across his eyes. "My mommy wants me?"

Christine tried to hide her sorrow as she looked at him. "You bet your britches, she does. But we need to keep you in a safe place until the policemen arrest Tommy."

Nathan looked confused. "The police are going to put Tommy in jail. Mommy won't like for them to do that. She and Tommy are best friends, I think."

"She loves you more. You'll see. What Tommy did to you is against the law. Did Tommy ever come where you were to visit the man again after he sold you?"

"I didn't see him. The bad man kept me in the dark place. The only other person I saw was the creepy one, another boy who didn't like me being there, he said. He tried to hit me once, but I ducked."

Christine's heart melted at the pride on the boy's face. *This is a smart kid and a brave one, too. No wonder Jeremiah felt so protective of him.* "I think it's time we headed back to Jeremy's office. What about you, Jeremiah?" She stood and brushed the grass clippings off her pants. Chief stood as well letting the boy flop on the ground. Nathan giggled.

Jeremiah reached to help his charge up and threw him over his shoulder. "You've gotten heavy after the huge lunch you had. We both need a nap."

Nathan spoke from his upside down position. "I'm not tired. Big boys don't nap. Mommy said so." He giggled again as Jeremiah swung him to the ground.

Nathan placed his hand inside Jeremiah's considerably larger one and grinned up at the man. Then he looked at Christine and slipped his other hand into hers. Christine smiled toward the small boy. Chief walked right behind as everyone strolled back to Christine's car. Nathan chattered all the way.

Chapter Forty

Christine gingerly drove the car into the parking space in front of Goodman Investigations. She glanced at Jeremiah, but spoke directly to her tiny passenger in the backseat. "Nathan, honey, do you think you'd be able to tell Mr. Goodman about Tommy ... what he did to you and about Mr. Fine at the coin shop?"

Nathan's big brown eyes stared at her in the rear view mirror. His head dipped down toward his hands and then back up again. "I don't wanna talk about that stuff anymore."

Jeremiah reached his hand over the front seat to pat the boy on his shoulder. "I won't let anyone hurt you, young man. Do you trust me?"

Nathan nodded in Jeremiah's direction and stared toward Christine. His eyes found hers in the mirror again. "I guess, but ... will I see my mommy soon?"

Christine didn't hesitate. "When we can make sure you'll be safe. We'll tell the police about Tommy and the coin man, and then bring your mom to visit, okay?"

The child nodded silently. Christine shifted her gaze to Jeremiah and noticed his glassy stare. He twisted his body so he was able to focus on Nathan again, blinking to keep the tears at bay. Christine gazed in the rear view mirror and detected the reappearance of hurt all over Nathan's face ... *every time we talk about this*.

Jeremiah glanced at Christine and back at Nathan. "Bad people live in this world, like good people. What they did to you was wrong. Laws protect little guys like you. When you tell the police your story, they'll make sure the bad folks are punished." His gaze landed on Christine. He lowered his voice. "Will they place him in foster care?"

Christine signaled an affirmative as her eyes sought the child in the rear view mirror. She kept her voice slightly above a whisper. "Probably. I guess I hadn't given the idea much thought. I wonder if we can prevent the authorities from taking him. I don't want him victimized all over again and I've heard a few real horror stories of little guys like him in the system. I realize there are some nice places, with people who really care about the kids but ..."

" Jeremy might have another option. Let's wait to find out what he says. With his dad being a lawyer and all ... well, maybe they'll let him stay with me ... until his mother rids herself of the creepy live-in boyfriend or the police take Tommy into custody." Jeremiah opened his car door. He glanced back at Christine. "I can tell you are fond of the kid. You're a good person."

Christine blushed. "Just doing my job. Nothing more."

Jeremiah stepped out of the car and took note of Christine as she exited her side to open the back door for Chief and Nathan. He stared at her over the top. "It seems to me you're more involved than one more case. It used to be clear to me when someone was sincere about something. Since Amanda, I thought I'd lost any discerning qualities, but now I don't believe so. I misplaced them for a time, but my instincts tell me you're a lot more interested in this case than you want to admit."

Christine marched toward the front door to the office with Jeremiah right behind. Chief's pace matched Nathan's. "I have to work at keeping a distance between myself and my clients in some cases, I will confess. Not professional to get too close, but sometimes ..." She glanced at Nathan who had a firm hold on Chief's collar. She was amazed Chief let him. She snickered at the two and shook her head. "So much for keeping distance. Chief is supposed to be a service animal, not a pet, but look at him." She laughed.

Jeremiah smirked at the boy and dog combination. "The intuitive nature of the animal is meant for someone like Nathan, I think. Is he good at tracking people?"

"He is when he has his mind on the job and, for the most part, his work is satisfactory for my purposes, but I've not done a lot with him since I purchased him. Denny, our trainer, wants me to treat him as a partner, not a friend. He says the distance will help Chief focus better." She pulled the entrance open and stepped inside the cozy building. "Oh-h, I didn't realize how chilly the weather had gotten." She shivered. Her regard shifted to Nathan. "Come on in where it's warm."

Chief and Nathan wove past the adults in the doorway and made their way to Christine's office and Chief's water bowl. Jeremiah scooted to one side to let them pass and shut the portal behind them. He waved toward Jenna. "Jeremy in?"

"He is and he has some news." Jenna motioned for Jeremiah to follow her to the end of the hallway. She rapped lightly, but slipped in without waiting for a response. "Here's Mr. Burton," she announced.

"Tell Christine to come in as well. This may be of interest to her." Jeremy's words traveled down the hall.

Christine glanced in the direction of his voice, but decided to make sure Nathan and Chief were dealt with first. "I'll be right with you."

She moved into her office. Jeremiah disappeared into

Jeremy's private domain. *I wonder what Jeremy has up his sleeve.* She poured some fresh water into Chief's bowl. "Do you think you and Nathan can survive without me for a few minutes," she asked Chief. She pretended to listen when Chief talked back to her in a whine. "Oh, you will. Well okay then."

She grinned toward Nathan. "Chief says he'll take care of you while I go talk to Mr. Goodman. Would you like that?"

Nathan grinned. "Sure. Chief and I are friends." The boy sat on the floor in front of Chief, who had plunked his body down with an 'oooof' sound after drinking his fill. Nathan brushed the excess water from Chief's muzzle and the dog licked the boy's hand.

Christine shook her head, marveling at the comradery between the two. "I won't be long. Chief, you could speak to Nathan about how you grew up." Christine strolled toward the door.

Nathan appeared perplexed. "I don't understand dog like you do."

"Oh, well maybe you'll have to tell Chief a story. Is that better?" Christine grinned as Nathan began with once upon a time. "Be good." She left her door slightly ajar and motioned for Jenna to keep an eye on them. Jenna answered with a nod as Christine sauntered toward Jeremy's office.

Her knock was answered with "Come in, Christine."

Once seated, Jeremy offered her a cup of coffee. "Sounds good. I'm a bit chilled." She took a seat beside Jeremiah.

She noticed his hands shook a little holding his own coffee. "What's up?"

Jeremiah spoke first. "Amanda was here. Jeremy says she's out for bear. Gonna be a long fight."

Christine patted his knee. "From what Jeremy tells me,

she hasn't a leg to stand on. Jeremy, did you get the forms to all the financial institutions before she arrived?"

Jeremy handed Christine a cup, steam rising into the room. "Just. I'd walked through the door and sat down at my desk when she barged in here. She seemed surprised we got so much done in such a short amount of time. Pays to have connections with a good lawyer. By the way, Jeremiah, where do you and Nathan plan to spend the night? Christine and I ..."

Christine squinted at him and signaled him to say no more. Jeremiah spoke up. "The boy needs me. I was thinking he could stay with me until ... Christine, you've not told Jeremy what Nathan revealed to us."

"No, I haven't. I want Nathan to get accustomed to sharing his story, so I'll get him to tell Jeremy." She glanced at the younger of the two men and dropped her head. "What happened is pretty awful. But I believe the more times he describes the story, the better. You should have seen his countenance change after we finally got him to talk."

"Talking is good therapy, even for a four year old." Jeremy focused his attention on Jeremiah. "You don't possess a home any more, remember." Jeremy sipped his coffee and added, "At least not yet."

Christine noted the disappointment as it crept across Jeremiah's face. The older man glanced at his wrinkled hands and back to Jeremy. "I guess you're right. I will obtain someplace to live by tomorrow. I phoned Franny when we were at the park. She said I'd be able to stay with her, but she also saw a house with a lawn sign saying it was for rent down the block. I'd like to go check the place out as soon as we can."

Jeremy grasped the old man's arm and gave the boney appendage a squeeze. "Good for you. Did you happen to call your bank to see if ... "

"No. I mean yes, but, I need to go in apparently ... to fill out a new signature card and change my bank account number, too. They said when someone fraudulently uses one of their accounts, those are the rules. So I won't have access to funds until I follow their procedures. The woman did say that right now the account was frozen so nothing else will come out. I got the impression I had money, though." Jeremiah leaned back in his seat and glanced at Christine before shifting his gaze to Jeremy. "Good old red tape, eh?"

Christine nodded. "This is hard on you, isn't it? Did the psychiatrist say anything about getting a physical done? I mean, you obviously don't want to go back to your old physician. Was he working with Amanda do you think?"

Jeremy piped up. "I don't know, but I intend to find out. His doctor should have been able to refute Amanda's claims that Jeremiah was not competent. Jeremiah, when was the last time you had an appointment with him?"

The older man frowned, trying to remember. "I think I saw him right before Amanda had me committed to that place. At the home, there was a doctor on staff. Mr. Levey always made the appointments."

"The administrator told me he understood nothing was wrong with you. He didn't figure you needed to be one of the residents. Meadowood's physician would have given him that opinion. I wonder if you'd be able to use him as your doctor now. Do you trust him?" Jeremy finished the last swig of coffee and placed his mug on the table between them. He peeked at Christine. Her eyes held his over the rim of her cup.

Christine felt warmth creep up her neck and around her ears. She purposely turned her head in Jeremiah's direction. "The doctor may be obligated to report your whereabouts to the authorities. Mr. ..." She looked toward Jeremy again. " ... Levey, was it? I'm sure he's already gotten the cops involved in this, even though Amanda Prescott hired you."

Jeremy focused on Jeremiah. "I guess we'll need to deal with the cops. I'll call dad and instruct him, as your attorney, to let the police know you are safe and sound, staying with Christine."

Christine opened her mouth to protest, but Jeremy cut her off. "Until tomorrow. Till he can access his bank account and rent a house."

Jeremiah interrupted. "No, another night is too big an imposition. I'll stay in a motel or something."

Christine grimaced. She waved her hand in the air to stop Jeremiah's protests. "No. No. That's okay. How would you pay for your accommodations, anyway? Moreover, Nathan feels more comfortable with you than with anyone else. As long as he's with me, you might as well be too. Jeremy, what about ..." She looked from one man to the other. "You know. The other thing?"

Jeremy seemed lost in thought for a few minutes. Like a flash of thunder, the light went on. "Oh, you mean ... that. He doesn't know where you live, yet. After tonight, we may know more. Speaking of tonight, we ought to get home, get some rest. I don't know how long we'll be but ..."

Jeremiah switched his gaze from one to the other. "If I'll be in the way ... or Nathan and I .... well, we could go someplace close by for dinner ... if you'll lend me some money, Jeremy."

Christine grinned. "I guess filling him in won't hurt." She shifted her gaze to Jeremiah. "Your imagination is way off base. My parents used to live here and were murdered when I was five years old. Their house is across town and Jeremy said he'd take me tonight. We won't be too long. You and Nathan don't need to come. If you wouldn't mind putting him to bed, you can both stay at my house till we get back. As for supper, I don't cook. I'll pick us up some KFC. Is that okay?"

Jeremy piped up. "Oh-h. KFC. I love their chicken. Can I come, too?"

Christine glared in his direction for a second or two. "Oh, all right. I guess I owe you for helping me out this evening. Let's get going. Jeremiah, would you like to go by Franny's, take a peek at that house on the way to my place?"

"No. You guys are busy enough right now. If you're free, I wouldn't mind going first thing tomorrow, though." He picked up his jacket and slipped it on.

Christine watched Jeremy as he strode over to his desk, placed his coffee cup down and grabbed his coat. "Where should I put these?" She held up the cups she and Jeremiah had used.

"Leave them there. Jenna will deal with them in the morning." He handed her a twenty dollar bill. "Here's my share for supper."

Christine glared at the money and shook her head. "I can certainly manage to pay for the food." She frowned in his direction.

Jeremiah chuckled. "In my day, a young woman never paid. The man ..."

Christine coughed. "This is hardly a date. Besides ... " She flicked a gaze from one man to the other and noticed the twinkle in both their eyes. She groaned. *I fell ... hook, line, and sinker. Wish they'd stop teasing.* "Oh, you." She smirked, tilted her head to the ceiling and rolled her expressive orbs heavenward as she strode pass them out the door. "Come on, Chief and Nathan. Protect me from these two."

Chapter Forty-One

Christine put the shift lever into park, turned off the ignition, and used the remote to shut off the alarm system. She grabbed the parcels containing their dinner and opened her door with her free hand as Jeremiah exited on his side of the vehicle. "The smell of this food is driving me nuts." Her stomach growled as if in reply.

Jeremiah stared at her over the hood of the car. "I appreciate what you mean. It doesn't seem that long since we had lunch, but I'm starving. Apparently being on the street, not knowing when your next meal will be, can cause an insatiable appetite."

"I've heard that." She unlocked the back door to let Nathan and Chief escape the confining restraints. They bounded across the yard and tumbled into a pile of leaves. Chief barked happily while Nathan squealed in delight.

Christine chuckled. "I think Chief will miss the boy

when he goes home, if he does." She turned toward the house as Jeremy pulled into the empty spot beside her car.

He honked his horn after turning off the ignition. When he stepped out of the truck, he hollered toward Christine and Jeremiah. "You're going to have a hard time getting them to come in."

Christine whistled for Chief and demonstrated how the dog herded the boy to the front door. "No problem. Chief is simply doing the job he was trained for." She decided to check out Jeremiah's reaction and observed the twinkle in his eye turn to sadness.

He stood still, reminiscing. "I remember when Amanda was little, we bought her a dog. They became inseparable until he got hit by a car and had to be put down. Amanda never wanted another pet." He looked toward Christine and grabbed the bucket of chicken she held.

Christine reached into her handbag for her keys. She inserted one into the lock and opened the door, quickly disengaging the house alarm system. "Let's go eat before my stomach does another summersault."

She led the way inside, but Nathan and Chief almost ran over her as they bounded down the hall toward the bathroom. "Wash your hands while you're in there," she bellowed after them. "Come on, gentlemen. I hope I have enough for both of you. I've never had to feed a man before, never mind two."

Jeremy chuckled, as he stepped inside right behind her. "What? No boyfriends over for a meal?"

She glared toward him. "None of your business. I don't cook, remember."

Jeremy was curious. "Didn't your cousin teach you the finer art of cuisine? I mean ... "

Jeremiah dropped the package he held on the counter,

and hung her coat, along with his, on hooks beside the back door. Jeremy followed the older man's example. Christine opened a cupboard. She handed Jeremy some plates while she retrieved cutlery from its appropriate drawer. "We had better things to do on the ranch and besides we had a cook." Her eyes froze on Jeremy as he added napkins beside each place setting.

Jeremy's stomach growled, the sound rumbling through the tiny kitchen. "I'm so hungry. This is going to be a lot better than the TV dinner in the freezer at home."

Christine glared at him. "So you don't cook either. Why is it okay for a man to not have cooking skills but a crime when a woman doesn't? Tell me that, eh?"

"The way to a man's heart is through his stomach, don't ya know. How ya going to get a husband if you can't cook?" Jeremy chuckled as he added some empty glasses from the cupboard without asking her permission.

"Make yourself at home, why don't ya. If that's all a man wants, then I don't want him. Seems to me you'd be able to handle yourself in a kitchen. There are probably other men who know how to cook, at least." Christine spied the crinkle lines frame Jeremiah's mouth. "Well it's true. Men can prepare a meal."

Nathan and Chief barged into the kitchen. Christine pointed Nathan to a chair with a pillow added for more height for the youngster. She waved a hand for Jeremy and Jeremiah to sit and she brought a jug of iced tea from the fridge.

Jeremiah placed the bucket on the table and sat while Christine added the rest. "When my Lily and I met, she was a wonderful cook. In the beginning, I will admit, her cooking drew me. Back then, women worked out of their home. None of this going to an office. They had enough to do right where they were."

"Barefoot and pregnant." Jeremy added and couldn't help laughing at the indignation on Christine's face. "Oh, come on. Life was simpler then." He reached for a helping of chicken and chips.

Christine placed some food in front of Nathan and scowled in Jeremy's direction. "Men." She bit into a chicken breast from her own plate. Everyone else sat silent ... waiting for something. "What? We missing anything?"

Jeremiah spoke first. "Grace."

Christine choked and quickly swallowed. "Go ahead. Sorry. I'm not used to religious people being in my home."

Jeremy bowed his head, placed his hand over Nathan's to still him, and began, "Lord, thank you for today, for your provision for this meal and for the things that were accomplished for Jeremiah. Thank you for bringing Nathan to us and help us this evening. May this food nourish us to your honor and glory. Amen."

Nathan waited for Jeremy to give him permission to eat, now that the prayer had ended. "Mr. Miah asked me to pray once, but all I know is 'Now I lay me down to sleep'. Nothing 'bout food." He stuffed a French fry into his mouth. "Yum-m-m."

"Me, too." Jeremy popped a few fries into his own mouth. "Yum-m-m." He picked up a chicken leg. "I'm a leg man." His eyebrows waggled up and down lecherously.

Jeremiah laughed. "Old joke. Used it on my wife a time or two." He obviously enjoyed every mouthful too.

Christine glanced around the table and marveled how only a couple more people filled her kitchen to capacity. *Kinda warm too. In a nice way.* She thought of Jeremy setting the table. *He definitely knows his way around a kitchen ... unlike most men.* Her heart seemed to thump a little harder at the idea of Jeremy in an apron. She scowled.

Jeremiah caught the look between her and Jeremy. He smiled. His gaze returned to Christine's slightly pink countenance. He grinned some more. She slapped his arm and glowered all the harder. Changing the subject seemed appropriate. "Nathan, will you tell Jeremy what happened to you?"

Nathan's smile of culinary satisfaction quickly turned to a frown. He set the drumstick he was holding on his plate and placed his hands in his lap. The defeat his posture reflected swam unencumbered through the room.

He glanced at Jeremy who forced a smile to his lips. "Go ahead, little man. Tell me your story."

"Well." He swallowed, his tiny Adam's apple bouncing up and down. "Tommy, that's my mom's boyfriend, he ripped the screen and pulled me through. He had pants and this shirt. He told me to get dressed and that's when the other man came to the fence with a puppy. When I finished putting my clothes on, I walked over to see the dog. Tommy said I could. I passed through the gate around to the sidewalk, but that guy grabbed me hard. He handed Tommy some money, a bunch. Tommy said I was sold cause my mommy didn't want me no more. I tried to get away, but he was too strong." Tears pooled in his eyelids. He hiccoughed and used his sleeve to wipe his eyes.

Christine handed him a tissue. Nathan took a deep breath. "Do I have to say more?"

"No, honey. You've said enough for now. But after dinner, I want you to tell Jeremy the rest, okay?" She averted her gaze when her own eyes filled. She cleared her throat before looking toward Jeremy. His eyes seemed a little glazed as well.

Jeremy picked up his chicken and ate a big bite. "Nathan, you are one brave little man."

Jeremiah patted the boy on his shoulder. "He is. Now finish your supper before the food gets cold." He glanced from one adult to the other.

Christine saw her emotions on the face of each of the men. They had to make certain that Tommy spent a long time behind bars. Whatever scheme he and the coin shop dealer ran, she'd try to guarantee they never hurt another kid. As soon as the idea of Tommy's incarceration flowed through her mind, she remembered the words spoken by Fine to the hooded person. *Get me another. He wanted an alternative to the one who'd gotten away and the creep, as Nathan called him, was obligated to find him. What an animal.*

Jeremy had begun a running conversation with the lad about his motorcycle. Nathan eyes lit up with wonder. "You mean it?"

"I sure do. As soon as spring hits and the weather is warm enough. I'll even get you your own helmet." He licked his fingers and reached into the bucket for another piece of chicken. Christine handed him a napkin and a clean fork. He made a face at her. "Women."

Jeremiah seemed to enjoy the comradery around the table, but Christine decided he'd been silent long enough. "Everything okay, Jeremiah?"

"Yeah. Been a long time since I enjoyed a family setting. The conversation feels good. While Lily lived, we'd eat in front of the television, but I always liked the table set for a meal. Especially if Amanda came for a visit." His face appeared sad again.

"Amanda Prescott. Who did she marry?" Christine wanted to understand what had happened to the girl he described as a child. "Why did she change?"

Jeremiah swallowed a mouthful and sipped his iced tea. "She encountered a man in college. They eloped. Never even met him till after they'd been married a few months. I didn't like him right off the bat, but I couldn't say anything. Lily tried to like him, but she wasn't able to warm up to him either. He lied, amongst other things. We caught on right away, but Amanda wanted to believe everything he said, I guess. Don't know how else she could have put up with him." He took another bite of food.

"Was that enough to divorce him over?" Jeremy entered the conversation as he folded his arms across the table in front of his empty plate.

"Not by itself and if he'd wanted to save the marriage, he'd have made changes. Amanda never disclosed any of this at the time, but he ran around with other women, too. Lots of them. One day Amanda had enough, I assume, and she walked out, leaving everything except her clothes behind. She filed and he got everything, even the money in their joint account. She's never recovered." Jeremiah shook his head. "Some men don't deserve to be married. They ruin a good woman."

Christine reached toward Nathan with a damp facecloth and washed his face and hands. "It's time for a trip to the tub."

"I can take care of his bath. You young folks have something else to do, don't you?" The older man wiped his hands on a napkin and stood beside his chair. "I'm not excusing what she did to me, but she changed and not for the good." He walked out of the kitchen.

Christine noticed the slump of his shoulders. *His daughter's treatment of him had hurt ... a lot.*

"What are you going to say to Nathan's mom?" Jeremy wasted no time in getting back to Nathan's story.

Christine took a prolonged sip of the cold beverage in front of her. "Meaning?"

"Well, I was thinking the courts are not going to allow Nathan to return to his house as long as the boyfriend is in residence. Teresa might lose custody all together, depending on the evidence concerning her involvement." Jeremy sat in the chair across from the young woman.

"I don't think she witnessed what Tommy did in any area of his life. Otherwise ... " She glanced at Jeremy. "Jeremiah and I talked on the way over here. Maybe the courts would give him custody instead of the kid going into the system."

Jeremy pondered the idea for a minute. "Aside from the fact Jeremiah doesn't have a home, the judge may decide he's too old. A youngster any age can be a handful. We need a plan B ... just in case."

Christine spent a few minutes assessing the situation. "Whatever happens, I want to get that guy and be there when the court locks him up for a long time. The poor kid. Breaks my heart." She shook her head. "Imagine telling him his mother didn't want him anymore. The first thing I said to him was how much she missed him and about her tears."

"Her tears could be faked. I've seen all kinds of so-called parents. Without God ... " He stopped, catching the grimace on Christine's face. "Well, He makes a difference."

"So Christians never abuse children?" Her skepticism wafted across the table.

"Not a true Christian. Unfortunately, many call themselves Christian but haven't a clue what it means to behave like one." He stood. "We'd better leave if we're going to get back in time to catch a few hours before the sun wakes the boy up."

Chapter Forty-Two

Jeremy pulled his truck over to the side of the road. Waiting for no one, Christine placed her hand on the door handle. "Wait just a minute." Jeremy turned the lights off and the ignition. He squinted through the dark shadows outside.

Christine checked around as well. "What are we looking for?" She saw nothing of interest except for the high stone walls surrounding a number of properties. "Which house is my parents'?"

Jeremy continued to stare out the windshield. "It's that one." He pointed to a property on the right hand side of the street. Two other homes existed between where he'd parked and the place he indicated. "We need to make sure no one is casing the place."

Christine leaned back in her seat. "I'm getting sloppy. Relying on you is not a good thing. If I'd been by myself, I'd have thought of that possibility."

Jeremy bristled. "So your lack of caution is my fault. Give me a break. And give yourself a break. I've been in this business a lot longer than you. You're not very teachable, are you?"

Christine bit right back at him. "Just because you've been doing this longer, doesn't mean that you're more experienced. I got careless, that's all."

"Okay, let's take a deep breath here." Jeremy sighed. "I meant no criticism. You are hard on yourself sometimes. You expect too much ... from both of us. A slipup could get you killed, too."

"How's that?"

"Well, if you spend so much time second guessing yourself, you'll miss what's right in front of you. It doesn't matter who thought of the idea. We need to approach your parents' house with caution. This would be a logical place for their killer to come looking for you." He shifted his gaze back to the street.

Christine placed her hands in her lap. She glanced outside again, but then looked at the man beside her. *My independence. It's getting in the way again.* "Jeremy, I'm sorry. I've been so used to doing whatever it takes to get the job done, not relying on anyone ... or in my case, a ranch hand ... to do things for me, I've never learned to work with someone. My independent streak was why I never joined the police department. They require teamwork, not lone rangers."

Jeremy leaned back in his seat again and gave her an intense once over. "We each possess skills which would benefit the other as far as this business goes. Maybe if Chief was with us, for instance, he'd let us know of any danger. You learned tracking, skills that I don't own. We'd make a good team, some of the time. I'm not suggesting we work all our cases together. Once in a while might be fun."

Christine's face grimaced. "May take a while, but I'll learn. I'm teachable ... at least some of the time. Conrad treated me as one of the men for most of the last few years I lived with them. It's hard to think in terms of sharing skills."

Jeremy heard the resignation in her voice. "Let's go. I can't see anyone out there. I think we still need to be careful, though. You never know. By the way, I picked up the key from Dad when I was at his office with Jeremiah earlier."

"Oh, my gosh. I planned to get back in the way I got out the last time I was here ... through the garage. But the garage is probably locked up, too. Right?"

"I think so." He opened his door and closed it behind him, making as little noise as possible. "I think a security company patrols this neighborhood now." He glanced at Christine as she closed her door cautiously. "Let's go over the fence in the yard next door. We'll enter your property from the back."

Christine followed Jeremy along the first stone fence toward the second. It was high, but not impossible to scale. Jeremy climbed first. He easily reached the top of the wall and extended a hand to help her up. They sat for a minute surveying the lay of the land. "There's my parents' yard. I recognize the wrought iron fence around the parking area. Appears deserted. Hope that's the case. Do you think these people have alarm systems in their yards? I don't remember whether my parents did back then."

Jeremy focused on the ground. "I'm sure they do. But if we cross the yard quickly, they might think we're an animal or something."

"Yeah, right. We're going to get caught." Christine decided to try something else. She stood, carefully, and balanced on the top of the wall. "We could walk along here until we're inside my parents' property. Then we wouldn't have to disturb these people at all."

"What makes you think the wall isn't armed. They might already know we're here. Besides, we'd be exposed."

"Well. So much for your idea of us being mistaken for an animal. How many animals would be able to jump this high?" She watched Jeremy jump to the ground. A twig snapped as he landed. "Sh-h-h."

"Come on, Christine. Let's just go and hope we won't be detected. We need to get to the house, do what we came to do and get out." He reached up to help her balance as she leapt to the ground. Christine stumbled, but ignored his out-stretched hand. She moved ahead of him toward the side of the yard and the wall separating this property from the one next door belonging at one time to her parents. *Not any more. Mine now.* This was not a happy thought.

Christine stood on tip-toes to peer over the fence surrounding her property, but the wall was too high. She glanced at Jeremy who linked his fingers to give her a leg up. She accepted his help this time. Oof-f-f. She made it and caught Jeremy's antics as he followed suit. They both sat still for a few minutes.

A cricket interrupted the silence of the night air. A nearby owl hooted his night call to anyone within hearing distance. The slight breeze rustled the branches, nearly deplete of leaves by now. Peace reigned supreme.

"What are you two doing?" Light flashed across their faces, blinding them to the gruff-voiced person waving the beam in their faces.

Jeremy jumped. He almost fell into the Romparts' yard. He shielded his eyes with his hand to see who had discovered them. The silhouette of a man stood a few feet to their left. "Who wants to know? We're just sitting here looking over this woman's property."

"Then you won't mind showing me some ID." His flashlight waved as he talked giving the two intruders a snap shot of some insignia on his jacket.

Christine was able to make out the size of the man around the glaring light. He appeared very large, even taller than Jeremy and much broader. "Do you know who owns this property?" She doubted Barkley Goodman would have let anyone know she was in town, even a security guard.

The man waved his flashlight toward them like a wand. His other hand was on the gun he had in a holster by his side. Christine glanced at Jeremy. Her raised eyebrows told him they really had no choice. She jumped to the ground. Jeremy landed right beside her.

Jeremy reached his hand into a pocket. The guard drew his gun. Jeremy held his hands in the air. "I'm just going for my ID."

"Take the card out with your left hand. Two fingers only." The guard portrayed a man who took his job very seriously. His eyes never wavered right or left. He kept his gun pointed right at Jeremy, but Christine never doubted he would shoot her if she moved, even a little bit.

Jeremy held his PI license toward the guard with his name and address printed on it. The guard read the information and shifted his attention toward Christine. "So who are you?"

Christine hesitated, but reached into her pocket where she still had some of her new business cards. She handed one to the guard. He checked the data and glanced in their direction. "So what are you two investigating?"

Jeremy and Christine exchanged glances hoping the guard would interpret their hesitation as indecision about how much to tell him. Christine chose to tell enough to prevent him from catching them in a lie. "We've been hired, by the daughter, to investigate the death of the people who own this property." *Most of that is true anyway.*

The guard held both their identification cards in his hand. "How come no one notified us you were coming?"

Jeremy spoke up. "Never crossed our mind. I guess we should have. Anyway, we weren't sure which security company had been hired to patrol the area."

"Not much of an investigator, are ya?" The guard handed them back their cards. "We've been responsible for the safety of these folks for about two years. As far as we know, this place is vacant now. Tenants left a few weeks ago."

"That's right." Christine waved her hands toward the house. "We needed to make sure the place was left in good condition and secure."

"And the only time you were able to come was at night and over a neighbor's fence." The guard holstered his gun finally, skepticism written all over him. "I'll go with you. Make sure you're not stealing anything."

"Man ..." Jeremy felt his temper rising. He took a deep breath and thought how he would react if the roles were reversed. "I gotcha man. Sounds suspicious, but the killer has never been caught so we were just being cautious."

"Killer. What killer? This is a quiet neighborhood. Nothing ever happens here." He took a step back from the duo as if he thought they might attack. His face registered shock and his body language became somewhat deflated at this piece of news.

"The owners were murdered over twenty years ago. The man who shot them walks around free as a bird. We believe he's looking for the daughter, the only witness. Seen any strangers here lately ... besides us?"

"Well, yeah. As a matter of fact. Two nights ago, someone reported a man was seen prowling around over here. By the time one of our guards got here, he was gone, but his footprints were all over the place. He'd tracked mud inside the house and everything."

The guard led the way toward the house. Jeremy walked by his side. "We have a key and want to get inside. Would like to get a cast made of those prints, too. Were you able to figure out the size of this man? The cast would help us identify someone later. And where there's footprints, we'll find fingerprints, probably."

The guard glanced back at Christine. "This is a funny business for a woman to be in, especially with a killer on the loose, if that's the truth."

Christine straightened her backbone. She was about to snap the man's head when Jeremy intervened. "Be careful. She may have to prove she's capable. You won't like that." He chuckled.

The guard sent a sobering glance toward the much smaller woman. "Yeah, well. I doubt that. I only meant with a killer on the loose ... you know. Not safe." He grimaced.

Jeremy placed a hand on his arm. "You're not helping yourself. She's stronger than she appears."

"Quit talking about me as if I weren't here." They'd reached the front door of the house she'd spent her first years of life in. She swallowed, emotion forcing its way up her throat like a glob of vomit. She glanced at Jeremy who produced the key for the door.

A simple click and a twist on the doorknob allowed them access to the large two story building. Before they stepped inside, a piece of the doorframe shattered, spraying Christine with shards of wood. Another shot followed in quick succession as the trio scooted for shelter inside. They slammed the door. "See." Jeremy glared at the guard who'd already drawn his gun.

Christine lay flat on the floor. She slid her body, soldier-like toward the nearest wall and out of the line of sight to the front door. Jeremy had flattened his body along the front closet doors away from the windows that flanked the door. The guard had his cell phone in his hand.

Jeremy sputtered. "What are you doing?"

"I need to call the shooting in." He hit a speed dial button and placed the phone next to his ear.

Jeremy grabbed the phone. "No. We want to catch the guy. If you call in the police, you'll spook him."

The guard fought to regain control of his cellular device. "How do you plan to do that? You're not even armed. I'm supposed to follow procedure." He grabbed his phone out of Jeremy's hand.

Christine spoke next. "Look. We need some time to get this guy. Can't you hold off for a few minutes?"

The guard stared at her as if she were crazy. "Lady." He threw his hands in the air. "All right. Ten minutes. But if something happens to you two, it's on your head. I'm not responsible." He shook his head.

Jeremy motioned for Christine to follow him. He headed toward the back of the house and the kitchen area.

Chapter Forty-Three

The black hooded figure slid behind the shrub. Branches scratched his skin even through the hoody. He brushed the offending plant parts out of his way and took aim again. Those punks disappeared. *They'll have to come out sooner or later.* He checked. The water was turned off as well as the electricity. *At least I know it's her.*

He lay on the ground, its coolness seeping through the light fleece. *Didn't come dressed for this*, he groused. His trigger finger twitched. He wanted the woman dead. He could taste victory on the end of his tongue. If he killed the other two bozos, no big deal. *The more, the merrier.*

He watched, his eyes never leaving the large oak door. He worked hard to ensure this would be the only way in or out. He remembered the sound of the drill as he closed off all the exits on the back of the house. This would be easy. *Like taking candy.*

His breath hung in the air. No breeze rustled branches this low to the ground. *Once that dame was dead, we'll be home free. The boss will let up... finally. Hounding him to finish the job. The old man never stopped.*

His skin itched where he touched those weeds the other night. *You'd think people would keep the weeds out of their yards in this neighborhood.* But then, he remembered the people who lived here were always at work. *Had the yard work done by hired help.*

That dame gotta come out sometime. Come on, baby. Come out, come out, wherever you are. Let's finish this. The excitement rumbled up in his chest. He could see her head explode with the perfect head shot. He could see blood all over the front entryway. *The nosey brat will cease to exist.*

Chapter Forty-Four

Jeremy led the way toward the kitchen. The large room was designed for entertaining. A huge butler's pantry was off to one side, he remembered. Christine expressed surprise that he was familiar with the layout. He filled her in. "I used to come here with my dad to inspect the house after tenants left."

"Boy, I don't remember much about this part of the house, but I do recall the cook. She was a nice lady and would let me taste the dough when she baked cookies or a cake. Mom and Dad entertained a lot. Of course, I was supposed to be in bed. My nanny slept in the room connected to mine, but every now and again, I'd sneak out in the hall and watch the people down below." Christine rubbed her midsection. Thinking about life in this house always gave her an unpleasant roiling in her abdomen.

Jeremy led her toward the kitchen door, through the butler's pantry. "Sounds like kids in the Sound of Music." He tried to open the back door. It wouldn't budge. "Is there a secret to this door? Can you recollect going outside through this exit?"

"No. But there's so many things I've worked hard to put

out of my mind. It hurts too much." She rubbed her stomach again. She watched Jeremy pull harder on the door. He'd already used his key to unlock it but the door was shut tight. "Maybe the thing is warped."

"Maybe." He pulled again. "The tenants would have told us if something needed fixing before they left." He checked around for another way out of the house. "Christine, where's that secret doorway to the garage you talked about?"

"Off the front foyer. At least, that's the only way I ever got to it. You can access it through that closet under the stairs." She led the way back down the hallway toward the front door.

"You've six minutes left before I call the cops." The guard stood beside the front door. Christine watched as he peeked through the glass where the frosted accents ended and clear glass took over.

She made her way to the one area of the house where her nightmare always began. She opened the door, slipped inside and ducked down. She reached for the sliding panel that led to the secret passageway.

Jeremy was right behind her. "Maybe I ought to go first."

Christine ignored him. "You're just as vulnerable as I am."

"Yes, but I don't think he wants me. I believe you're the target here."

She sucked in a deep breath. "We don't know that for sure. We're not familiar with the guy out there. Maybe he's out to get the guard."

Jeremy's loud harrumph sounded as if he were right beside her. "You know it's unlikely this person is anyone other than who you and I think he is. We recognized this was a possibility when we decided to come over here." He crawled on hands and knees, bumping into Christine once in a while.

Christine huffed. "This was a lot easier when I was little." She reached the door that appeared at the end of the passage. With one hand to balance with, she used the other to push the door outward. It didn't move. "I wonder if they nailed this shut after ... " She left the sentence unfinished.

"Here. Let me try." Jeremy squeezed past her as Christine flattened herself to one side of the rabbit hole they were in. At least that's what she imagined a rabbit hole would feel like when a childhood memory of her favorite storybook character flashed before her .

Jeremy pushed with every ounce of strength he had. Nothing happened. "Just like the back door. I wonder ..."

"What?" Christine began to retreat back the way they'd come.

"Well. Doesn't it seem like too much of a coincidence for both the back door and this door to be inaccessible? I mean ... could he have nailed them shut to make sure we have to go out the front door while he waits to pick us off." Jeremy's breathing labored. "Talking and scooting around on hands and knees is exhausting."

"Then don't talk. You make this guy sound like a monster."

"You don't think he is?" Jeremy scooted after Christine, through the panel and into the closet once again. "I mean ... if he is the guy who ..." He decided to let the subject drop. He stood, brushed his pants off and stalked past her to the foyer. "Do you recall any other way to get out to the back yard?"

"What about the windows?" Christine ran down the hall to the kitchen again. She stopped in front of the one in the breakfast nook. "These used to open from the bottom or the top." She gripped the lock, gave it a twist, and tried to lift the first one. "Ooff. It must be painted shut."

"Or nailed." Jeremy squinted his eyes down toward the outside to see if he could detect what was holding the window.

He saw nothing from where he stood.

In the meantime, Christine tried each of the other two in the large bow window. None of them would move up or down. "We might as well let the guard call the police. I sure don't intend to go out the front door as long as that shooter is out there."

"The police will scare him off for sure. We're gonna have to think of another way to catch this guy, I guess. At least he's keeping his distance. And the guard has a gun." Jeremy led the way to the foyer. The security guy already had his cell phone at his ear.

Jeremy pulled Christine aside. "Christine, what did you want to check here anyway? I've forgotten."

"I just wanted to see if any clues were left, something the police missed. But, of course, with tenants living here, I suppose that's wishful thinking. I'm going to check things out anyway." She started toward the large circular staircase. "I've thought about living here again. But this place holds so many bad memories, not enough good ones. Besides the house is too big." She placed her foot on the bottom stair and glanced back at the guard. "How long before the cops show up?"

"They said five minutes. Could be longer." He placed his phone back in the holder. "Couldn't find the back door?"

Jeremy strode toward him. When he reached the front door, he opened it a crack and peered outside. All was quiet. "Maybe he's gone already." He stepped sideways and placed one foot through the doorway. Next he slid his torso into the opening trying to make his silhouette as narrow as possible. A shot buzzed past his ear, nicking the appendage in the process. "Ouch" He propelled his body back inside. His hand automatically covered his injured ear. "He's still out there." He leaned against the closet door again.

Christine rushed toward him. "You okay?"

Jeremy grimaced. "Just a nick." He stared at the other

man. The guard's gun was ready for action. He relaxed his body against the woodwork. "Apparently all the windows and doors leading into the back yard have been secured. We can't get out that way. Could be weather, but I'll bet that man has been busy."

"How do you know the sniper is a man?" The guard obviously agreed with Christine.

Christine swatted Jeremy's bicep. "See. I'm not the only one who doesn't want to jump to conclusions." She headed back toward the stairs. "If you're okay, I'm going to check upstairs. Maybe I can see him from a window up there.

She took the stairs two at a time and didn't stop till she was on the second landing. She stopped and glanced around. A few pictures hung on the walls of the long hallway, but none of them appeared familiar. *I suppose they removed all my family's stuff when they moved the first tenants in. I wonder where all that stuff is?*

She moved past the rooms she remembered as hers and the nanny's and entered her parent's bedroom at the front of the house. Empty now, she remembered when she used to like to come in here and cuddle with her mother on the big bed that took up most of the center of the room. She shook her head. *No good thinking about that now.*

She slid closer to the window, making sure she kept out of the line of sight to anyone who might be watching for a shadow to pass by. *Good thing there's no electricity. No lights. No shadows.* She peered outside. The first sound of police sirens shrilled in the distance.

Christine scanned the front yard. If those shots were any indication, he was somewhere directly in front of the house. She scanned the bushes. *There.* A figure, all dark, scooted toward the high stone fence. He seemed short in stature from her vantage point, but he could be any height. She couldn't make out facial features, or any other identifying marks. He carried a high powered pistol, which kind she was sure the ballistics experts would be able to tell from the bullets they'd retrieve.

She looked around the empty room again, but by moonlight, there was a lot she couldn't see. *It'll be the same with the other rooms. We need to come back in the daylight. Yuck. A better target.* She made her way back downstairs as two police officers entered the front door.

Chapter Forty-Five

The police searched thoroughly before they decided the man was long gone. *If their attacker was a man*, Christine thought. She recalled the quick glimpse she'd had of him. It was hard to pick out any information to describe the figure she'd seen. "Jeremy, we might as well head home. I can't think of any other information to add to the police report. I wish I'd seen him, or her, more clearly."

Jeremy stared at the guard, as the man completed his statement to the cops. He glanced at Christine. "I wonder if he noticed more than he's letting on. After all, he said a prowler had been sighted yesterday or the day before. I can't remember exactly what he told us about the person, can you?"

"No. Maybe we need to get him to give us a better description. Let's try to speak with him after the police leave. Those bullet holes will need to be repaired before I can sell this house now." Christine rubbed her hands down the banister, caressing the strength of the wood and feeling as if she was disloyal to an old friend.

"Are you sure you want to do that? Maybe you could

turn the residence into a couple or three apartments, leave one for yourself and one or two to rent. That's what the people did to the house I live in. The house was once a single family dwelling, but now contains three homes." Jeremy kept his eyes on the guard and the police officers. He whispered to Christine. "Does it look to you as if he's telling them a lot more than he told us?"

"Yeah. Like I said, we need to talk to him. We also should make sure we're not followed back to my place. I guess it's a good thing we came in your truck. By the way, did the officers happen to ask you why we entered this property the way we did. Oh darn. We told the guard we were here looking at my property and that we'd been hired by the daughter." She studied Jeremy's face to see if he caught the discrepancy in their stories.

He did. "I tried to stop you from telling him too much, but at least it was a way to explain why we're both detectives ... considering that's what our cards say." He shifted his gaze toward the front door. "The cops are leaving. Now let's try to get some information from the security guard." He walked toward the man in uniform. "Do you have a minute?"

"Sure. The night's just beginning for me. I need to make my rounds soon, though." He settled his large frame on the steps leading to the second floor. "It feels as if I've been on my feet all night." He sighed. "You never expect anything to happen in this neighborhood."

"Yeah, I suppose it's usually quiet." Christine leaned against the large oak newel post. "The fence was added when I was four years old. I never understood why, but it sure changed how we left and returned to this house. Things got complicated after that. We used to be able to run from one yard to another, playing with our friends. The mom whose house we were playing at, always took responsibility to watch us. It was a nice place to grow up until ... "

The guard considered her closely. "So you're the daughter you said hired you to investigate?" He frowned. "I thought your story was a little too simple. And then ... those shots were meant for you." He acted as if he were checking off clues off his list.

"That's right." Jeremy stood beside Christine. He placed a protective hand on her shoulder. "And we think you guessed more than you've told us so far. Do you have a description of the prowler who was seen around here ... was that yesterday or the day before?"

The guard appeared a little miffed he was being questioned by the two people he thought of as intruders. "I guess I figure the information is for the police, not you." He hung his head. "But ... I guess ... you were the one shot at." He looked at Christine. "You have a right ... "

"Take it easy." Christine stiffened at his sympathetic demeanor. "We don't know I was the target. Maybe it was you for all we know. What did the man look like? Did you actually see him?"

"No. But your neighbor did. I can call ... see if they want to talk to you. They're relatively new to the area, but they seem friendly enough."

Jeremy interjected. "Arrange it, ... please. Did you get a look at the guy tonight?"

"No. I only saw the flash of his muzzle when he shot at you the second time. He was well hidden behind those bushes out there or I'da ..." He patted his gun in its holster.

Christine noticed. "By the way, why weren't you using that thing? You never shot back at the guy."

Jeremy continued to stare with interest at the guard. He waited, with a glance at Christine, for the answer to her question. "Seems to me you could have caught the sniper. What's the name of your security company?"

The sentry swallowed, his neck muscles moving up and down. He seemed to be stalling. He cleared his throat noisily.

"I've never killed anyone before. Don't want to either. I wasn't hired to shoot people, just to guard and protect." He chuckled at his witticisms. He quickly replaced his smile with a much more sober look when he noticed the reproach in the eyes of the two in front of him. He stood. "I gotta go. I'll get back to you with information about whether or not your neighbor will talk to you." He started toward the door.

"Wait a minute." Christine grabbed his sleeve. "We want to talk to them tonight, not whenever."

"That's right. This information could be very important to Miss Finder ... er ... Smith." Jeremy could have kicked himself.

"Which is it ... Finder or Smith?" The guard's smug expression indicated he thought he had the upper hand now. "I guess I'll just let the police learn you have an alias."

"Speaking of which, what exactly did you tell the officers?" Christine placed her hands on her hips and moved a little closer to the guard, ignoring his comment. "You were talking to them a long time."

"I told them exactly what happened tonight. I also described how I found you two. I know they're going to want to talk to both of you some more." He smirked and moved closer to the front door. "You will lock up when you leave, right?"

"We're leaving now, but we'll be back." Jeremy followed the guard to the door. He gave Christine a look that silenced any further protest. He motioned for her to follow. "We might as well go back out through the main gate instead of the way we came. Didn't help much anyway."

Christine followed silently behind. She reached for the doorknob just as Jeremy reached for it as well. As soon as their hands touched, the sensation of electricity shot up her arm. She jerked her hand back and checked his face to see if he noticed. Jeremy acted as if nothing happened. *Good.*

They walked down the long tree lined drive as soon as

the door was secured, following the path the guard had taken. He was only a few steps in front of them. Christine observed Jeremy place his fingers on his lips. She wondered why he wanted her to keep quiet. *He's got something up his sleeve. Wonder what.*

They observed the hired security drive off and then walked the last few steps toward their own vehicle. Jeremy unlocked the truck door and flipped the latch from his side to allow Christine to access her side. As soon as they settled into the interior of the truck with the doors closed, Christine leaned back, folded her arms across her chest, and glared at Jeremy. "Okay. What's up?"

"Did you get the impression the guard evaded our questions on purpose? I'm wondering if he was part of what went on tonight. Working for the security company would be a good way to keep an eye on your house without raising any suspicions, don't you think? And now he's discovered you are connected to the Finders and are Romparts' daughter. Your cover is blown if he's working for the drug cartel."

Christine's eyes opened wide as saucers. "How can we find out for sure? I have Charlie at RCMP headquarters, but ... does a company like that do background checks?"

Jeremy inserted his key into the ignition and then stopped. He stepped out of the vehicle and scrunched down to look under the chassis. Christine watched through the opened door. "You think they may have attached a bomb ... " She stepped out her side and scanned the underside of the truck as well.

Jeremy's voice was a little muffled. He was looking under the hood of the truck. "I don't know, but I'd rather be cautious than dead."

Christine nodded even though she understood he couldn't actually see her. "I'll be so glad when I catch this guy ... or guys. Man, if the security guy is working for the drug dealers ... " She shook her head. "I'm not going to be safe anywhere until they're caught ... and even then ... they could always send someone else after me." Tears glistened in her eyes as sheer fright welled up in her chest.

"Christine, the drug cartel is not your problem. They don't care if you're alive or dead. There's no evidence to put them behind bars. However, the monster ..." He emphasized the word. "... who did your parents ... this is his gig. Besides, he could have recruited help." He returned to sit back in the truck. "Nothing out of place. I even checked the brake lines. Now all we need to do is make sure we're not followed."

"I think I need a disguise of some sort. If that guy saw me, even if the guard isn't working for them, I'm vulnerable now. I should have thought about that before coming here in the first place. You were right, though. If I'd come alone ... "

Jeremy started the truck and steered it onto the street. "It might be a good idea to stop by tomorrow, use our IDs and speak to the neighbors. Forget about the sentry. We can find out the information we need ourselves. In the meantime, have Charlie check on him. He should be able to tell whether or not the company does background checks or if the RCMP does them." He steered into traffic flowing away from Christine's house. "We'll lose that guy on the perimeter, with less traffic to hide behind. If there is someone following."

They rode a few miles in silence before Jeremy turned onto the freeway that surrounded the city's circumference. It was a limited access freeway, but at this time of night, there were only a few vehicles in sight. No one turned onto the highway after they did. "I think we're home free, but we'll travel a while to make sure."

Christine shivered. "I don't know what made me think I was capable of handling myself against this guy. I probably wouldn't have checked under the chassis or anything. I guess I don't understand evil the way you do."

"I don't walk alone, Christine."

"What do you mean? I mean ... yeah, there's the two of us so no, you're not alone now, but ... "

Jeremy looked at her closely. She could see the indecision in his face and heard it in his voice. "You want to know or are you just talking for the sake of talking?" His gaze returned to the road ahead and every once in a while, he checked the rear-view mirror.

"I want to know, of course. I wouldn't have asked if I didn't want an answer." She folded her arms to make her point.

"I walk with the Lord. I'm tuned into His voice. He keeps me sharp." Jeremy glanced at Christine and for the first time, saw interest instead of skepticism.

"God talks to you?"

"In a way. It's a still small voice sometimes. At other times, it's a feeling, knowledge that a course of action is needed, like checking the underside of the truck and under the hood before we left just now. As I was putting the key into the ignition, the thought came to me. I attribute that to God. And I try to listen. Don't always succeed, but most of the time I do." He looked skyward and mouthed the word thanks. "This time there was nothing, but the next time, there could be a bomb or cut brake lines ... any number of things."

"But doesn't God know whether someone tampered with your truck or not. Why would He tell you to check when He knows no one did anything?"

"I thought you didn't believe in God. Are you saying you're willing to consider His existence?" Jeremy's eyes shone, hope sitting just below the surface.

"It just seems to me that by myself, I might be dead now. But you're here and you believe. Your faith seems to make a difference in your life. You've lasted longer in this game and maybe the fact there is a God protecting you is why. To ignore the existence of God, after growing up in the surroundings I did, would be stupid. Beauty everywhere and seasons, the stars, all of it. So, answer my question. If God knows all, then why?"

"I think He's teaching me to be sharp. To always be on my toes. At least, that's what Dad says. He follows his inner God voice all the time. It's what's made him such a good lawyer, he says." Jeremy turned off the highway and headed back to the center of town.

Christine stared out the window at buildings that slipped by as they traveled. She filed this new information into her brain, but the questions kept coming. She sighed, thankful that Jeremy respected her silence. He didn't preach at her. *Just answered my questions. He really believes that stuff, too. Maybe ...*

Chapter Forty-Six

Christine rolled over onto her side. Sunlight streamed through the sides of the blinds covering her bedroom window. She glanced at her clock. *Yikes. Not again. And this time no nightmare for an excuse. Hey. That's right. No dreams.*

She jumped out of bed, rushed to the bathroom and splashed cold water on her face. She snatched her bathrobe from the hook behind the door and slipped it on while slipping her feet into slippers. She checked her appearance in the mirror, grabbed a comb and ran it through her hair, and then stepped to the door leading down the hall to her living area. As soon as she walked past the frame, she could hear voices, one deep and the other excited.

She glanced into the room. Two male figures sat on the sofa in front of the television. Nathan was laughing, a sound she hadn't heard much from the little boy. Jeremiah was attempting to keep him quiet.

"Good morning, guys. How'd you sleep?" She smiled as much as she could without her first cup of coffee for the day.

"Christine." The boy clambered toward her as soon as he slipped off the sofa.

Jeremiah returned her smile. "I hope we didn't wake you. I tried but ... " He nodded toward the child.

"Oh goodness. No. I need to be up. In fact, I should have been up a long time ago." She accepted a warm hug from Nathan. Over his head, she told Jeremiah she had some things to check out today and pointed toward the boy. Jeremiah nodded his understanding.

"Do you think I could take him with me to see that house Franny talked about before you drop me off at Jeremy's office? At least I assume those are your plans." Jeremiah stood and walked behind Christine to the kitchen.

"Let's talk about the day over breakfast. Did you help yourself, or were you waiting for me?" She noticed the coffee had already been made.

Jeremiah pointed to the dirty dishes in the sink. "I hope you don't mind, but the boy was hungry so we helped ourselves to some cereal. You're out of milk now, though."

Christine poured herself some coffee. "No need to explain. I told you to make yourself at home. Thanks for making coffee. I don't function too well in the morning without it." She opened a cupboard and pulled out a loaf of bread. "I'll just have some toast."

Jeremiah refilled his coffee cup and sat across from her at the table. Nathan scooted up on another chair and stared at the toaster. "Can I have some toast, too?" he asked.

Christine laughed and Jeremiah pretended shock. "After that big bowl of cereal." He glanced toward Christine. "He's the one who finished all the milk." The chuckle that accompanied his words spoke of the comradery between the two, man and boy. "I think he's gotten his appetite back."

"I'm glad. That means ... " Christine let her words hang

in the air.

"I fathom a change." Jeremiah nodded, his smile covering his face. They both wanted what was best for the boy, it seemed.

Christine looked at the diminutive figure dwarfed by the table and the adult chair he sat on. "I think a slice or two of toast and some ... " She walked over to the cupboard and pulled out a jar of peanut butter. Nathan grinned and his head bobbed up and down in anticipation. Christine giggled, pulled a jar of strawberry preserves from the fridge, and returned to her chair. She looked toward Jeremiah. "You want some toast, too?"

"Naw. I'm good. Don't want ta eat ya out of house and home." He leaned back in his chair and folded his hands on the table in front of him. "Now about that trek over to Franny's neighborhood."

"No problem. Right after I get dressed. Don't worry about eating too much. I have another loaf in the freezer. Hey, where's Chief?" Just then a bark sounded at the back door. Christine jumped up and walked swiftly to let him in. Chief barged through the portal as soon as she opened it. "What're you doing out there?"

"Oh, Christine. I'm sorry. I put him out when we got up and got busy with Nathan. I forgot about him." He stood and walked over to Chief. He patted the dog's head. "Sorry boy."

Christine slipped four slices of bread in the toaster and rose to add some food and water to Chief's dishes by the kitchen counter. She walked over to the freezer and grabbed another loaf of bread and returned to her seat. She smiled toward Jeremiah. "Can you take Nathan with you to see the house? I could drop you off and get some errands done while you visited with Franny and pick you up later."

Jeremiah grabbed the toast as it popped up. While he buttered the four slices, he watched Christine add four more. "There's something about the smell of fresh toast that wets an appetite," He added some peanut butter to a slice for Nathan, and cut it into four pieces for his smaller hands. "I see no reason why Nathan can't come with me. You going to check out ..." He left his sentence unfinished, but nodded toward the boy.

Christine watched the child demolish his toast as if he'd not eaten in a week. She chuckled and ruffled his hair before looking at Jeremiah. "We have to be sure he'll be safe before we take him back."

Nathan looked up at her and then turned his gaze on Jeremiah. "Can't I stay with you for always?"

Christine swallowed the lump that formed when she saw the look of hope in Nathan's eyes. "Nathan, don't you want to go back to live with your mother? Don't you miss Darcy?"

The child hung his head to hide the tears that surfaced in his eyes. "I do miss Darce, and Mommy, too. But ... I'm afraid. Tommy ... "

"We're ... I'm going to make sure Tommy can't hurt you again. We won't let you go home until we know it's safe. Isn't that right Jeremiah?" Christine blinked, trying to keep her eyes from overflowing and scaring the boy. Chief licked her hand and moved over to stand by the boy. "Chief will help too. Won't you?" The dog used his indoor bark to let everyone know he was on board.

Jeremiah added more jam to another slice of toast. He took a big bite and hummed his satisfaction. "Franny loves little kids. We'll have a great time visiting her and I am looking forward to seeing that house. She said it had some furniture in it but I'll probably have to get more ... as soon as I can get my money back from Amanda." The twinkle disappeared from his eyes. "Families can be disappointing."

Christine nodded. "The three of us have a little in common. In my case ... well it wasn't my parents fault really. And I guess it really wasn't Teresa's fault either. Just bad choices. My mom and dad too. But for all of us, our families have ... " The doorbell cut her off. "I'll bet that's Jeremy."

Nathan went racing toward the front door with Chief right on his heels. He placed his hand on the doorknob.

Before he could open the door, however, Christine cautioned him. "Nathan. We don't know for sure who's on the other side of that door. I'll look through this peep hole and when we know it's safe, we'll let our visitor in. Okay?"

Nathan stepped back, out of her way so she could peek through the hole in the solid wood door. "It's Jeremy," she announced as soon as she looked. She waved Nathan forward to open the door.

Jeremy strode into the room, a smile attached to his face like a beacon. "I did some checking this morning. I think you might find it interesting that one of your neighbors, or at least one of the neighbors to your parent's house, is a Mr. Fine, a coin collector."

Christine gasped. "Do you think ...?"

"I don't think it's a coincidence this Mr. Fine is also a coin collector." His attention shifted to Nathan. "Did the man who Tommy sold you to take you any place else besides that place downtown?"

"Just there." He scrunched his eyes upward to look into Jeremy's. "But ... he left at night and didn't come back till morning. I was scared."

Christine bent down to give the boy a hug. She dipped her eyes as soon as she caught Jeremy taking note of her heightened color. She wrapped her arms around Nathan and held him tight. Then she glanced back toward Jeremy. "We need to talk."

Jeremy nodded and then looked toward Jeremiah. "Amanda came for a visit first thing this morning. She's decided to settle out of court. Apparently my dad filed some papers with her and she's taken our ... or your threat seriously. Surprised her, I guess."

The corners of Jeremiah's mouth turned downward. "What did she think I'd do? Just forget she stole from me? How much was your dad able to recover?"

"We don't know yet. It seems she invested a lot of it, but she's turned over those investments. Once we've gone through your records, we'll know how much she took and what she's given back. Anyway, at least we won't need to go to court." Jeremy grinned. Then he looked serious again. "Somehow I expected her to fight harder, though."

Christine straightened up and wrapped her bathrobe tighter around herself. "What time did you get up anyway?"

"I'm always up at five am." He grinned toward her and winked. "I guess you slept in." His finger touched the neck of her robe. He shrugged and folded his hands behind his back. "Do you have any coffee? I'll wait for you to get dressed. Then we can get started finding out what we can about Mr. Fine."

"Coffee's in the kitchen. Help yourself. I'll be ready in a flash." She looked toward Nathan and Jeremiah. "Are you done eating?"

Jeremiah grinned. "We'll finish and clean up. You just get ready." He patted the side of his leg. "Come on, Chief. Let's let Christine have some uninterrupted time." He led the way toward the back of the house and the kitchen area. "Jeremy, did your dad say how long it would take to clear my funds?"

"No. I'm sure there are a ton of variables. Like where they are invested." He waved toward Christine as she headed down the hall to her bedroom. She waved back over her head.

Christine pulled the robe tighter around her neck and shivered. She walked through the door to her bedroom, closed it tight, and strolled nonchalantly to the bed to throw the covers over the pillows in a make-shift attempt to straighten things. A few steps to her closet and she was staring inside, trying to determine what she'd wear for the day. *If we're going to the neighborhood around Mom and Dad's house, maybe I can pretend I'm moving in and want to meet the neighbors. Let's see ...* She grabbed a nice pair of slacks, a matching blouse and a jean jacket to go over it. *Casual but expensive looking. Nice touch.*

I wonder what kind of person would carry on two lives like that. She stepped into her bathroom, opened the shower curtain, and turned on the faucet. Jeremy's face floated through her mind. *Go away.* She took a wash cloth and some facial cleanser and began to look after the facial treatment she'd practiced since she was sixteen. *Connie sure believed in looking after one's complexion.*

She remembered all the things that Connie Finder had taught her as she stepped into the shower. Her facial cleanser rinsed away, leaving her skin soft and smooth. Connie had treated her like a daughter. *She wanted me to wear dresses though and I hated them. I'm not the feminine type, I guess.* She'd wanted nothing more than to ride a horse and be out with the ranch hands all day. That meant jeans.

Christine lathered her hair. She recalled a conversation she'd had when Connie invited a young man from a neighboring ranch over for dinner. It ended with Christine putting on her one dress, but fidgeting all evening wishing her legs were covered in denim. *The boy ... er ... I guess he was a man ... seemed not the slightest bit interested and couldn't wait to leave.* She shrugged as the hot spray poured over her head and shoulders. *Men.* Then Jeremy came to mind.

She turned off the spray, stepped out onto the rug, and grabbed a towel. *Better hurry or I'll have company in here.* Leave in conditioner made her comb run smoothly through her locks. She grabbed handfuls and scrunched them into some curl and hurriedly completed her preparations for the day, splashing some cologne over her collar bone and wrists. *Why am I getting all dolled up? It's just Jeremy.*

She used her hair blower to dry her tresses, added a hint of blush to her cheeks and some lipstick. She was ready to go.

She glanced around the room until she located her handbag. She still had her cache of weapons inside.

She heard voices coming from the kitchen as she approached. Jeremy was telling a story about when he was a boy. She stopped to listen just outside the door.

"My dad used to bring me to work with him all the time. I remember one time, when he wasn't paying attention, I climbed up on his desk and tried to find a game on his computer. Dad didn't play computer games. Anyway, I thought if I pushed enough keys, a game would appear. Well the computer crashed and dad was so mad at me. He was trying to deal with a client and had to look after me instead. I forget where my mom was."

Christine stepped into the kitchen. "Sounds like you were a trouble-maker." She looked around at the three male figures who dwarfed her kitchen. "You guys ready?"

Chapter Forty-Seven

The cab of Jeremy's truck reverberated with sound on the drive to Franny's house. Christine smiled as Nathan talked non-stop, excited Jeremiah was going to check out a house that might allow him to remain with his older friend. "A bedroom all to myself. I won't have to see Tommy."

She angled her body toward him from her position beside him in the back seat. "Remember, Nathan. This is only temporary. When the police arrest Tommy, and they will, we'll make sure your Mom's house is a safe place for you. You'll get to go home. Won't that be fun?"

Nathan stared at her with defiance in his eyes. "Don't wanna go back there. Wanna stay with Jeremiah."

Christine began to wonder if the boy was getting used to all the attention. "Jeremiah is a nice man." She assessed the older man sitting in the passenger seat. Then her gaze drifted back to Nathan. "But he ... " She was about to help the child understand that Jeremiah did not want to be saddled with a kid when she caught the look in the older man's eye.

He reached back and patted the hand she'd rested on the back of the front seat. "It's okay. Leave it for now. We can make small changes as things get straightened out."

He's right, of course. The child is too young to understand he needs to be with his mom. Speaking of which, I need to pay her a visit today. Christine looked toward Jeremiah and nodded. She rested against the seat cushions. Chief was struggling to sit upright with Nathan's arm hugging him so tightly.

She loosened the boy's grip. "Chief will come with me while you and Jeremiah go house hunting. We'll pick you up later this afternoon. Jeremiah, do you think Franny will mind you being at her house most of the day?"

Jeremiah swiveled his gaze toward Christine and chuckled. "That woman loves to care for people. She'll be tickled pink. At least the idea came across loud and clear when I called her this morning." He studied his hands for a few seconds and smiled just before returning his focus to Christine again. "She is always worrying about someone or other. Nathan will give her someone else to fuss over. She'll be in heaven."

Jeremy spotted Christine in the rear view mirror. "Are you sure you want to go back to your parents' house today. We could go there another time, after we get these two settled in their respective homes."

"I want to go visit Teresa Brent." She nodded towards Nathan. "I want to find out whether she has any misgivings about Tommy. You know ... feminine instincts. She may think she's imagining things, but ... sometimes we comprehend things without understanding what we're seeing."

Jeremy chuckled. "Sounds a little convoluted to me, but I've not ever been able to figure out women so ..." He saw storm clouds return to her face and quickly retracted his words. "Never mind. That won't take very long, though. Will she be open to talking with me there?"

"Well, you could wait in the truck. I also want to go

back to the coin shop. I want to discover if those thugs are always hanging around there or if they just come when Mr. Fine orders them to do so. In other words, do they work for him or is he under their control?"

Jeremy kept his eyes on the road as they turned down the street in front of Franny Morris' house. "I can't imagine a scenario where they control him. Since he's rich enough to own the house near your family home, he's the one calling the shots, I'll bet. But doing some snooping won't hurt, I guess."

"I need to be clear what their relationship is and I'd sure like to prevent another kid from being abducted by them." Christine peeked at Nathan. The boy was staring out the window.

Nathan turned his head and looked directly at her. "What's abducted?"

He was listening. "That's what happened to you." She placed her hand on his shoulder. "We don't want another little boy to be hurt like you were, do we?" *I'll have to watch what I say around this kid. He hears everything.*

"No." Nathan turned back toward the window as Jeremy parked the truck at the curb in front of Franny's house. "This your friend's house, Jeremiah?"

Christine watched the child dip back behind his inner wall, trying to forget. It was as if he looked for ways to think about something else. She unbuckled her seatbelt and released Nathan's. Jeremiah opened the door beside the child and helped him to the grass on the edge of the sidewalk. Christine slipped out her door and walked around to the passenger side of the front seat. "You two enjoy yourselves. Jeremiah, you have our phone numbers. If you need anything, call us." She stepped up into the truck and took the seat vacated by Jeremiah.

Jeremy gazed across to the open door on the passenger side. "Jeremiah, we'll try to give you a heads up when we'll be back to get you." He winked. "Wouldn't want to interrupt anything."

Jeremiah hooted. "Not too likely. Franny's a friend. Nothing more." His face seemed a little pinker than usual to the two who observed him.

Christine decided to save the man. She closed the door and gave Jeremy one of her scowls. "Leave the man alone. It's okay for men to have friends of the opposite sex without some ulterior motive." She waved as Jeremy, amidst lots of laughter, pulled the truck back onto the street. "Take us for example."

"Oh. So, we're friends now. When did our stormy relationship change?" He grinned toward the windshield, keeping his eyes focused on the traffic ahead. "Where to first?"

"The Brent home." Christine sat in silence for a few minutes, distracted over her remark about her and Jeremy being friends. *Are we?* She glanced out the window. *We're friendly toward each other ... most of the time. But friends?* She stole a look in Jeremy's direction. "I guess we're not quite friends. More like colleagues."

His quick glance in her direction gave nothing away about his thoughts on the subject. "Colleagues I can handle ... for now. Now, fill me in on the Brent woman."

Christine leaned back in the seat. She reached around beside her and lowered the seatbelt to more easily match her shorter height. "Teresa was worried sick when she hired me to find her son. If she'd not cared, she'd have left it in police hands and never even contacted me. In fact, it was she who contacted the police in the first place. I think she wants her son found."

"What about her poor choice in boyfriends?" Jeremy's facial expression told her he had no patience for someone who'd put her kids in jeopardy over a man. "Bad judgment on her part, don't ya think?"

"Loneliness can make some women do strange things. I think she really believes Tommy is innocent. Or at least, wants to believe the premise that he loves her and therefore has her best interests at heart. We'll see what she thinks now after her son's been missing for three days."

"Are you going to tell her what Nathan said about him?" Jeremy studied the street signs.

"I think I'll play that by ear. What do you think?" Christine sucked in a breath and bit her lip. *Why am I asking his opinion? This is my case.* Before he could answer, she cleared her throat. "That's what I'll do."

Jeremy glanced in her direction again. "Being sounding boards for each other's cases could be a good thing, I imagine."

Darn the man. It's like he read my mind. "Maybe. But I think I understand the woman better than you at this point. I'll handle this while you make some phone calls, like we agreed in the first place. You said you needed to talk to your father about Jeremiah."

"I'll pray for you, then, while you're talking to Teresa. God might give you the right question to ask to determine Teresa's complicity or lack thereof." Jeremy turned down the street leading to the address Christine had given him. "Remember when I told you about the still small voice? If God places a concern on your heart, go with it. Don't ignore it. It might be just the right direction to take with this woman in order to find out how much she really suspects."

Christine considered the man at her side. "Jeremy, I've never met anyone who talks about God as if He's interested in our lives like you do. I mean ... "

"He is. Interested, I mean, in the details." Jeremy glanced at the nearest house number. "We're here." He motioned toward the small house Christine had seen two days ago for the first time.

"Great. I'll get this over as quick as I can. When you talk to your father, ask him if he has a recent real estate appraisal on my parent's house. I'd also like to meet with the board of directors for my Dad's company, since they've been looking after the inner workings until I returned to the scene of the crime." Christine grimaced over her use of the word, but then shrugged. "I think I need to unload the past and all it contains. I need to get on with my life."

Jeremy nodded in her direction. "I'm not sure I agree with you, but that's your choice, of course. You go ahead. I'll be right here."

Christine stepped out of the truck and then turned back toward Jeremy. "Ask your father anyway. I won't make any decision without discussing it with him first. After all, he is my attorney." She closed the door and walked toward the little fenced yard.

She set her foot on the front walkway just as the front door to the house opened. Teresa stood, holding her hand against the door to keep it open for Christine. "I wondered when you'd be by. I drove to your office, but the security guard said you'd moved out. What's going on?"

Christine walked up the steps. "Is Tommy home?"

"Yeah, he came back. Won't leave again. Why you want him anyway?" Teresa's eyes drifted past her to the street. "What're they doing here?"

Christine turned around. "I don't know." She shifted her gaze toward the police sergeant striding purposefully up the front walk.

The uniformed officer glanced from one woman to the other. "Mrs. Brent, is Tommy Devine at home?" He took the steps two at a time.

Christine viewed two other officers walk around to the back of the house. She noticed Jeremy exit his vehicle, but waved him off. "What's going on Sergeant?"

"Police business, Miss Finder. Is he home, Mrs. Brent?" The man had not arrived to get just a few questions answered. This was more intense.

Teresa fussed with the waistband on her dress. She glanced down and then back up toward the police officer. "Why do you want to know?"

"Is he here or not?" The officer clearly was in a take charge mood.

Christine interjected. "She told me he was."

Teresa glared at Christine. Betrayal floated across the distraught woman's facial features. "He is. He's sleeping. Why? What's he done?" She moved aside, but then stepped in front of the sergeant to block his entrance into her home. "You bring a search warrant?"

"No, an arrest warrant. Now move aside." He stalked into the house and surveyed the room. "Which way?"

Teresa pointed up the stairs. "First door on the right." She squinted her eyes at Christine. She hurried after the officers who'd made short work of the staircase. Before she managed to go up more than four steps, raised voices could be heard from the upper floor of the house. Teresa backed down and stood beside Christine.

They gawked at Tommy, hands cuffed behind his back, as he descended to the first floor. He was followed closely by the sergeant and one other officer. They sat him on the first chair they came to in the living room. "Now Mrs. Brent. We need you to come downtown as well. You're not under arrest. There are some things we need to clear up is all."

Christine beheld the frightened woman's face as she stared at the stern countenance of the officer. She decided to ask a question of her own. "Do you suspect Tommy of something?"

"We'll fill you in downtown, Miss Finder. Since you're helping with this case and you supplied ..."

Christine interrupted. "I'll be at your office as soon as I can get there. Is that okay?" She turned toward Teresa. "It'll be okay. Be truthful. Do you have a lawyer?"

Chapter Forty-Eight

"What happened?" Jeremy was the first one to speak as soon as Christine returned to the truck. "I saw the police cruiser, but didn't have time to warn you."

"As you saw, the police arrested Tommy. He went willingly enough once they rousted him out of bed. Teresa was shocked, but she didn't appear as surprised as one would think ... if she truly cared about the man she was hiding her emotions well. I don't understand how that was possible ... unless ..."

"You didn't get a chance to ask your questions? Did you tell her about Nathan?" Jeremy turned the key in the ignition. The truck rumbled to a start and he steered it onto the street. "Where to?"

Christine grabbed her seatbelt. "The sergeant said I could meet him at the station and he'd fill me in." She fidgeted with the seat belt lock, finally got it latched, and turned toward

Jeremy. "I was just about to tell her we'd found Nathan when the sergeant asked her to come downtown with them for some questions. He said he wasn't arresting her, but I suggested she get a lawyer anyway. That creep might implicate her."

"You really don't think she had anything to do with Nathan's abduction? I guess I'm a little less convinced. Where was she when Tommy was selling her son?" Jeremy turned onto the street where the police station was located. "Did you tell the police where Nathan is right now?"

"I did. But yesterday, I obtained a lawyer for him through your dad. A childs advocate lawyer." Her gaze slipped toward the side window and then back at Jeremy. "This way, he'll be represented if it goes to court."

"When did you find time to do all this?" Jeremy appeared impressed. "I know you were busy most of yesterday."

Christine took the time to shift her focus to the back seat where Chief had made himself at home. "I think Chief likes riding in your truck more than my car. More room." She reached behind and patted the dog as much as she could without undoing her seatbelt.

She decided to fill Jeremy in. "I talked to the police, as soon as I left you guys, while you were dealing with Jeremiah's stuff. I paid a visit to Charlie and he called in the sergeant. I wasn't sure when they planned to arrest Tommy so I didn't say anything, but I understood that was the plan. I didn't want Nathan to hear about that just yet. And the coin dealer as well. I hope they arrested him already ... before he can abduct another little boy. As far as arranging for a lawyer for Nathan, a simple phone call did the trick."

Jeremy pulled his truck into the only free visitor slot in the police parking lot. He turned off the engine. Both he and Christine scrutinized the scene in front of them as Tommy was hauled through the back door, closely followed by the sergeant and Teresa. "I need to find a way to tell her that Nathan has been found ... if the sergeant hasn't already told her."

Jeremy stared out the window in Teresa's direction. "She seems a little miffed. I wonder what he said to her. Oh, well. I guess we'll find out. Come on, let's find out what the authorities have for us." He stepped out of the cab of the truck and Christine slid down the other side to the pavement.

She blocked Chief's exit from the back seat. "Stay here, boy. We won't be too long." She closed the door, made sure it locked and led the way into the station. "It's nice when the weather cools down. I can leave Chief in the vehicle for a few moments instead of dragging him everywhere with me."

Inside, she stepped up to the front desk and told the officer in charge who they were and who they wanted to see. Then she took a seat to wait. Jeremy plunked down beside her. "How long have you had a relationship with this Charlie character?"

"I met him when I first moved to town. I thought I'd be able to access the files on my parent's case since I am their daughter, but was soon informed that the case files were not accessible to me. I was too involved they said. Duh. Anyway, after that I purposed to get close to an officer who could access them and ... "

"Charlie fills you in on what's going on so you give Charlie the information you've discovered in your cases, too." Jeremy lowered his voice when he noticed a few more officers walk through the front door. "Sounds like a good working arrangement to me. I have someone in the RCMP who can access police records and traffic data bases, too, as well as other things. It pays to have a relationship with someone in the cop shop when you're a PI."

Christine looked toward the floor. "Charlie's a good friend too. Not just someone I use to get information. He and I have gone out a couple of times, but only as friends. He's a good man. I trust him."

"And there're not many men who you trust, I take it?" Jeremy reached toward her, but then pulled his hand back.

Christine noticed. "I'm cautious, that's all, especially now that I'm back in Canada. With this killer on the loose, I have no other choice." She slipped her gaze over the heads of officers and visitors nearby to see if the sergeant was coming yet. "They're sure taking their time. I wonder if we should rattle some cages ... squeaky wheels and all that."

"Probably couldn't hurt." Jeremy stepped toward the visitor's desk. But he was saved from saying anything when he noticed a tall, rough-around-the-edges officer head their way. He motioned for Christine to join him.

Christine smiled a greeting at the sergeant who'd been at Teresa Brent's home. "I guess you've secured Tommy already. Sergeant, this is my business associate, Jeremy Goodman. Jeremy, this is Sergeant ..."

Jeremy extended his hand toward the man in uniform. "Sergeant Irving I'm familiar with. We go back a ways, don't we Bill? We've worked a few cases in tandem over the years." Christine's eyebrows lifted with this disclosure.

The larger hand belonging to Sergeant Irving enveloped Jeremy's. "Jeremy's helped a few times. Right now, we need to figure out who's involved in the abduction of this kid." He motioned for the two to follow him toward the back of the room and down a long hallway. They passed a couple of interrogation rooms.

Christine tried to peer inside to see where Teresa was, but there was no viewing access from the hall. "Where's Teresa Brent? I need to tell her Nathan has been found."

The sergeant glanced in her direction. "I figured you'd want to be the one to tell her. She's in the room on the right back there. Tommy is across the hall. I'll let you see her as soon as we ..." He pointed at the three of them. "... complete our conversation." He opened the door to another small room, similar to the others they'd passed.

Christine followed Jeremy inside. Jeremy settled himself in a chair as if he'd done this before. He probably had. "Did you find anything to prove that Nathan's story is true?" Christine took the chair beside Jeremy.

The sergeant walked over to the mirror on the wall and then moved back to the only other chair available. "Tommy is good for this. We just have to get all our ducks in a row. Did Nathan understand what was going on between the coin dealer and Tommy?"

Jeremy stared at the sergeant. "Bill, the kid's been hurt. Badly. He doesn't like to talk about what happened, but with the right person asking the questions, I'm sure he can fill in the details. Whether he fully understands or not ... that remains to be seen. He is only four years old, after all."

"Where's the boy now?"

Christine placed her hands on the table separating them from Sergeant Irving. "We have him in a safe place for now. When I tell Teresa we found her son, she's probably not gonna like the idea we're keeping him away from her. Until we can assure Nathan he'll be safe, he doesn't even want to go home."

"We could get child protective services involved to make sure." Sergeant Irving liked to follow procedure to the letter it seemed.

"He's been through enough already and he's developed an attachment to Jeremiah Burton, the man who found him. Nathan doesn't need any more traumas in his life right now and tearing him away from Jeremiah would be traumatic, I think." Jeremy looked toward Christine.

Christine nodded in agreement. "Besides, as long as he feels safe, and he does, he'll be more likely to tell his story when the time comes. He's told us Tommy took him out of his window and received money from the coin dealer when he handed him over."

The sergeant shook his head. "Tommy Devine is some piece of work. For what purpose, do ya think, besides the money?"

Christine piped up. "I think Fine and Tommy are in business together. I don't know what, but I was going to go by the place later today to snoop around some more. There's a gang connection, I think, too."

For the next few minutes, Christine filled the sergeant in on her suspicions. "I've already told Charlie most of this, but everything is still so sketchy. Is it okay if I talk to Teresa now?"

"Sure. Jeremy and I need to clear up some other unfinished business." He glanced at the younger man. "I'll be right back." He opened the door and stood back to allow Christine to go ahead of him. "Christine, there'll be someone listening to your conversation with Teresa Brent. We haven't ruled her out yet."

They walked slowly down the hall toward the room he'd indicated. Christine glanced in the tall man's direction. "You don't really seriously think she had anything to do with her son's kidnapping, do you? The woman was overwrought when she contacted me. She wanted her son found. I'd stake my reputation on it."

Chapter Forty Nine

Sergeant Irving escorted Christine to the first interrogation room where Teresa Brent had been left cooling her heels. The irate woman stood as soon as the door opened. Visible relief washed over her face. "Oh, Christine. Thank goodness. These guys ..."

"Hush. Everything's okay Teresa. There are some unanswered questions to clear up." She turned towards the sergeant. "Thanks. I'll let you know when we're finished."

Teresa's face reflected confusion. Christine watched her face change from relief to caution as she took a chair across from the woman. "Let's get comfortable. Do you want some coffee or something?"

"Are you working for the police now? These questions they keep talking about, you gonna be the one asking?" Teresa ignored Christine's attempt to help her relax.

"No. I'm not working for the police. I work for you. And Teresa, we found Nathan." Christine couldn't help her feelings of justification when she saw the obvious relief bring tears to the other woman's eyes.

"You found my boy. Where is he? Is he alright?" Questions tumbled all over themselves. "Where'd you find him?"

"Whoa. One question at a time. Are you sure you don't want some coffee?"

"Sure. Coffee's good. Black."

Christine glanced at the mirror on the wall and nodded. "The coffee will be here right away. Now, first off he's fine. A little scared but outwardly in good shape. I think a good counselor will be needed and a medical exam to fully understand what he's been through, but otherwise he appears okay. He's staying with the man who found him."

Teresa slapped her hands on the metal table. "He's with a stranger, another man. Maybe he's the man who took my boy. How do you know he's safe? When can he come home?"

The door opened and a young policeman entered with two cups of steaming black brew. Christine sniffed and stared at the liquid in her cup. "I'll bet a spoon would melt in this stuff. Should help keep us awake, as if we needed that at this time of day. Thanks anyway." She chuckled. Then she shifted her gaze to Teresa. "The man was in a nursing home the night your boy was abducted and besides Nathan has told us how he was taken. Tommy ..."

"Tommy had nothing to do with the abduction. He couldn't. He wants nothing to do with the kids, but he'd never hurt them." Teresa's voice had risen to a high pitch. Christine watched as her white fingers gripped the cup of coffee as if the ceramic mug was held in a vice.

She patted the table in front of Teresa. "Stay calm, Teresa. You need to listen." Christine proceeded to tell Teresa what Nathan had told them. She watched the face of the other woman crumple as tears formed in her eyes. Teresa didn't utter a word until Christine had finished.

"My poor boy. Oh, my poor boy." She rocked back and forth in the chair she sat in, her hands holding both sides of her head as if she thought she might disintegrate where she sat. Then the wailing began. Teresa's pain was palpable and something anyone watching could not deny.

Christine's eyes glistened with empathy for the distraught woman. "Teresa, like I said. He's okay, but for now, he can't come home until we're sure Tommy will not be able to hurt him again. The police are holding him for now, but if we don't get more evidence to substantiate Nathan's story, it's just his word against Tommy's. Do you know of a man who collects coins that Tommy had any dealings with?"

"No-o-o. I would have told you when you found the coin. Tommy goes out at night and I never know when he's coming home, but I never met any of the people he hangs with. Oh-h-h, I've been so stupid. I put my kids in danger." She swiped her sleeve across her nose and reached for a tissue from the box in the center of the table. Teresa took a long sip of hot coffee.

Christine sat still for a moment. She also dabbed at her eyes with a tissue. "Teresa, how long have you known Tommy?"

"I met him two years ago ... at the bowling alley where I sometimes help out when they have a party to cater. He was with a bunch of guys, but they didn't bowl. He was just there for the party, I thought. Anyway, we hit it off. I get lonely sometimes." She hung her head. "I think I need to move out of the city, find myself a decent job so I won't be so alone all the time. Then my kids ... " Her tears started all over again.

"Teresa. Here's another tissue. Why would Tommy sell Nathan? Was he hard up for cash?"

"No. Not that I know of. The bills got paid and there was always a little money left over at the end of the month. I thought we were doing okay. But if I was wrong about Tommy, I may be wrong about a lot of things." She turned tear-filled eyes toward Christine. "You keep my boy away from us, you hear. I don't want him hurt no more. Oh-h-h. What about Darcy? I gotta protect her."

"Do you have someplace else you can go until this is all over?"

Teresa glanced at her watch. Her agitation evoked distress immediately. "I gotta go. Darcy's getting home early today from school. Where's that sergeant. I need to go get her." Teresa stood and moved frantically toward the door. "Let me outta here. My girl needs me." She raised a fist to pound on the door, but the lock clicked open before she hit the heavy metal barrier.

A police woman of indeterminate age walked through the door and quickly closed it behind her. "Calm down, Mrs. Brent. I sent a police officer over to your daughter's school. They'll bring her here to the station. Is that okay?"

"Yeah. I guess so." She gazed from the officer to Christine. "How much longer do I have to be here?"

Christine stared pointedly toward the officer waiting for an answer. They were met with a wall of silence.

Chapter Fifty.

    Jeremy filled Sergeant Irving in on his discovery of the whereabouts of Jeremiah Burton. "The daughter had the characteristic of an abuser, right from the start. She was obviously used to being in control. She had made sure she had access to all her father's assets long before she even placed him in the home and, of course, at the time, he was so distraught over his wife's death, he let her. Complete trust."

    The sergeant folded his hands on the table. "I remember when my father-in-law moved in with us. It took a while to adjust, but my wife and I would never treat him harshly. The kids enjoy a great relationship with their grandpa. He has enriched their lives, as well as ours, so much. I can't imagine someone treating an older person with so much disrespect. But I see the abuse all the time."

    "Do you think elder abuse is on the rise?" Jeremy finished the coffee the sergeant had brought back with him when he'd taken Christine to see Teresa. "I wanted to hit the woman."

    "I understand, believe me. The stories make you so

mad. These seniors sacrificed their whole lives to make sure their kids access all the advantages they never had and that's the thanks they get. I wonder if there are more cases because people are living longer. Statistics say the new middle age is sixty to seventy years old. People that age used to be at death's door and now ..."

"I know. My dad is in his late fifties and still hangglides or scuba dives whenever he can. No rocking chair for that man. I hope I'll still be riding a motorcycle long after I retire and I am acquainted with some guys who actually do. Being a senior is a state of mind, I guess." Jeremy stood. "I think I'd better go see how Chief is doing."

"Who's Chief?" Bill Irving stepped around the table to lead the way to the locked door. As he reached the metal barrier, the lock was opened from the outside.

Jeremy walked through ahead of the sergeant. "Christine uses a service dog proficient in tracking to find missing kids. That's what she does. By the way, her name is now Smith. Christine Smith. Are you familiar with her story?"

The stockier man walked beside Jeremy to the front of the building. "Yeah, a little. Charlie told me some of the details. Isn't Rompart her real name? I thought Finder was her cover."

"No, Finder was the name of the cousins who raised her in Texas. A murder was committed at the Finder ranch recently and a picture of Christine as a young girl found near the body. It looks as if they've trailed her here, too, considering that attempt on her life last night. You hear about the incident at her parents' house?"

"Yeah I did. But I don't think there's any proof that the sniper attack was anything other than a scare tactic. No one was hurt, were they?" The sergeant thanked the officer who had released them from the locked room. He glanced back at Jeremy. "So Smith it is. I'll make sure the paperwork says as much. What do you have to do with all this?" Bill Irving had been with the force long enough to remember the Romparts' murder was a cold case.

"I've been hired by Conrad Finder to protect Christine. Right now, she's moved into my extra office space and we've changed her name. She also enhanced her security at the house, but she's not necessarily any safer than she was before. We need to catch this guy, Bill. He's out there. He wants her dead. She's the only one who can identify him. Although, the time frame says his looks are changed. I'm sure." Jeremy moved toward the door leading to the outside. "I'll be back as soon as I walk Chief a little. Don't want any accidents in my truck."

"Bring him back inside with you. I love those dogs. They're so intelligent." Sergeant Irving waved and moved back toward the interrogation rooms.

Chapter Fifty-One

The weather's getting colder. He pulled the toque over his ears and shrugged more deeply inside the collar of his coat. He imagined his breath float upward. His bones ached. *It's her fault.* He'd never been known to take responsibility for his actions.

The sky was clear which made it all the colder. Last night he'd seen lots of stars, as much as you could see with street lights blocking the view. He rubbed his hands together. *I need a fix.* He watched the house across the street. The boy hadn't returned. The mother had left with the police as had Tommy. He chuckled. That dude was in handcuffs. *Serves him right.*

I need to get that kid back. He walked a few steps toward the city center and then turned and walked back. *I wonder where they stashed the kid. If he's not here, then maybe the police found him. I suppose I need to watch the cop shop instead of the kid's home.* He scratched his arm for the hundredth time since his vigil began. Blood surfaced, but he kept scratching.

He leaned against the brick wall in the alley way. There was a time. He remembered growing up on the farm, going out at night and seeing so many stars that the sky was hidden behind them, it seemed. They seemed close enough to touch. This place smelled. The odors in the country always seemed cleaner somehow, even the smell of manure. *Should definitely go home.*

He decided to figure out what he could find near the police station. Perhaps someone saw something. *Gotta get that kid back. Fine won't give me what I crave if I don't give him what he needs, the pervert.*

He began the long trek to the large gray brick building, one he usually avoided. His eyes scanned the people he passed. He hoped to find another street kid who might know something. They all kept their ears and their eyes open, but they also kept their mouths shut ... most of the time.

He passed a couple of restaurants, but ... no money. He shrugged. *Clothes too dirty for them places anyway.* He placed one foot in front of the other. His head was down most of the time, but he scanned passersby and listened through the knit cap, keeping his vigilance to himself. Every now and then, he'd spot another junkie, hanging out, waiting for a fix ... just like him.

Home life had not been good, so he'd been told since Fine had taken him. Fine had used him as a slave, making him work for his room and board, more so after he'd become too old to please the man any other way. *Always work to do. Shoveling snow in the winter, mowing lawns in the summer. Not my scene.* He'd tried to leave, but he always went back. *Now he just uses me to find more boys.* Life on the street was dangerous. Drugs, prostitution, and perverts. Hunger and stale beer didn't go together. They sure didn't keep a person warm in the winter. Fine was all he had. *Gotta find the kid.*

He brushed shoulders with a large teenager as soon as he rounded the corner near the police station. A couple of blocks down the street, he spotted the cruisers lined up along the sidewalk. The dude beside him elbowed him. "Whatcha doin' down here?"

"Nothin'. You been watchin' the cop shop long?" He hoped the other man had some useful info. He lifted his eyes to study the other's face. It was a good way to know if he was telling the truth or not. Junkies are poor liars.

"Naw. Just watched a friend of mine get hauled in, though. What're the cops lookin' for, I wonder." He sniffed and raised his arm to wipe his nose. A droplet of fluid remained on the end. He sniffed again.

"Gotta go. See ya round." He continued his trek toward the police building.

"Hey. You score?" The young man hollered after him, but he ignored him as was expected. That was not the information one shared with anyone on the street.

He found a space between two houses located across the street and ducked inside. He leaned against the wall of one building, stuck his hands in his pockets and prepared to wait. That's when he saw the dog.

The dude, a big guy, was walking the animal into the cop shop. *That's her dog. What's he doing with her dog? Bet she's inside, helping the cops. She's one nosey broad.* He swiped his sleeve across his face and groaned. His arm hurt where he'd scratched it. It felt as if thousands of bugs were burrowing under his skin, and following his veins inside his body. He shuddered. *I need a fix.* He'd coax Crow to give him something.

He decided to find the boys, his gang. *I'll be back, see what's going on. I'll get that kid back.* He trudged back the way he'd come, careful to avoid the dude who'd run into him before. He scurried like a rat toward Portage Avenue and the abandoned building he called home when he wasn't running errands for Fine.

Chapter Fifty-Two

Jeremy approached Bill Irving just as the man was leaving one of the interrogation rooms. Bill reached down and scratched Chief behind the ears, but the dog's menacing growl forced him to snatch his hand back with lightning speed. "What's with him? I like dogs and they usually like me."

Jeremy chuckled. "He's focused on finding Christine. He's in work mode. She's warned me I shouldn't treat him like a pet, but he likes me." He chuckled again. "He even rests his head in my lap from time to time. Makes Christine crazy." He smirked. "I guess I have the touch."

Sergeant Irving scowled. "Well, I told Christine she could take Teresa Brent home. The woman had no idea the scum she was living with was such a deadbeat. She had nothing to offer up either, so we're no further ahead in getting the evidence we need to put this guy away for a long time."

Jeremy shrugged. He thought about what he and Christine had talked about. This man never was trustworthy and they intended to prove it. "Christine and I plan to stake out the coin dealer again. What would happen if you let Devine go and we followed him for a couple of days? See what we find out."

Sergeant Bill pursed his lips in thought. He squinted his eyes in Jeremy's direction. "Are you serious? That could be dangerous. I think this guy is connected."

"Do you have the personnel to go after him?" Jeremy shifted his weight from one leg to another and struggled to hang on to Chief when Christine walked out of the small room down the hall. He decided to release the dog, leash and all. "Bill, we can do this. We use a means of protection and with the two of us, we could come up with some real evidence."

"Okay, Okay. I don't wanna know. Just remember. I need a trail of evidence to hold up in court. When you think you've found something, call us and we'll take it from there." He watched Christine bend down and give her dog a hug. "Not a pet, huh? Appears to be just that."

Jeremy waited while Christine ushered Teresa toward them. He smiled toward her and then held out his hand toward Teresa. "I'm Jeremy Goodman. Christine's associate. You have one cute kid."

"You've seen Nathan, too?" Teresa shook her head. "I don't wanna know where he is. You promise me, you'll keep him safe." She glanced from Jeremy to Christine and back again. "What happens to Darcy? Will the officer bring her home now, instead of here?"

"We'll make sure that happens and we will certainly keep Nathan safe. Now let's get you home. At least Tommy won't be bothering you anytime soon." Christine began to walk with Teresa toward the front of the office.

Jeremy cleared his throat. "Um-m. That's not entirely true. The police plan to let Tommy go ... in a while ... closer to nighttime. We," He glanced at Christine and made a motion with his hands to include her. "You and I will follow him and find out what he's up to." He shifted his gaze toward Teresa. "Is there a safe place you could take your daughter for a few days?"

Teresa looked a little confused. "Do you mean you're going to let the man who sold my boy out of jail, to go free? How can you do that?" Her voice grew louder on the last words, enough for a few people to check her out.

"Sh-h-h. We don't want word to get out." Bill Irving gazed around the room and smiled reassuringly toward the other officers nearby. "We haven't uncovered enough evidence to hold him. Jeremy has agreed to find that evidence for us. We need to see what his connection to Fine is and we need to know what Fine is really into ... besides being a pervert."

Teresa held her hand over her heart. "I don't want my boy in any danger. Is that understood?" She regarded each face in front of her with a stern countenance. When she saw their nods of agreement, she continued. "An aunt lives in Brandon. Darce and I will go there until you call, Christine." She straightened her body in an attempt to show strength for the decision. "You do what you need to in order to make my Nathan safe again. Put that scum behind bars."

Christine watched the faces of Jeremy and the police officer. Obviously they believed Teresa. *That fact will go a long way in making sure Nathan is returned to her when this is all over.* She smiled in Teresa's direction. "Okay, let's find Darcy. Sergeant, you did say someone picked her up from school. Where is she?"

He pointed toward the large room where most of the cop's desks were located. Sitting in a chair near one of them was a little girl with a pink ribbon in her hair and a pink jacket over very pink pants. Christine chuckled. "I take it her favorite color is pink."

Teresa grinned. "Ever since she was old enough to make a decision about the clothes she wants to wear, it's been nothing but pink. Her bedroom looks like a pink bomb exploded in it." She rushed toward her daughter.

Christine watched the mother hug Darcy. "The woman deserves better than she's gotten. Perhaps when this is all over, we can find her a decent job so she can be home when her kids are home, but working when they're at school. Maybe a work-from-home job." She spoke to no one in particular.

Jeremy responded, "Whoa. Let's concentrate on one thing at a time. First thing is to get her home so she can pack and get out of there. She does own a car, I assume?" Jeremy zig-zagged slowly through the people gathered all over the squad room.

Christine followed and motioned for Teresa to come as well. She held tightly to Chief's leash and cautioned a few people to keep their hands to themselves. Chief wove his body past legs of all shapes and colors before they reached the cooler air outside.

The small troop headed toward Jeremy's truck, Darcy Brent chattering a mile a minute. It seemed her jaunt in a police car was the highlight of her day. "Mommy, the lady let me talk into the radio ... just a few words ... but someone spoke back to me and she let me press the button for the siren ... but only for a second. It was fun and ..."

Teresa laughed. "Whoa. Hold on there, little girl. Police cars are not fun. If you're bad, they'll arrest you and ..."

Christine peered at Jeremy and then glanced toward the back seat and Teresa. "Do you think it's a good idea to give her the impression the police are bad people? If it weren't for a cop, I might be dead. It was a police officer who made sure I was protected when my parents ... well, you know."

Jeremy nodded his agreement as he turned onto the main street that went past the cop shop. He headed toward the area of town where the Brents lived. "You never know when the police will come in handy. The only people who should be afraid of cops are the bad guys."

"I just don't want her to enjoy being in one of those

cars." Teresa thought for a moment. "Darcy, the police were very kind to us today, weren't they?" Teresa placed her arm around the child.

"I had fun, mommy." She leaned against Chief who was sitting beside her. Her large blue eyes stared at the back of Christine's head. "What's your dog's name?"

Christine turned her body as much as the seatbelt would allow. "His name is Chief. Remember we came to your house when Nathan went missing. Chief tracks ... he sniffs people out with his powerful nose."

The child's face grew solemn. "Oh, right. Nathan. Where is he?"

Teresa smiled. "Nathan is safe. Miss Find ... er ... Smith found him a safe place so no one will hurt him ever again. When our home is safe again, he'll come home. Is that okay?"

Darcy's eyes drifted thoughtfully from one adult to the other. "I-I guess so. Did someone hurt him?"

Teresa gazed at Christine before she answered. Then her eyes landed on her daughter again. "He'll be fine. He's having fun where he is, too."

"Oh. Good." The child reached toward Chief and patted his back. "Hi Chief. You're a good dog."

Teresa relaxed against the back of the seat as Christine turned toward the front again. She glanced at Jeremy and then shifted her gaze out the side window. Buildings whizzed by as Jeremy maneuvered the truck through downtown traffic. It was a sunny day today with clear blue skies. People were shopping and conducting business as if they hadn't a care in the world while her life was in turmoil. *One day.*

Christine leaned her head back against the seat. Life on the ranch had been rather peaceful ... most of the time. *Wish I was back there sometimes. But that thug found the ranch too.*

Chapter Fifty-Three

He trudged through the broken boards that were intended to block access to the building. The musty smell assailed his nostrils, but he'd become so used to the odors he hardly noticed them anymore. Rat droppings scattered beneath his feet as he moved toward the staircase. At least with the colder weather, the flies had disappeared.

The effort to climb the stairs to the second floor took every ounce of strength. He was exhausted from the walk and the lack of food or sleep. But Crow might have something for him. He wanted a fix so bad; he already imagined what it would feel like. His skin continued to crawl, but he stilled his fingers before they could open his wounds again with fresh scratches.

He reached the threadbare carpet that remained attached to the second floor hallway. It was covered in stains, some blood he was sure. He shuffled toward the doorway where they hung out when they were high. He peeked his head around the corner cautiously. *Don't want to alarm anyone. Might get dead that way.*

"Crow, you in there?" He took a step inside. "It's me. Spider. Anyone here?"

"Quit yer hollerin'. I'm over here." The voice came

from the far side of the room, near the doorway to the only working bathroom in the place. "Where ya bin?"

"Aw-w Fine has me lookin' for that kid. He won't give me anything until I find him. You got a hit?" His whining voice carried through the dankness in the dark room. A little light filtered past the cardboard that had been nailed over the only window. Dark was the preferred atmosphere.

Crow cackled, making the sound of a crow. "What's in it for me, I give you a hit?" He stomped his foot and Spider could feel him move closer.

Spider cringed. He knew from experience that the older and more powerfully built man was no match for him. Crow had proved his prowess more than once. Crow's voice sounded as if it was near his right ear. "Got something to trade?" he hissed.

Spider took a couple of steps back hoping to put a little distance between them. "I think the kid is staying with that broad, the one we took a bat to her car. The nosey one. We could find where she lives. Tail her and see where she stashed the kid. Maybe steal something worth a lot from her."

"I know where she lives. Been there. Just to warn her, but she could have some good stuff. Nice place, near the park." Crow was silent for a few minutes. Spider assumed he was thinking about the deal. "I have some stuff over here. You get straight and then, you and me go to her house and see what's what."

Spider slunk over to the part of the room Crow had staked out as his. He eased his body down on the thin mattress waiting for the larger boy to give him the stuff he needed. The crawling on his skin was driving him nuts. He couldn't think straight, but soon.

"Where you got veins?" Spider could just make out the syringe Crow held out to him. Crow was stronger. Never used the stuff he provided to everyone else ... for a price. "I'll do it."

Crow expertly inserted the needle into the vein that popped up on Spiders arm once the tourniquet was tied tight.

Spider relaxed back against the wall, waiting for the drug to take effect. He closed his eyes. His skin stopped hurting almost immediately and the euphoria he would sell his soul for, came over him in waves. He heard everything, but he didn't want to respond to the world around him. His face broke into a smile of sorts. His body floated and the urine smell emanating from his clothing evaporated. This was heaven.

Chapter Fifty-Four

Franny offered Jeremiah and his young guest a cookie from the plate she held in her hand. "You boys like the house?"

Jeremiah smiled in her direction. "You were right, Franny. The place is perfect. At least until I get my own place back. The furniture is nothing to write home about, but those pieces will serve the purpose for now, won't they, Nathan?" He leaned a shoulder closer to the little boy.

The child had gobbled up one cookie and reached for another before Franny could set them on the coffee table. He mumbled though his mouthful of cookie and shook his head.

Jeremiah placed an arm around his small charge. "Nathan is going to be my houseguest for a while. When do you think the house will be ready for occupancy?"

Franny took a sip from the teacup she held. "I believe it's available right now. All you need is the first and last month's rent and you can move in. At least, I think so. Do you want to talk to the owner?"

Jeremiah thought for a minute. "I'll need to visit with my lawyer to determine how much of my funds are accessible. In the meantime, it couldn't hurt to talk to the landlord. What da ya think, Nathan?"

The boy nodded again, his mouth still full of cookie. Jeremiah saw him swallow and then run his tongue over his teeth. "Will my mommy be able to come visit?"

Franny glanced at Jeremiah when the older man's face turned serious. "I don't know, young man. We'll wait until Christine and Jeremy get back ... see what they found out when they went to visit your mom." Jeremiah had filled Franny in as soon as they'd arrived at her house. "Franny, do you have any toys a big boy like Nathan might enjoy?"

"As a matter of fact ..." She walked behind the large reclining sofa and pulled a wicker basket from its hiding place. "Here, take a peek. Notice anything of interest?" The adults chuckled as Nathan wiped his hands on his pants after swiping the milk mustache from his mouth with the back of his arm. "I guess I should provide a napkin next time, eh Nathan." Franny giggled.

The boy began to rummage through the toys Franny supplied. The grown-ups leaned back in their respective chairs to keep an eye on his progress. Jeremiah gazed toward Franny. "Thanks for all the help, old girl. I don't know what I'd do without you."

Franny lifted a hand to shoo away his declaration. "I can't stand to sit back and watch someone being taken advantage of and your daughter was surely doing that. Did your lawyer say what would happen to her?"

Jeremiah scrunched his face up as if he still hadn't figured everything out yet. "The funny thing is, she gave up instead of going to court. Turned over the bank accounts, everything. Now all we have to figure out is how to undo some of the choices she made with my investments and get the house back ... if I can. Mr. Goodman ... he's my lawyer... says if the sale was legal, I may not have a leg to stand on."

"That seems so unfair. Can't you still go after her for elder abuse? She did break the law." Franny clenched her fists, outrage clearly visible in her body language.

"Forgiveness is a good thing." Jeremiah hung his head and then he gazed intently at Franny. "I don't want pay back. Revenge is mine saith the Lord. I only want what's mine." His sad eyes turned down at the corners, the wrinkles gathering speed across his face as he spoke. "I desire a relationship with the woman one day. She's my only family."

"I don't believe it. How can you forgive her after all she's done to you? She's certainly luckier than she deserves." Franny stood as soon as the door bell sounded and moved toward the front of the house. "Must be your friends."

Jeremiah hadn't heard the doorbell. He leaned back and waited for Jeremy and Christine to enter. He knew Jeremy understood why it was important to forgive, but the two women in the room didn't. He hoped to one day be able to share his faith with Franny. Living a few doors down from her would ensure they ran into each other often. *Maybe more than I'll want.* He chuckled. *That's Franny.* "Hi, you guys. You're back earlier than I expected." His eyes shifted from Jeremy to Christine. "Got everything done you wanted to?"

Casting a furtive glance toward Nathan, Jeremy chose to ignore the question. He introduced Christine to Franny instead. "How did the house hunting go?" He waited for Franny's answer rather than Jeremiah's.

Franny grinned. "I think we've rented a house. It'll be fun having Jeremiah close again." She winked at the older man and observed the color rise up past his collar. "Oh boy. I gotcha there." Her laughter floated through the room.

"Franny makes all the old folks at the home laugh ... at least, that's what Randall Levey said." Jeremy grinned. His gaze landed on Jeremiah. The senior smirked.

"You young people just keep your ideas to yourself. Franny and I are friends, right Franny?" He squirmed a little in his seat and the adults burst into a gale of laughter.

Jeremy added, "Couldn't hurt." He laughed some more when a look of consternation passed over Jeremiah's face.

Let's get this show on the road." Jeremiah decided to change the subject ... fast. "I need to see your dad. Right away. Is there time?"

"We'll make a point of it." Jeremy ran his hand down the older gentleman's arm. "So ... the house will work for you until Dad can figure out how to retrieve yours?"

"I was asking Jeremiah the same thing. I can't believe he may not get his house back. That woman ..." Franny stopped when exasperation flitted across Jeremiah's face. "I know. You may have forgiven her, but I haven't." She placed her hands on her hips and glared at her guests. "Surely something can be done to see that she pays for abusing her father."

Christine decided to add her two cents. "If Jeremiah was my client, I'd make sure he'd never have to see the woman again." She looked toward Nathan. "But since my obligation is to that little boy over there, I have more control over his situation than Jeremiah's."

Franny nodded in Christine's direction. "At least someone besides me thinks the woman should pay for what she did."

"Franny." Jeremiah had clearly had enough. "Give it a rest. I told you I wanted a relationship with her one day. I meant it. Forgiveness is important, not only for her, but for me too. Since none of this affects you, you need to leave the decision about Amanda to me."

Franny's eyes grew glassy. She turned her body toward the door, an attempt to hide the affect his words had on her. She drew in a deep breath and faced the room again. "I was just trying to help. You're a friend. I hate it when someone takes advantage of another person. But I'll butt out."

Jeremy glanced toward Christine and his eyes landed on Jeremiah. "I think Jeremiah needs to feel as if he has some control over his life after losing so much these last few years. Right, Jeremiah?"

"I do." He studied Franny's body language for a few seconds. Contritely, he took the couple of steps needed to reach her side, and placed an arm around her shoulders. "I'm sorry. I didn't mean to snap. But ... " He bowed his head, lines of remorse where a grin was a few minutes ago. His blue eyes stared straight into hers. "I'm sorry. Jeremy's right. I shouldn't have taken my frustration out on you."

Christine piped up, "We're all tired. I think we need to leave the meeting with Barkley until tomorrow. Let's go home, relax and watch a little TV instead of trying to solve the world's problems all at once." She glanced toward Nathan. The boy seemed to be having a good time with the toy box. "Nathan, ready to leave?"

His large brown eyes stared at her for a second and then he resumed playing with the toys. Without lifting his head again, he asked, "Tommy going to be at my house?"

Christine walked swiftly to his side. "Oh, no, Nathan. When I said let's go home, I didn't mean your house. I meant mine, okay?"

The child shuffled a few Legos from one spot to another. "Is my mom okay?" He glanced from one adult to another, waiting for someone to speak.

Christine slipped her eyes toward Jeremy. She shrugged her shoulders as if to ask how much she should tell him. She decided to give Nathan the condensed version. "The police had Tommy in custody, but there isn't enough evidence to hold him ... yet. So your mom agrees you have to stay away from her until things are settled. She'll drive over for a visit in a day or two ... with Darcy. Is that alright?"

"Yeah, I guess so. Does she want me to come to live

with her again ... later?"

"Nathan, your mother was so happy to know you're safe. She loves you. I am certain of that. Jeremy thinks so, too. Right Jeremy?" Christine began to pick up some of the toys and place them back in the toy box.

Franny scooted down beside her and smiled at the little boy. "You are welcome to come visit anytime."

Nathan sniffed and brushed a hand across his nose. "I'm glad. Do the police believe me? That man said they wouldn't."

Christine scowled. "They do, but they need more information, evidence or proof, to back up your story. That's where Jeremy and I come in. We'll get the proof they want and then ... well, you'll be safe to go home."

Jeremiah and Jeremy moved to the front door. "Christine, why don't I drop you and Nathan at your house while I take Jeremiah to visit Dad." He glanced toward the older man, "You need money for a deposit on your house, I'll bet."

Jeremiah stopped midstride. "I do. But can your father free up some of my funds so quickly?"

"If he can't, there's a contingency fund at my office for such a time as this. Come on troops. Let's go." He herded Christine and Nathan out the door. "Thanks Franny. Things will settle down, you'll see."

Franny waved as the three adults and the child joined Chief in the truck. Childish squeals of delight filtered through the late afternoon shadows toward the woman who wanted nothing more than to put her feet up. Christine gazed out the side window as the gray head disappeared inside. "That was nice of Franny to find you a place, Jeremiah. I know it's not the one you owned, but it sounds like this place will do until Barkley can get your home back."

"Franny's nice enough. I ..." Just as he was about to say more a phone rang from its perch on Jeremy's hip.

Jeremy flipped the device open and spied the caller ID. "Hi Dad." Christine continued her perusal of the outside as they drove the short distance to her house.

Chapter Fifty-Five

Christine's stomach rumbled. It had been a long time since she'd made mac and cheese, but she assumed any little boy would enjoy the treat. She thought about the day's activities as she checked on the boiling pasta. The police kept Tommy overnight but when they released him that morning, she and Jeremy had been ready to follow.

She shook her head. *That was a waste of time.* Tommy returned to the motel he'd been staying in since Teresa kicked him out the second time. They'd parked themselves down the street with a good view of the room's door, but Tommy had remained inside. She snagged one noodle to test for doneness and peered out her kitchen window. Night shadows crept across her back yard. *The days are getting shorter.* She listened for the sound of movement from her living room. All was quiet except for the chipmunk voices coming from her television.

They'd hoped to catch Tommy with some incriminating evidence but ... *I guess it'll take longer than we thought.* She drained the pasta. With the milk carton poised over the empty pot, the alarm sounded as if every emergency siren in town had gone off at once. She rushed into the living room. Her fingers itched to punch in the numbers to quiet the alarm, but she remembered the instructions from the security company to make sure it was a false alarm before turning it off.

"Nathan, did you try to go outside?"

"No, I been watching the chipmunks. They're funny." He pointed toward Chief. "Chief been growling ... a lot."

Christine watched the dog as he stood at the front door. The hair along the back of his neck stood on end. "You hear something boy?" She walked to the peep hole in her front door. The screeching hurt her ears.

The telephone jangled twice. Before she could get to it, the ringing stopped. She picked the handset up and listened. *Nothing. Not even a dial tone.*

Christine walked back to the peep hole and peered outside. She could see no one near her door. She marched with purpose toward her bedroom, not wanting to scare the child. He had his hands over his ears, but was still trying hard to hear the television.

She extracted her weapons from inside her night table, selecting the spray can first. She gave a cursory glance at the instructions on the bear spray. She charged back to the main room, slowing only when she was in sight of Nathan. She glanced at the living room window. *They had to be locked in order for the alarm to work. I wonder if someone set off the new yard alarm. The mugger may have returned and tried to get into the house.* She decided to check all the windows and doors, just in case. *I hope the alarm company sent someone to check on us.*

Christine turned off all the lights. She sat with Nathan for a few minutes explaining why the alarm had sounded. "Someone outside may want to steal stuff from the house. You need to stay down on the floor, away from windows, while I check things out." She gripped the can of spray so tightly her hands began to ache.

Nathan whimpered. "I'm scared. Maybe that creep has found us." He slid closer to the sofa and tried to shimmy underneath the base. The sofa, however, was built too close to the floor. Christine watched as the small boy tried to make himself invisible. She wrapped her arms over his body in an effort to comfort him, but she knew she had to be proactive. The alarm coursed through her ears in a manner meant to distract.

Crawling toward the kitchen, she decided to begin to check the windows and doors in that room first. As she entered, the shadow of a short man made its way across her kitchen window above the sink. His masked face rested against the pane of glass in an attempt to peer inside. *Ski mask, eh? Could be the guy who assaulted me the other morning.* A second figure materialized behind the first one.

Christine willed her neighbors to be home. *Surely, someone would come to see what's going on.* Her eyes followed the men as they went past the window. *I guess they figured these windows are locked. They didn't even try to open them. I'd better get back into the living room and check those windows.*

She scurried on all fours back to the living room. Chief pranced, sniffing the air, but he remained beside Nathan. He obviously wanted to protect the frightened child. "Good boy." Christine whispered.

"Are they gonna get us?" Nathan had streaks of tears running down his cheeks.

"Not if I can help it." She brandished the bear spray. "This'll stop them. They won't be able to see anything when I spray it in their eyes." The window on the side of the house nearest the living room rattled. *Those guys are pretty confident the alarm isn't going to alert anyone. They're not even attempting to disconnect the wires. Or maybe they're searching for a way to cut the connections.*

She scooted toward the last window in the room and rose up a little to inspect the latch. Her eyes spotted it, securely locked in place, but then she ducked back down just as one of the shadows approached from the other side. *That was close. Maybe they'll think we're not home.*

She rolled her body back toward Nathan. "Someone will come help us." She spoke to the boy with more confidence than she felt. *If anyone was coming, surely they'd have been here by now.* She also knew the perpetrators had probably seen the lights go out so they were aware someone was home. The front door rattled.

Christine wrapped her arms around Nathan. Chief growled and lunged toward the front door. His growl turned into a loud angry bark. Christine had never heard him sound so menacing. The hairs on the back of her neck stood on end. Someone pounded, the sound reminiscent of a battering ram. The door might give way.

The pounding grew even louder. The door shook. "Christine. Are you in there?"

Jeremy? Is that his voice? Christine jumped to her feet. "Stay here, Nathan. Till I am confident we're safe." She walked over to the door and peeked through the tiny hole in the center. "Jeremy, are you there? Someone's trying to break in."

"I know. The police have them in custody. We need you to come out and identify them, if you can." Jeremy rattled the door knob again.

Relief flooded her body. Christine reached for the alarm pad, punched in the appropriate numbers and then unlocked the front door. She peered around the edge, cautiously. Jeremy stood on her front step. His face was not smiling. "It's a good thing the alarm was turned on. A neighbor called the police. I just happened to be talking to Bill Irving on the phone about Tommy Devine when the call came into the police station." He glanced into the living room. "Is Nathan okay? I'll bet he's scared spitless."

Chief inched his way around Christine's body. His low growl turned to a bark of recognition. He pushed Christine aside to get through the door. He acknowledged Jeremy, but continued into the yard toward the cop car sitting at the edge of the driveway. Jeremy and Christine watched as he jumped toward the back door.

Christine raised her voice to command level. "Chief, come. Everything's okay, boy." She looked toward Jeremy. "You think I might recognize these guys?"

"They seem to remember you. At least the one who's doing all the talking said you're the broad ..." He made quote marks with his fingers. "... they chased off with baseball bats. They came to get Nathan back, apparently. Now we have someone in custody who has more information than Nathan. Hopefully the cops can get them talking enough that they'll have the evidence they need to put Tommy and Fine away for a long time." He studied Christine's face. "We might not have to tail Tommy again after all."

She squeezed the bear spray can tighter. "How did they find out where I live? Was it a lucky guess that we had Nathan? I'm not sure I can identify anyone. They wore ski masks the other night too. When I noticed one of them in the kitchen window, I thought he might be the guy who mugged me the other morning. But ... I wonder if the person who took a shot at me the other night is part of this gang, too."

"Man, I don't know how this all ties together yet, but I'll bet there's a connection. Could be the killer you're looking for is not here after all. He may still be in Texas or anywhere for that matter. But we'll not know the whole story until we get these guys talking. Come have a look. See if you can recognize anyone."

Christine walked with Jeremy, keeping his body between her and the police cruiser until she saw the two thugs restrained in the back of the cruiser. An officer opened the back door as soon as she approached close enough to view the interior. She looked at both men, slowly searching one face and then another.

The one closest to the door spit at her and she had to jump back to avoid the spittle. He laughed, a menacing jeer meant as a form of intimidation, she was sure. She stood taller, and looked back at him. "He's one of the thugs who accosted me the first time I went to the coin dealer's shop. A gang of them have nothing better to do, it seems, than hurl insults and intimidate women."

"Yeah, well it worked, didn't it? You got yourself an alarm. Maybe a gun, too, eh?" He threw his shoulder toward her.

The police officer slapped him back into his seat. "What about the other one, miss?"

Christine smiled. "Yeah, that one I recognize as the person Nathan calls the creep. I overheard Fine telling him to get another kid. I guess he decided to get the same one back again. Fine was pretty upset with him."

The second thug hung his head. "I didn't want ta, but Fine made me."

Jeremy guided Christine back toward the little boy standing in the doorway. Chief blocked his body from going outside. "Good boy, Chief. Nathan you okay?"

"Did the police get the bad guys?"

"Yes, they did and before they could figure out a way into my house. The alarm worked even though the alarm company couldn't call me." She looked toward Jeremy. "They must have cut the phone line. It rang twice and then went dead. I'll have to get the phone company out here tomorrow. Imagine, I was so busy trying to figure out how to protect us, I forgot to use my cell phone to call the security company. I'd better make the call now."

She crossed her arms over her chest and walked inside with Jeremy close behind. "Where's Jeremiah?"

"He's with Dad. I thought it better to leave him there until I could check out what was happening here." Jeremy sat down on the edge of the sofa. "Smells like supper. Thought you didn't cook." He chuckled.

Christine made a face at him as she listened to a person answer the phone at the security company. "Hi. I'm Christine Smith. My alarm went off and my phone went dead. The police are here and they have the culprits. Thought I'd let you know." She listened to some more instructions and hung up. "They want me to call them as soon as the phone is fixed." She shook her head as if to clear it. "My ears are still ringing."

"The noise hurt my ears, too," Nathan said as he moved back toward the television. "Aw-w-w. The chipmunks is over."

Jeremy chuckled. "I'm sure Miss Smith can find you another show. Christine, will you be okay now. I'm going back to get Jeremiah and after we've had something to eat, I'll bring him back here. Will that work for you?"

"Yeah. I was making some mac and cheese for Nathan and I. I can do simple meals as if that's any of your business." She stuck out her tongue at Jeremy to soften her words. "I gave the security company my cell number in case the alarm goes off again before the land line is fixed. We'll be okay. Right, Nathan?"

Nathan shook his head, his eyes the size of small saucers. "Those guys scared me." He looked toward Chief and walked to the dog's side. "Chief protected us."

Christine placed her hands on her hips. "Well. What about me? Didn't I help?" She grinned and then walked Jeremy to the door, not expecting any answer from the boy who was once again engrossed in a TV program.

"You okay?" Jeremy asked.

"Yeah, we'll be fine. See ya later."

Chapter Fifty-Six

Christine sat across from Jeremy at the large conference table in Barkley Goodman's office. The morning had been exhausting for all of them. She glanced toward Jeremiah Burton. "Jeremiah, when do you move into your new house?"

"Considering there's nothing to move, I'll take over the lease today. Jeremy said he'd drive me to the nursing home to pick up my stuff, but clothing is all I have to transport." He gazed at Jeremy. "I want to thank you for loaning me enough to get some dishes and bedding ... and food, of course. Franny said the house comes with all the furniture we saw when we inspected the place. Not lots, but enough. She'll take me shopping after we get the key."

Jeremy chuckled. "I think that woman's taken a liking to you. You'd better watch out or you'll be married again before you know it."

Jeremiah sputtered, a little outraged at the idea. "I got a wife. She may not be with me now, but one day I'll be with her again. Don't need anyone else. No siree." He quickly composed himself and shifted his gaze in Barkley's direction. "You'll let me know when you've figured out how to get my investments and my bank accounts back in my name, won't you?"

Barkley nodded his head and smiled. "I certainly will and I'll work as quickly as I can. Sure you don't want to prosecute Amanda?"

"No, not a good idea. Not if I want to rebuild what we lost. She's my daughter, after all." He placed his hands on the table and folded one over the other. "God devised a plan already and one day, He'll let me in on the secret, but I studied His Word enough to understand what He wants us to do. So ... "

Christine frowned. "I just don't get this God stuff. I appreciate what Jeremy said and the death of my parents doesn't make me mad any more, but ... sometimes I think you all depend on Him too much instead of looking to your own resources."

All three men in the room spoke at once. "Exactly." They laughed and then Jeremy spoke in a solemn tone to Christine. "God created us. He fathoms our complexities better than is possible for us to understand and He discerns our future, something we can't possibly comprehend. So why not rely on Him and trust Him. Besides He loved us enough to die for us. No one else would do that."

Christine shook her head. "There's just too much to take on faith and not enough tangible evidence. Speaking of evidence, that was some turn around in the Brent case. When the kid, Spider, told us his real name, I thought the police were going to throw a party. The authorities have been looking for him for almost twelve years."

Jeremiah stared at Christine with interest. "He's the one whom Nathan calls the creep, right."

He leaned his forearms on the table. "Spider had been kidnapped when he was four years old. His parents never gave up. He's a mess now, but with some therapy ... He may need to serve time for his involvement in the kidnapping of three other little boys over the last five years. He rolled on Fine, though, so his cooperation may help the courts decide in his favor. He's still a juvenile, too.

Christine nodded toward the three men. "Right. He also admitted to shooting at us that day we went to my parents' house. He said he only wanted to scare us, but Fine told him to get rid of us. Apparently, Fine got a little nervous when we showed up in his neighborhood. I think I went a little paranoid for a while, seeing the killer around every corner, especially when we got over there."

"You're entitled. After all, someone did kill one of the ranch hands in Texas and left your picture lying around." Jeremy leaned back in his chair. "You know, maybe he wanted someone to find the picture. Can't imagine why ... other than intimidation."

"Did those guys tie the boyfriend to any of this?" Nathan had a special place in Jeremiah's heart. "I'd hate for the boy to get hurt some more."

"As a matter of fact, Spider identified Tommy as the one who Fine paid for Nathan, thereby corroborating the boy's story. They don't know why yet, but at the rate Spider is spilling his guts, I expect they'll be able to file a lot of information regarding Tommy's activities before the day is out. The police already have enough to put Devine away for a long time." Christine got up, stretched, and helped herself to some cold water. She took a long sip before continuing. "Of course, the outcome depends on the courts, but the Crown Prosecutor is planning on asking that no bail be set, citing Tommy as a flight risk."

Barkley piped up. "I doubt he'll be successful. Tommy's crime is not a capital offense. As much as we'd like him to fry for what he did to Nathan, he never actually hurt the kid physically. Fine did. If he turns on Fine ... they may let him off with a much lighter sentence. But ..." He looked at each face in the room. "... there's the other thing." All three fixed their eyes on him. Barkley hesitated, as if he might keep the rest of the information to himself.

"Come on, Dad. You can't leave us hanging here. What else?" Jeremy fetched some water for himself, Jeremiah and his dad. He sat back down and stared hard at the lawyer in the group.

"Well, I don't have all the facts yet and neither do the RCMP, but ... it seems ..." He looked toward Christine. "Tom Devine is working for someone in your dad's company, apparently. The creep is using the information as a bargaining chip."

"Working how? What can the men who run my father's business dealings possibly have in common with a low-life like Devine?" Christine's incredulous stare swept the room. A similar expression was firmly planted on Jeremy's face. "My dad may have laundered mob money, but did his business partners have any inkling that illegal activities were part of the program? Were they involved?"

"Christine, I wasn't supposed to say anything, but the RCMP have had those guys under investigation for a long time. They never understood the connection between Devine and the company before, that's all." Barkley's face softened a little. "I know you want to meet the men who've kept your dad's company alive but ..."

Christine put her hands on the arm of her chair and pushed herself to a standing position. "As soon as this case with Nathan Brent is over, I want to see those guys and let them know I intend to run my father's holdings ... with their help, of course. Now more than ever."

Jeremy's scowl was a clear indication of his disapproval. "Christine, Dad's right. You need to keep your distance until this is settled. I don't know what their involvement is ..." He glanced at his dad. "... and I don't suppose you're going to tell us, but when the police find out ..." He shifted his gaze to Christine again. "... you don't want to be caught up in any illegal activity."

"No, of course not." She yawned, placing a hand over her mouth. "I didn't get much sleep last night after all our excitement." Her gaze swept the room. "Just when I'm sure I've figured things out, something else crops up. I chase one shadow expecting it to lead somewhere, and another takes its place in an entirely different direction. I want peace in my life and I want my parents' killer caught so I can get on with my life. I can't relax as long as he's free to come after me." She yawned again. "I gotta get home. Jeremy, are you planning on taking Nathan to stay with Jeremiah tonight? He'd be safer someplace other than my house, I think. Just in case."

Jeremy stood and placed a hand on Christine's shoulder. "As long as a killer is on the loose, I intend to earn my pay. Conrad wanted you protected so maybe we need to find you a different address. But, yeah, I'll pick Nathan up. Oh, that's right. I don't have to." He glanced at Jeremiah. "He's already with Franny, remember."

"So that's where you stashed him." Christine giggled. "Jeremiah, you are going to owe her so many meals. She is one spunky lady and so-o-o helpful. Must be love."

"Cut it out. I told you guys ... Oh-h never mind. He's safe at her place, that's all." Jeremiah displayed the grumpiest face he could and grinned mysteriously toward the two youngsters in the group. "One day it'll be payback time. Don't forget what comes around goes around. Or something like that." He left the room humming mysteriously.

Jeremy and Christine crinkled their brows and stared in confusion at each other. "What is he talking about?" Christine was the next one to leave the room. "I'm going home. Tomorrow's another day. I'll be here bright and early. I'm glad this case is done, but we need to clear up the details of my parents' estate, whether I meet those men or not." She opened the front door and walked out into the waning sunlight.

EPILOGUE

Christine stretched, arching her frame toward the warm body at her side. She reached her hand to the soft fur and rolled to cuddle her best friend in her arms. Chief grunted his response, clearly not ready for the day to begin. She chuckled. "Come on, boy. Let's go for a run."

She nudged the large animal off the side of the bed. Chief landed with a thump, a whoosh of air indicating his lungs had connected with the floor. "Good thing it's such a short distance. Come on, get up. Need to run." Christine pranced by the dog's side, reaching her hands toward the ceiling. "Do you know how long it's been since the dream hasn't interrupted my sleep? I feel as if I've slept for three days." She looked out the window. "Such a beautiful day, too."

She skipped toward the hook where she hung her jogging clothes. Whipping her night gear off, she tugged a sweatshirt over her head and stepped into fleece pants. "We'll need to dress warm. It looks like it snowed last night." She added some extra heavy socks to her attire. Chief, although on all fours, stretched his front legs by leaning as far forward as he could without losing his balance and then the dog performed a perfect lunge forward to stretch his back legs. "You been practicing yoga behind my back?"

She started to trot, legs raised high, down the hall. "Maybe we need to pay a visit to Denny's facility for a refresher today." She stopped at the peep hole in her front door. A cursory check indicated no one was about ... at least as far as she could see. She moved toward a sofa table, popped the drawer open, and retrieved her spike. She never left home without it. Then she punched in the code to deactivate her alarm, grabbed her remote for the yard system, and opened the front door. She sighed. Chief nosed past her. "One day, I won't need to be so careful."

Christine stepped out into the crisp morning air. Two weeks had passed since she'd had a client. She wasn't too concerned about it though. *Thanks to mom and dad's legacy, I can be lazy once in a while.* She started down the driveway. Swinging her body around to jog backwards for a few feet, she used the remote to activate the yard alarm. *Just in case.*

Turning forward again, she trotted after Chief who had already reached the park. He was sniffing to his heart's delight, but it was clear from his body language, he knew exactly where she was at all times. *He's more protective now than he was when we began to look for Nathan Brent. I think he's learned something.*

Her mind continued to think about Nathan as they jogged, keeping her pace steady and her breathing deep. When she'd visited Teresa and Nathan yesterday, the boy seemed to be happier than she'd ever seen him. Moving back with his mother finally had been a good thing. She'd wished Teresa the best when she'd said they were making a permanent move to Brandon. "The doctor said getting out of this city will help Nathan recover," Teresa had told her. She'd also wanted Jeremiah's phone number to thank him for caring about a stray child walking the streets.

Christine smiled. *I love it when a plan comes together.* She jogged in place for a few seconds, waiting for Chief to complete his mark on a nearby tree. Tommy was awaiting trial for kidnapping, but the authorities were keeping a close eye on his activities with Fine and his connections to Rompart Industries. Fine also waited in jail for the justice system to prosecute him for sexual abuse, pedophilia, and several other charges. Fine seemed unaccountably calm so the authorities were checking into his connections as well.

Jeremy had recounted to her yesterday what Jeremiah told him about his first visit with Amanda. Christine continued to pump her feet up and down. *He isn't letting any grass grow under his feet in establishing a relationship with his wayward daughter. Jeremy said he even shared his faith with the woman, although how he can forgive what she did is beyond me.*

Chief completed his task and the two of them took off, racing as fast as the slick sidewalk allowed. She felt her muscles warm and become as lithe as they always did when she gave them a good work-out. *Jeremiah won't get his house back, but Jeremy said he's settled where he is. That's good. Nice man.* She thought about the older man's investments. *I'm sure Amanda was only looking after herself, but the increase in his investments was a nice surprise.*

The sky was clear blue. Her frosty breathe hung in the air, the absence of a breeze made the morning run a pleasant experience. *I wonder if anything will come of Jeremiah's friendship with Franny. That woman cares about him ... a lot.* She chuckled. *Now I've become a matchmaker.*

Christine and Chief covered their two mile course in record time. Turning around to head back, Christine heard the caterwaul of an alarm in the distance. *Wonder who forgot to turn their car alarm off.* She slowed to a steady jog, cooling down in the process.

The closer she got to home, the louder the alarm wailed. She picked up speed. Chief's ears perked up as well and he began to grumble, low in his chest. *Can't be. I wasn't expecting anyone.* She ran faster. The alarm grew shriller, startling the few remaining birds in the area. She noticed a neighbor standing on his porch as she exited the park gates.

Who'd set off her alarm? She jogged in place, scanning the neighborhood for an unidentified visitor. *No one.* The only other person in sight was the not-too-friendly occupant of the house across the street. He shook his fist at her. "Shut that thing off. I worked last night. Need some sleep." He yelled as if she had intentionally tripped her alarm.

There was no one about, but a large box the size of a small appliance stood just inside the perimeter of her yard. *Someone's been here.* But they'd left. She continued to gaze from yard to yard and down the street, looking for anything that would indicate who had left the container. She decided to turn the alarm off. *If it was a standard delivery man, he must have wondered why the alarm had gone off when he'd not been near the house yet.*

Chief walked closer to the box. He sniffed and then began to whine. "What's wrong, boy?" She glanced at the man still standing in his pajamas on his front porch. His scowling countenance was fixed on her actions so she decided to pry the top open with her spike. *It won't hurt for him to see I can protect myself.* She loosened the first flap and then the other larger one.

An unpleasant odor emanated from the box, combating the once fresh, crisp air. She flipped the last flap open. She screamed. And then screamed again. Her body slumped to the ground. Chief stood beside her, his body in protective mode as he emitted a vicious snarl at the neighbor approaching from across the street. But she wasn't aware of anything other than the smell and the black coffin that closed over her consciousness.

Dear Reader

If you liked Shadow Stalker, I would appreciate it if you would help others enjoy this book, too, by recommending to friends, family, and book clubs, and/or by writing a positive review for Amazon, Goodreads, and Smashwords.

If you do write a review, please send me an email at barbarawrites14@gmail.com. I'd like to add you to my e-newsletter list so that you can get updates about upcoming new releases. Thank You.

Watch for Book 2 in the
FINDERS KEEPERS Mystery Series
spring 2014

More books in the Wilton/Strait Murder Mystery series

Book 1

Vanished! That's what Andrea Wilton and Brian Strait discover when they come to visit their best friends one evening. Where could they be and does God answer prayers, two questions they find the answers to as they journey to another world of voodoo, murder, and more missing people. Andrea and Brian also discover each other as they learn to scuba, fight a common enemy, and search for the proverbial needle in a haystack.

http://amzn.to/VjW34a

Book 2

Andrea Wilton and Brian Strait, from *Shuster Detective Agency*, take on another case to find a missing person. This second book in the series introduces DJ Wiebe, a biker who rides with The Sons Riders, a Christian biker ministry. Another biker, a member of The Demons Raiders, is missing and presumed dead. DJ, his friend, hires *Shuster Detective Agency* to find him. He initiates Andrea and Brian into the biker culture, a world that encompasses motorcycles, leather, drugs and murder.

http://amzn.to/HO63y7;

Book 3

Brian Strait and Andrea Wilton discover that relationship and intrigue go together when they embark on their third adventure, back to the Caribbean. A visit cut short, the two sleuths uncover a plot that challenges their faith when they search to clear a friend of murder. Their hunt for truth brings them head to head with the black market, human contraband, and culprits who will stop at nothing to line their pockets.

http://amzn.to/HHSfmB

Book 4

Brian Strait and Andrea Wilton leave behind a cruise ship at the Miami harbor for a short visit in the bustling metropolis. Their plans are to purchase wedding finery before flying to the Dominican Republic to marry.

A surprise awaits Andrea when she arrives at the bridal boutique. Trent and Diane Michner, best friends, are waiting to share their special day with them. Andrea believes everything is perfect.

Fate has other plans, however, when Diane and Andrea are kidnapped by Chechen mafia members who spirit women away to several other countries into slavery. Andrea fears for her friend's life when Diane is taken elsewhere. In captivity, she wonders if her wedding was just a pipe dream and where God is in all this. She also encounters a young girl who is hurting and in need of a Savior.

Brian, with the help of Trent and a young friend from the Dominican Republic, Troy, begins a frantic search for his bride-to-be, encountering drug addicts, dirty cops, and murder victims. His faith in God is stretched as he wonders why this has happened to them at this time in their life.

http://amzn.to/13WlYaW

More books by Barbara Ann Derksen

Fiction
Vanished
Presumed Dead
Fear Not
Silence

Children's Books
Shih-Tzu Puppy Adventures
Scruffles Finds a Home
Squirrels Are People, too

Devotionals
Straight Pipes
Two-Up, Riding with the Lord
Chrome, Shining Faith
Chaps
Road Trip
More Than Bells

<u>Other</u>
Dance With a Broom
Second to None, Warrior Voices

All books can be purchased and shipped directly to you from www.barbaraannderksen.com or email: barbarawrites14@gmail.com to find out more

Watch For
The second book in the *Finders Keepers Series*
Coming May 2014

344

Made in the USA
Charleston, SC
26 October 2013